George Lawrence

Reminiscences of Forty-Three Years in India

Second Edition

George Lawrence

Reminiscences of Forty-Three Years in India
Second Edition

ISBN/EAN: 9783337268343

Printed in Europe, USA, Canada, Australia, Japan

Cover: Foto ©Raphael Reischuk / pixelio.de

More available books at **www.hansebooks.com**

FORTY-THREE YEARS IN INDIA

LONDON: PRINTED BY
SPOTTISWOODE AND CO., NEW-STREET SQUARE
AND PARLIAMENT STREET

REMINISCENCES

FORTY-THREE YEARS IN INDIA

BY LIEUTENANT-GENERAL

SIR GEORGE LAWRENCE, K.C.S.I., C.B.

INCLUDING THE CABUL DISASTERS
CAPTIVITIES IN AFFGHANISTAN AND THE PUNJAUB, AND A
NARRATIVE OF THE MUTINIES IN RAJPUTANA

EDITED BY

W. EDWARDS, H.M.B.C.S.

AUTHOR OF 'PERSONAL ADVENTURES IN THE INDIAN REBELLION' ETC.

SECOND EDITION

LONDON
JOHN MURRAY, ALBEMARLE STREET
1875

CONTENTS.

CHAPTER V.

Surrender of the Ameer Dost Mahomed Khan—His Deportation with his
Family to India—Unprecedented Tranquillity of the Country in con-
sequence of the Ameer's Surrender—The Result on the Mind of Shah
Soojah—Disturbances at Khelat and Murder of Lieutenant Loveday—
Brigadier Shelton's Operations in the Nuzeran Valley—Arrival of
Elphinstone—His Feeble State of Health—Return of the Court to
Cabul—Outbreak in the Ghilzye Country . . . .

CHAPTER VI.

Despatch of a Force under General Sale to Jellalabad—Attacked by
Ghilzyes—Sale Wounded—Sir A. Burnes nominated to succeed Mac-
naghten—Sudden Outbreak in City of Cabul—Measures proposed for
its Suppression—Ordered to proceed to Bala Hissar—Sturt Wounded—
Shelton's Brigade occupy Bala Hissar — His deplorable Inactivity—
Sir A. Burnes Murdered—Envoy's Energetic Measures

CHAPTER VII.

Position of the Cabul Cantonments—Protest of the Envoy against the
Choice of a Position for Commissariat Stores—Return of Griffiths'
Force — Trevor and Mackenzie forced to abandon their Position —
Commissariat Fort Abandoned and Stores Lost—Brigadier Shelton
Summoned from Bala Hissar

CHAPTER VIII.

Post of Charèkar Taken and its Garrison Destroyed—Major Pottinger reaches Cabul—Massacre of Woodburn's Detachment—Negotiations with Kuzzulbashes—Village of Behmaroo Attacked—Defeat of
our Troops—Fresh Negotiations—Mahomed Shurreef's Fort Abandoned.

CHAPTER IX.

Military Authorities Propose to Retreat—Their Views Opposed by Sir W.
Macnaghten—Proposal to Occupy Bala Hissar Rejected—Envoy Meets
Chiefs and Submits Draft of Treaty, which was accepted by the Sirdars—Our Troops Evacuate the Bala Hissar—Second Interview with
the Chiefs—Macnaghten Murdered—Trevor Killed—Mackenzie and
myself taken Prisoners

CHAPTER X.

CHAPTER XI.

CHAPTER XII.

CHAPTER XIII.

CHAPTER XIV.

CHAPTER XV.

CHAPTER XVI.

CHAPTER XVII.

CHAPTER XVIII.

CHAPTER XIX.

CHAPTER XX.

CHAPTER XXI.

REMINISCENCES

OF

FORTY-THREE YEARS IN INDIA.

CHAPTER I.

RECEIVE APPOINTMENT AND PROCEED TO INDIA — JOIN MY REGIMENT —
INTERVIEW WITH THE GOVERNOR-GENERAL, LORD W. BENTINCK—WIT-
NESS A SUTTEE—ORDERED ON SERVICE—MY REGIMENT JOINS ARMY OF
INDUS AT FEROZEPORE—RUNJEET SINGH—MARCH TO QUETTA—CANDAHAR
AND GHUZNEE.

AFTER attending the Military College of Addiscombe,
I received my appointment from the Honorable East India
Company of a cornetcy of cavalry on their Bengal establishment; and on the 5th of May, 1821, I proceeded to
India, arriving in Calcutta on the 10th of September of
the same year, and was immediately posted to the 2nd
regiment of Light Cavalry.

I remained six weeks in the Cadet Barracks in Calcutta. The chief incidents during my stay there were
my getting a severe fall the first time I mounted a horse
in my cavalry uniform, from, I fancy, using my spurs
unnecessarily. I was picked up senseless and taken into
a good Samaritan's house in Chowringhee. The other
was a dinner at the Governor-General's, Lord Hastings,

who gave me the good advice of 'Mind you study the native languages, sir!' On my way up the river Ganges my companion, Cornet Bradford, and myself were nearly drowned. While bathing, Bradford got beyond his depth. He could not swim, I could, and tried in vain to save him, when my servant, a khitmudgar, seeing us being carried down by the current, jumped in, and took one under each arm to the shore. He was so well rewarded that he left me at Sultanpore to return to Calcutta. I joined my regiment at Keitah, in Bundlekund, on the 15th of January, 1822; and nine months after was placed in charge of a troop. Two years later I became a lieutenant, and was then appointed adjutant of my regiment, a post I retained until September, 1834, when I resigned it.[1]

During this time India was in a state of profound peace, and my life was one of common routine in an Indian cantonment, merely diversified by a change of quarters, and by a visit in the summer of 1827, on sick leave, to Simla, then just becoming known as a sanatarium. While there I had the honor of an interview with the Governor-General, Lord William Bentinck, the circumstances of which I may here relate, as illustrative of his character. On entering his room, his lordship addressed me with, 'Well, sir, what do you want?' 'Nothing, my lord, for myself,' I replied. 'Well,' said the Governor-

---

[1] The regiment when I joined was commanded by Colonel Frank Johnston, who gave me the adjutancy. He was succeeded by Major Hubert De Burgh, then by Major Shadwell, then by Colonel Harry Tufnel Roberts, one of the smartest and most efficient officers in the service, and well remembered in India as having raised and commanded one of the first corps of Irregular cavalry employed in the service. Colonel Adam Duffin succeeded Roberts, and was the first officer who died on the Cabul campaign. I attended him in his last moments, and buried him at Ahmedpore. He was succeeded by Colonel H. F. Salter, from the Hyderabad Contingent.— *Geo. S. P. Lawrence.*

General, 'you are the first man I have met in India who gave me that answer; but you *must* want something?' 'Yes,' I answered, 'for my brother Henry, an artillery officer. I wish your lordship to be good enough to nominate him to the Revenue survey, for which he is qualified. For myself I want nothing, as I am adjutant of my regiment, and perfectly content.' 'Well, sir, I never promise, but go to my military secretary, Benson, who will put your brother's name down, and I will see what can be done.' I thanked his lordship and retired, and in six months thereafter my brother received the appointment he desired.

I may here mention an incident which occurred at this period as illustrating bygone times. One morning on dismissing the regiment from parade, the havildar major (native adjutant) requested my permission to attend a 'tomasha' (an extraordinary sight). On inquiry it turned out that a suttee was about to take place in the neighbourhood of the cantonment of Neemuch, and I resolved to witness it myself. On reaching the spot I found a large crowd collected around a funeral pyre on which the poor victim about to immolate herself was seated. Seeing a number of my own troopers in the crowd I asked them if they would stand by me if I attempted to rescue the woman from her dreadful fate, and finding that they were quite willing, I approached the pyre near enough to address her, saying I was ready to save her life if she desired it. She expressed her gratitude, but refused, saying she was willing to die. Immediately afterwards the flames enveloped her, and in a few seconds she was burned to ashes. Her calm intrepidity was most astonishing, especially as she had not even the excitement of her husband's body to be con-

sumed with her, only a portion of his clothes, as he himself had died far from his home.

'It is a long lane that has no turning,' and at last, in
September, 1838, came the welcome order to prepare for
service in the field. My regiment was ordered to join
the army of the Indus, then being concentrated at
Ferozepore on the Sutlej for service in Affghanistan, to
restore to his throne the Ameer Shah Soojah-ool-Moolk.

We marched from the cantonment of Meerut on the
30th October, 1838, reaching Ferozepore on the 28th of
the following month, and joined the army collected there
under the immediate orders of the Commander-in-chief,
Sir Henry Fane. The Governor-General, Lord Auckland,
with his suite, had already proceeded to this place, to
hold an interview with the famous Runjeet Singh, the
founder of the powerful kingdom of the Punjaub. Dur-
bars, to which I had great difficulty to get admission, and
reviews were held in his honor, and on Runjeet's taking
leave of the Governor-General his lordship presented him
with two finely ornamented horse artillery 9-pounders,
fully equipped for service. On leaving the durbar tent,
his Highness proceeded, with the Governor-General and
Commander-in-chief on either side of him, to inspect the
handsome present, which he most highly valued. Runjeet, at the time an infirm old man, stumbled and fell just
before the muzzles of the guns, and Lord Auckland and
Sir Henry Fane at once raised him to his feet. A murmur
of horror rose from his sirdars and retinue at the ill omen
to their chief, the head of their empire, thus falling pros-
trate before the British guns. Their hearts were comforted, however, and the unlucky nature of the omen
averted, by some one happily saying, 'Well, if his Highness did fall before the British guns, the highest repre-

sentatives of the British government restored him to his feet.'

During the time the grand army remained at Ferozepore, intimation of the raising of the siege of Herat, and the retreat of the Persian forces, reached the Government, and in consequence it was determined greatly to diminish the strength of the force about to proceed into Affghanistan. Sir Henry Fane's services were no longer considered necessary to command the army on its reduced scale, and indeed he declined to act as subordinate to Mr. Macnaghten, the political chief, so his Excellency made over the command of the Bengal column, to which my regiment was attached, to Sir Willoughby Cotton, who was ordered to proceed at once to Shikarpore. Sir Henry Fane asked Brigadier-General Thackwell to appoint me one of his aides-de-camp, but preferring regimental duties I declined, which was fortunate, as Mr. Macnaghten placed me on his own staff at a later date as his military secretary and political assistant, after I had declined the Cavalry Brigade Majorship offered me by Brigadier Arnold. Although no longer in immediate command, Sir H. Fane accompanied this column on its march down the left bank of the Sutlej and Indus as far as Bukkur, which place we reached without any incidents of importance, and by the ordinary marches, on January 20, 1839.

Sir Alexander Burnes, the political agent, had, ere we arrived, concluded a treaty with the Ameer of Khyrpore, to cede temporarily to the British Government his stronghold of Roree Bukkur, built on an island in the Indus. The Ameer was naturally most reluctant, when the time came, to make over the fort, but after sundry delays, he at last consented. Sir Henry Fane, attended by Sir Alexander Burnes, proceeded in state to take possession, and I accompanied the party. On landing, the old warder of the fort handed over the key to Sir Henry, who proceeded to the gate, and unlocking it with his own hand, entered and took possession, in the name of the British Government, of this ancient stronghold of the Ameers of Scinde. A bridge of boats was here thrown across the Indus, and by it the whole army, consisting of the Bengal and Bombay columns, which was now collected under the command of Sir John Keane, crossed the river, without accident, to Sukkur on the right bank, whence we proceeded to the large town of Shikarpore. Here Shah Soojah-ool-Moolk, a fine old man with a superb black beard, and the envoy and minister to his court, Mr. Macnaghten, had already arrived with the Shah's own troops. On the 23rd February we marched from Shikarpore for Dadur, distant 146 miles, crossing the desert which commences at a place called Rajghan. This sterile tract, extending for twenty-three miles, is pestilential during the extreme heats of summer, and becomes a swamp in the rainy season, in June and July. At this time of the year it presented little difficulty to troops marching across it, except from the scarcity of water and grain. We arrived at Dadur, the entrance of the Bolan Pass, on the 10th March, and were delayed there some time owing to the desertion of many of our syces and dooly bearers. On the 15th, the force entered this most formidable pass, my regiment forming a portion of the advance. About two miles from our camp the road lay over loose stones and boulders, passing over a mountain-torrent of a depth varying from one to two feet, no less than seven times during the march. While crossing the last time, I allowed my horse to drink, when he suddenly lay down in the stream, wetting me thoroughly, but doing no further damage to me or himself. The Beloochee marauders here commenced their depredations, and attacked and plundered our mail runners. I rejoiced that I had sent my wife and family to England, so that neither they nor I were liable to the worry and disappointment such events were causing to many others in our camp. Our second march through the pass, to a place called Kurlat, very much resembled in character the first. But on the 17th we entered a narrow defile; on one side flowed a rapid river and on the other rose precipitous mountains, where it would have been impossible for cavalry to act, even if required. The fourth march brought us through the dry bed of a torrent, nine miles, to a place called Beebee Nanee. Many camels succumbed to the severity of the marching and the difficulty of the road, and had to be abandoned. One of the officers of the 16th Lancers, who had forty servants, although prohibitory orders had been reiterated limiting the number for each officer, had his baggage plundered and his cook killed, by some of the thieves watching their opportunity, while hiding among the rocks of the defile.

The fifth march, again a distance of nine miles, brought us to Abeyjoon, where we encountered a terrific storm of wind and rain, which levelled a great many of our tents. Marching from thence, the road became so difficult that much of the baggage of the troops had to be abandoned and burnt to prevent its becoming the prey of the robbers infesting the pass. The infantry soldiers had also to assist the guns into camp, the horses and cattle being quite exhausted. On the 20th, after a march of ten miles, we encamped on the top of the Pass Sir-i-

Bolan, 5,000 feet above the level of the sea. On the 21st we commenced our descent by a narrow zigzag road, covered with boulders and with high precipitous rocks on either side, and halted at a spot bearing the inauspicious but well-deserved name of the Dusht-i-beh-Dowlut—'the unlucky plain.' Leaving this miserable place on the 22nd, our road lay through a fine grassy valley. Oh! how grateful to eye and ear was this march —the horses no longer grinding and crunching through stones and shingle as they marched, but stepping lightly and noiselessly on the grassy plain, smooth as velvet. We had now left behind us the dreaded Bolan, which extends for a distance of sixty-six miles from Dadur. Quetta was now distant from us ten miles, but instead of finding, as was anticipated, ample supplies for the army there, little or none could be procured. I and other officers were detached to forage for kurby and grain among the neighbouring villages, and I visited several on this duty, but with no success. Quetta, which we now reached, is only a village of some 500 houses, with a miserable mud fort. The former governor, Zullal Khan, who had lately been killed in a foray, was very civil to Arthur Conolly on his visiting Quetta some time ago, asking him, in the pride of his heart, if he had ever in his travels seen anything in the shape of a fortress stronger or more imposing than his own. He said to him also, with almost prophetic sagacity, ' that he knew he (Conolly) had some ulterior object in visiting Quetta, and not the mere love of travelling; that he was in fact the forerunner of a British army.' So it has now turned out, although the old man has, perhaps happily for himself, not survived to prove the accuracy of his prognostications.

The climate of Quetta is deliciously cool and bracing at this season. The whole army, including Shah Soojah and his troops, were collected here by April 4, by which time supplies became so scarce that the troops, much to their discontent, were put upon half rations, and to escape starvation, Sir J. Keane wisely determined to advance at once through the valley of Shawl to Candahar.

The army marched on April 7 to Koochlak, and next day to Hykalzie, a distance of twenty miles. I was on baggage guard with my troop. After advancing a couple of miles we reached the banks of the Lora river, where there was a complete stoppage in order to get the camels across, and the confusion and crowding were terrible. A fine wheat-field was close at hand, and I improved the opportunity by letting my men graze their poor starved horses for an hour in it. By this time the baggage had crossed the stream, and we pushed on another two miles, when we had again to cross the river. We came up to my regiment at the ford, the men having dismounted; a number of the troopers being required to assist a camel battery to cross the stream. This operation lasted two hours, but at length, with great trouble, we got over, and reached our camp at Hykalzie, after a very fatiguing march through ravines and barren country. Our horses suffered much from fatigue and starvation, and many of them had to be abandoned and destroyed. On April 10 we made another long and fatiguing march, losing on the way no less than fifty-eight horses—eight of them belonging to my own troop. The artillery horses were so completely worn out that they had to be unyoked, and the guns hauled along by the soldiers. We marched on the 11th through the Pisheen valley to the mouth of the Kojuk Pass, which we had to traverse before reaching

Candahar. This defile is, for four miles of the distance, so narrow, that even after all the efforts of our engineers, only a single camel could advance at a time. Sir John Keane consequently issued an order to diminish each camel load as much as practicable, as in the event of any animal falling on the road, he and his load must be thrown over the precipice to prevent those in the rear being stopped. Considerable delay occurred before the troops could enter the defile, and it was only on the 15th that it came to our turn to advance. I walked the entire way through the pass. The road for the first four miles was wide and good; then it became very steep and narrow, the hills closing in on each side to within fifty yards of the track. Much baggage, many tents, and a considerable quantity of stores had to be abandoned on the road, which the Beloochee robbers, hanging on our rear, soon appropriated. It was not until April 18 that the entire force, having passed through this formidable defile, was collected together at a place called Dándee Goolaiee. There the climate became rather trying, causing considerable sickness among the troops, the thermometer registering 54° at sunrise, and rising to 100° by noon.

Having halted at Dándee Goolaiee for some days, we marched on the 24th to Killah Abdullah, and the next day to Killa Quazee. These two were our most trying marches since leaving Ferozepore, the heat being intense, and no water procurable, as the Affghans had cut off the stream which previously flowed through the valley by diverting it into a new channel at its source in the hills, some sixteen miles distant. The troopers had to dismount and drive their horses before them; and I really believe that if attacked, not a hundred effective men could have been mustered in the three regiments—the 16th Lancers, the 2nd and 3rd Light Cavalry—to oppose an enemy. Numbers of native women, with their children, notwithstanding many prohibitions, had accompanied the army from India, and the sufferings of these poor creatures from thirst and heat were most terrible; a great many dropped down and died on the line of march. I saw a trooper of the 16th Lancers, who had a soda-water bottle half full of water, pour the whole contents down the throat of a poor native woman's child, who was just dying of thirst. I could have hugged the fellow for his noble and disinterested act.

Upon the 23rd, our camp was pitched on the bank of the Dooree river. Its flowing stream was indeed a most refreshing and delightful sight to us, who had so lately undergone such intense misery from the want of water. From hence we moved on the 24th to Dilkazee, seventeen miles from Candahar, a considerable village of some 2,000 houses, but entirely deserted, the inhabitants having abandoned their homes on our approach. Rumours reached us that we should probably be attacked by the Baruckzye sirdars, the brothers of Dost Mahomed, who were in force in the neighbourhood, but instead of offering any opposition, they fled with their troops, leaving Candahar to be occupied, without any show of resistance. Shah Soojah was formally installed here as king of Affghanistan, without, however, any symptom of the interest or enthusiasm which we were led to expect on the part of his subjects, at the restoration of the ancient Doorannee dynasty.

The whole of our army had, by April 27, reached Candahar, and was encamped on the plains near the city. The appearance of the town greatly disappointed me, as I expected to find the capital of western Affghanistan a far larger and more imposing place, instead of being merely composed of mud houses, surrounded by a wall of sun-dried bricks.

The Shah held a reception of the British officers while the army remained at Candahar. We were, one after another, presented to his Majesty in due form, and were the only persons who congratulated his Majesty on his accession. None of his own subjects came in to pledge their allegiance, and the country was clearly against us. Their hostility was unmistakeably shown by attacking a party of our officers who had proceeded a short way from camp, killing Lieut. Inverarity, of the 16th Lancers, and wounding severely another officer; the murderers, of course, escaping without detection. We remained at Candahar until June 27, when the army made its first march towards Cabul, leaving behind a garrison in Candahar, and with them, unfortunately, the heavy battering guns, as we expected to meet no opposition at Ghuznee, on our route to the capital. The country, until we passed Khelat-i-Ghilze, was most uninteresting, bare and rocky, but afterwards became well cultivated, intersected by flowing streams and watercourses, with numerous and apparently flourishing villages, surrounded by clumps of large fine trees. The country people willingly sold us grain, and brought in goats and sheep of the large broad-tailed Doombah species.

Upon July 20, intelligence having reached Sir John Keane of the probability of an attack on our camp, the Quartermaster-General, Major Garden, was ordered to make a reconnaissance to the front, and I was directed to proceed, with thirty troopers, as his escort. We pushed on to within half a mile of the celebrated fortress of Ghuznee, seeing only a few of the enemy's horsemen on the distant hills.   On our return we fell in with a well-dressed Affghan horseman, who told me he had visited our camp and seen our troopers, saying with much contempt, ' You are an army of tents and camels : our army is one of men and horses.' ' What could induce you,' he added, ' to squander crores of rupees in coming to a poor rocky country like ours, without wood or water, and all in order to force upon us a kumbukht (unlucky person), as a king, who, the moment you turn your backs, will be upset by Dost Mahomed, our *own* king ?" '

It was not for me to enter into a political discussion with my friend, who, in my opinion, however, spoke with great truth and sagacity.

We here received intelligence that Ghuznee was held by a garrison of 3,000 men, under Sirdar Hyder Khan, son of Dost Mahomed, while another of the Ameer's sons was in the immediate neighbourhood, with a large force of cavalry, and intended to make a night attack upon our camp. In consequence of this information we slept for two nights at our horses' heads, ready to mount at a moment's notice, but no attack was made upon us, and both nights passed quietly away.

It was now clear that we should meet with serious opposition at Ghuznee, and therefore it was determined that the army should advance upon it in battle array, and proceed at once to attack that celebrated fortress. That a serious mistake had been made in leaving the battering train at Candahar, 230 miles in the rear, was now very apparent.

CHAPTER II.

STORM AND CAPTURE OF GHUZNEE—APPOINTED ONE OF THE PRIZE AGENTS—
ADVANCE TO CABUL—PURSUIT OF DOST MAHOMED KHAN—RETURN FROM
BAMIAN—SHAH SOOJAH ARRIVES IN CABUL.

UPON the morning of the 21st our army, consisting of five
columns, advanced in battle array, and arrived before
Ghuznee at 7 A.M. Our light companies immediately
advancing, dislodged the enemy from some walled gardens, when the fortress opened fire upon us with heavy
guns. Our artillery was soon moved up into position,
and for two hours maintained an unceasing fire of shot
and shell upon the place, without apparently making any
impression, except carrying away the head of a brave
Affghan, who stood upon the parapet waving a flag, and
calling upon us to advance. The artillery were then
withdrawn, and the engineers, under an escort of a company of the 13th Light Infantry and a squadron of my
regiment, sent forward to reconnoitre the town and the
defences. The party drew down a heavy fire upon themselves, but fortunately without receiving any damage.

The cavalry regiments were at this time dismounted,
standing by their horses in a part of the plain supposed
to be beyond the range of the guns of the fort. Considering ourselves quite secure, we were watching the proceedings with much interest, when down came a 64-pound
shot, fired from the great gun called Zubbur Jung—'the
lord of war'—and by our men 'Long Tom,' and falling

in the midst of us killed one man outright, and took off a
horse's leg. Towards evening we commenced pitching
our camp, and just as half the tents were up we were
ordered to take up a position on the Cabul side of the
fortress. To reach our ground we had to pass a most
formidable morass; and had we been opposed by an enter-
prising enemy, the consequence might have been very
disastrous. The baggage, on carts and camels, got all
jammed together in a state of most inextricable confusion,
so that no amount of men at our disposal could have protected it had we been seriously attacked. Fortunately
for us the enemy contented themselves with a fire at intervals of five minutes from wall pieces and matchlocks,
which inflicted no serious damage. The baggage continued coming into camp all night, and a miserable night
we had of clamour and confusion. By daylight, however,
by a good Providence over us, almost all was brought into
position. I was on rearguard all the time.

On the morning of the 22nd I accompanied my regiment round the city to hunt up marauders, who were
reported to have plundered and carried off during the
night some of the baggage. We came on the dead bodies
of about a dozen camp followers, and from among the
mass suddenly rose up a living man, who had escaped the
fate of his companions by shamming death. The poor
creature was in such a state of exhaustion and fright that
he had to be sent in a dooly into camp.

On our return we saw the Lancers and 3rd Cavalry
proceed in support of Christie's Horse to dislodge a body of
Affghan cavalry from a neighbouring hill. The enemy
was soon driven off the hill, and were then followed by a
body of the Shah's Juzzailchees, under Outram and Lieut.
Nicholson, who put them entirely to flight, killing about

fifty, and taking many prisoners. During these proceedings our regiment was directed to remain in front of the camp, watching the fortress, lest the enemy should attempt a sortie. The men and officers dismounted, and while the latter were standing under the shade of the standard guard tent, a 64-pound shot from Zubbur Jung came lobbing in among us, passing quite close to me, and through our fourth troop, without doing any damage; at length carried off a horse's leg, then that of a trooper at his dinner, and finally lodged in the body of a camel close to my tent.

Having no heavy battering train with us, it was determined, at the suggestion of Captain Thomson of the Bengal Engineers, to attempt the storm and capture of Ghuznee by blowing in the Cabul gate of the fortress with powder, as it was known it had been built up by the garrison. Accordingly, in the night of the 22nd the storming party under Colonel Dennie, supported by the main column under General Sale, was held in readiness near the gate. Captain Peat of the Bombay Engineers, aided by Lieutenants Macleod and Durand of the Bengal Engineers, silently laid the powder bags against the gate, without apparently attracting the notice of the garrison within. At four A.M. on the morning of the 23rd, the gate was successfully blown in and the fortress stormed by our troops, with a loss of 17 killed and 165 wounded, among the latter being 18 officers. My regiment, with the rest of the cavalry, had remained on duty all night, and succeeded in killing and capturing many of the Affghans who were escaping from the fort.

On returning to camp after the storm, I led my troop through the town, and most sad and deplorable was the sight. The dead bodies of hundreds of men and horses strewed the streets. The Affghans, when driven to bay, had fought gallantly with their swords, and succeeded in wounding several of our men, even when themselves transfixed with the bayonet. Some 600 Affghans had fallen, and 1,600 been taken prisoners, but I am proud and thankful to say the women had been all spared. Ghuznee having been stormed, the plunder became the prize of the victors. I was appointed prize agent by the Bengal column.

The city of Ghuznee, although for two centuries the capital of a powerful empire, which in Sultan Mahmood's time reached from the Tigris to the Ganges, and from the Indian Ocean to the Jaxartes, is but a poor place now, containing only about two thousand houses and a very scanty population.

The fortress is situated on the western end of a range of hills, and is defended by a deep ditch. The citadel, an irregular square, is placed on a mound, with two ramps leading to it, the walls being loop-holed, and had it been defended, might have caused us much trouble to capture.

The old town of Ghuznee is three miles to the east, and contains the tomb of the famous Sultan Mahmood, the conqueror of India. It is a spacious building, covered with a cupola, the doors being of sandalwood, said to have been brought as a trophy from the celebrated Hindu temple at Somnath in Guzerat, which Mahmood sacked in his last expedition to India. The climate of Ghuznee is said to be very fine, and the country abounds in fruits; grapes, melons, apples, plums, &c., &c., growing in great perfection. The fort is reported in former times to have stood a siege of one year, and as it contained provisions for three or four months for the garrison, and was supplied with large stores of ammunition—powder and lead and cannon balls, we may consider it very fortunate that the *coup de main* by which it fell into our hands was so successful. The force remained at Ghuznee until the 4th August, when we marched towards Cabul. When about fifty miles from the capital, authentic information reached us that Dost Mahomed had fled with his family and property to Balkh. His escape was regarded with dismay by the Shah and the Envoy, and it was determined to make every effort to follow, and if possible to capture him. The first I heard of the intention was from the Adjutant-general, Major Craigie, who asked me if I felt inclined to form one of the party about to proceed under the command of Captain Outram in pursuit of Dost Mahomed, who had fled over the Hindu Koosh. I confess I was a good deal startled when he explained the plan it was proposed to follow, the means appeared so inadequate, and the employment of Affghans so injudicious. It seemed to me a proposal replete with difficulty and danger, which success alone could justify, but still, it was one of great daring, which I could not refuse to share in, having been once invited. I made but one stipulation, to be allowed to call for fifty volunteers from my own regiment to accompany me on the expedition. This was acceded to, and on making known the circumstances to the regiment, not fifty volunteers only, but the whole corps turned out to accompany me. I accordingly was enabled to select my own men. Besides my own fifty troopers, the party consisted of twenty-five troopers of the 4th regiment of Irregular Horse, twenty-five of the Poona Horse, and 125 of Christie's Irregular Horse under his own command, and a body of Affghan horsemen under the command of an Affghan of influence named Hadjee Khan Kakur, who alone of his countrymen had at this time professed allegiance to Shah Soojah.

The officers were Captain Outram, commanding, Captains Wheeler and Lawrence, 2nd Bengal Light Cavalry, Captain Colin Troup, of the 48th Bengal Native Infantry, then employed in the Shah's service ; Captain Backhouse, Bengal Artillery, Captain Keith Erskine, Poona Horse, Lieutenant Broadfoot, in the Shah's service, Bengal 1st European Regiment, Lieutenant Ryves, 4th Bengal Irregular Horse, Lieutenant Hogg, of the 2nd Bombay Grenadier regiment. We arranged to march in the lightest possible order, few of us taking more than the clothes we wore. Of the 500 Affghans under Hadjee Khan Kakur, 300 only were well mounted, the other 200 riding mere ponies. Upon August 3rd we left our camp as soon as it was dark ; the Hadjee recommended our following the high road by Mydan, but Outram determined at once to strike into the mountains, so as to avoid observation. We marched all this night, only halting occasionally for stragglers to close up, crossing several ranges of hills and passing along the dry beds of several rivers, the road being for a good part of the way merely a goat track. On the morning of the 4th we halted at seven A.M., at a village called Goda, situated in a narrow but lovely valley, having marched thirty-two miles. Of our Affghans, only about 100 were up with us ; the remainder continued to drop in during the day, in parties of six and seven, loaded with plunder of all sorts they had picked up along their route. At five P.M. we resumed our march, contrary to the protest of the Hadjee, who expressed himself most unwilling to proceed, alleging the dangerous and precipitous character of the road for a march by night. It was quite apparent his heart was not in the cause. His objections were not listened to, and we proceeded by a very bad road, over high hills and along the dry channels of mountain streams, for ten miles, when we halted and lay down by our horses, until the moon rose at two A.M. of the 5th. We then continued our march until seven A.M., crossing a lofty range of hills and through a difficult pass to Killah Suffeid, a pretty village, where we halted. Not fifty of our Affghans reached the ground with us; the rest came in during the day. Here we received intelligence that the Dost was at a place called Youk, only one march ahead of us. Hadjee Khan again showed great reluctance to advance, begging Outram to halt here, as the Dost had 2,000 good horsemen with him. Outram, however, ordered the party to march at four P.M., and on mustering the Affghans found they numbered 350 men, but most of them badly mounted.

After much difficulty and long altercation with the Hadjee, we marched in the full hope of overtaking the Ameer before gun-fire in the morning. Our Hindustanee troopers were full of pluck and in high spirits, although they had had only parched grain to eat all the day. After proceeding for some miles and descending a very precipitous mountain into a sort of punchbowl, a cry arose from the front that the guides had disappeared. The night was pitch dark, and there was no help for it but to lie down where we were halted, bridles in hand, until the light enabled us to proceed. Videttes were planted to keep a look-out, and then we lay down on the bare ground with large stones for our pillows, until day broke, on the morning of August 6, when we resumed our march to Youk, which we reached at seven A.M., only to find the Dost had left and proceeded to Hurzah, sixteen miles in advance, where we heard he was halting.

Our Affghans were far in the rear, and nothing could

induce the Hadjee to advance at once, promising that he would go on in the evening if we would wait until then. Situated as we were, there was no help for us, so we were obliged to agree. At 4 P.M. we were all mounted and ready to proceed, but not one step would the Hadjee advance, and not an Affghan was in the saddle. Vexed and disappointed at this delay, which prevented all chance of our coming up with the Dost, we had no course but to dismount. Outram strongly remonstrated with the Hadjee, who seemed to yield to his arguments, and promised to make a double march the following day. Instead of this, the Hadjee, when day broke, talked loudly of the folly of the pursuit any further, as the Dost had treble our number of men, with horses all fresh ; and as they were fighting for their families and their lives, we should certainly be beaten by them if we overtook them. To these remonstrances Outram only urged that we had to perform a duty, so everything must be done to obtain success. We accordingly marched, and reaching Hurzah found the recent traces of the Dost's encampment. Here the Hadjee halted, and declaring his men to be famished, and their horses done up, endeavoured to persuade us to remain also. We steadily pushed on, and a mile beyond Hurzah fell in with some deserters of the Dost's party, who informed us that they had only left him early that morning at Keeloo, where he intended halting. Outram rode back to inform the Hadjee, and urge him to advance, but without any effect. He declared that we were mad, rushing on our own destruction, for not a man of us would escape to tell the tale if we encountered the Dost, while only disgrace would be the result to the Shah. Outram told him in reply that he was determined to advance to Keeloo without delay, and if he found the Dost there, would at once attack him at all hazards; and if we failed the Hadjee would have to answer for it with his head to Shah Soojah. We advanced alone, and reaching Keeloo at 3 P.M. found the Dost had left some hours before, and must by that time have crossed the highest pass of the Hindu Koosh. To follow him, therefore, with our tired horses, and our men wanting rest, was quite useless, as we had been then nine hours in the saddle. Not a single Affghan was with us, all having remained behind with Hadjee Khan Kakur.

On the morning of August 8 we were joined by Captain Taylor, of the 1st Bengal European Regiment, and Trevor, of the 3rd Bengal Light Cavalry, with fifteen troopers of the Bombay 1st Cavalry, and the same number of the 3rd Bengal Light Cavalry, and 300 Affghans. This accession of force induced Hadjee Khan Kakur to follow us; but on reaching Keeloo he only reiterated his remonstrances against proceeding any further without additional reinforcements, enlarging on the risk we ran by encountering desperate men; more especially as, if we came up with the Dost, not an Affghan of our party would fight against him, but join in attacking us. Outram only replied that he was ordered to intercept, if possible, the Dost, and this must be done at all risks; and if the Affghans refused to fight they must answer for their conduct with their lives to the Shah. Finding arguments of this kind of no avail, the Hadjee, removing his turban as a last resort, and seizing the skirt of Outram's coat, implored him to advance no further. However, it was no use; off started all our party, leaving the Hadjee to follow us, which we saw him and his followers slowly doing when we got half way up the pass, as if ashamed of their conduct. So steep was the ascent over the Hindu

Koosh, that we had to dismount and lead our horses for more than a mile. Descending, we reached a village quite deserted, where we halted for stragglers to close up and to rest the wearied. While halting here, we were joined by the Hadjee and his Affghans, who reiterated his arguments to induce Outram to halt and return, only receiving the reply that we should march at 2 P.M., and push on to Bamean. He then begged Outram at least to postpone moving until daybreak, as none of his Affghans would consent to march at night. To this Outram at length acceded, as our horses were much fatigued. Some of the officers, however, went on in advance at 3 P.M. to reconnoitre.

Just as we were remounting on the morning of the 9th, information reached us that the Dost, instead of halting at Bamean, had, on the forenoon of the previous day, proceeded to Syghan, some forty miles beyond the limits of the Shah's territory, and had placed himself under the protection of the Wullee of Khoolum. Outram then told the Hadjee that if this news proved true, he must be held answerable to the Shah with his head for the Dost's escape. On reaching Bamean, a distance of twelve miles, we found seventy of the Dost's horsemen, who had been dismissed by him, and also two of our own, all of whom confirmed the reports that had already reached us of the Dost's movements, who was still accompanied by a force of some 2,000 men.

Finding it, therefore, useless to continue the pursuit any further, we were reluctantly compelled to give it up, and halted three days at Bamean to recruit and recover from our fatigue. When we expected to overtake the Dost, we officers agreed among ourselves if we found the Affghans or our men unwilling to attack, to charge him *en masse*, and either take him prisoner or kill him. It probably was well for us we had not to make the attempt from our failure to overtake the party.

While at Bamean we met with a caravan of Affghan merchants, who had come from Russia *viâ* Bokhara. We purchased from them tea, sugar, cups, saucers, and some handkerchiefs. We found that the British name was well known and honoured in these regions, for these merchants refused our cash, which we could not conveniently part with, and merely wanted our bills on Cabul, offering us money as a loan to a very considerable amount.

Upon August 12 we commenced our return to Cabul, which we reached on the 17th, having marched sixteen miles each day. Our arrival was hailed with much satisfaction as well as surprise, as a horseman had come into camp and reported that he had witnessed our total destruction. Of course we had to bear the usual fate of the unsuccessful; friends kindly remarking, 'what madmen we were to go on such a wild-goose chase; what other result could have been expected? we were only too lucky to return with our heads on our shoulders,' &c.; Sir John Keane winding up the chorus by saying 'he had not supposed there were thirteen such asses in his whole force!' Indeed, I entertained some such thoughts myself as to the rash character of our expedition, but still, as a soldier, I could not have shrunk from undertaking what my superiors deemed was within the verge of possibility. Besides, I think that had we been accompanied by a stronger body of our own troops, and no Affghans, with only trustworthy guides, we should have succeeded in our enterprise. At any rate, the expedition was thus far satisfactory, as showing the good stuff our troopers, regular and irregular, were made of. During this expedition, occupying fifteen days going and returning, our Hindustanee troopers, Brahmin, Rajpoot, and Mussulman, behaved most admirably.   Nothing could exceed the patience, fortitude, and good humour with which they underwent fatigue and exposure of no ordinary kind ; without any cooking utensils for preparing their usual meals, and with no other covering than the clothes on their backs.   It was delightful to return to a comparatively civilized life after our nomad one, although the latter was not without its charms.   It was no small enjoyment for a dozen of us to sit down round a large cauldron borrowed from the Hadjee, to prepare our meal, consisting of half-a-dozen fowls and half a sheep, all thrown into the pot together, with peas and beans gathered as we marched along, all forming together a delicious fragrant stew which an alderman would envy.   We had but one glass among us, in which Outram doled out to each a glass of sherry and one of brandy.   Keith Erskine, with his songs, wit, and drollery, was the life and soul of our party, and our mirth used at times to astonish the grave, long-bearded Affghans, who could not understand our joyous spirits in circumstances which they considered perilous and critical enough. Stern, bigoted Mahomedans as they were, some of them did not hesitate to partake of our stew, or even to take a nip of brandy, which they evidently greatly · relished. During our absence the Shah had made a sort of triumphal entry into Cabul, proceeding in state, and accompanied by the British officers and troops, through the streets to the citadel of the Bala Hissar, the inhabitants manifesting the most complete indifference to their new sovereign, and expressing no sign of welcome or satisfaction at his accession to the throne.   Evidently their hearts and affections were with their previous sovereign, now a wanderer beyond the Hindu Koosh.

CHAPTER III.

Now that Dost Mahomed had fled the country, and no active opposition to the government of Shah Soojah was manifested in any quarter, affairs were considered to be so secure that Mr. Macnaghten and the married officers of the army determined to send for their wives and families to join them, as there appeared no prospect of an early return to Hindustan. Lieutenant Conolly, a relation of the Envoy and Minister, was despatched to India to conduct the ladies to Cabul. I was nominated to succeed him as political assistant and commandant of the envoy's escort, consisting of a rissalah of picked men of Skinner's Irregular Horse, and a volunteer company of native infantry. My duties, though nominally of a military character, were in reality almost entirely political and civil, and indeed, from the first I was actually, though not till afterwards duly installed military secretary to Mr. Macnaghten. The transition from purely regimental to civil duty was sudden and complete, and at first not a little embarrassing. My position was by no means the sinecure the secretary of an embassy is represented generally to be, who has only to look solemn and mysterious; on the contrary, my employment was incessant, and any leisure I could snatch had to be devoted to the study of Persian, as without an intimate knowledge of that language it would have been impossible for me to carry on the multifarious duties devolving on me.

Our sense of fancied security was not a little strengthened by the arrival on the 4th of September of the heir-apparent, Shazâdah Timour, who had been escorted from India by Colonel Wade, our political agent on the north-west frontier. This able officer had, by a judicious mixture of negotiation and force, conducted his charge, without serious opposition, through the much dreaded defiles of the Khyber pass, his escort consisting of a small number of regulars, and a large medley of irregular native troops. With these troops he succeeded in capturing the fort of Ali Musjid, a strong fortress in the middle of the defile, and entirely commanding the road.

In order to give the idea of confirmed power and unquestionable stability to his government, the Shah now instituted, after the manner of other sovereigns, an order termed the Dooranne, or Pearl of the Age, to reward those who had merited the distinction by their services in restoring him to his throne.

The recipients were entirely composed of British officers of the force, as none of his own subjects were regarded as worthy of the honor. Scarcely was the day of the installation, which had been conducted with much pomp, past, than we were shocked by the intelligence of the murder, while proceeding with his regiment, the 37th Bengal Native Infantry, from Candahar to Cabul, of Colonel Herring, a very able and meritorious officer. While encamped, apparently in complete security, on the 3rd of September the Colonel had walked out unarmed a short distance beyond the tents, when he was set upon and murdered by a band of Affghans prowling about the camp. His body, bearing no less than seventeen wounds, was brought in and buried in Cabul.

Two days afterwards the gallant and indefatigable Outram, accompanied by Captain Peter Nicholson, started with a body of Christie's Irregular Horse and some Affghan cavalry to punish the murderers, a duty which he very completely performed, having succeeded in catching nearly the whole band, who were summarily executed.

Notwithstanding this event, from which the feeling of the people towards us might have been judged, the Bombay column commenced their return to their own Presidency on the 18th September. On the 15th October following Sir John Keane returned through the Khyber pass to India, accompanied by Her Majesty's 16th Lancers, the 2nd Troop 2nd Brigade Horse Artillery, the 3rd Bengal Cavalry, and 4th Local Horse, making over the chief military command in Affghanistan to Sir Willoughby Cotton.

For some time after the departure of these troops the country remained to all appearances perfectly tranquil, when suddenly alarming rumours reached Cabul of Dost Mahomed's having arrived at Bamean with the view of commencing a Juhad, or religious war, against us, who were regarded by all orthodox Affghans as infidels. To counteract the Dost's intentions, a force consisting of the 4th Troop Bengal Native Horse Artillery, the Shah's 4th Goorka Regiment, and 200 Affghan horse were despatched to Bamean under Captain Garbett of the Bengal Artillery. The idea of raising the country by proclaiming a religious war against us had never been anticipated, and was one well calculated to produce deep anxiety, as it

was a cause which would enlist the sympathy and secure
the hearty co-operation of the tribes, otherwise bitterly
hostile to each other, and living in a state of chronic
civil war. As these tribes had failed to coalesce as a
nation to oppose our entrance into Affghanistan, and
had apparently acquiesced in our policy of imposing upon
them a king who had been an exile from his throne for
thirty years, we were unfortunately led to conclude that
the Affghans were indifferent on the subject, and so divided
by mutual jealousies and blood feuds, that they could
never be induced to act together for any national purpose.
This false view of the national character threw us off our
guard, and insensibly induced that want of preparation,
in consequence of which an émeute which might have
easily been repressed at the moment if active measures
had been taken, was turned into a most formidable and
successful rebellion. Besides this false estimate of the
state of the nation, there was something in the Affghan
individual character which also tended insensibly to put
us off our guard.

Possessing many noble natural qualities, such as individual courage, hospitality, and generosity, of fine and
commanding appearance and presence, good horsemen,
capable of enduring, without complaint, much exposure
and fatigue, fond of all manly sports, and frank and
social in their bearing and manners, there was much
calculated to prepossess us in favour of the Affghans as
a people on first acquaintance. Further experience, however, proved them to be destitute of all regard to truth,
treacherous, revengeful, and bloodthirsty, sensual and
avaricious, to a degree not to be comprehended by those
who have not lived among them, and thus become intimately acquainted with their character.

Such being the people we had to deal with, it is perhaps not surprising that we did not quite comprehend at first the dangers and difficulties of our position as foreigners carrying out a policy distasteful to the nation, and were lulled into a false security.

Not, however, that due precautions were not, to some extent, taken ; for, on Sir Willoughby Cotton assuming the chief command, the army of occupation was distributed as detailed below, in salient positions, best calculated in the opinion of the military authorities for overawing the population and maintaining the general security.

In the Bala Hissar, the citadel of Cabul, were stationed her Majesty's 13th Light Infantry, three guns Light Field Battery, and the 35th Bengal Native Infantry, the whole under the command of a very able officer, Colonel Dennie.

The fortress of Jellalabad was garrisoned by the 48th Bengal Native Infantry, a detachment of Sappers and Miners, the 3rd Bengal Light Cavalry, 3 guns Light Field Battery, and one rissalah of Skinner's Horse.

At Candahar, under the command of Major-general Nott, were the 42nd and 43rd regiments of Bengal Native Infantry, one company European Bengal Artillery, one troop of Shah's Horse Artillery, one regiment Shah's Irregular Cavalry, and two regiments Shah's Irregular Infantry, her Majesty's 40th and 41st regiments of the line.

At Quetta, one regiment Shah's Irregular Infantry, one troop Shah's Horse Artillery, and a force of Irregular Cavalry.

The Kojuck pass was watched over by a corps of Affghan Irregular Horse, stationed at Killah Abdoolah, under the command of Lieutenant Bosanquet, of the Bengal infantry.

The fortress of Ghuznee was garrisoned by the 16th Bengal Native Infantry, one rissalah of Skinner's Horse, and some guns of the Shah's Horse Artillery, the whole under the command of Major Maclaren.

At Bamean, as already stated, a small corps of observation had been posted to watch the movements of Dost Mahomed, and check his progress if he advanced at the head of an invading force.

A political officer was stationed at each of these posts, whose duties consisted in obtaining the earliest intelligence on all important matters, and communicating all details of interest at once to the government at Cabul. They were also the channels of communication between the highest civil and military authorities and the chiefs, and people within their respective charges.   Sir Alexander Burnes, in charge of Cabul, and myself, were the assistants in immediate attendance on the Envoy and Minister of Cabul; Major (now General) Sir George Macgregor was stationed at Jellalabad; at Peshawur, Major Mackeson, and Major (now General) Sir Henry Rawlinson had succeeded Major Leach at Candahar, on the latter being sent to Kelat-i-Ghilzye. In the Ghilzye country, Captain Peter Nicholson; at Ghuznee, Lieutenant Burnes; at Bamean, Dr. Lord; and in the Kohistan, Major Eldred Pottinger, the gallant defender of Herat. The most of these officers had already earned distinction in the field, and were eminently suited for the important duties they were called upon to discharge.

On November 4, 1839, Shah Soojah, attended by the Envoy and Minister, proceeded to Jellalabad, to pass the winter months, as the climate was less severe than that of Cabul.   The cold was, on that day, so intense, that icicles formed on our beards and on our horses' manes and tails.

The roads were execrable, nothing more than the mere beds of mountain streams winding through the hills. Nothing of note occurred until the 14th, when, in camp at Neemla, a son of the Shah's died, and his body was carried for interment to a shrine of much celebrity in the neighbourhood, and held very sacred as the supposed burying-place of Lamech, the father of Noah.

On this day I met, for the first time, Major Eldred Pottinger, who, before taking up his appointment as political agent in the Kohistan, was proceeding from Herat to Calcutta to meet the Governor-General, Lord Auckland, and confer with his lordship respecting the affairs of Persia. He gave us many interesting details relative to the siege of Herat; both besiegers and besieged were, he asserts, thoroughly afraid of each other, and a single British regiment could, in his opinion, have taken the fort with ease.

From Jellalabad the Envoy proceeded with an escort to Peshawur, in order to meet with, and if possible to conciliate, the turbulent tribes in that neighbourhood. The political agent, Major Mackeson, whose head-quarters were at Peshawur, and the fort of Ali Musjid in the Khyber —had, we were informed, just succeeded in concluding a treaty with the Khyberrees, by which they bound themselves, on certain conditions very favourable to themselves, to keep the pass open for the unmolested passage of our troops and people at all times. On the strength of this engagement the 37th and 48th regiments Bengal Native Infantry, under Colonel Wheeler, proceeded on November 22 from Ali Musjid towards Peshawur. Mackeson, however, not very sanguine himself how far the solemn conditions of his treaty would be respected by the Khyberrees, had advised the troops ' to trust in Providence and keep their powder dry,' rather than in the stipulations to which the Khyberrees had bound themselves. It was well for the force that they took Mackeson's advice, for as they entered the pass they found the heights covered with bodies of armed men, who did not molest their progress, seeing they were well prepared for resistance, but, on the contrary, welcomed them, waving their hands to encourage the troops, bidding them pass on, ' as *they* were their faithful allies.' No sooner had the main body passed, and the baggage commenced to defile through the pass, than 300 of our allies swooped down upon it, and succeeded in capturing 150 camels, slaying their conductors and guards. Colonel Wheeler was fortunately near enough to hear the shouting, and immediately retracing his steps with two companies, attacked the marauders before they could get off with their plunder, and recovered all the camels, killing twenty and wounding eighty of the Khyberrees. In this affair our loss consisted of two European officers wounded, two European soldiers killed, and twenty-five sepoys wounded. The force was then permitted to proceed without further molestation to Peshawur. Notwithstanding the severe lesson the Khyberrees had received on this occasion, it was not deemed expedient for the Envoy to attempt to proceed to Peshawur without an additional escort. Accordingly the 48th and 37th regiments Native Infantry were sent back to the fort of Ali Musjid to conduct our party to Peshawur, which we consequently reached without meeting with any opposition.

The Khyber pass is a narrow defile of twenty-eight miles long, between lofty perpendicular hills, the road during its entire length passing over rocks and boulders, which render a speedy advance or retreat of any body of men impossible.

The heights on either side entirely command the defile, and are scarped so that they cannot without great difficulty be scaled. They are also perforated with numbers of natural caves, the secure haunts of the savage robbers who have for ages held possession of the pass. The crests of the hills are further defended by stone breastworks called Sungahs. A small valley called Gurhee Lall Beg, about six miles from the western entrance of the pass, is the only open spot to be met with during the entire distance. Shortly before we passed through, a regiment of Sikhs, escorting the political agent, Major Mackeson, was attacked and destroyed to a man in the pass, Mackeson himself escaping with great difficulty, and losing all his baggage. On our arrival at Peshawur we were hospitably entertained by General Avitabile, an Italian officer in the Sikh service, and governor of the district, —a man of singular energy and determination, whose iron rule alone was able to maintain the peace of the turbulent district over which he presided, and secure some measure of prosperity for the town of Peshawur. At Peshawur Lieut. Conolly met us with the wives and families of the officers he had escorted from India, among the rest, Mrs. Macnaghten. Conolly at once resumed his appointment as commandant of the escort. I continued, however, to act as political assistant and secretary to the Envoy. We remained at Peshawur until December 15, when the Envoy returned to Jellalabad, meeting with no difficulty or opposition in the pass.

Both the chaplains previously attached to the army having returned to India, I was requested to conduct divine service each Sunday in future, a duty which I most gladly undertook, not only for the benefit to be derived by ourselves from regular worship on the sabbath, which had been too long interrupted and neglected by us in this strange land, but because the Affghans might see and believe that we really had a religion and worshipped our God, of which fact they had hitherto, I lament to say, too good reason for expressing their doubts, which they did very freely.

While the Shah remained at Jellalabad, it was deemed requisite to take the opportunity of chastising Syud Moshem, the petty chief of Koonur, a valley some twenty miles N.E. of the fort. Accordingly, a small force of infantry and cavalry, with a party of sappers and three 9-pounder guns, under the command of Colonel Orchard, was sent out to attack and destroy his stronghold of Pushoot. This force reached its destination at 5 A.M. of January 18, 1840, and the guns at once opening on the fortress soon made a practicable breach in the wall on each side of the main gate. It was, however, perceived, to the mortification of the party, that there remained still an inner wall and gate which could not be breached. Lieut. Pigou, commanding the sappers, immediately volunteered to blow in this second gate, and went up with a bag of powder for the purpose. Owing to the powder being damp from the rain then falling, and from its inferior quality, the attempt to blow in the gate twice failed, and the attacking party had to be withdrawn into shelter until the weather should clear. On advancing, after a short interval, to renew the attack, the fort was found to have been evacuated by the enemy. We lost one gallant young officer, Lieut. Collinson, of the 37th Regiment, mortally wounded in this affair.

Upon February 23, while at Jellalabad, information reached the Envoy from Dr. Lord, the political agent at Bamean, that Dost Mahomed Khan, having abandoned his reported design of raising a religious war for our expulsion, had sought refuge with the Ameer of Bokhara, and had been made a prisoner by his treacherous host, who was endeavouring to get the Dost's family also into his power. Dr. Lord intimated the probability of the family seeking an asylum from the British Government, as they had been warned not to trust themselves to the Ameer, who was well known for his treachery, and the political agent sought instructions how to act in the event of the family asking his protection. The Envoy instructed Dr. Lord to promise the family a safe asylum should they desire it, but to intimate to them at the same time that their ultimate destination would rest with the Governor-General alone.

Our Ambassador, Colonel Stoddart, was at this time a close prisoner at Bokhara, and it often occurred to me that we might be required to invade Balkh and Bokhara to effect his release and chastise the Ameer. The Governor-General, Lord Auckland, however, wisely set his face against any such forward movement at this time.

Upon March 3 the common routine of our life at Jellalabad was enlivened by the arrival of the Sultan of Bajore, Meer Alum—whose country is the Switzerland of Affghanistan—to tender his allegiance to the Shah as his liege lord, making an offering, among other articles, of three slave girls from Kafferistan. By Macnaghten's advice the Shah had these girls married to three of his own suite. The Sultan had scarcely had time to tender his allegiance, when the startling intelligence reached him that as soon as he had proceeded beyond the frontier of his own country, a usurper had seized the government. The Sultan was consequently forced to supplicate the Shah for assistance to recover his lost authority. Petty chiefs, such as this Sultan, scarcely able to maintain their own position, tendering their allegiance, was of no political value to the Shah, but rather a source of trouble and anxiety.

Sir Alexander Burnes, who was left as agent in Cabul, communicated to us at this time alarming reports, which he seemed disposed to credit, of the advance to Khiva of a powerful Russian force of 24,000 men and seventy-two guns. Intimation had previously reached the Envoy from the Court of Directors in England of the despatch of a Russian force of 4,000 men to Khiva, but which had not reached its destination. I could not but regard the reports forwarded by Burnes as greatly exaggerated. The equipment and despatch of so large a force as Burnes represented could scarcely have escaped the attention of the Government in England, and would have been certainly reported to the authorities in India. Russia had, no doubt, very just grounds for advancing to Khiva to release its subjects, where so many were known to be in slavery, and also to prevent such proceedings in future. Such a measure, at the same time, could not but be embarrassing to us, and in order to remove all cause of offence on this ground, the political agent at Herat, Major Todd, thought it expedient to depute his assistant, Major Abbott, to Khiva, to represent to the Khan the great danger he incurred by provoking the Russians to attack him, and to urge him, as the only way of averting such an event, immediately to release all Russian slaves, and to prohibit his subjects in future from capturing or retaining in slavery any Russian subjects. Shortly afterwards we received intelligence from Major Abbott himself at Khiva, that the Khan, having heard that a Russian force had advanced to within twenty-six marches from Khiva, had in consequence become seriously alarmed, and was anxious to depute Abbott as an ambassador on his part to St. Petersburg.

We were informed that a Russian ambassador had arrived at Bokhara, and was received with much distinction by the Ameer, who at the same time had placed in confinement, and was treating with much rigour, our ambassador, Colonel Stoddart. Although this intelligence was rather discouraging, I could not help considering that the only sure and satisfactory way of checking Russian designs on Central Asia was by direct remonstrance from the Cabinet in Downing Street to that at St. Petersburg, and not by isolated efforts of ours, either by armed expeditions or negotiations with the Heads of these petty states, who never could aid our Government in any material way, or prove efficient or faithful allies.

CHAPTER IV.

RETURN OF SHAH SOOJAH TO CABUL — INTRIGUES OF THE SIKH DURBAR— DISTURBANCES IN DIFFERENT PARTS OF THE COUNTRY — SUCCESSFUL OPERATIONS OF COLONEL DENNIE IN THE BAMEAN DISTRICT—DEATH OF E. CONOLLY — SALE'S OPERATIONS IN THE KOHISTAN — CAVALRY ACTION OF PURWAN DURRAH, AND REMARKS THEREON.

ON April 30 Shah Soojah left Jellalabad on his return to Cabul, and on May 3 entered his capital, accompanied by the heir-apparent and another of his sons, amidst the acclamations of crowds of his subjects, whose demonstrations of welcome, although tardy, might still lead to the conviction that he was the most popular of sovereigns. Very different, however, was the reality, for shortly after we had settled down into our ordinary course of life at Cabul, intelligence reached us of a rising in the Ghilzye country, and of an attack by some 2,500 of that tribe at Tezeen, between Candahar and Ghuznee, on a British force under the command of Captain Woodburn. This attack was happily repulsed, and the enemy driven off with considerable loss to themselves. This first outbreak of the insurrection was summarily punished and suppressed by the energetic action of General Nott, who lost no time in sending out a force from Candahar, which successfully attacked the Ghilzyes, and destroyed several of their forts and strongholds.

Rumours reached us at this time of the Sikh durbar, which, since the death of Runjeet Singh, had manifested a decided spirit of hostility to the British

Government, having commenced secretly intriguing with the Ameers of Scinde. They had also, we heard, forwarded money to Dost Mahomed, promising at the same time to aid the Ameer if he made an effort to recover his crown. Several intercepted letters fell into our hands, addressed by many of the leading chiefs throughout Affghanistan to Dost Mahomed, urging him to come forward and head his countrymen in a holy war for the extermination of the infidels, whom they represented as ' a mere handful,' whereas they were ready to join him with lakhs of men. Threatened as we thus were by enemies on all sides of us, the Envoy lost no time in pressing on the Governor-General, Lord Auckland, the immediate necessity of sending a reinforcement from India to Cabul of not less than one European and two native regiments, a troop of horse artillery, and a regiment of light cavalry.

The Bamean frontier now became seriously disturbed, and collisions continually occurred between our foraging parties and the turbulent tribes of that region. The political agent, Dr. Lord, after using all means of conciliation, which were met by defiant threats and insults, was forced to act on the offensive, and captured a fort belonging to Shah Nuzzeer, an important chief of the Huzārāh. This most laudable exhibition of energy on the part of Dr. Lord was of little real avail, for on August 30 a son of Dost Mahomed attacked, with 500 Usbeg horse, Dr. Lord's assistant, Lieutenant Rattray, who was stationed with a small force at Rajgah. The attack was repulsed, but Rattray wisely considering that this force was only the advanced guard of a greater, which he would be unable to resist, retired on Syghan, where reinforcements joined him, consisting of Captain Hopkins's regiment of the Shah's Affghan infantry, and a newly raised regiment of Jan

Bāz cavalry under Captain Hart, some Bamean horse, and two 6-pounder guns. Rattray thinking he was consequently strong enough to make a forward movement, advanced into the valley of Jumrood, where he hoped to find the enemy. Intelligence, however, having reached him that Dost Mahomed, accompanied by Murad Bey, of Koondooz, and other powerful chiefs, had actually raised the standard of a holy war, and was advancing to attack him, Rattray found it necessary to retreat and retire beyond Syghan. It was fortunate for him he did so, as the Affghan levies, as soon as the retrograde movement took place, abandoned their colours, and plundering their officers, joined Dost Mahomed in a body. The other troops with Rattray fortunately remained faithful, and retiring in excellent order, were joined by Dr. Lord with strong reinforcements, which on the first indications of the storm he had wisely got together.

Affairs now assumed so serious an aspect in this quarter that Colonel Dennie, of H.M. 13th Light Infantry, was despatched with the 35th Native Infantry and 200 horse, to assume the command of the troops at Bamean, which he reached on September 13. On the 17th, intelligence was brought in that some Usbeg cavalry was entering the Bamean valley, and had attacked a village belonging to a friendly tribe. Dennie lost no time in advancing with a third of his force to drive them back, which he easily did, when, on crossing a ridge in pursuit, he suddenly found that they formed only the advance guard of an army of some 6,000 men, chiefly Usbegs, who had got possession of the forts commanding the valley. Without waiting to be reinforced, and undismayed by the superiority of the enemy in numbers, Dennie at once advanced to the attack, and while the active little

Goorkhas of Rattray's regiment drove the enemy from the heights, Dennie fell on the main body, and throwing in round shot and grape from his guns, caused such a panic that the Usbegs broke and fled, and the cavalry charging completed the work, slaying numbers, among them many of our Affghan deserters. The Dost, his son, and the chiefs of Kooloom and Koondooz, fled early from the field. The two former sought an asylum in the hills of Nijrow, while their allies, considering the Dost's cause for the time a losing one, sought their own safety by offering to conclude treaties of peace with us. This success was very opportune, for the disaffected among the townspeople at Cabul had spread many evil reports of serious disasters having happened to our force at Bamean. They alleged that our troops had been defeated and dispersed, with the loss of all the guns, by the Dost's army, which, ' Inshallah,' they said, ' would soon rid the land of Feringhees, who would be destroyed to a man, with their Kaffir king.'

On September 20 I was deputed by the Envoy to wait on Shah Soojah and offer his Majesty his congratulations on the defeat of Dost Mahomed and the dispersion of his allies. The King was very affable and gracious on the occasion, as indeed his Majesty usually was to me. His Majesty, after receiving my congratulations, remarked that offers had been made to him by several individuals to bring in Dost Mahomed, and he, therefore, would be glad to have the Envoy's opinion on the subject. I replied, ' I was well aware that it was the earnest wish of the Envoy that the Dost should be captured, for so long as he remained at large it was certain that there would be neither peace nor comfort for your Majesty or himself.'

'But,' remarked his Majesty, 'if in apprehending the Ameer it should so happen that he be killed, what then would be the Envoy's opinion?' Knowing well what his Majesty meant by the inquiry—nothing less than that a reward should be offered for bringing in the Dost, dead or alive—I merely observed that it was beyond my province to say, but that the Envoy would himself communicate with his Majesty, and then taking leave returned to the residency to report the result of my interview.

The appearance of Dost Mahomed at the head of an army, although temporarily defeated, tended no doubt greatly to elate his partizans throughout the country, and Southern Affghanistan had, in consequence, by this time become seriously disturbed. Some of our troops, in attempting to quell the insurrectionary spirit, had unfortunately met with some reverses, especially in the Kohistan and country about Ghuznee. It became consequently apparent that some more vigorous measures were required to restore tranquillity to the country than the mere detached efforts of our political agents. With this view, a small force was sent on September 24 into the Kohistan, under General Sale, to restore order in that quarter. Another force was sent out from Jellalabad to act against some refractory Wuzzeeree tribes. General Sale succeeded in reducing several forts and strongholds at the entrance of the Ghorabund pass, leading into Turkestan. At the assault and capture of one of them, called 'Ali Khan,' fell, shot through the heart when reconnoitring, my brave and valued friend, Edward Conolly, a relative of the Envoy, and one of his assistants. The body was brought into Cabul and buried with military honours, the Envoy, the General and all his staff, and many Affghans, being present on the sad occasion; it was all I could do to read the service over the remains of my valued friend without breaking down.

Sale's operations, although successful, did not overawe the enemy so completely as was expected, for on October 18 a night attack was made on his position, which, however, was successfully resisted, the assailants being beaten off with loss. On November 1, while encamped near a fort called Bhàg Alum, intelligence was brought to Sale that Dost Mahomed was at hand, having arrived at Purwan Durrah, a small valley close to his camp. This valley was studded with small forts and orchards, and crossed by a narrow stream, and was altogether a strong position to occupy.

On the morning of November 2 Sale moved out towards Purwan Durrah. The advance guard, under the command of Colonel Salter, consisted of two squadrons of the 2nd Light Cavalry, six companies of her Majesty's 13th Light Infantry, the flank companies of the 37th, and one company 27th Bengal Native Infantry, with two 6-pounders and the Shah's 2nd Cavalry. The force marched through a rich, well-wooded country, but difficult to traverse, being intersected with aqueducts, watercourses, and ravines. While crossing the stream which passed through the valley, a small fort opened fire upon them, but with little effect. The cavalry, which was somewhat in advance of the main body, came suddenly in sight of Dost Mahomed and his force, consisting of about 400 horsemen, just as these were emerging from Purwan Durrah and the adjacent forts, and forming upon an elevated piece of ground. Our cavalry prepared at once for action, the guns coming rapidly to the front, when unhappily Dr. Lord, the political agent, proposed that they should take up a position on the enemy's flank, in order to prevent the Affghans

attempting to turn our flank.   The order to retire was
accordingly given, and the two squadrons, consisting of
some 220 troopers, had already gone 'threes about,' when
Captain Fraser, commanding, seeing the enemy coming
down upon them, instantly gave the word, '*Front; draw
swords!*' and, advancing well in front, ordered the charge.
Fraser with the other European officers dashed into the
mass of the enemy before them, never dreaming that their
men were not following close behind them. Alas! it was
not so; both squadrons followed their officers, but scarcely
at a trot, which soon subsided into a walk. Cavalry
waiting to receive a charge and assaulted are lost, and our
men, after feebly crossing swords with the enemy, who
cut several of them down, turned and fled, leaving their
officers to their fate.   Of these, two—Crispin and Broadfoot—were instantly killed; the political agent, Dr. Lord,
who joined in the charge, managed to extricate himself,
only to receive a shot through the heart immediately after
from one of the forts.   Ponsonby was severely wounded,
and his bridle being cut, he was saved by the riding-
master, Bolton, with the greatest difficulty; the other
officers escaped by a miracle. The high-minded and
brave commander, James Fraser, was saved by the activity and strength of his horse, who carried him right
through the enemy.   He was just able to ride up to the
infantry column, his right hand nearly severed at the
wrist, and bleeding profusely from other severe wounds,
and to detail what had occurred, which he did with won-
derful calmness and precision.   He was then taken to the
rear, stricken far more deeply in his heart than in his
body by the foul dishonour attaching to his standard, and
the bitter disappointment of having had Dost Mahomed
Khan almost within his grasp, only to escape him.

The instant the truth flashed on the commanding officer, Colonel Salter's, mind, from observing the Dost's red banner borne aloft in the midst of our cavalry, he formed line and advanced to retrieve the day. The gallant old Ameer, who had been foremost in the fight, encouraging his men with his turban in his hand, now planted his flag in defiance on some high ground just in front of our force.

The triumph of the Affghans was very short, for a company of the 37th Native Infantry, under Lieutenants Reed and Mayne, and covered by Lieutenant Dawes's guns, quickly advanced, and with great judgment and gallantry drove the enemy off, maintaining their position on the high ground until recalled. On this occasion Lieutenant Mayne greatly distinguished himself by his daring courage. The troops were then withdrawn, and the camp pitched, all remaining accoutred for immediate action, and looking forward to a decisive success the following day. Their hopes of victory were, however, disappointed, as in the morning it was found that the Ameer had disappeared, and his host dispersed in all directions.

I must now remark on the conduct of these two squadrons of my regiment, on which I had prided myself hitherto as a model corps of Light Cavalry, having on many previous occasions behaved with great gallantry. What could have caused such dastardly conduct in the face of the enemy as they exhibited? In a body of men *all* cannot be really cowards so as to flee in a body. The regiment had no doubt discontented spirits amongst them, yet the feelings of even such men were not likely to influence them when called on to follow their officers in charging an enemy in their front.

It appears to me that this deplorable result can alone be accounted for by a fatal combination of circumstances, which in themselves trivial, yet *together* produced this disastrous event. Just as the squadron were preparing to attack, the recall, it may be remembered, was unhappily sounded, and in obedience to it, they had gone threes about. At that moment the determined advance of the enemy caused Fraser to countermand the previous order, and suddenly to give the word 'Front; draw swords.' On the very instant the squadron received a brisk fire from the enemy's infantry sharpshooters, who having been carried close up, each behind a horseman, had dismounted and poured in their fire. Ere our troopers' swords were well out of their scabbards, or their officers had time to close up their ranks and to cheer their men by a few inspiriting words, the opportunity of making an effective charge had passed away. The officers indeed gave their men a noble example by charging alone into the midst of the opposing mass, but even this impetuosity, heroic and devoted as it was, may not have been without its evil influence on the men. The officers did not give themselves time, although the Affghans were not advancing at speed, to see that they were followed closely by their men, and the troopers, just as they were about to advance, saw themselves cut off from their officers, some of whom were immediately slain, others severely wounded, and all this in so short a space of time that the men, scarcely knowing what they were about, hesitated and wavered. Hesitation with cavalry verges on, and soon produces fear, and then all is lost, for the charge, to be effective, requires the energy of body and soul of each individual trooper, to be conveyed again, by some occult influence, to his charger, so as to animate

and inspire the animal with confidence while rushing into
the battle.   At such a moment, to be checked by even
trivial causes is often disastrous, producing hesitation,
ending in panic, among men who were the instant before
full of high courage, ready and eager ' to do or die' in
discharge of their duty.   Thus it was, I believe, with
my unhappy regiment, which was consequently disgraced
for ever.

CHAPTER V.

SURRENDER OF THE AMEER DOST MAHOMED KHAN—HIS DEPORTATION WITH HIS FAMILY TO INDIA—UNPRECEDENTED TRANQUILLITY OF THE COUNTRY IN CONSEQUENCE OF THE AMEER'S SURRENDER — THE RESULT ON THE MIND OF SHAH SOOJAH — DISTURBANCES AT KHELAT AND MURDER OF LIEUTENANT LOVEDAY — BRIGADIER SHELTON'S OPERATIONS IN THE NUZERAN VALLEY — ARRIVAL OF ELPHINSTONE — HIS FEEBLE STATE OF HEALTH—RETURN OF THE COURT TO CABUL—OUTBREAK IN THE GHILZYE COUNTRY.

UPON the evening of the 4th November the Envoy and I were returning from our customary ride, attended by four sowars of the escort, both of us sad and cast down by the evil tidings from Purwan Durrah, and at the same time rather indignant by the receipt of a very desponding letter from Sir Alexander Burnes, urging an immediate concentration at Cabul of all our forces. Just as we were approaching the Residency, we were surprised by a horseman suddenly riding up, who, pushing his horse between the Envoy and myself, asked me 'if that was the Lord Sahib.' On my saying yes, he caught hold of Sir William's bridle, exclaiming 'The Ameer, the Ameer!' The Envoy, surprised and agitated, called out, 'Who, who? Where, where?' Looking behind me on the instant, I saw another horseman close to us, who, riding up, threw himself off his horse, and seized hold of the Envoy's stirrup-leather and then his hand, which he put to his forehead and his lips as a sign of submission. Sir William instantly dismounted, and said to the Ameer, ' You are welcome, you are welcome;' and then led him through the Residency garden to his own room. Dost Mahomed, on entering, prostrated himself in Oriental fashion, and taking off his turban, touched the floor with his forehead. On rising, he delivered up his sword in token of surrender, saying 'he had now no more use for it.' The Envoy, immediately returning him his sword, assured the Ameer of every consideration being shown to him, notwithstanding he had so long opposed the views of the British Government. To which the Ameer replied that ' it was his destiny, and he could not oppose it.' The appearance of the Dost was rather disappointing, quite different from what I had imagined. He was a robust, powerful man, with a sharp aquiline nose, highly arched eyebrows, and a gray beard and moustache, which evidently had not been trimmed for a long time. His first inquiry was for his family, in our safe keeping at Ghuznee, and then he requested a moonshee might be sent for, to write letters to his sons from his dictation. His first letter was to his son, Mahomed Afzul Khan, then in Nijerow, desiring him to proceed forthwith to Cabul to surrender, as he himself had been received with much kindness and respect. Not having his seal with him, the Dost, in order to satisfy his son of the authenticity of the letter, attached to it, by a string taken from his waist, a small clasp-knife, which he said his son would recognise at once. He addressed similar letters, enjoining immediate surrender, to his two sons, Azeem Khan and Shere Dil Khan, who were then in the Zoormut valley raising followers, having on the 25th September both escaped from Ghuznee, where they were in custody.

Having despatched his letters, the Dost conversed freely with the Envoy, observing that ' they had told him that the Envoy was an old man, whereas he did not appear to be so,' and on the Envoy saying 'he was just fifty,' the Ameer replied that 'he himself was also exactly that age.' He then told us that previous to the action at Purwan Durrah, he had made up his mind to surrender, and his temporary success in that affair did not in the least alter his determination, of which all his followers were quite ignorant, except his tried friend and follower, Sooltan Mahomed Khan. With this chief and four other followers he had ridden off from the field, and doubling round our camps, travelled by unfrequented mountain paths, and after having been twenty-four hours on horseback, reached Cabul about five or six o'clock in the evening. Covering his face and head with a part of his turban, to prevent his being recognised, the Dost, avoiding the city, fortunately arrived without interruption at the Peshawur gate, just at the time the Envoy and I were returning from our ride. Following us at some distance the Dost was challenged by our sentries, but was allowed to pass on his representing himself to be a courier with urgent despatches from Nuzeran for the Envoy. He then sent on his companion, Sooltan Mahomed Khan, to announce his arrival, and finally surrendered himself to the Envoy in the manner already described. Several Affghans had by this time entered the room, and cordially welcomed the Ameer, shaking him familiarly by the hand, and applauding his wisdom in at last surrendering himself. Among these was Shere Mahomed, 'Chapper Bashee,' noted as the swiftest mounted messenger in Affghanistan, who exclaimed, as he grasped his hand—'Ah, Ameer, you have done right at last; why did you delay so long putting an end to all your miseries?'

Tents were then pitched for the Ameer's reception, who was put under my immediate care, and a most anxious duty it was. I scarcely closed my eyes during the two nights he remained under my charge, every now and then getting up and looking into the tent to see that he was still there ; it seemed all so much like a dream that *at last* we should have the Dost safe in our hands, that I could hardly credit it except by frequent visits to the tent.   Sir W. Cotton wished to put a European guard over him, but at my suggestion the Envoy declined.

Upon November 6 I gladly made over my charge to Captain Peter Nicholson, who had been selected to escort Dost Mahomed to India, where the Envoy had determined to send his Highness without delay.

Our exhilaration at the surrender of the Ameer was somewhat damped by the intelligence which reached us simultaneously of the murder of the political agent at Khelat, Lieutenant Loveday. A detachment had been sent from Candahar by General Nott, to re-occupy that fortress, which had fallen into the hands of the rebels, who evacuated it on the approach of our force, carrying Loveday along with them. They were followed by our troops, who surprised and defeated them with much slaughter, taking their camp, in which was found the body of poor Loveday, cruelly murdered. This gallant officer might have escaped on several occasions, but he unfortunately confided in the good faith of those barbarians, and fell a sacrifice to his sense of duty.

Upon November 13, the Ameer, under charge of Captain Peter Nicholson, and accompanied by his son, Mahomed Afzul Khan, left Cabul for Hindustan. I accompanied the party some little way, and the Dost recognising the charger I was riding as having belonged to his son, Mahomed Khan, which I had purchased at auction some time before, requested me to make over the horse to him, to which I consented with some reluctance, as he was a very fine animal. The Ameer's family followed him on the 29th of November to India. Among his wives was a sister of Shah Soojah, whom the Dost had compelled to marry him some years before. The Shah was most anxious to get her back into her own family, and was very indignant with the Envoy for preventing his doing so.

Upon December 4, the Shah and his court proceeded to Jellalabad for winter quarters, the Envoy and his staff accompanying him. A scene occurred *en route*, most illustrative of the wild justice obtaining among these people. A woman rushed up to Timour Shah, the heir-apparent, demanding justice, stating that her husband had two wives, herself being one, that his servant had murdered his master and taken possession of the other wife, and she demanded that the murderer should be given up to her. Prince Timour demurred, and offered to pay the blood-money if she would grant the man his life. This she refused absolutely, and the murderer having been seized and given up to her, she rushed upon him and repeatedly stabbed him with that most formidable weapon, an Affghan knife. The poor wretch, though of course desperately wounded, still lingered, and his relatives, who quite admitted the justice of his fate, put an end to his torture by cutting his throat.

We arrived at Jellalabad on the 16th December, on which date Sir Willoughby Cotton was installed by the Envoy with great pomp as a Knight Commander of the Bath. Sir Willoughby returned shortly afterwards to India, and was succeeded in the chief command by General Elphinstone. Sir Willoughby, on delivering over charge, observed to the General, 'You will have nothing to do here. All is peace.'

The tranquillity which for the time prevailed in Affghanistan, the result of Dost Mahomed's surrender, was as remarkable as it was unprecedented. The wild tribes seemed suddenly to forget their old feuds and lawless habits, and to subside into peaceful subjects, while our European soldiers were able, for the first time since our arrival, to walk out in all directions for miles, unarmed, with the most perfect safety. The consequence was, that the Shah, regarding his position more secure than hitherto, and feeling less dependent on us to maintain him in it, began to evince some impatience at our presence, and to show how irksome he felt the restraint, necessarily imposed by the Envoy, on the full exercise of his despotic authority. The first symptom which came to our notice of this change of feeling was from some intercepted documents, purporting to be official, and bearing Shah Soojah's seal, addressed to the chiefs of the Kohistan, urging them to rise and expel the British. No doubt these were forgeries, some persons about the Shah having taken advantage of their position to make use of his seal without his knowledge or permission. Whether they were regarded as genuine or not by the chiefs is uncertain, but the tranquillity we were enjoying did not last long, for on the 21st February it was deemed expedient to send out a force from Jellalabad under Brigadier Shelton, who had lately arrived in the country in command of the 44th Foot, from India, to coerce the Sunghoo Khail, a turbulent tribe in the Nuzeran valley, near Pesh Bolak, which had recently rebelled, and to dismantle some of their forts and strongholds.

The force, after operating successfully against the refractory tribes, and destroying about 100 forts throughout the district, returned on the 18th March to Jellalabad, having lost two very valuable officers, Lieutenant Pigou, killed by an explosion, the fuse being too short, when blowing in a gateway, and Captain Douglas, Assistant Adjutant-General, who had joined the force as a volunteer, shot through the head.

Intelligence reached us at this time of the dismissal of our mission at Herat, by Yar Mahomed, and of their being on the way to join us at Cabul, a very perilous journey. This news was not a little disconcerting, considering that it was with the view of preventing the acquisition of that important place—regarded as the key to Hindustan—by Persia, under Russian instigation, that the expedition to Affghanistan had been originally undertaken. The Envoy, deeply impressed with the importance of maintaining a secure hold on Herat after the retreat of the Persian army from it, had repeatedly urged on the Governor-General the expediency of annexing the town and province to the kingdom of Cabul. Lord Auckland, however, always discountenanced the proposal as too full of risk and uncertainty, which no doubt it was; but yet that measure seemed the best calculated to give strength and consistency to the policy he had himself initiated.

Upon April 15 Shah Soojah left Jellalabad on his return to Cabul, accompanied by the Envoy and General Elphinstone. I had frequent opportunities during the journey of becoming acquainted with the General, an 'intelligent, amiable man, but who had served but little out of Great Britain since the close of the great war, and was necessarily altogether without Indian experience. He was evidently in very weak health, suffering acutely from chronic rheumatic gout, so much so that it was understood he had for a long time declined, on account of his infirmities, to accept the command in Affghanistan, and only consented when so urgently pressed upon him by the Governor-General, that as a soldier he could no longer refuse. The Shah's reception on his return to his capital was apparently as enthusiastic as on the previous occasion. His family, consisting of some hundred females, joined his Majesty about the end of May from India, escorted by Captain Broadfoot, of the Madras army. He had much difficulty in getting his charge past Peshawur, as the Sikh troops there were in open mutiny, and at first refused them a passage, only permitting the party to proceed on hearing that a force was in movement from Jellalabad to coerce them, and had proceeded as far as Jumrood for that purpose.

The country was at this time tranquil, and everything seemed so secure that several of us, the Envoy and myself among the number, had built houses for ourselves. All went on until the month of September in the usual routine; but evidently the Shah felt his position more and more irksome and distasteful, and showed that he would gladly be rid of the Envoy's controlling supervision and authority, although these were exercised in the manner least likely to offend his Majesty, and only when absolutely requisite. Macnaghten himself was desirous to retire from the scene of so much labour and anxiety, and was glad to accept the post of Governor of Bombay, which was offered to him in the month of August, it being arranged that Sir Alexander Burnes should act in his place until the pleasure of Government was known. My own health had begun to fail from incessant labour, and I was ordered by my medical advisers to seek relaxation, and leave the country for a year. I was therefore greatly pleased by the arrangement made by the Governor-General, at the

Envoy's request, as a recognition of my services, that I should accompany Sir William to Bombay. Seldom, however, in history has there occurred such a complete subversion of human plans and frustration of all hopes, as was destined to take place in our unhappy case.

In the month of October, when the Envoy was about to make over charge of his office to his successor, Sir Alexander Burnes, intelligence reached us that the eastern Ghilzye tribes had risen *en masse* in rebellion, and cut off all our communications with Jellalabad and India by that route. An annual subsidy of 3,000*l.* had been, on the accession of Shah Soojah, assigned to the heads of these clans, as the surest way of securing their allegiance and the safety of our communications with Hindustan. This subsidy was nominally paid by the Shah, but *actually* contributed by our Government to his Majesty's treasury for this purpose. Suddenly, the Governor-General, Lord Auckland, in direct opposition to the strong and repeated remonstrances of the Envoy, ordered this payment to be discontinued, on the ground that the Shah had been long enough supported by British funds, and his Majesty must for the future maintain his position and authority from his own resources. The chiefs, indignant at what they regarded, and with some justice, as a breach of faith, flew to arms, and commenced operations by plundering a rich kaffila at Tezeen, and then taking up a strong position in the Khoord Cabul defiles, closed the pass, and bade defiance to the Shah and his European allies. Thus commenced a conflagration which soon spread over the length and breadth of Affghanistan, producing most unlooked for and disastrous results.

CHAPTER VI.

DESPATCH OF A FORCE UNDER GENERAL SALE TO JELLALABAD—ATTACKED BY GHILZYES—SALE WOUNDED—SIR A. BURNES NOMINATED TO SUCCEED MACNAGHTEN—SUDDEN OUTBREAK IN CITY OF CABUL.—MEASURES PROPOSED FOR ITS SUPPRESSION—ORDERED TO PROCEED TO BALA HISSAR—STURT WOUNDED—SHELTON'S BRIGADE OCCUPY BALA HISSAR—HIS DEPLORABLE INACTIVITY—SIR A. BURNES MURDERED—ENVOY'S ENERGETIC MEASURES.

THE rising of the Ghilzyes necessitated immediate operations, and Sir Robert Sale's brigade, which was under orders to return to Hindustan, and which the Envoy, General Elphinstone, and I were to have accompanied, was directed to proceed at once to coerce the rebels and open our communications with Jellalabad.

The Brigade consisted of H.M. 13th Light Infantry, the 37th and 35th Regiments of Bengal N.I., a detachment of Sappers under Captain Broadfoot, a squadron of the 5th Cavalry under Captain Oldfield, and two guns under Major Abbott. A portion of this force marched on the 9th, and the remainder on the 11th October. On the morning of the 12th I was directed by the Envoy to carry some despatches to Captain Trevor, then acting for Macgregor as political officer with the brigade. I started at gunfire on a pony, escorted by two horsemen, and on reaching Bootkhak—the limit I was told to go—found the troops had advanced at 6 A.M., and were then engaged with the enemy some five miles on in the pass. I immediately proceeded to join them, and reached while the fighting was yet going on. It was very interesting and exhilarating to see the gallant bearing of the European and native soldiers, emulating each other in ascending and driving the enemy from the heights hitherto deemed inaccessible. In the middle of the pass I met General Sale, who had immediately before received a shot in the ankle, and Lieutenant Mein of the 13th dangerously, it was supposed mortally, wounded by a ball in the head, but from which he ultimately recovered. He told me afterwards that he plainly heard me say, as I stood over him, ' Poor fellow, it is all up with you.' The enemy retired, and the pass had been nearly cleared, when I returned with my report to the Envoy, having ridden about twelve miles without any molestation.

It may be taken as a pretty clear proof how secure we regarded our position in Cabul at this time, notwithstanding this outbreak, that when the property of General Elphinstone, who was about to accompany the brigade to India, and resign the command on account of ill-health, was disposed of by auction on the 12th, and that of the Envoy on October 23, the prices the different articles fetched, were extremely high.

Upon October 24 I breakfasted with Sir Alexander Burnes, who resided in the city, and found him in high spirits at the prospect of succeeding Sir W. Macnaghten, and exercising *at last* the supreme authority in Affghanistan. Burnes felt he could do this more securely and effectually than his predecessor, as the Governor-General, at length persuaded by the Envoy's incessant and urgent representations, had increased the force in the country by one or two additional regiments. Lord Auckland and his advisers had entered on the expedition to Affghanistan under the impression that Shah Soojah, when once restored to his throne, would rule over a loyal and willing people, who were ready and anxious to receive and acknowledge the representative of their ancient race of kings, and that when once the Shah was on the throne, our troops, being no longer required to support his Highness, could be finally recalled within the limits of our own dominions. Very different was the result. For the past three years, ever since our entrance into the country, the population of Affghanistan, with one or two short intervals, had been in a state of rebellion against the Shah's authority. To live in a state of constant insurrection and turmoil is, indeed, congenial to the taste and habits of the people, and our presence rather encouraged than kept under their natural propensities. Their previous ruler, Dost Mahomed, was strong in the allegiance and fidelity of his own Sept, the Baruckzyes, one of the most numerous and powerful in the country. His intimate knowledge of the internal feuds and divisions of the different clans, and the unscrupulous manner in which he made use of it, on the ' Dividè et impera ' principle, gave him great opportunities of maintaining and consolidating his own power. Added to this, the Dost's energetic and determined character, fearing neither God nor man, and holding all pledges even of the most solemn description as mere moonshine when they stood in his way, rendered him a very fit person to rule over and to keep in subordination, through dread of his authority, this turbulent and implacable people.

Very different was the position of Shah Soojah. If left to himself, and able to exercise unquestioned despotic authority, he might by similarly impressing his subjects with a salutary dread of his power have *perhaps* commanded their allegiance. But this was impossible, on account of the controlling and superintending power exercised by the Envoy, who, as the representative of a civilised government, which had placed the Shah on his throne, was bound to interpose to prevent every questionable exercise on his part of despotic authority. Hence was imposed on the Envoy the hopeless task of ruling and controlling a savage and lawless community on the principles of modern and civilized government. Of course the attempt failed, and the Governor-General at length convinced, as already noticed, by the arguments and continual representations of the Envoy—that the only mode of maintaining the Shah's authority and the general pacification of the country was by the presence of a large British force, imposing enough to overawe the turbulent Affghan nation, and to convince them of the hopelessness of resistance— had reluctantly consented to send reinforcements into the country. Sir A. Burnes, therefore, had just cause of congratulation that he would enter upon the duties of his office as Resident at the court of Shah Soojah under far more favourable circumstances than those in which Sir William Macnaghten had held the post of Envoy. Little, however, did Burnes or I anticipate, when thus discussing the future, how speedily and awfully his high hopes and anticipations were destined to be overthrown for ever.

Upon the 24th October I dined with Major Skinner, whose house was in the city of Cabul, and remained the night, returning with only a single companion next morning, everything in the city then bearing the appearance of complete tranquillity. The rising of the eastern Ghilzyes had of course annoyed the Envoy, as occurring just at the close of his administration; little importance, however, was attached to the movement, and the only precaution we ourselves adopted in consequence, was to strengthen the mission escort by the addition of some Native Infantry and some Irregular Horse. Thus matters continued until the 2nd November, 1841.

I had just returned from my morning walk, about seven A.M. on that day, and was about to sit down to my

desk as usual, when a messenger whom I had sent into the
town to make some trifling purchases, returned breathless,
in the greatest state of excitement, reporting that the shops
were all closed, and crowds of armed men filling the
streets and surrounding the houses of Sir A. Burnes and
Captain Johnstone, which had been set on fire. I instantly
rose and sought the Envoy, whom I found about eight
A.M., in earnest consultation with General Elphinstone
and his aide-de-camp, Captain Thain, Captain Grant,
Assistant Adjutant-General, and Captain Bellew, Quartermaster-General. On my coming in, Sir William placed
a note from Burnes in my hand, begging for aid, as from
a tumult in the city he feared his house might be attacked.
On reading it, my opinion was asked, and I suggested
that not a moment should be lost in marching a regiment
from the cantonment to proceed straight to Sir Alexander
Burnes' house in the city, and thence detach strong
parties to the houses of the chief persons who were
causing the insurrection, and who were understood to be
Ameenullah Khan of Logur, and Abdoollah Khan
Atchukzye, and to seize their persons. My proposal
was at once set down as one of pure insanity, and under
the circumstances utterly unfeasible. I then urged that
at any rate Brigadier Shelton's force should be sent from
the Seah Sung Lines to occupy immediately the citadel
of the Bala Hissar, from whence it would be in a position
to act as circumstances required, and as might be
directed by the King and the General. This proposal
was agreed to by the Envoy and General Elphinstone, and
Lieutenant Sturt, our sole engineer officer, was ordered
by the General to proceed immediately to Brigadier
Shelton with instructions *to march, not on the moment,
as I had suggested,* but to have his force in readiness

to move on the Bala Hissar as soon as informed that
the Shah required his presence to occupy the citadel.
The Envoy directed me at the same time to proceed instantly to the King in the Bala Hissar, a distance of about
two miles, and inform him of this order. I started forthwith, mounted on a powerful horse of Sir William's, and
taking four troopers of the escort with me, directed them
to keep close up to me, to use their spurs if necessary,
but on no account to pull up or stop. So little was the
outbreak in the city expected that about 100 workmen
employed at the Residency had come as usual in the morning from the town to resume their daily work. These
men, hearing of the outbreak, and becoming anxious
about their families, ran alongside of us on their return
home, asking us eagerly what had happened. When
near the fort of Mahomed Khan, an Affghan rushed from
a ditch on to the road, brandishing a huge double-handed
sword, and made a furious lunge at me, which I avoided
by throwing my stick at him, drawing my sword and
making my horse plunge towards him. One of my
escort, as we afterwards ascertained, for I had no time to
see or inquire, killed the fellow with a shot from his
carbine. It was well for us we did not halt to look after
him, for just as we emerged from the road we were met
by a shout and a rapid fire of musketry from a party of
men concealed in a ditch. Our rapid pace, and the firing
being too high, alone saved us from destruction. On
reaching the Bala Hissar and dismounting, I was ushered
into the presence of the Shah, who was walking in great
agitation up and down the court before the throne.
His Majesty exclaimed, 'Is it not just what I always told
the Envoy would happen if he would not follow my
advice?' evidently alluding to his recommendation to

the Envoy to be permitted summarily to seize and execute certain refractory chiefs, but which measure Sir William of course could not sanction.

I then informed the King of the object of my visit, and requested his Majesty to authorise me to order up Brigadier Shelton's brigade to occupy the Bala Hissar. 'Wait a little,' the King replied; 'my son, Futty Jung, and the prime minister, Mahomed Osman Khan, have gone down into the city with some of my troops. I have no doubt they will suppress the tumult. Sir A. Burnes, I am happy to say, has escaped.' I accordingly waited, as his Majesty desired. Reports were from time to time coming in that Futty Jung's efforts to restore order were becoming successful, and indeed the gallantry of that young prince, with his undisciplined levies, was nearly accomplishing what *ere then we should have effected ourselves.* Believing from their reports that things were taking a better turn, I proposed, half an hour after, to the King, to proceed to Brigadier Shelton to delay his advance. The King, however, refused, saying, 'I have seen the peril you have already run. You must incur no more risk. Write to him.' I did so, informing the Brigadier that all was quiet *just then* in the palace, and that he had better stand fast until hearing from us again. Scarcely had I written and despatched this letter when Lieut. Sturt rushed into the court, sword in hand, bleeding profusely, and crying out that he was being murdered. He explained that just as he was dismounting from his horse at the gate he had been stabbed three times in the face and throat by a man who rushed out of the crowd, and then made his escape through some adjoining stables. The King, calling his Master of the Horse, desired him, on pain of losing his head, immediately to search out and arrest the assassin. I washed and staunched poor Sturt's wounds, and he was sent back in one of the King's palanquins, under a strong escort, to the camp. At this time several of the King's adherents and servants were urging his Majesty to recall his son and the prime minister from the city, on the plea that their valuable lives would certainly be sacrificed. The Shah then turned to me, and asked my opinion. I answered, 'Let them stay where they are, as they can do much good,' at the same time deeply lamenting mentally that our troops were not aiding them, *as surely they should have been.* The old King, however, influenced by his paternal affection, after hesitating for a short time, recalled his son and the prime minister. The latter, a bold, honest, uncompromising man, came in panting from the fray, and, greatly excited, said in an angry tone to the King, ' By recalling us just in the moment of victory your troops will be defeated, and evil will fall on all.' It was, however, no use his urging the Shah to allow them to return, and as the firing still continued heavy in the town, I entreated the King to send me with an escort to summon Shelton's brigade, and at last his Majesty consented. I soon reached the Seah Sung cantonment unhurt, and Shelton, under my instructions, set out at once for the Bala Hissar with a force consisting of a squadron of the 5th Light Cavalry, a company of the 44th Foot, a wing of the 54th Native Infantry, four Horse Artillery guns, and the Shah's 6th Infantry. Shelton asked me to accompany him as interpreter, but I said I must first give in my report to the Envoy, and then, if permitted, would speedily join him in the Bala Hissar. In the meantime I pointed out Captain Hopkins, of the 6th Shah's Infantry, as fully qualified to act as interpreter.

F

I then proceeded to join the Envoy, who was surprised and pleased to see me, as a trooper had come in a little before and reported having seen me slain. Having reported the position of matters, and stated Shelton's wish that I should join him, Sir William reluctantly assented, directing Captains Troup and Johnston, and a strong escort, to accompany me. Before starting I went to see Lady Sale, to comfort her about her son-in-law, Sturt's, state, and assure her that, though severe, his wounds were not dangerous. We then all three left the Residency, and reaching the Bala Hissar about 3 P.M., found the King still walking about the court, with most of his officers round him. His Majesty's first inquiry was for intelligence of Sir A. Burnes, and he was much disappointed when we could give him none. I then sought Brigadier Shelton, whom I found directing a fire on the city from two of his guns, which the enemy returned by a sharp rattling fire from their juzzails. These weapons carry a long distance, and Captain Macintosh, of the 5th Native Infantry, major of brigade, received a shot through his forage cap as we stood talking together. Brigadier Shelton's conduct at this crisis astonished me beyond expression. I had always regarded him as an intelligent officer, and personally brave. I knew he was unpopular with his own corps, but I did not attach much weight to the fact, as popularity is no sure proof of merit. He was doubtless well acquainted with all details of discipline, and strict in maintaining them. But he was apt to condemn all measures not emanating from himself, and call in question and depreciate the merits of others, after alluding to what he himself would do were he in their position. I confess to a doubt having crossed my mind before then, as to whether, if tried, he would not be found a failure, but

I as often dismissed it as unjust to the man.   Added to all this, he was dissatisfied with his position, a great croaker, and anxious to return to India.   Such was the man who, alas! was destined to exercise so baneful an influence over our fortunes at this period of unexampled peril.   Shelton, on my joining him, seemed almost beside himself, not knowing how to act, and with incapacity stamped on every feature of his face.   He immediately asked me what he should do, and on my replying ' Enter the city at once,' he sharply rebuked me, saying, ' My force is inadequate, and you don't appear to know what street firing is.' ' You asked my opinion,' I rejoined, ' and I have given it. It is what I would do myself.'   Finding further expostulation vain, I begged that two guns might be placed on a platform in an elevated spot of the Bala Hissar, so as to fire down effectively on the very limited portion of the city to which the disturbance was *then* confined, and which was fully exposed to artillery fire from where I was standing.   To this Shelton assented, and directed Captain Nicholls to take up the guns.   Nicholls, however, represented that his horses were unequal to drag the guns up such a steep ascent.   At this I lost patience, and turning to the Brigadier, exclaimed, ' Really, sir, if you allow your officers to make objections instead of obeying, nothing can be done.   We had better unharness the horses, and two companies of the Shah's own Native Infantry will soon put the guns in position.'   This was done, and fire opened. The King at this time asked me more than once why the troops did not act, and seemed to be, as well he might, deeply annoyed that they did nothing. Shelton well knew the King's anxiety that he should take active measures for quelling the disturbance, but he was in fact quite paralysed,

and would not act.   Finding that my suggestions were un-
attended to, and the Brigadier determined to do nothing,
I felt that my remaining any longer in the Bala Hissar
was useless, and therefore towards the evening I took leave .
of the King, as it happened for the last time, and returned
with Captains Troup and Johnston to the cantonments,
escorted by the squadron of the 5th Light Cavalry which
was considered useless in the Bala Hissar.

We found that Sir William, accompanied by his wife,
had left the Residency, and removed, for greater security,
within the entrenched cantonment, leaving in the mission
premises his own escort and two squadrons of the 5th
Light Cavalry.   Towards night accounts reached us that
the mob had burnt Sir A. Burnes' house, and Johnson's
treasury, plundering its contents, amounting to 17,000*l.*,
having first cut in pieces Sir Alexander, and his brother,
Captain Burnes, and Captain William Broadfoot.   We
further received intelligence that Captains Trevor and
Mackenzie, who both held detached fortified posts in the
city, were successfully holding them with great determination and gallantry, though each had only a handful of men.
Both officers sent urgent and repeated messages for aid,
and I proposed to General Elphinstone to order out two
companies immediately to reinforce Mackenzie, and throw
fresh ammunition into his fort, volunteering to lead them
by a way passing through only a short street, so that
they would be very little exposed to the fire from the
houses.   My proposal was condemned by the staff as most
imprudent, as they feared exposing their men to street
firing.

What a contrast to the vacillation of our military commanders did the conduct of these two gallant officers
exhibit, proving by their successful resistance, although

unaided, the weakness at that time of the mob, and how easily we could have quelled the insurrection had we only firmly and instantaneously used the powerful force at our disposal! But alas! vacillation and incapacity ruled in our military councils, and paralysed the hearts of those who should have acted with energy and decision. By their deplorable pusillanimity an accidental émeute, which could have been quelled on the moment by the prompt employment of a small force, became a formidable insurrection, which ultimately involved the ruin of a gallant army, and brought down upon our country a stigma from which, in the *East at least*, she will never totally recover.

Of those in authority, the Envoy alone comprehended the gravity of the crisis, and showed his usual resolution and energy of character. In his position, however, he could do no more than urge his views, which were for immediate action, on the chief military authorities ; he had no power to enforce their obedience. Situated as he was, he hesitated not to use the authority he *did* possess promptly and judiciously, by despatching messengers to Sir R. Sale, directing him to return by forced marches from Gundamuck, where he was encamped, and ordering Major Griffiths—who had been left behind by Sale at Kubbur-i-Zubbur to keep the pass open—to march at once to Cabul, with the force under his command, consisting of the 37th Bengal Native Infantry, the Sappers, and two mountain train guns.

Sir William had also sent messengers to Candahar, directing General Nott to detain the Bengal brigade, about to return from thence to Hindustan, and to march them with all expedition to Cabul, with the addition of a troop of Horse Artillery and a troop of Irregular Cavalry.

The energy and decision which characterised the chief

civil authority, were, alas! altogether wanting in our military leaders. General Elphinstone, although a skilful soldier, well versed in all branches of his profession, and a naturally brave man, cool and undaunted in danger, was unfortunately so prostrated in mind and body, by severe and protracted suffering from fever and rheumatic gout, that he was perfectly incapable of exertion.

Well aware of the extent of his bodily infirmities, he had, as previously stated, only assumed a command, for which he felt himself unfit, at the earnest solicitation of the Governor-General, who urged it in a way no soldier could refuse. Finding on his assuming the chief command in Affghanistan, that his forebodings as to his own physical incapacity were but too correct, he had requested to be relieved, and was on the eve of leaving the country. To cast the blame of these disasters, then, on this veteran soldier, would be as ungenerous as it would be unjust; but great and heavy is the blame attaching to those who, for their own purposes, imposed, against his own protest, a command on a high-spirited and patriotic officer, for which, as was well known, he was physically unfit.

Enfeebled as he was in body and mind by disease, General Elphinstone was completely in the hands of his staff, and although there were several noble exceptions among them, as a body they were characterised by the most deplorable vacillation and absence of energy. No representations or remonstrances could move them or make them sensible of our salvation depending on immediate strenuous action,—that to remain on the defensive was certain destruction, cowing our friends and encouraging and multiplying our enemies. They declared and maintained, on the contrary, that it was impracticable, with the means at their disposal, to act upon the offensive, and at the same time protect their own position in the cantonments.

Thus the 2nd November slowly waned away, and at last closed in apathy and confusion. Sorely cast down in mind and greatly fatigued in body, I went to rest, with many a sad foreboding for the coming day.

CHAPTER VII.

POSITION OF THE CABUL CANTONMENTS—PROTEST OF THE ENVOY AGAINST
THE CHOICE OF A POSITION FOR COMMISSARIAT STORES—RETURN OF
GRIFFITHS' FORCE—TREVOR AND MACKENZIE FORCED TO ABANDON THEIR
POSITION—COMMISSARIAT FORT ABANDONED AND STORES LOST—BRIGADIER
SHELTON SUMMONED FROM BALA HISSAR.

BEFORE proceeding further with my narrative of these
disastrous days, it may be convenient to explain that the
cantonment we now occupied was a space of 1000 yards
in length by 600 in breadth, surrounded by a rampart
with a bastion at each corner, and by a narrow ditch.
With a strange contempt for all military science, the
cantonment was placed in low swampy ground, overlooked
and commanded by a low range of hills, and several small
forts, as Zoolficar's, Mahomed Khan's, Mahomed Shurreef's,
the Rikhab Bashee, and others within musket range. One
of these forts had been purchased by the military authorities from the owners, and fitted up for the reception of
the commissariat stores. The Residency enclosure adjoining the cantonment contained the Residency and
buildings for the accommodation of the officers and guards
attached to the Embassy. The site of the cantonment had been selected by Sir Alexander Burnes and the
military officers during the absence of the Envoy at
Jellalabad, who entirely disapproved their choice, but had
no authority to interfere, as it was a purely military
matter. Sir William, however, protested against the
commissariat stores being located outside the entrenched

position as being highly dangerous, but was informed that there was no room for them within the cantonment, which was all required for barracks. He further repeatedly requested Lord Auckland to sanction the purchase from their proprietors of the forts commanding the cantonment in order that they might be levelled, but his lordship declined, on the score of the great expense which would be thereby incurred.

On the morning of the 3rd November I was awakened by loud firing, and on turning out was gratified by seeing it proceeded from Major Griffiths' force, the 37th Native Infantry, and a wing of Broadfoot's Sappers and two mountain train guns, which had marched immediately on receiving the Envoy's summons to return. The force had been assailed by swarms of Affghans, and had to fight their way from the Khoord Cabul pass until within sight of the cantonment. They had by their bold bearing and discipline utterly baffled their enemies, arriving in perfect order with their followers, tents, and baggage, having had only two or three Sepoys and one officer wounded. These troops had bearded the lion in his den—the Affghan in his almost inaccessible defiles—after which they would think but little of street firing. The arrival of this brave body of men greatly cheered the spirits of our troops, but did not seem to give much encouragement to our military chiefs, or arouse them to greater energy.

Brigadier Shelton was, however, in consequence, reinforced by one 9-pounder, one 8-inch howitzer, and two $5\frac{1}{2}$-inch mortars, and the remaining wing of the 54th Native Infantry, and he was directed to keep up a hot fire on the city.

An attempt, which proved through Shelton's negligence unsuccessful, was at the same time made to establish a line of communication between the cantonment and the Bala Hissar, by the road leading through the Lahore gate of the city. With this view Major Swayne of the 5th Native Infantry, with one company of that corps and one of the 37th Native Infantry, and two Horse Artillery guns under Lieutenant Waller, were sent to co-operate with a detachment which Brigadier Shelton was instructed to send to meet them from the Bala Hissar. Major Swayne advanced three-quarters of a mile, defeating on the way a body of the enemy who opposed his progress. Seeing or hearing nothing of the party he expected to meet, he was at length compelled to retrace his steps, as his men were exposed to a very heavy matchlock fire from the enemy concealed under cover of the adjoining forts and the ditches which line the road. Any further advance on his part, without the co-operation from the Bala Hissar, which he had been led to expect, would only be to sacrifice his men in vain. In fact Brigadier Shelton was determined not to act, and it was hopeless to expect him to do so, for although already supplied with a force superior in numbers to that which had shortly before carried the strong fort of Khelat by assault in open day, he had remained totally inactive for two days and a night. Thus was this second precious day frittered away in endless discussions and abortive proposals instead of in vigorous instantaneous action. Even so obvious a measure as securing the Shah Bagh and Mahomed Shurreef forts was totally neglected, although these lay between us and that containing the commissariat stores, on which the very existence of the force depended. Neither of these strong positions had been up to that time occupied by the enemy in force. On the morning of the 4th November Captain Trevor and his wife arrived in camp, having held his post as long as he retained any hope of receiving the succour he had so repeatedly requested. When none arrived, seeing no object to be gained by sacrificing his men, he effected his retreat into the cantonment, reaching it safely. His men, composed of Affghans of the Jan-baz and Hazir-bash corps, had remained faithful to him, some of them carrying his children before them on horseback. Trevor confirmed fully my previous conviction, that had troops been thrown into the town on the 2nd and 3rd November, the insurrection would have been stifled at the commencement.* He asserted that the Kuzzulbashes, or Persian descendants of Nadir Shah's troops, numbering some 15,000 and occupying one distinct part of the city, had up to that moment held aloof from the rebels, as also did Dost Mahomed's own powerful clan, the Baruckzyes, both parties watching events, undetermined which side to espouse. No doubt had we made any powerful demonstration, the Kuzzulbashes, always known to side with the strongest, would have decided on joining us, but by our vacillation we lost the support of this powerful section of the inhabitants of Cabul. About the forenoon of this day the Affghans took possession of the Shah's garden and Mahomed Shurreef's fort lying between the cantonment and the commissariat fort, which latter was distant about 400 yards from the south-west bastion, and was garrisoned by only a guard of eighty sepoys under command of Lieutenant Warren of the 5th Native Infantry. This officer reported that the enemy were undermining the fort, and unless relieved he

---

* So little did the chiefs themselves anticipate success, that at a later date, when I was a captive, they told me they had their horses ready saddled, to escape as soon as our troops entered the city, as they fully expected they would have done that day.

could not hold his position for any time. General Elphinstone then despatched a few companies under Captain Swayne to relieve Lieutenant Warren, but meeting the enemy in considerable force they were repulsed with the loss of a number of men and two gallant officers, Captain Robinson of the 44th, and Lieutenant Gordon of the 37th, killed, and Captain Maine wounded. Towards evening a party of the 5th Cavalry was sent out with the view of drawing the fire of the enemy, and occupying their attention while the garrison should evacuate the commissariat fort. This miserable attempt failed as it deserved ; and the cavalry, unable to act in a wooded country intersected with watercourses, and fired into from the enemy under cover, suffered severely, and were forced to return with the loss of twenty-two men. Their commander, Captain Hamilton, had his horse killed under him, and was only able to escape from the knives of the Affghans by fortunately catching and mounting the horse of a dead trooper. In the meantime Captain Mackenzie had been, notwithstanding his repeated calls for aid, left to his own resources. Finding his ammunition exhausted in his gallant three days' defence of his important post, which contained the commissariat stores for the Shah's force in the Bala Hissar, he was forced to evacuate his position, and although wounded himself, succeeded in effecting his retreat into the cantonment with all his party. With his small force, consisting of ninety of Ferris's Juzzailchees, twenty sepoys of the Shah's Infantry, and fifty of Broadfoot's Sappers, without a single European officer with him, Captain Mackenzie had not only for three days held his own, but made several successful sallies, inflicting great loss on the enemy. He reported that with aid, and a supply of ammunition, he could have held his post for any time.

What a comment was his spirited defence on the supine-ness of our commanders !

The commissariat officers now reported that there were only two days' supplies for the troops in the canton-ments. The vital importance, under these circumstances, of securing the commissariat fort being too evident, the Envoy sent me about eight in the evening to the General, to urge him to send out troops immediately to take possession of Mahomed Shurreef's fort, and then adopt measures for preventing the evacuation of the com-missariat fort by Lieutenant Warren's detachment. It will be scarcely credited that so obvious a measure, in-volving the very existence of the force, was discussed for three hours and then negatived. At last common sense prevailed; the previous decision was overruled, and I was directed to return and inform the Envoy that the fort would be assaulted at four o'clock the following morning. My grief, indignation, and amazement were great when early in the morning of November 6 I found that the assault had been countermanded until daylight by the General, on the plea that he dreaded the effusion of blood. When the force was at last about to advance, it was found to be too late, for Lieutenant Warren, unable to hold out any longer, had evacuated the fort and marched into the cantonment, leaving the Affghans in possession of it. Shortly after, the enemy could be seen in swarms remov-ing all our stores, the daily bread of our troops, and ap-parently perfectly careless about any ill-conceived and futile demonstration we could make to prevent them.

Later on of the day, November 6, it was at last de-termined to attack Mahomed Shurreef's fort, which, after being bombarded for some time by three 9-pounder guns, was gallantly carried by assault by Major Griffiths, with three companies of the 44th Foot, and the 5th and 37th regiments Native Infantry, with the loss of Ensign Raban of the 44th, shot through the heart while waving the colours on the wall. A brilliant and successful charge of cavalry, led by Major Thain, aide-de-camp to General Elphinstone, an officer of rare merit, entirely dispersed the enemy, who were followed into the town, and many sabred in the streets. Captain Colin Mackenzie at the same time, with his Juzzailchees, drove out the enemy from the Shah's garden. In short, it was quite apparent that the insurgents could not successfully oppose us in the field, and that strenuous and united exertion was only requisite to re-establish our authority. This, alas! was wanting, and these partial successes being unsupported by reinforcements from the cantonment, were but of little avail. The troops retired at night-fall without having attacked the commissariat fort, which up to that time was not half emptied of its contents, and to recover which was of course the chief object in view in sending them out.

Now that this fort and its stores were thus finally lost to us, the chief object of our anxiety was how to feed our troops. The Envoy, anticipating what might occur, had previously endeavoured to meet the exigency of our situation by entering into arrangements with the chief of the village of Behmaroo, situated a short distance in rear of the cantonment, to furnish us with supplies of grain. The immediate prospect of starvation was thus averted, but it was nevertheless deemed necessary to reduce the troops to half rations. This resource, after the loss of the commissariat fort, was not to be much depended on, as the supplies, although purchased at very high rates, came in but slowly, and it became too evident that Khojah Mahomed, the owner of Behmaroo, was in communication with the insurgents, whose aim was clearly to starve us out. The fort and village of Behmaroo completely commanded the Residency and the rear defences of our camp, and if once occupied in force by the enemy would have rendered our position very insecure. The Rikhab Bashee fort, commanding the left rear of our camp, was also a strong position, and the Envoy, seeing its importance, had frequently endeavoured to induce the owner, who was at that time friendly to us, to permit a body of our troops to garrison it, but was met with the most decided refusal. There was, besides these two forts, a long range of buildings within 100 yards of our ramparts, which, if occupied by the enemy, would have made the side of the cantonment adjoining them untenable. The Envoy had repeatedly warned the General of the necessity of occupying the Behmaroo and Rikhab Bashee forts, and of destroying this range of buildings, but his expostulations and my own earnest entreaties utterly failed, and were met with apathy and indifference; so much so, that even a request for some sappers to assist me in blowing up this contiguous range of buildings was refused. I was fortunate, however, to procure the services of some sixty camp followers, with whose assistance I succeeded in levelling them, so as no longer to be available for the enemy to occupy and annoy us.

The gloom and despondency now becoming apparent in our private soldiers, who are quick to discern all signs of weakness and incompetency in their leaders, were sufficient to awaken the most serious apprehensions, tending as they did to destroy all confidence and spirit of enterprise in our men. The Envoy, fully alive to the gravity of our position, and seeing that it was useless to expect any energetic action on the part of the General, by whom and his advisers all his own suggestions were either negatived or indefinitely postponed, adopted the extreme measure of urging Elphinstone, on the ground of his own physical inability, to recall General Shelton from the Bala Hissar, and devolve the general guidance of military affairs upon him, as Shelton was at any rate in the enjoyment of good health, and therefore better able to undertake the duty. General Elphinstone at last consented to adopt this measure, and Shelton was accordingly sent for, and reached the cantonment on the 9th, escorted by two guns and the 6th regiment of the Shah's Infantry.

Our forebodings as to the probability of the enemy occupying positions in the rear of our cantonments were destined too soon to be verified, for on the morning of November 10 the Envoy and I being out early, observed crowds of the enemy's horse and foot assembled on the Seah Sung hills, evidently with the intention of seizing the Rikhab Bashee fort. Once in occupation of that position the insurgents would cut off our communications with the country in the rear, and stop all the supplies hitherto received from that quarter. The Envoy, comprehending the greatness of the emergency, immediately went to General Elphinstone, requesting him, while not yet too late, to send out some troops to occupy the fort and prevent the insurgents getting possession of it. His proposals meeting as usual with a decided refusal, the Envoy for once assumed the responsibility himself, and demanded that his requisition should without delay be complied with. Compliance was thus forced upon the military authorities, but so tardily did they act that it was not until past 3 P.M., when the best part of the day had long passed, that Brigadier Shelton, with two Horse Artillery guns, H.M. 44th Foot, the 37th Native Infantry, and the 6th Shah's

Infantry, proceeded to attack the fort, which in the meantime, in consequence of this delay, had been occupied by the insurgents in great force. Captain Bellew, Assistant Quartermaster-General, volunteered to blow open the gate with a bag of powder, but by some unfortunate mistake blew in a wicket only wide enough to admit a single man at a time. Nevertheless, the men pressed in one after another with the greatest gallantry, and drove the enemy out. Suddenly a cry was raised by the troops outside that 'the cavalry was upon them,' and the whole column fled panic-stricken, suffering considerably from the Affghans, who although beaten out of the fort had rallied outside and attacked them. I met Bellew in the cantonment covered with blood and dirt, who told me to my dismay that all was lost, as neither European nor native troops would fight, but had run away. The news appeared incredible to me, and rushing to the rampart immediately facing the fort I saw the attacking column drawn up at some distance from it, and Brigadier Shelton, with great courage and coolness, rallying his men. Some European soldiers just at that moment ran out of the wicket-gate, followed by Affghans sword in hand, one of whom, I grieve to say, I saw cut down three soldiers of the 44th Regiment in succession, who had thrown away their arms to facilitate their flight. Brigadier Shelton having at length succeeded in rallying the column, led them again to the attack and carried the position. Several officers and soldiers had been left behind in the fort when our men fled; among them were Colonels Mackerell and Macrae of the 44th Regiment, and Captain Westmacote of the 37th Native Infantry. The two latter were found dead on our men re-entering the place, and Colonel Mackerell so desperately wounded that he soon afterwards died. Westmacote,

G

a gallant soldier, and clever, well-informed officer, had recently joined his regiment from furlough, and had taken leave of me in the morning, saying, as he was first for duty, the odds were we should not again meet, and so, alas! it turned out. Lieutenant Bird, an officer of the Madras army, was found alive, having had a marvellous escape. Finding himself alone with only one sepoy of the 37th Native Infantry, he had closed the main gate with a bayonet through the loop. The Affghans, finding all was quiet within, soon summoned up courage and returned. By cutting a hole in the gate they were able to remove the bayonet, and opening it, rushed in. Bird and the sepoy had just time to dash into an adjoining stable and bar the door, and this post they held until relieved by their comrades on retaking the fort. Having two muskets, they had succeeded in killing some thirty of their assailants, Bird firing while the sepoy loaded.

The abandonment of the Rikhab Bashee, after having once been taken, and the heavy loss which ensued, can alone be attributed to the unfortunate panic which occurred. Probably this would have been avoided, even although our men did not on this occasion display their usual indomitable daring, had not Shelton unfortunately sent back the detachment of cavalry ordered to accompany him; which would no doubt have kept back and overawed the enemy. Shelton deserved great credit for the gallant and energetic manner in which he rallied his troops and led them on to retake the post. The Ghilzyes had during the attack appeared in great force for the first time on the Seah Sung hills, waving banners and firing *feux de joie*; but they precipitately retired on our troops advancing towards them. Four forts in the immediate neighbourhood of the Rikhab Bashee, which had been evacuated by the enemy, were then destroyed ; a large quantity of grain was recovered in them and brought into cantonments.

These operations, although accompanied by heavy loss to ourselves—no less than 200 soldiers, chiefly Europeans, having fallen—so completely overawed the enemy that for three days following not an Affghan was to be seen, and our commissariat camels were able to proceed unmolested several miles into the country, bringing back supplies and forage. I myself walked three miles from the cantonment without seeing an enemy. There is small doubt that had our success on this occasion been vigorously followed up, as it ought to have been, the occupation of the city would have been the result, and once in our hands, backed up as we would have been by a commanding fortress, the Bala Hissar, then garrisoned by our own troops, our position would have been impregnable against any force the enemy could bring against us. But our military chiefs had long abandoned the idea of so safe and obvious a proceeding as seizing the town, and by their supineness, our partial successes tended rather to weaken us than improve our prospects, as their only result was the loss of valuable lives and the diminution of our garrison. Indeed, the most obvious suggestions made to the General and his advisers were disregarded until it was too late. The Envoy urged, for instance, the immediate seizure of Mahomed Khan's fort, a very strong position, situated midway between the Bala Hissar and the cantonment, *then* garrisoned, as we had ascertained, by only twenty or thirty Affghans, although it was regarded by them as a most important post. The proposal was met with the usual objections of the great risk of failure, and the certainty of increasing the already large list of killed and wounded, thus weakening the garrison still further. The large number of casualties was indeed chiefly owing to the miserable system pursued by themselves of doling out the troops in insufficient numbers for those operations they *did* see fitting to undertake.

Encouraged by our supineness during these precious days, the enemy, in large numbers·of horse and foot, with two guns, appeared on the 13th on the Behmaroo hills, and opened a fire on the cantonments. At noon the Envoy, seeing the danger, urged the General to send a force out immediately to dislodge them, but being met with the usual excuses and objections, Sir William insisted that his suggestion should be complied with, and a few men were in consequence tardily prepared for the duty, under Brigadier Shelton's command. No indication of any advance being made on our part until 3 o'clock in the afternoon, the Envoy went himself to ascertain the cause of the delay. On his return he informed me that, exasperated at the waste of precious time and the stubborn opposition shown by Brigadier Shelton, he had been obliged to address him in a most peremptory manner, saying, ' Brigadier Shelton, if you will allow yourself to be thus bearded by the enemy, and will not advance and take these two guns by this evening, you must be prepared for any disgrace that may befall us, and to-morrow you may find yourself obliged to do *that*, with treble the loss and risk, *which* can be done to-day with comparative ease and safety.'

Notwithstanding all this urgency on Sir William's part, it was not until 5 P.M., as the night was closing in, that the column moved out, consisting of two squadrons 5th Light Cavalry, two rissalahs of the 2nd Irregulars, one of Skinner's, and the 4th Irregular Cavalry, six companies of

the 44th Regiment, six companies of the 5th and 37th
Native Infantry, four companies Shah's 6th Infantry, one
mountain train, and one Horse Artillery gun. As the
Envoy prohibited my leaving him, I took charge of the
rear face of the cantonment with the infantry portion of
the escort and some men of the Shah's 6th Infantry.

The troops marched in double column of divisions for
a gorge in the centre of the hills, distant about half a mile,
the cavalry taking the right, the infantry the left, it being
intended that both should meet on the top of the gorge.
On the infantry reaching nearly the summit, they were
charged with such impetuosity by a body of some fifty
Affghan horse, that the column fairly reeled to and fro,
and as a volley they had just delivered had not emptied
one saddle, I for a moment trembled for the result. Our
cavalry had, fortunately, by this time crowned the height,
and charging to the rescue, the Affghans fled, hotly pursued
by our troopers.

Our infantry then advancing in order of battle, the
enemy fled with such precipitation that they abandoned
their two guns, and our troops might have easily followed
them into and taken the city, had not the night come on.
Brigadier Shelton thus gained a brilliant success against
his own will, but his previous procrastination had rendered it impossible to reap any real advantage from the
victory.

In this combat several officers distinguished themselves
greatly, especially Captain Anderson of the 2nd Irregular
Cavalry, who killed several of the enemy in personal
encounter, and rescued Captain Bott of the 5th Cavalry,
who was severely wounded, by sabring an Affghan who
was about to cut him down. Major Thain, aide-de-camp,
ever present at the post of danger, was severely wounded

while gallantly leading the infantry column; and a valuable and brave officer, Captain Paton, Assistant Quartermaster-General, had his arm shattered, and was obliged to suffer amputation. During the action a desultory attack was made by some matchlockmen on the cantonment, which, however, did no damage, and they were easily beaten off.

The success of this operation could not fail to inspire our soldiers with contempt of the enemy, showing that Affghans never would withstand a steady and determined advance of our troops. Would that it had produced the salutary effect of inspiring more vigour into our military councils, but in this, alas! it failed.

CHAPTER VIII.

POST OF CHARÈKAR TAKEN AND ITS GARRISON DESTROYED—MAJOR POTTINGER REACHES CABUL—MASSACRE OF WOODBURN'S DETACHMENT—NEGOTIATIONS WITH KUZZULBASHES—VILLAGE OF BEHMAROO ATTACKED—DEFEAT OF OUR TROOPS—FRESH NEGOTIATIONS—MAHOMED SHURREEF'S FORT ABANDONED.

MUCH anxiety was at this time felt respecting Major Pottinger, the political agent in the Kohistan, and the Goorkha Regiment stationed with him at Charèkar. Towards the end of October the chiefs of that district had risen in rebellion, and threatened the post so seriously that Pottinger had repeatedly asked for reinforcements, which it was not in the Envoy's power to send. Great was my delight, therefore, on the morning of November 15, to see Pottinger and Haughton, adjutant of the Goorkha regiment, arrive at my house, although both were desperately wounded. I put Pottinger at once into my own bed; and after getting Haughton's wounds dressed, sent him to Eyre, where he would, I was confident, receive the utmost kindness and most tender attention. Pottinger had a sad story to communicate. He and his assistant, Captain Rattray, resided, with a guard of Goorkhas, at the fort of Lughman, distant about two miles from Charèkar. On November 3 the leading chiefs of the district, with their followers, waited upon Pottinger, ostensibly for the purpose of negotiating, but really with treacherous intentions. At a meeting held with them outside the fort, Rattray was cut down, and Pottinger with difficulty escaped within the castle, and subsequently was forced to retreat to Charèkar, which was speedily attacked by the enemy in large numbers. After desperate fighting for several days, in which the commanding officer, Captain Codrington, and Ensign Salisbury, were killed, the remainder of the garrison, reduced to 200 men and three officers, Haughton, Rose, and Dr. Grant, with Pottinger, evacuated the post on the night of November 13, and commenced their retreat to Cabul. Of these, only Pottinger, Haughton, and one sepoy succeeded, after incredible escapes, in reaching the cantonment, the rest having been all slaughtered by the way. The loss of the important post of Charèkar, and of the entire Goorkha regiment, necessarily produced much depression among us, which was increased by the disastrous news following immediately afterwards of the massacre of Captain Woodburn of the 5th Shah's Infantry, with 150 men, at Shekabad, within thirty miles of Ghuznee. It appeared that he and his men had been inveigled into the courtyard of a fort by fair promises of being hospitably received and sheltered. When all were inside, the gate was suddenly closed, and the whole party shot down by a fire opened on them from a tower which completely commanded the enclosed space. In this miserable manner fell this brave officer, who but a short time before completely defeated, with 400 sepoys, at Secunderabad, on the river Helmund, no less than 5,000 Affghans under Mahomed Akram Khan.

General Elphinstone had for some time been pressing on Sir William Macnaghten the expediency of entering into negotiations with the enemy, and these disasters rendered him more urgent on the subject. The Envoy, from his intimate knowledge of the Affghan character, was well aware that the only hope of negotiating successfully with the chiefs was after some decided advantage had been gained on our part, when they were smarting under the humiliation of recent defeat. To attempt to treat, while they saw clearly that we were afraid to act on the offensive, was, he knew well, merely to encourage their hopes and stimulate them to more vigorous and united action against us. Thinking that Shelton's late success, and the consequent temporary depression of the enemy, offered a favourable opportunity for making advances to some of their leaders, the Envoy authorised Moonshee Mohun Lall to offer considerable sums to the head men of the Kuzzulbashes, on condition of their separating themselves from the general confederacy. Mohun Lall was moonshee of the city, and since his master's murder had been secreted in the Kuzzulbash quarter, where he was protected and well treated. From the information furnished by him to the Envoy, Sir William considered it highly probable that an important diversion might be made in our favour by sowing distrust and dissension in this manner among the chief men of the insurgents.

At the same time Sir William urged that advantage should be taken of our late success and the consequent lull in the operations of the rebels, to throw a supply of ammunition into the Bala Hissar, and this reasonable and indispensable measure was adopted, after having been strenuously opposed by General Shelton. Sir William at this time renewed his previous suggestion that Mahomed Khan's fort might at once be attacked, as it was a most formidable position, the occupation of which by our troops might yet retrieve our fortunes. This proposal was at first, though after much discussion, acquiesced in, and a force told off for the duty, but afterwards it was countermanded and nothing was done. Messengers had been once and again despatched to Ghuznee, Khelat-i-Ghilzye, and Candahar, and also to General Sale at Jellalabad, pointing out our critical position and requiring aid. Our chief reliance was on Sale, but at last it became clear that it was quite out of his power, from the number of his sick and wounded and the deficiency of carriage, to come to our assistance. As there was now but slight hope of our being reinforced from any other quarter, the Envoy, on November 19, brought to the notice of General Elphinstone the pressing necessity of immediately considering our position, and what course we should eventually pursue. Sir William strongly urged our holding out to the last, and vehemently opposed the idea of retreat, already broached, which would not only be disastrous but dishonourable, to be contemplated solely in the very last extremity; for we must in that case have to sacrifice a vast amount of valuable property belonging to our Government, and also abandon the King, to support whom was the main object of our original entrance into Affghanistan. He pointed out that even if we could make good our retreat, we could carry with us no shelter for our troops, who would in consequence, at this inclement season, suffer immensely, while our camp followers, amounting to many thousands, must inevitably be utterly destroyed. As to any hope of successful negotiations, it appeared to him vain, so long as there was no party among the insurgents of sufficient strength and influence to insure the fulfilment of any treaty we might enter into. He therefore inclined to regard it as the wisest ultimate course to throw ourselves into the Bala Hissar, although this might also be to some extent disastrous, as involving the sacrifice of much Government property. Upon the whole he considered that we should maintain our present position for eight or ten days more, by which time a more correct opinion could be arrived at of the wisest course to pursue.

Upon November 22, the enemy appeared in force in the neighbourhood of the friendly village of Behmaroo, from which we had hitherto been able to procure a considerable quantity of grain for the troops. Once in the possession of the insurgents we would be cut off from our supplies, while the enemy would be able to approach under cover close to the mission premires, and so render them untenable. In order, therefore, to forestall them, a force under command of Major Swayne was sent out on the 22nd to occupy Behmaroo, but he contented himself with merely skirmishing from an adjoining orchard, and returned without seizing the village, as was intended, and with the serious loss of Lieutenant Eyre, wounded, shot through the hand.

The same night we heard that Mahomed Akbar Khan, the favourite son of Dost Mahomed, and a person of considerable influence, had arrived in Cabul from Bamean. During the night of the 22nd a council of war was held, and on the Envoy pointing out in the clearest manner the necessity of occupying Behmaroo, it was resolved that a force should be at once told off for the duty. Before dawn of November 23 the troops under General Shelton moved out of the cantonment, and taking the Kohistan road, ascended the gorge on the extreme left of the hills, dragging up, with no small difficulty, the single gun which had been sent with them. On ascending the gorge they moved to the north-east, to a part of the hill just above the village of Behmaroo, and opened fire with grape on a square, where, from the number of the watchfires, it was thought the enemy was congregated in the greatest number. The enemy, in great confusion, immediately abandoned the open space, and concealing themselves in the houses, opened a fire of matchlocks. *Now* was the time for assaulting the village, for the enemy were seen leaving it in shoals, as was pointed out to Brigadier Shelton by Captain Bellew and others, but he declined to give the necessary order for the assault. Towards daybreak, however, when the enemy, reassured by our inaction, had recovered from their panic, and returned to the village, the order *was* given to Major Swayne to storm the place. Unfortunately he missed the main entrance, and came to a small wicket, which, while endeavouring to force, he was himself shot through the neck, and losing several men, he was recalled by Brigadier Shelton, although the fire of the defenders had by that time so greatly slackened that it was supposed their ammunition was exhausted, as was afterwards found to have been actually the case.

At sunrise the drums sounding on all sides proclaimed the advance of the enemy in considerable force. Leaving Major Kershaw, of the 13th Light Infantry, and a party of the 37th Native Infantry to watch the village, General Shelton took up a position in close column on the brow of the hill overlooking the gorge and the hill beyond it, from whence a heavy fire of jezzails soon opened upon our men, doing considerable execution on our closely-formed ranks. Our single gun was at this time served with great effect, and a shot killing one of their chiefs a panic ensued, and the whole body fled towards the city. Of this panic, unfortunately, no advantage was taken by our troops, and the Affghans recovering from their alarm resumed their attack upon the position so injudiciously and unfortunately selected by General Shelton. Favoured by inequalities of the ground a number of the enemy crept up unobserved by our men, and making a sudden rush, captured our single gun.

Our troops were ordered to charge and retake it, but not a man would move. Several officers advanced to the front setting them an heroic example, but in vain, none would follow them. I saw from my post in the cantonment Captain Macintosh, 5th Native Infantry, and Lieutenant Lang, 27th Native Infantry, slain while rallying their men in the most noble and dauntless manner, even throwing stones at the enemy, as if in contempt of them. A single combat then took place between an Affghan and a brave sepoy of the 37th Native Infantry, both falling dead together. At last the gallant bearing of their officers prevailed with the men, who advancing, retook the gun, the enemy falling back. The Brigadier was then urged and entreated to seize the decisive moment to charge the enemy, but from some unexplained cause nothing could induce him to stir from the hill. Fresh horses, a limber, and ammunition had in the meantime been sent out from cantonments for the rescued gun, which now reopened its fire; but the enemy rallying, made another rush, and then, alas! our squares broke, all order was at an end, and infantry and cavalry fled down the hill together. The stanch artillerymen dashed, sword in hand, through the Affghans, but were obliged to abandon their gun at the foot of the hill. I could see from my post our flying troops hotly pursued and mixed up with the enemy, who were slaughtering them on all sides: the scene was so fearful that I can never forget it. On came the fugitives pouring into the cantonment, which we fully expected the Affghans to enter along with them. Fortunately for us, and most unexpectedly, the Affghan cavalry suddenly swept to the right, directed, as we afterwards heard, by Mahomed Osman Khan Baruckzye, who was one of the chiefs then in communication with Sir W. Macnaghten. From the walls we kept up a hot fire of musketry on the enemy, and a fresh troop of the 5th Light Cavalry formed outside the cantonment, under cover of whom some of our flying horsemen rallied, but though the poor decrepit General with heroic devotion placed himself at their head, he could not induce them to charge. Captain Walker at this moment was mortally wounded, vainly endeavouring to induce his Irregulars to follow him. In this fatal action we lost 300 men, and among the slain was Colonel Oliver, a gallant soldier, but from the commencement of our troubles most desponding and despairing of ultimate success. He appeared to have courted death, for when our men were ordered to lie down on the hill to shelter them from the enemy's fire, Oliver could not be persuaded to screen himself, but stood erect until shot down. We recovered his body, and those of several others, all terribly mutilated, and gave them a soldier's burial.

But who can depict the horror of that night, and our consternation, for we felt ourselves doomed men? Nothing of course could justify the conduct of our troops; but the total incapacity of Brigadier Shelton, his reckless exposure of his men for hours on the top of a high ridge to a destructive fire, and his stubborn neglect to avail himself of the several opportunities offered to him throughout the day—by the temporary flight of the enemy, to complete their dispersion and prevent their rallying—go far to extenuate the soldiers, who had lost all confidence in a leader who had proved himself so incapable to command. It may appear to bear hardly on the character of a departed officer to state these facts exactly as they occurred, but it is at the same time an act of simple justice to the memory of the gallant officers who fell on this occasion, to show that no blame can justly attach to

them.   Their heroic devotion, had their leader possessed
common judgment and ability, must have insured success ;
but when that was seen to be hopeless, they hesitated not
to sacrifice their lives in the endeavour, so far as in them
lay, to mitigate a catastrophe they were powerless to
avert.

The Affghans, considering our feelings must be
similar to their own under similar circumstances, deemed
that the proper moment had arrived for entering into
negotiations with us, as our recent reverse must, in
their judgment, have alarmed and humbled us.   Accordingly, they sent two deputies, whom Trevor and I,
on behalf of the Envoy, met at the bridge on the Cabul
river, in front of the cantonment.   After a long and
fruitless discussion on our parts, we deemed it necessary
to bring them to the Envoy, by whom they were speedily
and indignantly dismissed, their demands being of the
most preposterous and inflated character.   The same day
General Elphinstone officially reported to Sir William
Macnaghten that he considered it impracticable to hold
our position any longer without receiving reinforcements,
and as these were not to be expected, he recommended
the Envoy to come to terms with Mahomed Osman Khan,
who was, he knew, friendly to us, and had interposed most
opportunely on our behalf the preceding day, by turning
the Affghan cavalry, and so preventing them entering the
cantonment with our flying troops.

Upon the 26th the insurgents appeared in large
masses on the Behmaroo Hills, and towards evening,
as negotiations were going on, and hostilities suspended
for the time, they passed close to our ramparts, exclaiming ' that the war was over.'   We were curious to see the
style of troops who had the day before successfully

encountered our soldiers, and we accordingly scanned them closely. To our deep humiliation, we found that instead of being stalwart and devoted clansmen, following their hereditary chiefs to battle, the troops who had chased the British banner from the field chiefly consisted of tradesmen and artizans of Cabul, so that we had not even the melancholy satisfaction of knowing that we had been contending with the soldier tribes of the country. As yet we had not suffered from want of provisions, and our single defeat should, instead of daunting, have rather stimulated and moved us to energetic action. To strike now a decisive blow, would not only retrieve our own honour, but also, by bringing down the enemy's confidence, induce them to offer us better terms than before. But although the garrison were ready enough to undertake any enterprise, nothing could arouse to action our imbecile military leaders, who actually permitted a small number of the enemy to attempt, unmolested, the destruction of the bridge in front of our camp, our only means of communication with the Seah Sung Hills and the Bala Hissar.

Upon November 27 fresh negotiations with the leaders of the insurgents were entered into, but as their proposals were of the most humiliating character—requiring us to abandon Shah Soojah, lay down our arms, and surrender unconditionally, our lives only being spared—the Envoy broke up the conference, indignantly exclaiming, ' I prefer death to dishonour, and leave the issue to the God of battles.'

From the 1st to the 4th of December little occurred beyond an attempt of the enemy to occupy the tower on the hill above the Bala Hissar, which, if successful, would have rendered the citadel untenable. They were, however, defeated in a very spirited manner by some troops under Major Ewart, of the 54th Native Infantry. At this time the discipline of the garrison had fallen into a very lax state, and the troops were becoming thoroughly demoralised. I mentioned the subject to Major Thain, aide-de-camp, who, admitting the fact, replied that he had so repeatedly pointed it out to his superiors that now no one listened to him. He, however, made another attempt in consequence of our conversation, and the same evening an order of the day was issued, which restored some show of discipline for the time, and produced increased alertness in the guards. Upon December 5 the enemy successfully carried out their previous attempt to destroy our bridge, and actually carried away the timbers composing it before our eyes, not a hand being on our part raised to prevent them. Emboldened by this apathy, some Affghans, upon the 6th, finding a small passage into Mahomed Shurreef's fort, formed by an old mine which had been sprung by Captain Sturt, crept in, and suddenly showing themselves within, the garrison, composed of one company of the 44th Regiment and one of the 37th, fled precipitately, without firing a shot, abandoning their officer, Lieutenant Hawtrey, of the 37th Native Infantry, who only left his post when not a soldier remained with him. The Envoy, driven frantic on hearing of this disgraceful affair, rushed to the General, whom he found at the bastion just opposite this fort, and entreated that an attack should immediately be made, and this most important position recovered. His solicitations could not for very shame be refused, but the attack was, on one pretext or another, postponed until night came on. Sir William sent me to the General to reiterate his instructions. I found him with Brigadier Shelton still at the bastion discussing the matter, but doing nothing. The two companies who had abandoned their post so shamefully, had in the meantime volunteered to retake the fort, and were standing near, looking very crest-fallen, and waiting the order to advance. Lieut. Sturt and a sergeant of the Sappers had proceeded beyond the bastion to reconnoitre the approach to the fortress, and as they had been absent more than an hour the General became anxious for their safety, and I volunteered to proceed with two men of the 44th to look after them. My offer was accepted, but just as I was starting the proposal was held to involve too much danger, and, much to my annoyance, was abandoned. It was then determined that the fort should be attacked in the morning, and I returned and reported this to the Envoy. The same evening, while passing through the wicket of the Bazaar fort, which was occupied by a company of the 44th Regiment, I observed a sentry of the 37th Native Infantry in altercation with a private of the 44th, and on inquiring the cause the sepoy informed me that he had been placed there with orders to prevent any men of the 44th leaving the fort, as they had been in the habit of doing on one pretext or another. While standing there I observed two privates try to pass out, who were stopped by the sentry. I mentioned the circumstance to Lieut. Hogg, the adjutant of the 44th, who assured me I must be mistaken, but *there* was the indisputable and astounding fact of a Sepoy guard being placed to prevent English soldiers leaving their post. In the morning Sir William entreated the General to remove the 44th from the Bazaar, which was considered the post of danger, as no dependence could be placed upon them, and replace them by the 37th Native Infantry, and this was agreed to.

As to Mahomed Shurreef's fort, the determination to attack it in the morning came to nothing, and it remained in the enemy's possession, notwithstanding the Envoy's expostulations and entreaties.

CHAPTER IX.

UPON the 8th December, General Elphinstone addressed an official communication to the Envoy, which was concurred in by Brigadiers Shelton and Anquetil and Colonel Chambers, giving it as their decided and unqualified opinion that no more military operations could be undertaken by the troops in their present condition, and that therefore no time should be lost in negotiating for a safe retreat to Hindustan, without any reference to Shah Soojah or his interests, as their first duty was to provide for the honour and welfare of the British troops under their command. This proposal to abandon the Shah was in marked contrast to his Majesty's conduct towards ourselves, for we were aware, that although proposals had been made by the insurgents to him, inviting him to break with us and join them, his Majesty had summarily rejected them, and remained staunch and faithful to us. The Envoy had not at this time despaired of receiving reinforcements from Candahar, and with the view of giving time for their probable arrival, and also avoiding the renewal of negotiations with persons whom he

well knew to be so treacherous that no dependence could
be placed on their most solemn assurances, directed me
to wait on General Elphinstone, and propose to him to
capture the Khowjah Ruwash fort, distant some four miles
from cantonment, which we were aware contained large
supplies of grain. These stores, once in our possession,
would obviate the necessity of retreat, for the military
authorities urged that measure chiefly on the ground of
the failure of our supplies, although the scarcity had
hitherto not been felt by us. I delivered my message to
the General in the presence of Brigadier Shelton and the
staff, and perceiving from the manner in which it was
received that there was very little prospect of the proposal being approved of, I returned to Sir William, and
urged his going in person to press his proposal. He
accordingly proceeded to the General's quarters, and a
vehement debate ensued. At last his views were acceded
to, and a detachment commanded by Captain Hopkins,
of the Shah's 6th Infantry, was directed to be in readiness, to start at four next morning to seize the fort.
Brigadier Shelton proposed that I should accompany the
force, which I gladly acquiesced in, the Envoy sanctioning
my going. I then offered to take charge of the single gun
which was to accompany the party, two not being available, and General Elphinstone accepted my offer with
thanks. On leaving the room, I particularly requested
that the officer on duty at the Kohistan gate should be
ordered to have the drawbridge down before four A.M.,
and that grass should be laid on the bridge, to deaden the
sound of the gun passing across; and this, Brigadier
Shelton and Captain Bellew promised should be done.
At half-past three, next morning, I proceeded with the
cavalry and infantry of the Envoy's escort to the artillery

lines, where I found the gun all ready, and proceeded with it to the Kohistan gate. On my arrival there I found that no order had been given to the officer in charge to lower the drawbridge, so I ran to inform Grant, the Adjutant-General, who immediately went to Brigadier Shelton for the necessary order. What took place between these officers I know not, but Grant on his return directed me to accompany him to the Envoy, to whom he announced the fact that in the opinion of General Elphinstone and Brigadier Shelton, the attempt to capture the Khowjah Ruwash fort had better be abandoned. This was but another instance of the contumacious spirit in which all the suggestions of Sir William Macnaghten were set aside, which if carried out would have saved the force. Indeed it was abundantly clear that the military authorities were determined not to avail themselves of the many opportunities which at this period offered of procuring provisions, nor even to permit the Envoy's doing so. Their sole object was to retreat to Hindustan, and they were conscious that if the force were supplied with necessary provisions, their chief pretext for abandoning their position would be thereby removed.

At this time Captain John Conolly, with our trusty ally Jan Fishan Khan, came into cantonments from the Bala Hissar, in order to urge upon the Envoy the expediency of destroying all our stores which could not be moved, and then, abandoning the cantonments, to proceed to occupy the citadel. The Envoy, myself, and other officers had already frequently of late urged this course upon General Elphinstone as the safest and most expedient which under our circumstances could be adopted.

Captain Conolly's arrival afforded a fresh opportunity

for Sir William's again pressing his views on the General, which he did at a conference on the 9th December. His proposals were met by Brigadier Shelton with the most decided opposition, and even derision; and although Captain Conolly was able to show clearly how futile were the objections Shelton offered, he would not be convinced, but jeered at the idea, and said openly that he had brought round the General entirely to his views, and that retreat was the only measure which *could and must* be adopted. In this view General Elphinstone unfortunately expressed his acquiescence. It was most strenuously opposed by the Envoy, who justly regarded the clamorous desire of our military chiefs to retreat as the wildest infatuation, which must end in annihilation, as our route would lie through these terrible defiles, difficult at all times, and at this season blocked with snow, where the force would certainly be assailed by our bigoted and barbarous enemies, whose oaths and pledges for its safe conduct were only made to lure us on to our destruction, and were never for a moment intended by them to be binding.

His arguments were, however, all in vain, so, in closing the conference, Sir William said, 'If the General has determined to retreat, I cannot of course prevent him; but in that event I will throw myself into the Bala Hissar with the Shah's troops, and stand or fall with the King.'

Conolly and Jan Fishan, finding their arguments of no avail, returned at night to the Bala Hissar.

We this day received the melancholy intelligence from Candahar, that a force which had been sent to our rescue had retraced its steps from Tezeen about forty miles from Ghuznee, in consequence of a fall of snow which had alarmed Brigadier Maclaren, in command. We felt we were thus left to our fate, and had nothing to hope from Candahar, for we were well aware that any snow which could have fallen on this route so early in the season could never have deterred a force which was really determined to advance to our rescue. Upon the 10th one of our commissariat moonshees came in from the city, saying he could, if we desired it, reopen negotiations with the chiefs, and brought in as a proof a paper signed by the most influential of them, offering to meet the Envoy outside the cantonment in the morning. Sir William, knowing it to be the fixed determination of the General and Brigadier Shelton to retreat, considered it his duty to comply with this proposal, and the moonshee returned at night to the city, with an intimation that the Envoy would meet the chiefs. I saw the moonshee safely beyond our outposts—a very necessary precaution, as our sentries fired on all alike, friend or foe. Lady Macnaghten, with an instinctive presentiment of evil arising from the conference, did all she could, by tears and entreaties, to dissuade her husband from attending this meeting. Knowing, however, as he did, that it was quite hopeless to expect any energetic action from our military commanders, the Envoy was determined that no personal risk should deter him from doing what he could to deliver the troops in this dire extremity. Accordingly the next day, accompanied by Trevor, Mackenzie, and myself, he proceeded to a spot about 200 yards beyond our ramparts on the Cabul river, close to the bridge which had been destroyed, where we met nearly all the chief men of the insurgents, among them Mahomed Akbar Khan. After an interchange of the usual compliments, we all sat down on horsecloths spread for us on the ground, and the Envoy produced a draft treaty which he had drawn up, consisting of the following eighteen articles, and which he proposed for their acceptance.

'Whereas it has become apparent from recent events that the continuance of the British army in Affghanistan for the support of Shah Soojah-ool-Moolk is displeasing to the great majority of the Affghan nation; and whereas the British Government had no other object in sending troops to this country than the integrity, happiness, and welfare of the Affghans, and therefore it can have no. wish to remain when that object is defeated by its presence, the following conditions have been fixed upon between Sir W. H. Macnaghten, Bart., Envoy and Minister at the court of Shah Soojah-ool-Moolk, for the British Government, on the one part, and by Sirdar Mahomed Akbar for the Affghan nation, on the other part.

'1st. The British troops now at Cabul will repair to Peshawur with all practicable expedition, and thence return to India.

'2nd. The Sirdars engage that the British troops shall be unmolested in their journey, shall be treated with all honour, and receive all possible assistance in carriage and provisions.

'3rd. The troops now at Jellalabad shall receive orders to retire to Peshawur so soon as the Envoy and Minister is satisfied that their progress will be uninterrupted.

'4th. The troops now at Ghuznee will follow *viâ* Cabul to Peshawur, as soon as arrangements can be made for their journey in safety.

'5th. The troops now at Candahar, or elsewhere within the limits of Affghanistan, will return to India either *viâ* Cabul or the Bolan Pass, as soon as the necessary arrangements can be made, and the season admits of marching.

' 6th. The stores and property, of whatever description, formerly belonging to Ameer Dost Mahomed Khan, will be restored.

' 7th. All property belonging to British officers which may be left behind in Affghanistan will be carefully preserved, and sent to India as opportunities may offer.

' 8th. Shah Soojah-ool-Moolk will be allowed either to remain in Affghanistan on a suitable provision for his maintenance, not being under one lakh of rupees per annum, or to accompany the British troops on their return to India.

' 9th. All attention and respect will be paid to such of the Shah's family as may be unable to accompany him. and they shall be permitted to occupy their present place of residence in the Bala Hissar until their return to India, should the Shah resolve on accompanying the British troops.

' 10th. On the safe arrival of the British troops at Peshawur, arrangements will be immediately made for the return to Affghanistan of the Ameer Dost Mahomed Khan, his family, and all other Affghans detained in India.

' 11th. So soon as the Ameer, with his family, shall reach Peshawur on their return to Cabul, the family of the Shah shall be allowed to return towards India.

' 12th. For the due fulfilment of the above conditions, four respectable British officers will be left in Cabul as hostages, and will be allowed to return to India on the arrival of the Ameer and his family.

' 13th. Sirdar Mahomed Akbar Khan, Sirdar Mahomed Osman Khan, and such other chiefs of influence as may be so disposed, will accompany the British troops to Peshawur.

' 14th. Notwithstanding the retirement of the British

troops from Affghanistan, there will always be a friendship between that nation and the English, so much so that the Affghans will contract no alliance with any other foreign power without the consent of the English, for whose assistance they will look in the hour of need.

'15th. Should it hereafter be the desire of the Affghan nation, and the British Government consent thereto, a British resident at Cabul may be appointed to keep up a friendly communication between the two governments, but without interfering in any way with the internal administration of Affghanistan.

'16th. No one is to be molested on account of any part he may have taken in the late contest, and any person desirous of going to India with the British troops shall be permitted to do so.

'17th. From the date on which these articles are agreed to, the Sirdars above-named undertake that the British troops shall be supplied with provisions, on rendering payment for the same.

'18th. All British officers and troops who may be unable from any cause to quit Affghanistan immediately, shall be treated with all honour and respect, and receive every assistance until the state of the season and of their preparations admits of their departure.'

Mahomed Akbar Khan's bearing was at first very haughty, and on Sir William's reading out the first article, 'that our troops should march with all practicable expedition to Peshawur,' he broke in with the exclamation, 'Why should you not march to-morrow?' The Envoy's quiet and determined manner appeared, however, to over-awe him, and the other chiefs checking his vehemence, he was silent and apparently well disposed during the remainder of the interview, which lasted about two hours.

The articles were duly discussed, and in the main agreed to by the chiefs, who bound themselves to supply us with provisions, we agreeing to evacuate the cantonment within three days. Captain Trevor was made over on our part, and Moossa Khan, a confidential follower of Akbar Khan, on theirs, as hostages for the mutual due fulfilment of the treaty. Mahomed Akbar first asked for me as a hostage, but this the Envoy refused, saying, ' I was his right hand, and he could not spare me.' During our meeting a shot whistled over our heads, and at its close a large body of Affghan horse made a rush towards us, but were checked, and the conference broke up with mutual assurances of friendship and good faith. We had reason to believe afterwards that it had been Mahomed Akbar's wish to seize us on this occasion, but that he was overruled by the chiefs, whose specious courtesy towards us was all assumed, with the view of veiling their ulterior treacherous designs and removing any suspicions we might have.

Great excitement prevailed in cantonment on our return from the conference, as it was reported that the result was that we were speedily to evacuate the cantonment, and commence our retreat to India. Advantage was taken of these negotiations to throw a supply of ammunition into the Bala Hissar, for we had no lack of it, and to bring from thence a supply of grain, the duty being successfully performed by a party led by Lieutenant Le Geyt, of the 1st Bombay Cavalry. Captain Hay, of the 35th Native Infantry, was sent the next day with fifty picked men of the Envoy's escort to communicate to Shah Soojah the terms of the proposed treaty, and to warn our troops in the citadel to march out and join us. Hay was fired upon from the Seah Sung Hills as he rode rapidly towards the city, but reached the citadel

without loss.   On his return in the evening he had
to make a considerable détour to avoid the enemy, and
regained the cantonment, with the loss of one man and
three horses wounded or missing.   Hay reported that our
troops in the Bala Hissar were prepared to join us as soon
as they were supplied with transport, without which they
could not move.

The Doorannee leaders by this time became rather
alarmed at the stipulation contained in the proposed treaty
for the restoration to power of Dost Mahomed and family,
and with him his tribe, the Baruckzyes, on the abdication
of Shah Soojah.   With the view of avoiding a state of
things which would involve their humiliation and depression, some of the chiefs waited on the Envoy, and proposed
that Shah Soojah should continue on the throne under
certain conditions, and, with the Envoy's consent, the proposal was made by them to the Shah.   His Majesty suspected that they were insincere, but nevertheless assented,
though most unwillingly, to the proposal: nothing ultimately came of it, owing to the jealousies of the chiefs
among themselves.

Upon December 15th it was expected that we would
be joined by the 54th Native Infantry from the Bala
Hissar, which they were to evacuate under the terms of
the treaty, on being relieved by the juzzailchees of Ameenoolah Khan Loghurree, who, although one of the
most prominent leaders of the insurrection, was known to
be personally friendly to Shah Soojah.   The 54th had
actually marched out of the fortress, when they were
stopped by Mahomed Osman Khan Baruckzye, who
advised their halting, on account of some very suspicious
manœuvres on the part of Mahomed Akbar Khan's own
men, who came up to relieve our troops instead of

Ameenoolah's juzzailchees, as had been previously agreed upon. The impatience of Akbar Khan's partizans in forcing themselves between the rear of our troops and the gate of the fortress betrayed their design of occupying the citadel; and the Shah, suspecting treachery, ordered the gate to be shut, and a fire opened on them, by which many of them were killed, as also, very unfortunately, two sepoys of the 54th Native Infantry and John Conolly's horse. These casualties, which were purely the result of accident, were magnified by several in the cantonment into treachery on the part of Shah Soojah. His Majesty, however, clearly exonerated himself from all blame. Had Akbar's troops penetrated into the citadel, the consequences would have been disastrous to the King and his family, and instead of blaming the Shah, we could not but admire the promptitude and courage he had displayed on this very critical occasion, and heartily desired that similar energy might be shown by our own leaders, who appeared quite paralysed and incapable of adopting any measures to secure *our honour and our safety,* for both were inseparably connected and each dependent on the other.

Upon December 16 the 54th Regiment, with half of Nicholl's troop of Horse Artillery, evacuated the citadel and marched into cantonments. During the entire route they were fired upon by the Ghazees or Fanatics, and lost several men. One poor English artilleryman, who had been severely wounded, and was being carried in a waggon some way in the rear, was set upon by them and brutally murdered.

The chiefs, upon being remonstrated with for this outrage, declared that they were quite powerless to restrain their followers, which ought to have convinced the General and his supporters, who were so urgent for the conclusion

of the treaty, that no sort of dependence was to be placed
on the most solemn assurances of such savages, nor any
safety to be expected from a retrograde movement on our
part. Still their cry was 'Retreat, retreat!' as if by
that movement alone could our safety and honour be
secured.

Notwithstanding the stipulation of the chiefs under
the treaty to furnish us with all requisite supplies, little
or no provisions were being brought in, and such was the
scarcity that some of our Mahomedan soldiers and our
camp followers had to subsist upon carrion. General
Elphinstone officially addressed the Envoy on the 11th
December, pointing out that the cattle would soon be
unable to move from starvation unless forage were supplied for their support, and urging him to arrange with
the chiefs to send in supplies, which, if not treacherously
inclined, they could do in great abundance without
any difficulty. Sir William in consequence addressed
a communication to the chiefs, who replied in writing,
that so long as we held the strong position of the
magazine, the Masjid, the Rikhab Bashee, and Zoolficar
Khan's forts, close to cantonments, their people placed
no reliance on our stipulations to retire or leave the
country, and therefore they could not furnish any supplies until these forts were evacuated by our troops and
made over to them. The Envoy took this reply to the
General, who, naturally enough, demurred to complying
with such unreasonable demands. Sir William then
urged upon the General, as the only other alternative,
that he should march out at once in order of battle,
and enter Cabul, or fight the enemy beneath its walls,
expressing his own earnest hope that the General, now
that he had been reinforced by the fresh troops from

the Bala Hissar, would adopt this clear and obvious course. Elphinstone, however, declined, urging his inability to attack the enemy, and the forts were the same evening given up and immediately occupied by the Affghans. The Envoy and I stood on a mound near the mosque while the forts were being evacuated by our men, and I am not ashamed to say it was with eyes moistened with tears from grief and indignation, we witnessed these strongholds, the last prop of our tottering power in Cabul, which it had cost us so much blood to seize and defend, made over, one after another, to our treacherous and exulting enemies. Nuseerolla Khan, who had been sent in as an hostage for the fulfilment of the treaty on the part of the Affghans, was standing by us on this sad occasion ; I had been kind to the old man, and he evidently sympathised with us, and participated in the feelings of shame and anguish it was in vain for either of us to endeavour to stifle or conceal.

As was to have been expected, the enemy, instead of being conciliated by our making over to them the forts, only raised their demands. The Envoy, attended by Mackenzie and myself, held a conference with the chiefs on December 20, who demanded the immediate surrender of our 9-pounder guns, which the Envoy at once rejecting, the conference broke up. On our return from this meeting, Sir William, in my presence, proposed to General Elphinstone ' to break off all negotiations as futile and vain, and to take our chance in the field, as he felt sure we would beat them if we only marched out boldly and met the rebels in the open plain.' Instead of hailing eagerly this manly suggestion, the enfeebled old man, prompted by those who felt no manly shame in urging him on to retreat, merely reiterated his former excuses, and asserted that the abandonment of our position was

the only solution of our difficulties. On this day the
chiefs demanded four hostages to be made over to them,
as the security for our evacuating the cantonments and
commencing our retreat. John Conolly and Captain
Airey, aide-de-camp to General Elphinstone, volunteered
to go, and accompanied the chiefs, who promised, at the
earnest request of his wife, to send back Trevor, who had
been a hostage since the 11th, when the treaty was nego-
tiated. Little did she know, poor woman, what her unfortunate request for the return of her husband was to
cost her.

Several of the Affghan leaders had for some time been
endeavouring to induce Sir William to enter into separate
and distinct negotiations with them, but with that stern
spirit of integrity for which he was distinguished, the Envoy
resolutely declined their overtures, and expressed his fixed
determination to treat with the Sirdars only in their col-
lective capacity. The chiefs, however, had, as a body, up
to this time entirely failed to fulfil the terms of the treaty,
or to carry out any of their promises, never having sent
in, as they bound themselves to do, Captains Skinner and
Drummond, who had been concealed in the city since the
commencement of the outbreak on the fatal November 2.
Sir William was on this account more particularly careful
to avoid all suspicion of double dealing, as he well knew
that any one act of only apparent duplicity on his part,
though such might generally be regarded as a legitimate
exercise of diplomatic skill, would be at once eagerly
seized on by the Affghans as a full justification on their
part for their breach of faith, and for the darkest acts
of treachery, and also inevitably sever the very slender
hold the Envoy still had on their minds. On December 21 the Envoy had another stormy conference with

the chiefs, who pretended to be greatly incensed by the contents of an intercepted letter addressed by Major Leach, the political agent at Khelat-i-Ghilzye, to an influential banker in Cabul, urging him to assist us to the utmost of his power, and assuring him of being munificently rewarded on the return of our troops to reoccupy Affghanistan. The chiefs were very overbearing and disrespectful in their treatment of the Envoy, omitting the usual courtesy of dismounting from their horses, talking loudly and angrily of this instance, as they alleged, of treachery and breach of faith on our part, proving as it did that we had no real intention, whatever we said, of finally leaving the country. Sir William at length succeeded in pacifying them, by representing that the letter must have been written by Leach in complete ignorance of the pending negotiations, and the conference, though destitute of any results, closed amicably as far as outward appearances went.

Up to this time the Envoy, as has been already stated, had scrupulously abstained from receiving any overtures from any individual chief apart from the main body, explaining in the frankest manner to those who made them, that their mutual animosities were so inveterate, and their interests so divided, that he could only treat with them as a body, as he felt assured that no engagement would prove in the least binding to which each and all of the chiefs did not distinctly stand pledged.

It had, however, *now* become quite apparent that no trust was to be placed in the assurances and pledges of the insurgent leaders, *even acting collectively*, for no single stipulation to which they had bound themselves had been as yet observed. As, then, nothing was to be looked for from the chiefs *acting as a council*, the Envoy, as the sole chance of effecting his object, determined to alter his previous course of policy, and to negotiate separately with Mahomed Akbar Khan—who had made known his wish to treat—as he was the sole chief possessed of sufficient power and influence to enforce the due observance of any treaty entered into with himself individually.

On the evening of December 22, Captain Skinner, who had been since November 2 a prisoner in the city, came into cantonments on his parole, attended by Sirdar Selim Khan, a cousin of Mahomed Akbar's, and Surwar Khan, a Lohannee merchant, with proposals to the Envoy from Mahomed Akbar, contained in a document signed by himself. It happened that I was not present on this occasion, and next morning Sir William informed me of the proposals which had been made to him. These were to the effect that Shah Soojah should remain king, with Mahomed Akbar as his minister; that Mahomed Shurreef's fort should be garrisoned by one British regiment, and the Bala Hissar by another; that our forces should remain in Affghanistan until the spring, when they would evacuate the country, as the season would then be favourable for marching; and finally, that Ameen-oollah Khan, the chief instigator of the rebellion, should be made over to us. The Envoy said, he had summarily rejected the last proposal; but the rest he thought might be agreed to. He then stated his intention of meeting Akbar Khan in the forenoon by appointment to discuss, and if possible conclude, the treaty. Sir William informed me that he had already discussed the terms of the proposed agreement with General Elphinstone, and had requested him to have two regiments ready by noon for secret service.

At 11 A.M. I received a note from Sir William, desiring

Trevor, Mackenzie, and myself, with an escort of ten troopers, to accompany him to the conference. Accordingly we all three, with the escort, attended the Envoy at noon, who appeared unusually flurried and excited in manner. As we were leaving the cantonment, General Elphinstone met us, and expressed to the Envoy some fear of treachery, and his own misgiving about the business. Sir William answered, ' If you will at once march out the troops and meet the enemy, I will accompany you, and I am sure we shall beat them ; as regards these negotiations, I have no faith in them.' The General replied, shaking his head, ' Macnaghten, I can't ; the troops are not to be depended on.' These were the last words which ever passed between them.

As we moved out of the Seah Sung gate we found a crowd of Affghans, armed with juzzails and their long knives, congregated there, and I requested the officer on guard to order them off. After passing through the crowd, I noticed that the reserve guard was not on duty, so, turning back, I begged the officer to tell the field officer that the Envoy, being about to hold a conference with the chiefs, desired the guard to be brought out of cantonments, so as to be ready to meet any emergency. On my rejoining Sir William, he remarked to me how strange it was that neither General Elphinstone nor Shelton, although both were well aware of the critical state of affairs, should have nothing ready ; adding, with some bitterness, ' But it is of a piece with all the rest.' He then remarked that the escort was smaller than usually attended him on such occasions. I remarked that I had taken sixteen troopers with me, instead of only ten, as he himself had ordered. I then proposed going back to order Le Geyt, who was anxious to see the meeting, to follow with the remainder of

the escort. 'Do so,' Sir William replied; 'and tell him
to let Shelton know, as he also expressed a wish to see the
conference.' I rode back to issue the necessary orders,
and afterwards rejoined the party.

Some days previously Mahomed Akbar had communicated to the Envoy his wish to receive as gifts
from him a pair of double-barrelled pistols of mine, and
a fine horse belonging to Captain Grant, to which he had
taken a fancy. I naturally demurred strongly to giving up my pistols, as it was no time to part with such
useful weapons; but as Sir William made it a personal
favour, I could not of course decline, and the pistols
had been duly sent to the Sirdar. Grant was equally
reluctant to part with his charger, but he also at length
consented to transfer him, and now Mackenzie was sent
back to fetch the horse, which had been forgotten, and
which he accordingly brought. Sir William then warned
me, that at the close of the conference I should be
required to ride to the Bala Hissar to communicate the
result to Shah Soojah, and then expressed his strong hope
that he had secured Mahomed Akbar to our interests,
and that all would be satisfactorily settled at the conference. I expressed my hope that it might turn out as he
expected, but asked at the same time if there was not
some risk of treachery. 'Treachery!' he replied, 'of
course there is; but what can I do? The General has
declared his inability to fight, we have no prospect of aid
from any quarter, the enemy are only playing with us,
not one article of the treaty have they fulfilled, and I
have no confidence whatever in them. The life I have led
for the last six weeks, you, Lawrence, know well; and
rather than be disgraced, and live it over again, I would
risk a hundred deaths; success will save our honour, and

more than make up for all risks.' We had by this time reached the place fixed for the conference near the river, about 300 yards from the cantonment, in the direction of Mahomed Shurreef's fort, where Mahomed Akbar, attended by Mahomed Shah Khan, Sultan Jan, and other Ghilzye chiefs, had already arrived. After the usual salutations of Salaam Aleikoom, 'Peace be with you,' had been exchanged on both sides, Sir William, addressing Mahomed Akbar, said : 'Sirdar Sahib, here is Grant Sahib's horse for you, as you wished.' 'Many thanks,' said Akbar, 'and also for Lawrence Sahib's pistols, which you see I am wearing. Shall we now dismount ?' Sir William assenting, some horse-rugs were spread on a small mound sloping towards the river, which was freer from snow than the surrounding ground. The Envoy dismounting, reclined on the slope, and Trevor and Mackenzie sat down beside him. At first, on dismounting, I stood behind Sir William ; but on being importuned by Mahomed Shah Khan to be seated, I knelt on one knee, the escort being drawn up a short distance in the rear. I had on first arriving remarked to Sir William the unusually large number of armed Affghans congregated around us, and suggested his requesting Akbar Khan to send them to a distance, as the meeting was confidential. The Envoy, in consequence, mentioned the subject to Mahomed Akbar, who said, 'Oh, we are all in the same boat, and Lawrence Sahib need not be the least alarmed.' Scarcely were the words uttered, when my pistols were snatched from my waist, my sword drawn from the scabbard, and my arms pinioned by Mahomed Shah Khan, who raised me up from the ground, saying, 'If you value your life, come along with me.' I turned round and saw the Envoy, with his head down the declivity, struggling to rise, and his wrists locked in the grasp of Mahomed Akbar, horror and consternation being apparent in his face. Trevor and Mackenzie I noticed also in the same predicament as myself. Comprehending at a glance that resistance was useless, I said to Mahomed Shah Khan, 'Lead on ; I will follow you.' At the same moment swarms of Affghans, armed to the teeth, sprang up all around, yelling, and demanding that I should be given up as a 'koorbàn'—a sacrifice—to their vengeance. They were with the utmost difficulty kept off by Mahomed Shah Khan's retinue, who closed in and fought around me. On reaching his horse the Sirdar at once mounted, calling on me to get up behind him. I accordingly sprang up, at the same instant driving my spurs into the horse to rouse his mettle and keep him on his feet, for the frozen snow was slippery as glass, and once down I knew too well it would be all over with me. Nobly did he respond to the call, and rushed forward with his double burden, the guards closing in around us, keeping off with great difficulty the savages yelling for my blood, and receiving themselves many blows intended for me. One fellow, more daring and nimble than the rest, broke through our protectors, and springing under the horse's legs seized my sabretash to pull me down. I clung on for dear life to the chief, and the strap fortunately breaking, my assailant rolled over on the snow. As we hurried along, my relentless enemies pressed in upon us in increasing numbers, and had they fired their juzzails my span of life would soon have been over ; but strange to say, they were chiefly the retainers of my protector, Mahomed Shah Khan, and were restrained from firing lest they should slay or wound their chief, who under the circumstances was as likely to receive the bullet as myself. They kept, however, striking at me with the butts of their firelocks and long swords, shouting to Mahomed Shah, ' Drop the infidel !' ' Why spare the accursed !' ' Let us shed the kaffir's blood !'

Rapidly the noble horse bore us through the *mêlée* and the increasing tumult to Mahomed Shurreef's fort. At the gate a powerful body of horse was drawn up awaiting us, which opened its ranks to admit us, and closing again, stopped the infuriated mob from any further advance, and I was saved, thanks to the Almighty, whose outstretched arm alone delivered me, ' covering my head in the day of battle.' My poor friend Trevor was less fortunate. He was mounted, as I had been, behind a chief, but the horse falling on the ice just as they neared the fort, he was, as I afterwards heard, cut in pieces by the savages. I was brought inside the fort, and made to enter a low dark room, lighted by only a small grated window in the outer wall. I was aching from blows and contusions, but thank God, not otherwise injured. I had scarcely recovered my breath when a man entered, and hastily whispered something to Mahomed Khan, who followed him out, and almost immediately returned, bringing in Mackenzie. Filled with anguish and horror as I was, I cannot describe the glow of pleasure and delight which crept over me as I saw my friend brought in, auguring well as it did, I thought, for the safety of the Envoy and Trevor. Mackenzie was severely contused about the head and body, but otherwise unwounded. The horse he was riding fell just as he reached the gate, and he was only saved by the chief behind whom he was carried, falling upon him and covering him with his own body. We sat down together in a corner of the room, but the mob on the outside soon discovered us, and coming up to the small grated window, commenced cursing us and spitting at us through the bars, calling on the soldiers who were guarding us to deliver us up to them as a sacrifice. A severed human hand, clearly that of a European, was then held up for us to look at, while they shrieked out, ' Your own will soon be in a similar plight.'   A blunderbuss was then passed through the bars, and was just about being fired, when one of our guard struck it up.   Towards night-fall the crowd of bloodthirsty wretches gradually melted away, and then we were visited by several chiefs, who spoke kindly to us, assuring us no harm would befall us. I then ventured to relieve my intense anxiety about the Envoy, and on inquiring what had become of him was assured he was safe in the city with Trevor.

Sirdar Ameenoollah Khan then came in, and addressed us in the most savage manner, assuring us he would have us both blown away from guns.   Some moollahs then came in, and desired me to write a letter to the General, inform-ing him that the moment an attack was made upon the fort in which we were, we should both be put to death.   I . strongly recommended their applying to the Envoy, as General Elphinstone would of course pay no attention to anything we might write ; if he deemed it advisable to attack the fort, he would not stop his proceedings on our account.   The moollahs were inexorable, and at length compelled me to write a note to Elphinstone, in which I informed him of Mackenzie's safety and my own, and that they threatened to kill us if he attacked the fort, requesting him, however, to follow his own plans without reference to us, or giving our fate a moment's considera-tion.   The moollahs left us with the note ; but to our surprise soon returned and gave it back, saying it was un-necessary, as the General had no intention of attacking the fort, and had set at liberty all the Affghans who had up to that time been detained in the cantonment as dangerous and suspicious characters. Mahomed Shah Khan, my preserver, and his brother, Dost Mahomed Khan, who had saved Mackenzie, had both remained with us throughout, the latter relieving us of our silk handkerchiefs, watches, and rings. Parties of their retainers kept dropping in from time to time, to offer their congratulations on the successful issue of the day's proceedings, which they attributed entirely to these two chiefs. An old moollah who had travelled much and seen several countries was a noble exception to these sycophants. Standing up, like a prophet of old, he denounced the conduct of the chiefs as foul and treacherous in the extreme, and a disgrace to Islam, assuring them that they would draw down heavy vengeance upon themselves for their misdoings.

Towards night we felt hungry and chilly, and some sheepskin cloaks were supplied to us, the Ghilzye guard sharing their dinner with us. Then, thoroughly exhausted in body and mind, we lay down, and strange to say fell sound asleep, notwithstanding the awful events of the day and the perils with which we were surrounded.

CHAPTER X.

PARTICULARS OF SIR W. MACNAGHTEN'S MURDER—REMARKS ON HIS CHARACTER —EXPLANATION OF HIS NEGOTIATIONS WITH MAHOMED AKBAR KHAN—MACKENZIE AND I TAKEN TO HOUSE OF NUWAB ZUMAN KHAN—CHIEFS SUBMIT A NEW DRAFT TREATY TO GENERAL ELPHINSTONE—SUMMONED TO ATTEND AMEENOOLLAH KHAN—NEW HOSTAGES SELECTED—IT IS DETERMINED TO LIBERATE ME.

WE both slept soundly until midnight, when we were awakened by our guards and desired to follow them outside the fort, where we found horses ready for us. I was ordered to mount behind Mahomed Shah Khan, and informed we were to proceed to the presence of Mahomed Akbar Khan, who had sent for us. We passed through a large portion of the town of Cabul unchallenged, the streets being as silent and deserted as a city of the dead. We crossed one street which I knew led directly to the Bala Hissar, and I was at the moment strongly tempted to throw myself off the horse and run for the fortress, and was only deterred from doing so by fearing to endanger Mackenzie, who might have been killed in revenge, had I effected my escape. On reaching Mahomed Akbar's house we were told he was in bed; but he got up on hearing of our arrival and received us courteously, lamenting the sad occurrence of the day, and affecting even to shed tears, though he gave us no clue to discover the reason of his grief. After a short time he asked us if we desired to see Captain Skinner, and on our replying in the affirmative he led us into his room. I at once rushed up, and seizing Skinner's hands exclaimed, 'Here is a pretty business!' but being startled by the gravity of his looks, I asked him 'what was the matter?' 'Matter!' he replied, 'don't you know?' 'No!' said I; 'nothing more than that we have been lucky enough to escape with our lives, and are prisoners.' 'The Envoy is dead,' said Skinner, slowly and solemnly. 'I saw his head brought into this very courtyard; and poor Trevor is killed. His horse fell near the fort, and he was instantly despatched.'

Thus suddenly came upon me the dreadful and astounding intelligence of the murder of the man I loved and revered as a father, and of my companion and valued friend, poor Trevor. It appeared that on Mahomed Akbar's suddenly telling Sir William to rise up and follow him, the Envoy resisted, and pushed away the Sirdar. At that instant some one said, 'Our troops were coming out of cantonments,' when quick as thought Akbar shot Macnaghten through the body with one of my own pistols, which the Envoy had so lately presented to him. The Ghazees at once mutilated the corpse, no one interfering to save him except his faithful jemadar, who, rushing on Akbar with his drawn sword, was instantly cut to pieces. Sir William's mutilated body was dragged through the city, and his head stuck up for all to gaze upon in the Char Chowk, the most frequented and open part of Cabul. Trevor was carried off as we had been ourselves, but unfortunately the horse on which he was mounted behind an Affghan Sirdar fell on the snow just as he was nearing the gate of the fort, and a man named Moolah Mohseim struck him his deathblow as he lay entangled with the horse, exclaiming, 'Suggee, Trevor'—Die, dog Trevor.

Thus miserably perished, by an act of treachery, Sir

William Macnaghten, a man of the highest attainments in all branches of Eastern knowledge, a skilful politician and a most distinguished statesman, but above all, an upright, high-minded, chivalrous gentleman, a fitting representative of the British Government from his brilliant talents, entire devotion to the honour and interests of his country, and his undaunted personal courage.

Holding every species of intrigue in just abhorrence, he may be said to have fallen a victim to his own rectitude of purpose and unbending sense of honour. The proposals made to him on several occasions by Shah Soojah for the seizure and summary execution of several of the leading chiefs, Sir William had indignantly rejected. To effect their seizure as his Majesty desired would have required much dissembling on his part, and false protestations of friendship, which were abhorrent to Macnaghten's sensitive and straightforward nature. The leaders who were thus saved by his personal influence from a fate they richly deserved, were the very persons who treacherously compassed his death. When through the imbecility of the military authorities the Envoy was compelled, sorely against his will and his own judgment, to enter into negotiations with the hostile chiefs, he behaved with consummate prudence and strictly fulfilled to the very letter his own part of the engagements entered into with them, although every stipulation was evaded and every promise deliberately broken on their part. Finding their conduct to be so faithless that nothing could be hoped from negotiating with them *as a body*, the Envoy was perfectly justified in entertaining the proposals made to him by Mahomed Akbar Khan, a person of great weight and influence in the country, and whose regard for his own interest rendered it highly probable that he would be faithful to his engagements. His father, Dost Mahomed, and his family being prisoners in Hindustan, entirely in our power, constituted a powerful guarantee for the son's fulfilling his obligations, added to which was the certainty, in the case of failure on his part, of reprisals on ours, and the re-occupation of his country sooner or later by an avenging army. The position also which Mahomed Akbar was himself to occupy as Vizier would invest him with almost absolute power, and the large annual allowance secured to him would, it was very reasonably expected, prove sufficient inducements to secure his adherence to any engagements he might enter into with us. Added to this the well known and bitter hostility existing between himself and the leader of the insurrection, Ameenoollah Khan, would naturally induce him to grasp at any arrangement which would place his rival under his power, and give him an opportunity of dealing with him as he pleased. There were, in short, abundant good and sufficient reasons for inducing the Envoy, even at considerable personal risk, of which, however, he never took any account, to endeavour in a personal interview with Mahomed Akbar to bring these negotiations to a satisfactory conclusion. If they proved successful, the safety of our forces would be the result; if they failed, his own life and the lives of his staff might of course be sacrificed, but even then our army would be placed in no worse position than they already occupied. The Envoy did not attempt to disguise from himself the personal peril he was about to encounter, but an exalted sense of duty upheld him, and he was prepared to face any danger in the almost forlorn hope of at length rescuing his countrymen from a position of otherwise almost certain destruction.

Many a brave man has fallen in his country's cause, but no braver or more self-devoted a servant of the state ever sacrificed his life in the execution of his duty, more freely than my beloved and ever-to-be-lamented chief, nor in circumstances more depressing or less calculated to excite to acts of heroic daring and devotion. His own service and his countrymen at large have reason to be proud of him, and to respect and cherish his memory, falling, as he did, a martyr to his public duty.

On the 24th of December, the day succeeding the Envoy's murder, Mackenzie and I were again summoned to the presence of Mahomed Akbar, who bid us consider ourselves as his honoured guests, and to be under no apprehensions for our personal safety. With the view of securing us from molestation he directed that we should be clothed in Affghan dresses, so as not to attract attention. We were then escorted by Sultan Jan, a cousin of Akbar's, and several other chiefs, to the house of Nuwab Zuman Khan. Our escort had to close in around us as we passed through the streets and alleys, to protect us from the savage mob who yelled and screamed on all sides, demanding our blood. At Zuman Khan's we found Conolly and Airey, with all the principal chiefs, assembled in council. Meeting with Conolly in such altered circumstances (for the last occasion on which I had seen him was in company with the lamented Envoy) was too much for me. I had borne up stoically enough through the horrors of the preceding two days, but now I sunk down quite overpowered by my feelings, and could scarcely refrain from tears. Conolly begged the Nuwab to place us all together, but to this he would not consent. A long discussion then took place with the chiefs, who one and all, including his murderer Akbar, lamented the Envoy's death. They had

the audacity to blame him, however, for not having
fulfilled the terms and conditions of the treaty submitted
by him to them on the 9th December, totally forgetting
that they themselves had rendered that agreement a dead
letter, and practically annulled it by their own faithless-
ness, first by violating their engagements, and then by
exacting after conditions, which were never contemplated
at the time they professed to concur in and accept it.
After much discussion a draft was drawn up of the new
conditions on which the chiefs were now prepared to grant
our army a safe conduct to Peshawur. We endeavoured to
propose some modifications in it, but, as prisoners, our remonstrances had no weight whatever. They demanded
now that the ladies with our force should be made over
to them as hostages, but this they waived on our declaring
that such a proposal was utterly abhorrent to our feelings
and at variance with our customs. They, however, persisted in requiring the immediate surrender of all our treasure, ammunition, and guns. When the draft was ready,
it was sealed by several of the leading chiefs, Mahomed
Zeman Khan, Mahomed Akbar Khan, Sirdars Ameenoollah Khan and Osman Khan, and forwarded to cantonments by a special messenger. I took the opportunity,
which was not objected to, of sending a note to Lady Sale,
informing her of what had occurred, and inclosing a note
from Conolly to Lady Macnaghten, intimating to her her
sad bereavement. At the same time I wrote to Mrs. Trevor, acquainting her with the fearful end of her gallant
husband, an officer of rare merit and courage. To his
conscientious and unshrinking devotion to his duty, which
required him to carry out many measures of economy in
cutting down salaries, resuming pensions and jaghires, re-
forming other long-standing abuses, and having to reduce

numbers of insubordinate soldiers to something like discipline, may be attributed the dislike of the Affghans to him, and their murdering him as soon as the opportunity offered.

After the meeting was closed, Mackenzie and myself were reconducted to Mahomed Akbar Khan's house, where, although prisoners, we were treated with kindness. Mahomed Akbar Khan's confidential servant, Moossa Khan, remained in the next room to us, strictly preventing any one coming near us, and watching all our movements During these dreary days we were enlivened by our friend Skinner's account of his marvellous escape on the morning of the 2nd November, when the insurrection first broke out, and his preservation since that time. About seven A.M. Mr. Baness, a merchant who had lately arrived in Cabul with supplies of English goods and stores for the officers, rushed into his house, advising Skinner to quit it at once for cantonments, as a large crowd had assembled and had commenced making a disturbance. Skinner immediately dressed and ordered his horse, intending to follow this advice. While waiting for it, his servant rushed in, saying the mob were approaching his house. He had just time to disguise himself as an Affghan, and escape through a side door into the area of an adjoining house, when the mob broke into his own. The owner of the house, a little old lady, came up to him, and taking him by the hand led him inside and concealed him in her harem, thoroughly disguising him by putting a bhoorkah or veil over his head. From this place of concealment he heard the mob plundering his house and uttering many curses at not finding him within. He remained with this family a month, treated with the utmost kindness as one of themselves ; and though repeated search was made for him, they never betrayed him, and only made him over to a servant of Ameenoollah Khan's when Skinner himself insisted on the measure, fearing, as he did, that his further retention would ruin his protectors. The kind family only gave him up after extorting many solemn promises that his life should be spared. During the time he resided with them, the daughter of his hostess used to sit by him for hours, listening to his stories of his own and other countries, and deeply interested in all he told her.

The 25th December was a very sad Christmas to us. In the course of the day Mahomed Akbar Khan visited us, and brought me one of my own pistols which the Envoy had presented to him, requesting me to look at it, as one of the locks was out of order. On taking it it in my hand, I said, 'Look, both barrels have been discharged!' 'Oh yes,' he muttered, hanging down his head, 'I fired them both at the Ghazees when they attacked the Envoy.' The truth was that this false traitor had fired them both at Macnaghten, and stained his hand with a foul and treacherous murder. I felt quite sick at the thought, and returned his weapon to the assassin, without further remark, but with the deepest loathing and abhorrence. His half-brother, Sultan Jan, visited us later in the day, and while conversing with us in a very friendly manner, he at the same time inveighed most bitterly against our occupation of the country, and the indignities to which his countrymen, and women especially, had been subjected by our troops, and by some of our officers whom he named.

Early on the 26th I was summoned by a special messenger to proceed to the house of Ameenoollah Khan. Mackenzie seeing me look grave at so portentous a summons prepared to accompany me, but I declined his generous offer, thinking we should neither of us rush heedlessly into danger, but each take his own turn as circumstances might require. It was no wonder that both of us felt a shrinking from appearing in the presence of such a monster of cruelty as Ameenoollah Khan, who would not hesitate a moment to torture and put us to death, so utter was his contempt for human life. It was with a heavy heart, therefore, and full knowledge of the danger, that I bade my companion in misfortune farewell, and followed my conductor. To my great and pleased surprise, this blood-thirsty chief received me with courtesy and even kindness. I was personally acquainted with him, having often met him previously at the Envoy's, and in the presence of Shah Soojah, with whom he was on terms of friendship.

He said he had requested Mahomed Akbar to make me over to him, as General Elphinstone and Major Pottinger, now at the head of affairs, had requested me to be set at liberty, as they could not without my aid draw the bills on India, which were required to be prepared in regular form, for the ransom now stipulated to be paid by us under the new treaty. After a short interview, Ameenoollah ordered a room to be prepared for me, to which I retired. He ordered a guard to attend me, and every attention to be paid me, saying to his servants, ' Treat him like the son of a king.' In the evening I was again summoned to a conference with Ameenoollah and several other chiefs. They all rose up on my entrance, and Ameenoollah seated me next himself. He then commenced speaking in flattering terms of the late Envoy, but accused him of having offered Akbar Khan two lakhs for his head. *This accusation I instantly and most indignantly denied, asserting it to be entirely false. I admitted that the Envoy was anxious, and very justly so, to arrest Ameenool-*

lah, and retain him in confinement, as the chief leader of the insurgents, but declared in the strongest language that Sir William was incapable of bribing anyone to commit murder, and that offering a price for the blood of anyone was abhorrent to his character and principles, as I would pledge my life. Besides, I pointed out that from the confidential position I occupied as the Envoy's secretary, I must have known of any such proposal, had it been made by Sir William, and I most solemnly declared it never had been.[1]

The chiefs seemed satisfied by my denial, and then all proceeded to discuss anew the several heads of the proposed treaty, and renewed their demand to have the ladies and children made over to them as hostages. This, however, they abandoned, after my assuring them that it was impossible for us to consent to so outrageous and ignominious a proposal. I was then desired to name the officers who, from the positions they held on the staff of the army, were of a rank and importance to make them suitable to be received as hostages. They themselves mentioned Macgregor, political agent at

---

[1] I am perfectly well aware that subsequently to the return of our troops to India, documents were produced by Moonshee Mohun Lall which went to prove that he had been instructed to offer a reward for Ameencollah's head. But Mohun Lall never asserted that these instructions had emanated from Sir W. Macnaghten, or with his knowledge or sanction, or that the Envoy was in any way responsible for them. I here again most solemnly and sincerely declare, as I did at the risk of my life before these chiefs, that no such instructions were ever given by the Envoy, either directly or indirectly. The Envoy could not and would not issue any such instructions without my knowledge; indeed, had they been issued they must have gone through my hands. I assert and declare, therefore, with the deepest earnestness and solemnity, that such a course would have been abhorrent to a man of the Envoy's high religious principles and unswerving rectitude.—*G. St. P. Lawrence.*

Jellalabad, and a barrack-sergeant of the name of Deane, who from the extensive monetary transactions he had in the course of his duty to carry on with several of their number, must, they supposed, be an officer of high dignity and of great importance. I laughed on hearing the sergeant named, and said, ' Surely you don't want *him* as a hostage ; he is only a Gorah, an English private soldier, and not a Sahib or officer, although a very worthy man and excellent soldier, but not in a position to associate with officers.' My assertion respecting Deane caused a good deal of very animated discussion, and evidently raised an impression in my favour. In the midst of the hum of their voices I could distinctly hear hearty expressions of their approval of my frankness. ' Lawrence Sahib is truthful and to be depended on,' they said ; ' he might easily have passed off Deane on us as an officer quite fit for a hostage, but he would not deceive us. We shall trust him ; he is a man of truth.'

I then named the following officers as proper persons, by their rank and position, to be made over as hostages :— Captain John Conolly, assistant political agent, and commander of the late Envoy's escort; Captain Drummond, 3rd Light Cavalry; Captain Airey, aide-de-camp ; Captains Walsh and Webb, of the Shah's Sappers ; and Captain Warburton, Shah's Artillery. Macgregor, I told them, though in every respect eligible, was at Jellalabad with General Sale, and therefore was not available. I was then, after a cup of tea, dismissed to my room, where I lay down on my rug, but was not allowed to sleep much, my guard of four men pestering me with questions all night long.

On December 27th I had another interview with Ameenoollah, who informed me that I would be sent the next day into cantonments, spoke kindly, and on

dismissing me, gave me a present of fruit and sweetmeats.
The prospect of being set at liberty and of rejoining the
force was a source of extreme gratification to me, and on
the 28th December I waited very patiently for the
joyful order to depart. Hour after hour, however, passed,
and I had almost abandoned all hope of receiving my dismissal on that day, when a friendly Cashmeree merchant,
who had been much employed by Sir A. Burnes, visited
me, and explained the delay by informing me that in a
durbar which had just been held, Mahomed Akbar Khan
had so violently opposed my release, that an angry altercation ensued between him and Ameenoollah Khan, the
latter stating that he had pledged his word to release me,
and expressing his determination to quit the coalition
unless he was allowed to have his own way with respect
to me. He at length carried his point, and it was agreed
that I should be set at liberty the following day. Towards
evening Ameenoollah sent for me, and confirmed the
report I had heard from the Cashmeree of the discussion in the durbar, and the difficulty he had experienced
in fulfilling his promise to release me. I of course was
profuse in my thanks and praise of the truth-loving Sirdar. He then informed me that he would send me into
cantonments the next day, with a guard of some hundred
armed retainers under the command of his son, so as to
prevent any attempt, which was probable, on the part of
Mahomed Akbar Khan to capture me. I begged that
Mackenzie might be allowed to accompany me, but this
was decidedly and abruptly refused. Ameenoollah Khan
then expressed his doubt whether, although the new treaty
had been signed, our troops would quit the cantonments,
and that the plea of want of carriage was a mere blind, as
they had plenty. This I stoutly denied, instancing my

own case, and saying, ' Why, here am I, whom you are kind enough to consider as a person of some importance, without even one beast of burden belonging to me ; how, then, can it be possible that others of less influence can possess the necessary carriage ? ' The Sirdar then inquired what I wanted, and on my saying that three yaboos would carry all my property, he directed his servants to select three of his best animals and make them over to me, which was done.   He then strongly advised me to press on General Elphinstone the expediency of avoiding the Khoord Cabul passes in his retreat, as they were under the authority of Mahomed Akbar Khan and his Ghilzyes, who were not to be trusted, but to proceed through the Zoormut country, which was his own territory, and where he could effectually protect the army from all attack.   This I promised to do, and then with mutual good wishes I took leave of this formidable chief, whom, however, I found by no means so terrible a character as he was represented.   I met in Ameenoollah's house a Goorkha sepoy who had been taken prisoner at Charekar, where his corps was destroyed.   On my recommending him to return to cantonments with me next day, he declined, saying if he did he would only be either killed or again taken prisoner, as he was perfectly sure no man of the army would ever reach Jellalabad alive.

CHAPTER XI.

RECOVER MY LIBERTY—AM SENT INTO CANTONMENT—MY CORDIAL RECEP-
TION—STATE OF AFFAIRS IN CANTONMENT ON DAY OF ENVOY'S MURDER—
STURT AND POTTINGER'S PROPOSALS REJECTED—SCENE IN CANTONMENT
—KING URGES US TO REMAIN—ARMY EVACUATES THE CANTONMENT—
MISERIES OF FIRST MARCH—REARGUARD ATTACKED—ARMY COMPLETELY
DISORGANISED—AM MADE OVER AS A HOSTAGE.

AT 5 A.M. December 29, as the hour of prayer was being
proclaimed from the different mosques, I got up and found
Ameenoollah's eldest son ready to escort me to the cantonment with 100 of his father's armed retainers, horse and
foot. I was dressed as an Affghan, and my face completely
concealed by a fall of my turban, leaving only an eye exposed. I mounted the horse prepared for me, and proceeded, with the Sirdar's son on one side, and Ameer Ack-
hoonzadah on the other, and closely surrounded by the
horsemen, the foot soldiers closing up the rear. We passed
at a brisk pace through the city, challenged only by a
party of Juzzailchees, who gave us the Salaam Aleikoom
as soon as they heard the names of my conductors. Leaving the city we passed close to Mahomed Khan's—the
Yághee—fort, and halted within gunshot of the cantonments. I then proceeded, accompanied only by the servant leading the three yaboos which Ameenoollah had
given me, and who was to bring back to the party a watch
I had promised Ameenoollah Khan as a memorial of his
kindness to me. On reaching the Seah Sung gate of the
cantonments, we were challenged by the sentry, and on

my replying I was Captain Lawrence, the poor fellow shouted out with delight, 'Oh, sir, welcome a thousand times! We never thought to have seen you again.' On passing through the gate I proceeded at once to the General's, where I found Pottinger installed as chief political authority. My reception by him, and all the ladies, was most cordial; but my meeting with poor Lady Macnaghten and Mrs. Trevor was so heartrending that I cannot venture to describe it. My old Hindu bearer wept with joy when he saw me, and many of the sepoys of the 37th Regiment, and the escort, crowded round me, rejoicing at my escape, while they deeply lamented Sir William's untimely end, saying that 'with him had passed away their last hopes of deliverance from their present perilous position.' I now learnt for the first time, that on the seizure of the Envoy and his suite on December 23, the escort was fired upon and immediately fled back to cantonments, making no effort to rescue their officers. As they fled, they met the rest of the escort advancing under Lieutenant Le Geyt, and these immediately joined the fugitives, carrying their brave leader along with them. As had been already told us by Mahomed Akbar, only one man—a noble Rajpoot, named Ram Singh, a jemadar of Chuprassees—rushed forward, sword in hand, to endeavour to save the Envoy, and was instantly cut in pieces. The tale told by the recreant troopers on reaching cantonments was, that the Envoy and his suite had been seized, bound, and carried into the city. This report, vague in itself—proceeding from cowards who had fled from their duty—was nevertheless received as sufficient by the military authorities. Not a man was despatched to ascertain the exact truth, nor a party sent out to reconnoitre; no sortie made, nor even a gun fired; and though bodies of the enemy's horse and foot were seen hurrying from the place of conference towards Mahomed Khan's fort, and several officers declared they could see distinctly through their field-glasses two bodies lying on the ground where the meeting took place, and which must have been those of the Envoy and his brave jemadar, no attempt was made to recover them. Thus, almost within musket-shot of our entrenched position, and in broad day, a British envoy had been barbarously murdered, and his mangled body allowed to remain for hours where he fell, and finally to be carried off by a savage mob to be insulted in every possible way, and paraded through the city, without an attempt being made on our parts to save any of the party, or to avenge this unequalled outrage.

Captain Sturt told me that he had strongly urged the General to attack, with the two regiments which had been prepared for duty, Mahomed Khan's fort, and then to start the same night, without baggage, for Jellalabad. Major Pottinger at the same time urged the General to lead the troops, who were inflamed with fury and indignation at what had occurred, to attack the city, which in their *then* temper they would no doubt have stormed and carried. But the counsels of these two brave men were unheeded, and it was deemed sufficient to endeavour to calm down our excited soldiers by sending round the Adjutant-General to the heads of regiments, with directions to inform their men that the Envoy and his suite were safe, having been carried off to Mahomed Khan's fort to protect them from the Ghazees, who had appeared in force and broken up the conference. Towards night a camp follower of the 54th Regiment brought into cantonments from the city the intelligence of the murder of the Envoy and Trevor, but it was kept secret as wanting confirmation.   All doubts, however, were next day dispelled on the receipt of my letter to Mrs. Trevor, inclosing the one from Conolly to Lady Macnaghten.

The treachery of the Affghans and their utter contempt of all treaty obligations were now so apparent that Pottinger remonstrated most earnestly against any attempt to reopen treaty negotiations with the chiefs, urging in the strongest terms that our only means of safety was either to move at once into the Bala Hissar and remain there for the·winter, or to march straight to Jellalabad, unencumbered with stores or baggage.   Such was the infatuation of our military leaders, that even although information of the despatch of an army from India to our aid had reached us, they determined to reject both proposals and to accept the treaty proposed by the Affghans.   They bound themselves also, contrary to Pottinger's most vehement protest, to pay to the enemy twelve and a half lakhs for a safe-conduct to Peshawur, on the ground that Sirdar Ameenoollah Khan had represented, though most falsely, that the late Envoy had promised this sum for that purpose. This money was to be paid by bills on India, and I was ordered to prepare them.   I stipulated that the bills should be cashed only on the presentation of certificates from our political agent at Peshawur *of the safe arrival there of our troops,* and took care to warn the bankers of the city of this part of the stipulation.   This prevented the bills being marketable in Cabul, and the chiefs consequently could raise nothing on them.

During December 29 and 30, Captains Drummond, Warburton, Walsh, and Webb, were, with their own consent, sent into the city as hostages.   The sick and wounded were also forwarded to the city, under the command of Lieutenant Evans of the 44th Regiment, and under the medical charge of Doctors Berwick and Campbell. Most of the luggage and bedding of these poor creatures were plundered by the mob in transit to the city.

Provisions and cattle for transport were brought in for sale, and eagerly purchased; the unfortunate sellers were, however, immediately plundered of their gains by their own countrymen at our very gates. Orders had been repeatedly issued to fire on these marauders, but Brigadier Shelton thought proper not to follow them up. He would not direct the soldiers to fire, who were obliged in consequence tamely to endure the most insulting taunts from the mob. All this told frightfully against us, and ruined the discipline of the troops. Mackenzie and Skinner came in during the evening from the city, disguised as Affghans, without having been molested. I had on my first arrival from the city informed General Elphinstone of Ameenoollah's advice that we should retreat by the Jumrood, and not by the Khoord Cabul passes, but he objected on the ground that it would keep the troops longer in the snow, and therefore would not hear of the proposal. On December 31 abundance of provisions and cattle for carriage were brought in for sale. There was much plundering going on this day close to cantonments, but no attempt was made to stop it, although even the chiefs wished us to open fire on the robbers. Thus sadly closed this miserable year.

The new year opened on us most ominously. The snow was falling heavily, and all our Hindustanees looked cold and miserable. The cantonment presented a very singular, and under other circumstances an amusing scene. Crowds of Affghans were bartering all sorts of curiosities in exchange for articles the officers and men wished to get rid of to lighten their baggage. I gave my cocked hat to one fellow, who instantly clapped it on his head and galloped off to the city, narrowly escaping being shot by his friends, who fired at him supposing him to be a British officer. He afterwards informed me of his escape, and was much chagrined and offended at my laughing heartily at his story. Few of the Affghans credited the report of our intended departure, not supposing we could be so insane as to leave our position. Many among them, friendly to us, freely expressed their amazement, or shook their heads doubtfully, when informed we were actually to retreat. Several of the native officers of Anderson's Horse brought in most alarming reports of the treacherous intentions of the enemy, and declared that if we did move at all, our only chance was to march rapidly, sacrificing all stragglers and baggage. They also stated that Mahomed Akbar had made them offers to go over to him. The General was duly informed of these facts, but was recommended by Captain Bellew to attach no credit to such vague reports and statements. From the 2nd to the 4th of January the confusion in cantonments was fearful. Upon the 2nd the Kohistanees made an offer to General Elphinstone to come over to us, and, for a consideration, to escort us to Peshawur, offering to give hostages for their good faith. They repeated their offer the following day, but it was declined by General Elphinstone. The old King sent me, as the only officer now remaining with whom he was intimate, an urgent message begging of me to warn the General on no account to leave the cantonment, for no trust could be placed in the promises and oaths of the insurgents. As long as we held our position, the King urged, they could not hurt us, but if we once abandoned it we were dead men. The King dared not communicate with me in writing, but told his servant, by way of authenticating his message, to mention some words spoken by the late Envoy to his Majesty at an interview at which he and I were alone present with the King, and to refer to a circumstance of which his Majesty and I were alone cognizant. This mode of communicating confidentially and accrediting their messenger is common among the Affghans. A Kuzzulbash chief sent me a similar warning. Of these warnings I duly informed Pottinger, who took me to General Elphinstone, to whom I repeated both messages ; but as we could not guarantee that supplies would be furnished supposing we moved to the Bala Hissar, we were told that it would not do now to remain where we were, and that march we must. It appeared in orders in the evening, that we march to-morrow.

January 5th.—We were to have marched this morning, but the order was countermanded, as the escort promised by the chiefs did not appear, and they sent a messenger to say that they would furnish it next day.

A messenger came to-day from the King to Lady Macnaghten, urging her to withdraw from the army, who would all be destroyed, and offering herself and as many ladies as would accompany her, an asylum in the Bala Hissar. Upon this Pottinger proposed to me again to urge General Elphinstone, when the force marched out of cantonments, to order them to move straight into the Bala Hissar, without previously saying a word to anyone, instead of proceeding by the road leading to Jellalabad, provided I thought the King would receive us into the citadel. I replied that I was sure his Majesty would be delighted at such a movement, and volunteered to ride on in advance and announce our coming. Pottinger and I then communicated with General Elphinstone, who replied, 'Can you guarantee us supplies?' 'We cannot guarantee,' we replied, 'but we are pretty sure of sufficient supplies.' 'No, we retreat!' was the General's ultimatum, and orders were then issued for each fighting man to take three days' provisions in his haversack, and the force to be ready to march at daybreak the following morning.

The 6th of January at length dawned, but although the troops were under arms at eight A.M., no sign of the promised Affghan escort was to be seen. I had solicited to be placed in charge of the ladies and children, with the late Envoy's escort of cavalry and infantry, about 150 strong, and my place was assigned in rear of the advanced guard, which consisted of her Majesty's 44th Regiment, 600 men; Sappers and Miners, 220; 100 sabres Irregular Horse, and three mountain train guns, under Brigadier Anquetil. Next to my party came the main column, consisting of three Horse Artillery guns; Anderson's Irregular Horse, 500 sabres; 37th Native Infantry, numbering 650; and 5th Native Infantry, 700 bayonets, with baggage and convalescents, sick and wounded, under Brigadier Shelton.

The rearguard consisted of the 54th Native Infantry, 630 strong; Shah's 6th Infantry, 600; two squadrons of the 5th Light Cavalry, 250 sabres; and four Horse Artillery guns.

At nine A.M. the troops moved off, a crouching, drooping, dispirited army, so different from the smart, light-hearted body of men they appeared some time ago. Not an Affghan was then to be seen as we left the cantonment and slowly picked our way through the snow, the men sinking a foot deep each step, even in the regular track, and several feet if they missed it and wandered off. As we crossed the Seeah Sung Hills, and threaded our

way through our old and once jovial camp, now so silent
and deserted, my heart sunk within me at the remem-
brance of the past, and under the conviction that we were a
doomed force. I could not help casting a longing, lingering
look at the Bala Hissar, feeling assured that *even now* all
might be retrieved if only the order was passed to march
upon and occupy that fortress, instead of plunging into
the dreadful defiles before us, to our certain destruction.
I strove to drive away these melancholy and desponding
forebodings by riding as hard as my powerful horse, one
belonging to the late Envoy, could carry me, from the
head to the rear of my charge, striving by an assumed
air of cheerfulness to encourage the poor terrified women
and children. On the Seeah Sung Hill, we were halted by
an order from the rear, the Affghan Sirdars, as we were
informed, wishing us to retrace our steps, as their promised
escort was not yet ready. The General, however, thought
it too late then to countermand the force, as the greater
part had left the cantonment, and some of the enemy
from the Behmaroo village had already occupied it.
After having been detained here more than an hour, the
order to proceed was given. It was bitterly cold, freezing
hard, and I pitied from my soul the poor native soldiers
and camp followers, walking up to their knees in snow and
slush. It was no easy task to keep all my charge together,
some of the bearers hurrying on, others lagging behind
with the palanquins and doolies containing the women
and children. At last, towards dark, we reached in safety
our halting-place at Bagramee, having marched only four
miles. No camp was marked out, and only a few Pals—
the smallest description of tent—pitched for the ladies,
most of whom remained for warmth in their doolies and
palanquins, and as many of these as possible were placed

inside the Pals for shelter. Few of our servants had up
to this time arrived; three of mine, however, had, after
encountering great difficulties, reached in safety. These
faithful men, instead of caring for themselves, strove to
the best of their power to make me comfortable, and
pitched a Pal for me in a spot they had first cleared of
snow, and into it Le Geyt, Major Scott, and I crept, most
thankful for the shelter and some cold meat and sherry
which Lady Macnaghten was able to spare us, and without
which we must have starved.

The rearguard, which should have marched at noon,
were unable to quit cantonments before three P.M., and
then had to leave behind much baggage, and two guns,
which were spiked. No sooner had they cleared the
gate than they were attacked, and Cornet Hardyman
and many men were killed. The Affghans rushed in
crowds to occupy the abandoned position, and having
plundered the houses and barracks, set them on fire, burning, in their blind fury, the very carriages of the two
abandoned guns, thus rendering them permanently useless,
to their own great loss. The crowd of camp followers
and cattle became at once mixed up together in an
unmanageable mass, so that it was quite impossible to
protect them, and to add to the confusion the banks of
the canal had become so slippery as to be impassable for
the camels, who, poor animals, lay down in heaps, unable
to move. The rearguard had to fight the whole way
to Bagramee, and passed through literally a continuous
lane of poor wretches, men, women, and children, dead or
dying from the cold and wounds, who, unable to move,
entreated their comrades to kill them and put an end to
their misery. At length, at midnight, worn out by hunger and fatigue, and benumbed by cold, the rearguard

reached its ground, where, finding no shelter, food, or
fuel, they had to huddle together on the snow, to endeavour to impart some warmth to each other by mutual
contact. The night was pitch dark and excessively cold,
and many perished during it. The silence of the men betrayed their despair and torpor, not a voice being heard.
In the morning I found lying close to my tent, stiff,
cold, and quite dead, in full regimentals, with his sword
drawn in his hand, an old gray-haired conductor named
Macgregor, who, utterly exhausted, had lain down there
silently to die. Such was the first march of the retreat,
proving but too surely how correct was Sir William Macnaghten's conviction, that the measure which the military authorities regarded as the only one for insuring the
safety of the force, must, if persisted in, end in its
annihilation.

About seven A.M. of the 7th of January, the army, if
such it could be called, moved off, the rearguard of yesterday being the advance of to-day. Already all discipline
and order had ceased, and soldiers, camp followers, and
baggage were all mingled together. More than half of
the sepoys were, from cold and hunger, unable to handle
their muskets, and throwing them away, mixed themselves up with the mass of non-combatants. The majority
of the Shah's 6th Infantry and Sappers had abandoned
their colours and retraced their steps to Cabul, preferring
becoming prisoners there to the certain death which they
saw clearly must result from continuing any longer with
the main body.

I followed next to the advance guard with my precious charge, and we were fortunately unmolested, although some hundreds of horse and foot of the enemy
were seen moving parallel and close to us on both flanks,

and were supposed to be the escort promised for our protection. The bearers of the palanquins and doolies soon knocked up, and those carrying Lady Macnaghten were so thoroughly exhausted, that on hearing firing in the rear, and seeing Captain Troup gallop past to bring back a corps to support the rearguard, they declared themselves unable to proceed. It became of course necessary for Lady Macnaghten to quit the palanquin, and I induced her to mount before me. The horse was powerful and active, and I managed to get her on several miles, until, falling in with a camel with empty kajahwahs, I lifted her ladyship into one, balancing her with a bundle of clothes in the other. On reaching Bootkhak I found all my charge safe and well except Mrs. Boyd, who was nowhere to be seen. I immediately rode back several miles to the rear, in the hope of finding her. In searching for her I came upon Brigadier Anquetil, with the remains of his rearguard, which had been attacked shortly after leaving the last halting-ground. While passing a small fort a body of Affghans had sallied out and captured the mountain train guns ; their escort, a detachment of the 44th, not firing a shot to defend them. Lieutenant Green, a very gallant young officer, in command of the guns, had just time to spike them before they were carried off. He was frantic at their loss, which he attributed solely to the misconduct of the 44th. The Brigadier shook his head, and said 'it was too bad to speak about.' Their adjutant, Lieut. White, had been severely wounded when endeavouring ineffectually to rally his men. In this predicament Anquetil had despatched his brigade-major, Captain Troup, to the front, for assistance from General Elphinstone, who directed him to return with the 37th Native

Infantry. Their commanding officer, however, declared that the regiment was so worn out by starvation and the fatigue of the previous day, that they were unable to return, and this was quite true, for this gallant regiment never shrank from duty, but was ever forward, and an example to the army, never refusing to face a foe whenever called upon. Major Swayne then got together a few men of the 5th Native Infantry, and returned with them to Anquetil, but it was then too late, as the enemy had carried off the guns. On failing to find Mrs. Boyd, I returned to my party, and was rejoiced to see that she had already arrived there with her husband, with whom it appeared she had left my column on horseback, without my having noticed her departure.

General Elphinstone had intended pushing on without a halt through the Khoord Cabul pass, but this attack on his rearguard required him to halt, and when it came up he and his advisers deemed it too late to enter that dangerous defile. Two Horse Artillery guns had to be spiked and abandoned this day, in consequence of the horses being unable, from their starved condition, to drag them along. We only made five miles this miserable day. Sepoys and camp followers were all mixed up together, and the confusion and distress were terrible, increased and aggravated by the enemy attacking the centre of our baggage column, cutting up many camp followers, and carrying off much plunder. As night was closing in, we heard that Sirdar Mahomed Akbar Khan was present with the body of Affghan horse who had attacked us. He sent his confidential servant, Moossa Khan, to summon Skinner and myself to join him. I refused to go, saying I had had enough of him, but Skinner accompanied the messenger. On joining Mahomed Akbar, he was informed by the Sirdar that the chiefs had not been ready for our departure from Cabul, and that we should not have left cantonments before the escort promised by them had joined us. He had himself been deputed to escort us to Jellalabad, but that now six more hostages must be made over to him, to insure the force not proceeding beyond Tezeen until Jellalabad had been evacuated by our troops. Skinner was then sent back to make known this determination to the General. The enemy happily now ceased firing upon our camp, if camp that could be called which consisted of thousands of human beings and animals all promiscuously huddled together in such a dense mass that it was hardly possible to move through them. Most fortunately I had my Pal pitched, and having in vain hunted for Lady Sale and Mrs. Boyd to offer them its shelter, Le Geyt, Major Scott, and I again shared it, Lady Macnaghten giving us some food as on the previous night. The night was intensely cold, the thermometer marking ten degrees below zero. Most of the officers and all the men were forced to lie down upon the snow, without food or fuel. Who can adequately describe the horror and sufferings of such a situation ?

By dawn on the 8th January we had managed to get almost all the ladies into kajahwahs on camels, as their bearers were not to be depended on, and their palanquins and doolies had to be abandoned. As soon as they were ready I left them and proceeded beyond our pickets a little in the rear to look about me. Just then the enemy opened a dropping fire upon us, when suddenly the whole mass of soldiers, camp followers, and cattle appeared convulsed and to roll towards the rear like an enormous wave. I ran forwards and met Captain Anderson, commanding the Irregular Horse, who called out,

'The enemy are upon us; have you any of the escort ready?'

Fortunately I had ordered my troopers to mount, and directing the subahdar of the infantry portion, a fine brave old soldier, to close in his men round the ladies, I started with the cavalry at a trot to the front, whence the firing appeared to come. On getting clear of the living mass—no easy task—I found the 44th Regiment drawn up, and the enemy's Juzzailchees taking long shots at them, and creeping on gradually towards the brow of the hill on which the 44th were posted. I drew up my men on the right of the regiment, and looked in vain for any senior officer to give orders. Failing to find one, I took upon myself to send an orderly to Colonel Chambers, to tell him that two guns and a squadron of cavalry would be of much use. I then observed Major Thain, aide-de-camp, apparently reconnoitering in front, and I sent two orderlies to him to ask for orders. Presently he signalled to me to advance, which we did, and charged the enemy, who fled in all directions, their horsemen leading the way. Seeing a considerable body of them collected under the hills, I asked my men if they were willing to attack them? 'Yes, we will follow you any-where,' was their spirited reply. I then ordered the advance, but had soon to pull up, as the enemy, seeing us increasing our pace as we neared them, fled behind some hillocks which were occupied in force by their Juzzailchees. I am quite of opinion that even at this, the eleventh hour, we might, if properly led, have driven the enemy like sheep into Cabul, and ourselves have occupied the Bala Hissar.

Just as I halted my men a messenger reached me, saying I was wanted by General Elphinstone. I then desired my rissuldar to remain near the 44th, and support them until I returned, and if I did not return, to obey any orders he might receive. General Elphinstone, on my joining him, informed me that Akbar Khan had demanded me as a hostage, together with Brigadier Shelton and six others. I declined going, saying that I would much prefer remaining with the force, having a very important and honourable charge confided to me, and urging that this was not the time to leave it. Major Pottinger then offered to take my place, as he was wounded and could be of little or no use, whereas it was important that I should remain to take charge of the mission establishment, and he hoped that by his going Akbar Khan might be satisfied with fewer hostages. Pottinger then proceeded to join Mahomed Akbar, but in about half an hour he sent a note back stating that I must join him at once, as the Sirdar insisted on my being given over to him as a hostage. On my showing this note to the General he said he was sorry to lose me, but go I must. I therefore started in company with General Shelton, but had not proceeded beyond our own pickets when another note from Pottinger reached me, saying that Mahomed Akbar had agreed to dispense with General Shelton, and would be satisfied with Pottinger and myself, and a third officer, whomsoever Pottinger might select. He accordingly had named Captain Colin Mackenzie. I read the note to Shelton, who returned to the General, and I sent for Mackenzie to join me, which he did. We then proceeded, escorted by two of Akbar's dependents, through crowds of the enemy until we reached the Sirdar, whom we found seated on the side of the hill at breakfast, which he civilly asked us to partake of, ordering at the same time his men to take away our firearms. I had to

give up my rifle, slung at my back, and a pair of pistols,
but was allowed to retain my sword.   We then sat down
and partook of breakfast, not without a shudder I confess on my part, at eating from the same dish with the
man who had been so lately the murderer of the Envoy.
Mahomed Akbar then despatched messengers, by whose
orders the enemy ceased firing on our troops.

CHAPTER XII.

RENEWED ATTACK ON OUR TROOPS—INCIDENTS OF THE RETREAT—FURY
OF THE GHILZYES—DYING SERGEANT OF THE 44TH REGIMENT—MAHOMED
AKBAR'S PROPOSAL TO RECEIVE AND PROTECT LADIES AND CHILDREN—
THEY ARRIVE IN MAHOMED AKBAR'S CAMP — MARCH TO TEZEEN — DR.
MAGRATH'S ESCAPE.

FROM our position on the side of the hill, Pottinger,
Mackenzie, and I witnessed the march of our army.
Hardly had they moved from their ground when the
enemy rushed in shoals on the baggage in the rear, and
Mahomed Akbar then sent horseman after horseman to
the commanding officer, directing him to fire upon the
plunderers, which at length was done, and they fled on
all sides, but only to return after a short interval when
the guard had advanced some little way.   At noon we accompanied in their advance the Sirdar and some Ghilzye
chiefs on horseback. As we were starting, Sùltan Jan
asked me if I had a sword, and on my replying I had,
said, 'Well, then, use it if any man comes too close to you.
' Rely upon it I will,' was my answer, as I moved forward.
As we proceeded, we passed at every yard the mangled
corpses of our murdered camp followers, but saw those
of only three Europeans, who were evidently invalids and
killed while lagging in the rear.   As we neared the pass,
however, the bodies of our countrymen became more frequent.   Heavy firing was now heard to our front, and
Mahomed Akbar directed us to halt, while he and Sùltan

Jan rode on to stop it if possible.   We halted for half an hour, and then moved on under charge of Abdul Gheiass, a cousin of Mahomed Akbar's, with about thirty horsemen, who kept us well within their circle.   Soon we came upon more bloody scenes: sepoys and camp followers were being stripped and plundered on all sides, and such as refused to give up their money and valuables were instantly stabbed or cut down by the ruthless enemy with their long knives.   On seeing us the poor creatures cried out for help, many of them recognising me and calling out to me by name.   But what could we do?   We ourselves were quite helpless.   As we neared the centre of the Khoord Cabul pass, we came upon an abandoned gun, and near to it many bodies; among them was that of Captain Paton, a most gallant officer, and close behind him that of young St. George.

The Ghilzyes had now tasted blood, and clearly showing their tigerish nature, became very savage and fierce in their demeanour towards ourselves, demanding that we should be given up to them for a sacrifice, brandishing their long blood-stained knives in our faces, and telling us ' to look on the heaps of carcases around us, as we should soon be ourselves among them.'   ' You came to Cabul for fruit, did you?   How do you like it now?' they cried. It was most difficult to restrain oneself, and involuntarily my hand grasped my sword-hilt; but I controlled my anger, knowing that any offensive movement on my part would insure our instant destruction.   So threatening did their conduct at length become, that our conductor, fearing that they might rush in upon us and destroy us, recommended our quitting the road and sheltering ourselves under some overhanging rocks close by, where we could remain unnoticed.   This we did, and shortly after a wounded soldier of the 44th was brought to us by command of Mahomed Akbar, and also Captain Boyd's youngest son, who had been separated from his parents in the tumult. We were told that a lady was sheltering in the rocks near, but could not safely be brought to us until darkness set in. We remained under these rocks until evening, when it began to snow. The crowds had by this time considerably decreased, numbers of them having departed, laden with spoil. Sùltan Jan then joined us, and we moved on under his directions, the English lady having been first brought to us. She turned out to be Mrs. Bean, the wife of a private of the 13th Light Infantry; the poor creature was so stupefied from fear and cold, that I could scarcely rouse her sufficiently to get her up behind Mackenzie on his horse. As we moved on, the carnage became more frightful every step. Seeing the body of an Englishman lying close to the road, I rode up, when it moved, and the poor fellow raising his head and recognising me, cried out, 'For God's sake, Captain Lawrence, don't leave me here!' I jumped off my horse, and going up to the man raised him up, with the assistance of two of Sùltan Jan's men, who had dismounted by his orders. He was a sergeant of the 44th, and at first appeared only to have lost his left hand; but to my grief and horror, on raising him, I saw that from the nape of his neck to his backbone, he had been cut in pieces. 'What use is there in lifting him up?' said the Affghans; 'he cannot live many minutes.' I reluctantly assented, and on telling the poor fellow we could do nothing for him, he said, 'Then for God's sake shoot me.' 'Even this I cannot do,' I mournfully replied. 'Then leave me to die,' -he said, and this we were forced to do. As we proceeded we met numbers of the enemy's horse and foot returning to Cabul, laden with plunder of all kinds. One miscreant had a little Indian girl seated on his horse behind him. Towards the end of the pass we struck off to the right, and passing the Khoord Cabul fort, which we were not allowed to enter, proceeded on to another, two or three miles in advance. By this time it had become dark; there was no regular road, and none but Sùltan Jan seemed to know the way. The reflection from the snow had nearly blinded us, and we followed our leader in moody silence. At last, after considerable difficulty and delay, we reached the halting-place, a small fort, a room of which was immediately cleared out for us and a fire lit, round which prisoners and guards all crowded. We were treated with kindness, the guards sharing their scanty meal with us, after partaking of which we all lay down in a circle with our feet towards the fire. Little Boyd shared my postheen, and poor Mrs. Bean crouched in a corner a little way from us; and thoroughly worn out we fell asleep.

On awaking on the morning of the 9th, we were requested at once to mount our horses, who, poor creatures, had remained saddled all night, just as we dismounted from them, unfed, and of course ungroomed. I took up Mrs. Bean behind me, who showered blessings on our heads for not leaving her among these savages, as Sùltan Jan proposed. Mackenzie took up behind him the wounded private of the 44th whom I had carried yesterday, and an Affghan took little Boyd before him. After an hour's ride we came to the Khoord Cabul fort, the same we had not been permitted to enter the preceding night, and there found Mahomed Akbar. The Sirdar received us very graciously, and made us sit down on either side of him. After some general conversation he turned to me, saying, 'I have a proposal to make which reasons of humanity alone prompt me to offer, and which I am well aware may be misconstrued.' The Sirdar then proceeded to say, that from the occurrences of the previous day we must be well aware that the British camp no longer afforded protection to the helpless women and children, the Affghans having already carried off two of the latter. He therefore proposed that the ladies and their husbands, the children, and the wounded officers should be made over to him, and he would protect them now, and afterwards forward them under an escort to Jellalabad. I promptly and cordially approved the proposal, as also did Pottinger. Captain Skinner arrived from our camp just as the offer was made, and he also expressed his great satisfaction, as it was to propose their surrender he had now been deputed by the General to Mahomed Akbar. He said to me at the same time in a whisper, 'But they have all marched.' We begged Skinner to lose no time in returning to stop them, and Akbar suggested that the troops should halt that day, and promised in that case that he would send them food and fuel. It was not until evening that Skinner returned, bringing with him Lady Macnaghten, Lady Sale, Mrs. Sturt, Mrs. Boyd and two children, Mrs. Anderson and two children, one an infant ten days old, the third having been carried off by the enemy; Mrs. Eyre and one child, Mrs. Waller and one child, Mrs. Trevor and seven children, Mrs. Ryley and two children, and two wives of soldiers. The officers who accompanied them were Captains Waller, Troup, Trevor, and Eyre, wounded; Captains Boyd and Anderson, and Mr. Ryley, Sergeant Wade, and Mackenzie's Christian servant Jacob. Lieutenant Melville, of the 54th Native Infantry, in charge of the party, made them over to Mahomed Akbar, and then returned to camp to report to General Elphinstone their safe arrival. Anderson brought me a note from Le Geyt, offering to take my place, as he was aware how much I disliked my position. I had, however, no opportunity of sending a reply, as Lieutenant Melville left the moment he had made over his charge. Towards morning a note was received from the General, recalling Captains Boyd and Anderson, but it was then quite impossible for them to return to camp.

It was distressing beyond expression to see our countrywomen and their helpless children thus placed in the power of these ruffians, but there was no help for it. The extreme suffering of mind and body they had endured since the 5th was apparent in their worn and grief-stricken faces. Many of them during these four wretched days had tasted nothing but some dry biscuits and some sherry or brandy. With the exception of Lady Macnaghten, who had saved all her property, they had lost everything except the clothes they were wearing. The delight of Mrs. Boyd on seeing her little boy in my arms can be imagined, and was in striking contrast with the anguish of Captain and Mrs. Anderson at not finding their little daughter—who had been lost in the confusion —among our number, as they hoped and expected. Mahomed Akbar received the ladies very courteously, and desired me to explain to Lady Macnaghten and the others that they were his honoured guests, and should want for nothing he could give them, and that on the first favourable occasion he would have them escorted safely to Jellalabad. The ladies were then distributed among three small rooms in the inner court of the fort. A fourth small room was assigned to the gentlemen, and a sheep-

skin cloak or postheen was supplied to each. My three
faithful servants took the opportunity of joining me here,
bringing with them the most of my baggage. Its receipt afforded me the great gratification of supplying the
gentlemen from my stores with many necessary articles of
apparel. My servants informed me that two of my syces,
one of whom had been in my service eighteen, the other
nine years, had refused to accompany them, and had absconded with my two best yaboos, saying, ' The master's
throat is soon to be cut, and what is the use of our staying
to see it ? ' They were never heard of afterwards, and
doubtless perished with the others in the retreat.

At midnight food was supplied to us, consisting of a
mess of boiled rice with a small bowl of clarified butter or
ghee in the centre, which forms the usual daily food of
the Affghans. At first few of us relished the food, but we
all learnt very speedily to appreciate the full value and
sustaining properties of the dish. We remained the whole
of the 10th in the Khoord Cabul fort, and on the morning
of January 11 we were ordered to march. The ladies
were placed in kajahwahs on camels, while the gentlemen,
who had been allowed their arms, rode on horseback, and
all started for Tezeen, under charge of Sùltan Jan,
Mahomed Akbar's half-brother. If for the moment our
spirits were elated by the absence of immediate suffering
and danger, our hearts were soon torn and distracted by
the awful spectacle the road presented. It was strewn
in every direction with the stripped and mangled bodies
of our late companions, exhibiting every variety of the
ghastliness of death. At intervals small groups of
wounded and frost-bitten creatures were collected together for mutual warmth, to whom the boon of death
had not yet been granted, and who in hopeless misery

and silent despair saw us pass, well knowing we could not help or deliver them.

I recognised the body of the venerable old subahdar of the Envoy's escort, Appumbul Singh, lying on the road by the side of his dun horse. It was told me that the Affghans offered him his life, for he was well known to them, if he would go over to them. 'No,' replied the grand old soldier; 'for forty-one years I have eaten the Company's salt, and I will now show myself ready to die for them.' For sixteen miles we passed through these scenes of horror, until we arrived at sunset at the fort of Tezeen, belonging to Mahomed Khan. We there found Lieutenant Melville, of the 54th Native Infantry, who having been wounded surrendered himself a prisoner to Mahomed Akbar Khan, who dressed his wounds, and putting a turban on his head and a postheen on his shoulders, made him ride by his side so as to escape detection by the infuriated enemy.

On the morning of the 12th we resumed our march for the fort of Surroobee, which we reached at sunset. On the way we were joined by Dr. Magrath, of the 37th Regiment, whom we had long numbered among the dead. His escape was very remarkable. Observing a body of Irregular Horse he followed them, thinking they were about to attack the enemy, instead of which they joined them in a body. Magrath, on discovering the real state of the case, and finding himself separated too far from the force to allow of his rejoining them, drew his pistol, and kept all who desired to attack him at bay, until observing a considerable body of the enemy at some distance he galloped towards them, and making his way on the instant to their leader, Sirdar Khuda Buksh Khan, surrendered himself and was saved. Three poor privates of the 44th Regiment, observing the success of the doctor's manœuvre, followed his example, surrendered also, and were saved. As we passed through the valley of Tezeen, which exhibited the same scene of carnage, I recognised, near an abandoned Horse Artillery gun, the body of Dr. Cardew, a most gallant and fearless officer, termed by the troops for his bravery 'the fighting doctor,' and beloved as well for his professional skill as his generous kindness to them when sick or disabled. The doctor had been wounded early in the march, and the soldiers placing him on the gun-carriage, had protected him until the gun was lost, and in the attack upon it he received his death wound. He had come to Cabul from Ghuznee, on his way to India to meet his betrothed, whose anticipations of happiness were thus for ever blighted by the stern vicissitudes of war.

We had this night to bivouac on the snow, and by surrounding the ladies and children with Lady Macnaghten's trunks and my own, we formed a slight shelter for them from the piercing wind; and with some tea and sherry which she and I had saved, we passed the night with less suffering than we dared to anticipate.

We marched again on the morning of the 13th for Jugdulluck, passing through the same scenes of suffering and death as on the two previous days. The last two miles into Jugdulluck were literally lined with bodies of Europeans and natives, all stripped, and lying just as they fell, side by side. The body of poor Skinner was pointed out to me among them. He had been sent by General Elphinstone to parley with Mahomed Akbar, and was shot by a treacherous wretch named Sìr Bùlund Khan, who boasted of having committed the dastardly deed. Skinner was a highminded, manly soldier, the very impersonation

M

of honour, and was loved and respected by all of us, and
a great favourite of Mahomed Akbar's, whose confidential
servant, Moossa Khan, bound himself to me by an oath,
the only one I believe he ever kept, that he would carefully bury poor Skinner's body. I mourned for him with
unfeigned sorrow.

From among the miserable survivors I contrived this
day to save two, one a subahdar of the 37th Native Infantry, whom I took up on my horse, and the other an
old Hindù treasurer of Captain Bygrave's, whom I induced·
a good, feeling Affghan to carry behind himself on his
horse. I saw hundreds of miserable sepoys and camp followers huddled together on the sides of the hills on each
side of the road. They begged us with the most heartrending supplications to assist them, but alas! no aid
could we afford; and indeed, had it been otherwise, they
were beyond all human help, for the Affghans having
stripped them of all their clothing had left them to perish
of cold and hunger, and the greater number of them were
then, from the effects of the frost on their limbs, quite
incapable of ˝moving. I could not even do anything for
them by supplicating Mahomed Akbar on their behalf, as
otherwise I would have done, for the Sirdar had warned
me not to come near him unless he sent for me, and I was
surrounded by a guard of his own retainers.

My supply of tea proved this day of the greatest use;
one poor lady, who had been confined only a few days
before the army moved, declared she owed her life to its
sustaining qualities. During the whole of these trying
marches I felt truly proud of my countrymen and women;
all bore up so nobly and heroically against hunger, cold,
fatigue, and other privations of no ordinary kind, as to
call forth the admiration even of our Affghan guards.

At length we reached Jugdulluck, and there were received with much courtesy by Sirdar Mahomed Akbar, who had with him General Elphinstone, Brigadier Shelton, and Captain Johnson. From the latter I heard the following sad details regarding the fate of our army since we had left it.

At 8 A.M. on the morning of the 10th, as many of the remnant of our troops as could be collected, commenced their march for Tezeen. As soon as the rearguard moved off, the Affghans, who had bound themselves to protect them, commenced firing upon them, but our military authorities, who proved themselves as incapable in conducting a retreat as they had previously shown themselves in all the operations preceding it, had with the most strange perversity ordered our men on no account to return the fire. The consequence was that their ranks were forced in, and an indiscriminate slaughter of unresisting men followed all the way to Tezeen. The 54th Native Infantry were completely cut up, and their colours lost. On arriving at the halting-ground at Tezeen, the army was reduced to a few men of Her Majesty's 44th Regiment, and of the Horse Artillery, who alone maintained the appearance of discipline ; the rest consisted of a ghastly mass of maimed soldiers and camp followers, mixed up with the cattle, and reduced almost to their level from their unparalleled sufferings and privations. Faithful to their charge, though utterly hopeless of effecting their deliverance, many brave officers fell during this march in the vain endeavour to extricate their men. At night a deputation, consisting of Captains Skinner, Bellew, and Hay, was sent by General Elphinstone to wait on Mahomed Akbar to try if any terms could be made to save the remnant of the force. The result was that the

Sirdar offered them safety and protection, provided the soldiers surrendered and gave up their arms; the officers to be allowed to retain their swords. What better terms could the General have expected under such circumstances? yet they were rejected on the ground of the dishonour they entailed. No dishonour, however, could have resulted from surrendering at such a crisis, in order to save the lives of the rest of the army. The dishonour, and it was deep and indelible, had been already incurred in commencing a retreat which was clearly avoidable, but which when once commenced could not by scarcely any human means have turned out otherwise than utterly disastrous. The troops moved from Tezeen at 7 P.M., hoping in the darkness of the night to escape their assailants. The enemy was not aware for some time of their having marched, and they consequently proceeded without interruption, except for an occasional shot, as far as Bareek-i-ab, when from some adjoining caves volley after volley was poured into their rear. Instead of hurrying on as fast as possible, by the same sad fatality which attended the force throughout, the camp-followers were allowed to crowd up to the front, which so retarded the troops that it was 8 A.M. of the 11th before they reached Jugdulluck. The delay decided their fate, for Akbar Khan, as soon as he heard of their having left Tezeen, proceeded immediately with a body of his followers by a short cut across the hills to intercept them. The Ghilzyes also, having received intelligence of their approach, swarmed on the hills on each side of the road, and poured into the column as it passed underneath an incessant and most destructive fire from their long juzzails.

On arriving at Jugdulluck, the remains of the force sought shelter behind some ruined walls, but all in vain, for the Ghilzyes took up a position on some adjoining hills which commanded the place, and fired a succession of volleys into the crouching mass, which drove our miserable people from this temporary shelter. Some twenty European soldiers, headed by Captain Marshall, of the 61st Native Infantry, then charged the enemy, and drove them down the hills with great slaughter, but their brave leader fell desperately wounded in the charge. This produced a momentary lull, but as soon as our men quitted the hill the enemy returned and resumed their fire. About 4 P.M. Captain Skinner effected a communication with Mahomed Akbar, who through him invited General Elphinstone to a conference. At this time the force was reduced to 150 rank and file of her Majesty's 44th Regiment, sixteen dismounted Horse Artillerymen, and twenty-five troopers of the 5th Light Cavalry, but not a single infantry sepoy. The ammunition had all been expended, and what remained in the soldiers' pouches had been taken from those of their slaughtered comrades. The General and Shelton had under the circumstances, therefore, no other resource than to attend the conference, which they did, taking Captain Johnson as their interpreter. The Sirdar proposed that the surviving Europeans should be separated from the natives, and each mounted behind one of his followers, for the Ghilzyes were so infuriated that nothing would now prevent their slaughtering our men but the fear of at the same time slaying their own comrades. It was probable that the Sirdar was for the first time quite sincere in this offer, for the few survivors, less than two hundred, were no longer a source of dread, while their preservation might prove very useful for his ulterior purposes. But with the fatal indecision which adhered to all their measures, the General and Shelton demurred to the Sirdar's proposal on a point of honour. They had abandoned their post, their stores and treasure, when they had a well-equipped army of 5,000 men to defend them— had allowed some 8,000 camp-followers to be butchered and their fighting men to be reduced to less than 200— it was surely too late *then* to talk of honour, when to surrender was the only measure which could avert the annihilation of this remnant. Instead, however, of at once closing with the Sirdar's proposal, they spent the night in useless and vague discussions, and no decision had been arrived at, when a heavy musketry fire was heard, and a report was immediately brought to Mahomed Akbar, that, despairing of the return of the General and the Brigadier, the remaining troops had commenced, about dawn of the 12th, moving from Jugdulluck. On reaching the pass in their front they were stopped by two barricades, which the enemy had constructed while the force was halting, and in endeavouring to surmount these breastworks nearly all the sad remnant of the Cabul force perished. The few remaining mounted officers and men made a rush to the gap the infantry had made, and rode over them; the latter retaliated by firing on the horsemen. Despair seized the survivors: many submitted unresistingly to be murdered, and some crawled into caves and holes in the rocks to die.

Twenty officers, fifty men of the 44th, four Horse Artillery and cavalry troopers, and 300 camp followers succeeded, as we subsequently heard, in clearing the defile in the night, and favoured by the darkness, reached Gundamuck, where the greater number took up their last position on a height to the left of the road, having only twenty muskets among them. A few officers, however, pressed on, hoping by long marches to distance their pursuers. One of the party left at Gundamuck contrived to open communications with some Affghans who were seen coming towards them. At first these men seemed disposed to commiserate our unfortunate famished fellow soldiers, among whom they distributed some bread. Major Griffiths was engaged in talking with the leaders of the party, when unfortunately one or two European soldiers, almost in a state of frenzy, fired their muskets, which sealed the doom of the whole. Major Griffiths, Captain Souter, and a Mr. Blewitt were instantly made prisoners, and the rest butchered. Of the party of officers, consisting of Captains Bellew, Hopkins, and Collins, and Drs. Brydon and Harper, who had pushed on beyond Gundamuck, only Dr. Brydon[1] succeeded in reaching Jellalabad, desperately wounded. Thus perished our Cabul army, sacrificed, as the preceding narrative sufficiently proves, to the incompetency, feebleness, and want of skill and resolution of their military leaders.

[1] For Dr. Brydon's narrative of his escape, see Appendix.

CHAPTER XIII.

MARCH FROM JUGDULLUCK TO PUNJSHEIR RIVER—INCIDENTS OF THE MARCH —FORD THE RIVER—RESCUE AN OLD SERVANT—MARCH TO TEERGHURREE — INHABITANTS HOSTILE AND MENACING — PROCEED TO BUDEEABAD — QUARTERS ASSIGNED TO US IN THE FORT — CHANGE OF CUSTODIANS— MAHOMED AKBAR ADVANCES MONEY FOR OUR USE—REMAIN AT BUDEEA- BAD—INCIDENTS.

AT 8 A.M. on the morning of the 14th January we marched from Jugdulluck, and proceeded in a northerly direction, under the escort of Mahomed Akbar Khan, and of our own Irregular Horse, who had gone over to him in a body during the retreat. After passing through a valley we ascended a very steep gorge, so narrow that our camels, loaded with kajahwahs, could scarcely pass. At 2 P.M. we reached the lofty Budurnuck pass, the steepest and most difficult we had yet met with, ascending a height of 1,100 feet by a narrow pathway. From the top of the pass the view was most extensive of a succession of barren mountain ranges, without a trace of cultivation perceptible, except on the banks of the Cabul river far below us. The descent was almost as tedious and difficult as the ascent. In this march we met some hundreds of our miserable Hindustanees, who had, to escape the massacre, left the high road. They were all naked, wounded, and frost-bitten, huddled together round the remains of some bushes which they had set on fire. Alas! we could do nothing for those poor wretches, none of whom survived the next few days. As I was coming on in the rear of the party, I heard a voice crying out behind me, and turning my horse saw a camel on which I had placed two English private soldiers, fallen down and surrounded by Affghans, who were pulling the poor fellows out of the kajahwahs. I galloped up, calling out to them to desist, at which they looked amazed. Most fortunately for myself and the two men, some of Moossa Khan's servants came up and drove the marauders off. I took care to keep the men well in front of myself for the rest of the way. After a toilsome march of 25 miles we arrived towards dark at a small fort in a valley on the banks of the Punjsheir river. Here we hoped to receive shelter for the night, but were refused admittance and forced to bivouac in the open air. My own and Lady Macnaghten's trunks were, as on a previous occasion, made into a shelter for the ladies and children from the cold, biting wind. At midnight we were awakened to partake of our dinner, consisting of small pieces of boiled mutton and half-baked cakes. Moossa Khan conveyed to me the Sirdar's request that I should then, and in future, undertake the duty of dividing the supplies among the party. He took occasion then to profess great friendship for Lady Macnaghten and myself, probably because we were the only individuals of the party who possessed any baggage.

We all slept well, in spite of the high, cold wind and the dust, and marched early on the morning of the 15th January, reaching shortly after the ford of the Punjsheir river, which here divides into two rapid streams. The ladies had to be carried across behind the Affghan horsemen, and nothing could exceed Mahomed Akbar's and Sùltan Jan's anxiety until all had been safely got over, they themselves carrying across two of the ladies.

Mahomed Akbar desired me to remain on the bank until the whole cavalcade had crossed. While watching the party crossing, I observed an old attached servant of mine, who had been with me twenty years, holding out in vain his solitary rupee to an Affghan horseman to take him across. Dashing into the stream, I made him mount behind me, and carried him safely over; and it was well that I did, for scarcely had we got across when a body of Affghan plunderers attacked all those who remained on the bank, and many in despair threw themselves into the river and were drowned. By this time the party had got some miles ahead, and I started alone to follow them. As I was riding leisurely along I was joined by a Kuzzulbash horseman, who expressed his surprise at my riding alone so unconcernedly, when any men of the village we were just approaching might if they chose shoot me. Fortunately no one molested us, and we jogged on together in friendly conversation until we overtook the column, which proceeded in a northerly direction until reaching the Loghman valley we crossed a wide, rapid stream. The plain was studded with forts and high-walled villages, whose inhabitants heaped the most unmeasured abuse upon us as we passed. One ruffian nearly frightened poor Mrs. Mainwaring to death; she had unfortunately fallen from her pony, and was seated by the roadside with her baby in her arms, crying, when I overtook her, and putting her on her pony, rode by her until we rejoined the column. In this march we passed the Zeārut or tomb of Lamech, the father of Noah, a place of great sanctity, to which Shah Soojah had made a pilgrimage in 1840, and where he had buried one of his sons, as already narrated. About 3 P.M., after a march of sixteen miles, we arrived at the large village of Teerghurree, where we found a great number of Hindù shopkeepers residing, who were very kind to us, evidently deeply compassionating our forlorn condition. The 16th, Sunday, we halted here, and for the first time since our captivity were able to join together in divine worship. It was a melancholy but deeply impressive service, frequently interrupted by the tears and long-drawn sobs of some of our number. During the day some disturbance occurred in the village, shots were fired and some persons killed. In the evening the Sirdar informed me that he had been forced to cut off the ears of some plunderers, that Teerghurree being an open unwalled village was not safe for us, and that he must take us at once higher up the valley to a place of greater security. On the morning of the 17th we all assembled, and marched under protection of an escort of from 200 to 300 Juzzailchees. Mahomed Akbar, Sùltan Jan, and some others remained on horseback until the whole of the captives had passed, including some fourteen or fifteen sick and wounded European private soldiers. As soon as they had all passed, Mahomed Akbar and his horsemen closed up behind them, thus preventing the fierce Ghilzyes who swarmed around rushing in and attacking the column, as they were prepared to do. While we were getting ready for our march a friendly Affghan accosted Anderson and myself, and saying we were in a most perilous position, offered to go to General Sale at Jellalabad, or to do anything for us we required. We thanked him, but declined his kindness, saying we must now just take our chance. At Teerghurree several Hindù ' Baboos,' writers attached to our secretariat, and who had hitherto managed to keep up with us, left us, saying it had been given out that our hour was come and that we should be all killed. My servants, although Hindùs, however, remained faithful and accompanied us. During the march, Mahomed Akbar informed me of the total destruction of our army, as already described, and that only one officer, a doctor, had succeeded in reaching Jellalabad.

At 2 P.M. we reached Budeeabad, a newly erected fort belonging to Sirdar Mahomed Shah Khan. The fort, surrounded by a deep ditch, is a square building with walls thirty-five feet high and a bastion at each corner, and stronger and superior in appearance to any we had yet seen. There was no water inside the fort, which was supplied by a fine stream 100 yards off. Mahomed Akbar and Sùltan Jan brought us themselves inside the fort, which they told us was to be our residence for the present. They sat with us for some time, pointing out to us the apartments assigned for our accommodation. These formed the inner fort or citadel, occupying two sides of the square, raised about two feet from the ground, and much more comfortable than we expected. It devolved on me to distribute the rooms among the captives. Accordingly No. 1 was assigned to Lady Macnaghten, Mrs. Boyd and her two boys, Mrs. Anderson and two daughters, Mrs. Eyre and one son, and Mrs. Mainwaring and her infant, and an English orphan girl of the name of Hester Macdonald. No. 2, separated by a wooden partition from No. 1, was made over to Captains Boyd, Anderson, Eyre, and myself; this room was also used during the day as a mess-room for ourselves and the occupants of No. 1, the trunks being used for tables and chairs. In No. 3 were Lady Sale, her daughter Mrs. Sturt, Mrs. Trevor and her seven children, Mrs. Waller with one child, and Mrs. Ryley. No. 4, Captain Mackenzie and his servant Jacob, Mr. Ryley and Captain Waller, a clerk named Fuller, and a wounded soldier of the 44th whom Mackenzie carefully tended.   No. 5 was occupied by the bachelors, and three European women occupied a tykana or underground room. The soldiers who were able to move about were located in a stable, near which our horses and ponies were picketed. In a small shed lay a poor lad about sixteen, a son of Sergeant Wade, whose extremities had mortified from frost, and whose agony was beyond description until relieved in about a week from his sufferings by death.   In the same shed also lay a fine young soldier of the 44th, with both his legs broken by a gunshot, whose sufferings also were most acute.   After the accommodation had been all assigned, Mahomed Akbar Khan visited the ladies, and desired me to explain on his behalf to Lady Macnaghten, to whom he was invariably most courteous, and the rest of the ladies, that they were his ' honoured guests, that they should want nothing he could supply them with, and that as soon as the roads were safe enough he would forward them to Jellalabad; in the meantime they could write freely to their friends.'   On my complaining of one of his servants for having grossly insulted me, the Sirdar had the man soundly flogged, saying that ' if that was not sufficient I might have his ears if I pleased.'   He then turned to his servants, and in a loud voice warned them that any one venturing to insult any of us would be similarly punished. He then desired me to furnish him with a statement of all the articles we required for our daily consumption, and directed Moossa Khan to furnish the necessary quantity and to attend carefully to all our wants.   I then by desire of Lady Macnaghten presented to the Sirdar the fine grey horse, belonging to her late husband, which I had ridden hitherto.   We also gave him a gold repeater, and to Sùltan Jan a diamond ring, both of which articles I had saved from the government durbar stores.   Upon the morning of the 18th Mahomed Akbar, Sùltan Jan, and several of the other chiefs, took their departure, leaving Moossa Khan in charge of us. Desiring to propitiate him, I made him a present of my handsome silver hookah, and Lady Macnaghten presented him with a shawl he greatly coveted. I then gave him a list of the daily supplies of sheep, flour, rice, ghee, and wood we should require for our subsistence. My servants greatly assisted me in the daily duty of distributing the supplies, especially in killing, dressing, and dividing the sheep. We had no spoons or knives, and only a few plates and brass drinking vessels, but were otherwise well supplied. On the 20th our custodian, Moossa Khan, was sent for by Mahomed Akbar Khan, and his place supplied by an old horse-dealer named Mirza Baha-oo-deen, a friend of Troup's. Moossa Khan was a man of indifferent character and low habits, and his removal was not regretted by us. He had faithfully followed his master's fortunes, accompanying him to Bokhara when he fled, and was highly valued and trusted by Mahomed Akbar. Upon the 22nd, two chiefs named Dost Mahomed Khan, and his brother, Khojah Mahomed, paid us a visit, and were much amused at seeing me drilling the children, putting them through all kinds of manœuvres to give them exercise and amusement. On this day Lady Sale received a letter from her husband from Jellalabad, and Pottinger one from Macgregor, which cheered us much.

After divine service on Sunday, January 23, which Mackenzie and I read in turns, Mahomed Akbar paid us a visit, and on my representing our want of money, offered to send me 1,000 rupees, and on my giving him a receipt for it, tore it up, saying such things were only required among traders, not between gentlemen. He then requested

Pottinger to write a full account of the Cabul insurrection
for him to send to Macgregor, endeavouring to induce
Pottinger to insert in it directions to evacuate Jellalabad,
and scarcely believing his assurances that any such
instructions would be of no effect from one who was himself a prisoner. Poor General Elphinstone's state of
health was now becoming very precarious; in the retreat
he received a wound in his thigh, which did not heal, and
his mental anguish, which was intense, of course aggravated
his bodily sufferings. Pottinger's wound remained still
unhealed and very painful, but Lady Sale's and Troup's
wounds were nearly healed. On Monday, January 24, our
custodian, Baha-oo-deen, brought me the thousand rupees
from Mahomed Akbar, which I distributed, giving fifty
rupees to each of the officers and widows, and dividing the
rest among the European soldiers. I also distributed among
the ladies and women some chintzes and long cloth, with
needles and thread, which Akbar had sent us. On this day
I addressed a letter to John Conolly, with Shah Soojah
in the Bala Hissar, requesting him to do his best to
recover the Andersons' child reported to be in Cabul, and
regarding whom the parents were in the deepest anxiety.
Towards evening Sirdar Dost Mahomed Khan asked me to
walk out with him, which I gladly did, taking with me
two of Mrs. Trevor's boys. The country round the fort,
which is said to be only thirty miles from Jellalabad, was
highly cultivated, and the refreshment and exhilaration
were great in finding oneself in the open country, beyond
the walls of the fortress. Upon the 29th Sirdar Mahomed
Akbar came and endeavoured to induce Pottinger to alter
his letter, describing the incidents that took place at
Cabul so as to give a more favourable impression of the
part played by himself in the late operations. A Hindù

clerk of mine accompanied him, by whose means he learnt the contents of all our letters. He brought with him a most welcome supply of boots and shoes he had procured for us from Cabul. Abdul Ghuffoor, an Affghan acquaintance of my own and poor Trevor's, also arrived to-day from Jellalabad bringing letters and newspapers, and a supply of clothing, most generously contributed by the Jellalabad garrison, although they were themselves greatly in want of wearing apparel. From my letters I learnt that my brother Henry, Mr. George Clerk's assistant, was at Peshawur, with General Pollock's force advancing to Jellalabad. Our letters also informed us that poor Captains Hopkins and Collyer, and also Dr. Harper, had actually arrived within musket-shot of the walls of Jellalabad when they were massacred, their bodies having been found there by Oldfield's squadron of cavalry while out for exercise.

After prayers on Sunday the 30th, Sirdar Sùltan Jan invited those who liked, to take a walk with him beyond the fort. I gladly went, accompanied by several of the children, whom he feasted on sugar-cane. I felt so exhilarated at being again in the open fields that I took a run down to the river, giving Sùltan Jan's people, who thought I had fled, a pretty chase, much to the amusement of Sùltan Jan, who, as none of them could catch me, laughingly told his men they must keep a sharp look-out on me lest I should escape from them some day. Sùltan Jan was naturally a fine-tempered man and very fond of children, being particularly kind to little Edward Trevor, whom he always asked for; he is, however, very bigoted, and has an overweening idea of his own prowess and that of his countrymen, assuring me that one Affghan was equal to five European soldiers. 'Sirdar,' I instantly replied, ' you have never yet met a European in fair fight ; and now, little as I am, if Akbar Khan will promise to release me if I overcome you in single combat, I am ready to fight you to-morrow morning, big as you are.' ' Oh !' he laughingly replied, ' we all know you are a Bahadur '—or man of great prowess. ' I saw you myself very red in the face at the head of the cavalry at Bootkhak on the 8th December.' ' Yes,' I said, ' you saw me, and took very good care not to come too near me '—to which he made no reply. We heard to-day, January 31, that Sirdar Mahomed Akbar had dismissed our Irregular Horse who had deserted to him during the retreat, stripping them of their arms and accoutrements and taking away their horses, telling them contemptuously, that as they had been faithless to their own masters they would be of no use to him.

From February 1 to 15, nothing worthy of notice occurred. On that day, however, our friend Abdul Ghuffoor arrived, bringing us letters and papers, and accompanied by Major Griffiths, Captain Souter, and Mr. Blewitt, who had been taken prisoners at Gundamuck during the retreat. He told me that Mahomed Akbar Khan was greatly incensed at Pottinger and myself for having sent to Macgregor letters and reports for the government, by a kossid whom he had intercepted, declaring it to be a breach of faith on our part, as he had himself promised to forward all our letters to Jellalabad. We accordingly wrote to him to say, that as we had never promised not to correspond or communicate with our countrymen in Jellalabad in any way we found possible, we were guilty of no breach of faith ; *now*, however, that we were made aware of his wishes, we should abstain from forwarding any communications direct for the future.

N

Poor Major Griffiths is greatly reduced, suffering much from an open wound in his arm ; the limb appears wasting away. Captain Souter is also wounded, and looks very thin and ill. They have both undergone great hardships, having been confined in a small room, with other wounded prisoners, for twenty days. We hear that poor Baness, the Delhi merchant, a most worthy and industrious man, was taken into Jellalabad in a dreadful state from lock-jaw, brought on by exposure and suffering, and died shortly after his arrival.

The morning of February 19 was unusually close and hot. About 11 A.M., when I was exercising the children at drill, I felt the ground suddenly convulsed under my feet, and immediately the ladies rushed out of their rooms, large masses of the lofty walls falling in on all sides, and the whole fort seeming to rock to and fro. Lady Macnaghten's room sank several feet, and that occupied by Lady Sale fell in with an awful crash. Lady Sale and Brigadier Shelton were both on the roof at the time, and had a most miraculous escape, the portion on which they stood providentially remaining firm. Moore, the Brigadier's servant, a private of the 44th, rushed upstairs, and at the risk of his life brought his master down in his arms. We all assembled in the centre of the court as far from the crumbling walls as possible, and near a low building, the underground rooms of which were used for storing wood for fuel, when suddenly the entire structure disappeared as through a trap-door, disclosing to us a yawning chasm. The stoutest hearts among us quailed at the appalling sight, for the world seemed indeed coming to an end. The Affghans, accustomed as they are to earthquakes, were overwhelmed with terror at its unusual severity, and loudly called to Allah to spare them. Our horses, poor animals, trembled and plunged, and several of them getting loose rushed about the open space, adding greatly to the alarm and confusion. The bachelors' room was assigned to Lady Sale, as it had escaped uninjured, and we gentlemen slept in the open air, afraid to trust ourselves in the tottering buildings. The cold of the night was intense, and the dew very heavy. The earth continued agitated all the day and through the entire night.

On February 20 we heard that the neighbouring town of Paghree had been almost entirely destroyed, and many of its inhabitants had perished. All the forts in the valley had suffered more or less damage, and lives were lost in each. Thanks be to the Almighty, not one of our party had been injured, and our immunity, although equally exposed with themselves, greatly surprised the Affghans, some of whom declared it was a visitation of the Almighty upon them for their treacherous and bloodthirsty conduct to us, while others as confidently asserted that the calamity was inflicted upon them by God for sparing the lives of the infidels. Dost Mahomed Khan came to visit us, and reported that the walls of Jellalabad had been destroyed by the earthquake, but that the garrison, notwithstanding the injury to their defences, held out as before. Some days previously to this, Sirdar Mahomed Akbar insisted on our giving up our swords, and would listen to no remonstrance on our parts. We begged that at least Generals Elphinstone and Shelton might on account of their rank be exempted from this indignity, and this day their swords were returned to them, with a polite note from the Sirdar, expressing his pleasure in complying with our request, but refusing to give us back our own. Upon February 23, much to our surprise and delight, we were joined by Captain Bygrave, paymaster of the troops.

When the force was utterly disorganized he managed to extricate himself and hid among the ravines, coming out at night and hiding during the day ; at last he surrendered to Nuzam Khan, a Ghilzye chief, by whom he was made over to Mahomed Akbar. Bygrave had lost the entire toes of one foot and the joints of several on the other by frost-bites, and was greatly reduced in body and deeply depressed in mind.

Upon the 25th the brother of our custodian, Baha-oo-deen, who traded between India and Cabul, arrived from Peshawur, where, owing to the disturbed state of the country, he had been forced to leave his consignment of shawls and merchandise. We learnt from him that up to this time Sirdar Mahomed Akbar had not been successful against the Jellalabad garrison.

When the Sirdar left us to proceed to Jellalabad, he said to me boastingly that he would take the fort in two days. 'No, not in three months,' I replied ; 'you have not frost and snow to fight for you as at Cabul.' 'Never mind,' he replied ; 'Sale and his garrison will soon be with you.' On the night of February 28 we had another smart shock of an earthquake, but no damage was done. We were still living in the open air, and I maintained as yet good health, and contrived to get exercise daily by racing the Affghan guards every morning round the courtyard, generally managing to beat them, and I felt all the better for the excitement as well as the bodily exercise.

CHAPTER XIV.

MURDER OF LE GEYT—EJECTION OF OUR SERVANTS FROM THE FORT—SIRDAR MAHOMED KHAN REVOKES HIS ORDER FOR THEIR DISMISSAL—FALL OF GHUZNEE — ATTEMPT TO ASSASSINATE MAHOMED AKBAR — CHANGE OF CUSTODIANS—APPOINTMENT OF SALEH MAHOMED—SALE'S VICTORY—DEPARTURE FROM BUDEEABAD — ELPHINSTONE'S FEEBLE STATE — MACKENZIE DEPUTED TO JELLALABAD—·DEATH OF ELPHINSTONE—HIS BODY SENT TO JELLALABAD.

MARCH 1.—Mirzah Baha-oo-deen left us this morning at daybreak to visit Sirdar Mahomed Akbar's camp, who was busy making preparations for a grand attack on Jellalabad. He returned on the morning of the 3rd, and informed me that the body of my poor friend Le Geyt had been found at Neemla among some reeds, where he had hidden himself in company with a rissuldar of Anderson's Horse. Le Geyt was urged by his companion to shoot his charger, a fine old white Arab, lest the animal might cause their place of retreat to be discovered; but he refused, saying he had not the heart to kill the charger that had carried him so nobly to that moment. The rissuldar's conjecture, however, proved too true, for the horse having been seen near the reeds, caused the Affghans to search them, and finding Le Geyt, murdered him, and left the body where it had been now found and recognised. The Mirzah then told me he had received Mahomed Akbar's orders to search Lady Macnaghten's boxes and my own, as it was supposed we had much valuable property concealed in them. Lady Macnaghten no doubt had valuable jewels and shawls, which she contrived to secrete; but as for myself, beyond my regimentals I had nothing except the star of the Dourannee order and a medal for Ghuznee, both which the Mirzah took away.   He then proceeded to eject as many of our poor Hindustanee servants as were incapable of work from frost-bites, wounds, and other injuries, first plundering them of all they possessed.   Our remonstrances at his cruelty were all in vain, the Mirzah averring he was only carrying out the imperative orders of the Sirdar.   Having luckily received from the Mirzah a hint of what was to take place, I induced a good number of the servants to entrust their little savings to me, and I lent the amount, about 600 rupees, to several officers who wanted loans, to be repaid at some future time to the owners.   By this means the plunderers were to some extent disappointed in their gains.   The poor servant whom I had carried across the Cabul river was among the number turned out of the fort, as he had lost the use of his feet, his toes having fallen off, but I succeeded, with the Mirzah's connivance, in readmitting him and many of the rest after nightfall. Upon March 5 these unfortunate men were again ejected, so I wrote a note to Mahomed Akbar Khan, remonstrating against this act of cruelty and begging him to cancel his orders.   On this day Mrs. Mainwaring received a box of useful articles from her husband at Jellalabad, which she most liberally distributed among the rest of the ladies, who were much in need.   The Mirzah hinted to me this day that he knew Lady Macnaghten possessed much valuable property, which the gift of a pair of valuable shawls to himself might save her being deprived of; accordingly, her ladyship, on my advice, bestowed a pair of the handsomest on our keeper, which had the desired effect of saving the rest.

March 8.—I received to-day a reply from the Sirdar to my note, explaining that he had ordered only those servants to be sent away who were totally inefficient, as their maintenance involved a heavy expense. He expressed, however, his willingness that we should retain as many as we desired. Accordingly, as many of them as had remained in the neighbourhood of the fort returned to us. Upon the 11th we were visited by Dost Mahomed Khan, who was accompanied by Mirzah Imamoodeen Woordee, who had held confidential posts both under the Ameer Dost Mahomed Khan and Shah Soojah, and was a man of much intelligence, high character, and great influence. He privately informed Pottinger and myself that Sale's position at Jellalabad was very strong, having supplies in abundance, and that some of Sirdar Mahomed Akbar's adherents were becoming disaffected in consequence of his being able to effect nothing at Jellalabad. On the 12th we heard a report, false we trust, that Ghuznee had fallen, and all the garrison except eight officers had been put to the sword. On the 14th we received intelligence of Mahomed Akbar having been wounded in the arm by one of his own servants, who was roasted alive for his crime. This attempt to murder the Sirdar was of course reported to have been instigated by Shah Soojah or Macgregor, who, by the way, has a great name among the Affghans, who mention him in the highest terms of praise. Upon March 15 Mirzah Baha-oo-deen applied to Troup and myself to get him a certificate, signed by all the captives, testifying that he had treated us well, as he was about to be relieved from his charge. We gladly complied with his wishes, as he had deserved well of us all. He is an intelligent man, without the overweening conceit of his countrymen, and knowing well that the destruction of our army would one day be avenged, he thought it a prudent measure to provide himself beforehand with a document which would be of great use to him hereafter. Upon March 19 the Mirzah took his departure, and was succeeded by Nazir Saleh Mahomed Ghilzye, a tall, gaunt, savage-looking fellow, of whom we augured ill, as he immediately commenced maligning his predecessor, saying he knew he had fed us insufficiently, and asking what amount of money he had done us out of. We heard this day that Shah Soojah had been murdered, a not unlikely fate for the worthy old king, and I fear the report is too true. On Sunday the 20th, during prayers, we experienced two or three shocks of an earthquake, but no injury was done. The Sirdar sent us supplies of tea and sugar and of chintz and long cloth, and on me devolved again, the very disagreeable and invidious task of apportioning the whole among the captives, whom I found it impossible fully to satisfy, although I tried to the utmost to act without favour or partiality. Upon March 21 Sùltan Mahomed Khan, brother of Shah Khan, the owner of the fort, and the person who carried me off behind him on the fatal 23rd of December, at Cabul, visited us in company with our custodian the Nazir Saleh Mahomed, and hinted to us that ten lakhs of rupees would purchase our release. We however referred him to the authorities at Jellalabad, who might receive and consider his overtures. Ten camels were this day sent for our use by Mahomed Shah Khan, and as a few days previously a farrier came and shod our horses, we were under the impression that we were about to be removed from Budeeabad.

From this date until April 9 nothing of much interest occurred to vary the routine of our life in the fort, but on the latter date Mahomed Shah Khan came and corroborated reports which had already reached us, that Sale had on April 7 made a successful sally from Jellalabad, surprising Akbar Khan's camp, and capturing his tents and guns, and very nearly taking prisoner the Sirdar himself. A council of war was then held, when the defeated chiefs proposed to put all the captives to death, but Akbar Khan would not hear of it, resolving to move us from Budeeabad to a fort more distant from Jellalabad, and, therefore, more secure from any attempts which might be made to rescue us. In the evening Mahomed Shah Khan had a private interview with Pottinger and myself, when we urged him to take us to Sale and make terms for himself, but he refused, saying 'he must follow Akbar Khan's fortunes wherever they led him.' It was with much regret we found that we must now quit Budeeabad, which had been for eleven weeks a city of refuge to us.

On April 10 we had our goods and chattels packed up ready for our march, when orders were given us to give up our horses, for which yaboos were substituted, as a precaution against any attempt to escape. Mahomed Shah Khan then ransacked my boxes, taking from them, in spite of my remonstrances, my pouch, belt, epaulettes, and some stars of the Dourannee order I was conveying to officers in India. He then turned to Lady Macnaghten's, and appropriating some of her best shawls, desired her to produce her jewels, which he knew were secreted about her person. I recommended her ladyship to make a virtue of necessity and give up what otherwise might be taken from her by force, and this, after some natural hesitation, she did. We were now informed, much to our regret, that the poor private soldiers were not to be permitted to accompany us. Many of our servants, hitherto faithful, demurred to following us any further, believing we were all going to certain death; and a servant who had been with me twenty years determined to remain behind, showing that he regarded our position as desperate. We started in the afternoon from Budeeabad, and had not proceeded above four miles in a north-easterly direction, when a horseman was seen advancing from the south-east at full gallop, waving his turban, and shouting out some phrases in Persian which threw our escort into the most intense excitement. They wheeled round, flourishing their arms, and I really thought for a few minutes that it was a preconcerted signal for commencing our indiscriminate slaughter. However, after a short time they calmed down, and then it appeared that the messenger had brought orders for our return to Budeeabad, the necessity for moving us from thence no longer existing, as intelligence had been received of Sùltan Jan having utterly annihilated Pollock's army in the Khyber pass. The story was told us in so detailed and circumstantial a manner that for a time we really were inclined to believe it to be true. On our return to the fort we were directed not to unpack our baggage, as we would have to march the next day; and soon the real truth respecting our retrograde movement came out. It appeared that a serious dispute had occurred among the chiefs respecting our disposal, and Akbar Khan, fearing those opposed to him might seize us on the march, had determined on sending us back for the day to Budeeabad.

After breakfast on the morning of April 11 we left Budeeabad finally, and after proceeding about four miles on the Loghur road we took a westerly direction, skirting the hills, and then crossed a low ridge into the cultivated valley of Allishung, through which a river flowed, which having crossed we met Mahomed Akbar, seated in his palanquin near the road. He looked pale and ill, and carried his wounded hand in a sling; he returned our salutations very courteously. He smiled as I passed him, and beckoning me to join him, spoke in a free and soldierly manner of Sale's victory and his own defeat, praising the gallant bearing of our men, which nothing could exceed, with Sale conspicuous on his white charger at their head. He admitted that his force was fairly surprised, and fled precipitately, he himself having to get out of his palanquin and escape on horseback, and had our troops only followed up a few miles further to the bank of the river, he must have been captured, as he had to remain some hours until a raft could be prepared to take him across. We halted in this valley for the night, fortunately finding three tents pitched for us, as it rained in torrents the entire night. Our custodian, the Mirzah, made over charge of us here to a Sikh rajah, with eighty Punjabee sowars. This man had followed the fortunes of the Ameer Dost Mahomed Khan to Bokhara, and stood high in favour with Mahomed Akbar, by whom he had been employed to tamper with our native troops at Cabul before the retreat.

Before starting on the morning of the 12th the Mirzah informed us that our party was to be divided, the married men and ladies to be sent one way, and the bachelors a different one. Strongly objecting to this proposal, I went, accompanied by Anderson, to Mahomed Akbar's camp, and inquired if such was his order; on his replying in the affirmative, I remonstrated against it, pointing out how hard it would be for these helpless ladies who had no husbands to look after them, such as Ladies Macnaghten and Sale, and Mrs. Mainwaring,

Mrs. Sturt, and Mrs. Trevor. The Sirdar said, ' Then you and Troup may go with them.' I answered, ' Let us all proceed, as hitherto, together;' and to this, after a little pause, he assented. I then took this opportunity of saying how much more he would consult his fame and good name if, instead of warring with poor helpless women and little children, by dragging them all about the country and exposing them to fatigue and hardships they were ill able to sustain, he should send them at once to Jellalabad while he retained us, men, in his power. The Sirdar heard me patiently, and I thought, moved by my earnestness, was about to comply with my proposal, when unfortunately Mahomed Shah Khan coming up, sat down beside Akbar's palkee, who said, ' Do you hear what Lawrence Sahib says ? ' On my repeating my words, Mahomed Shah said, ' It is well for Lawrence Sahib to say this;' and then turning to me with a diabolical look, he added, ' but I can tell you that as long as there is an Affghan prisoner in India, or a Feringhee soldier in Affghanistan, so long will we retain you, men, women, and children. When you can ride you *shall* ride, when you cannot you *shall* walk, when you cannot walk you *shall* be dragged, and when you cannot be dragged *your throats shall be cut.*' I jumped up, exclaiming, ' Mahomed Shah Khan, you a warrior, and proposing to treat prisoners in such a manner! Warriors don't talk thus to men whose hands are tied.'

Mahomed Akbar quickly rejoined, ' Oh, Lawrence Sahib, do not mind him; he is only trying you, and does not mean what he says.' I then walked away, Mahomed Shah following me, declaring he did not mean to offend me. We then marched, and after some miles crossed a small stream, on the opposite side of which, among some reeds, we found our camp pitched. Two lean old goats were then sent to us to kill for our dinner, but we returned them, saying we could not eat such things, and demanded sheep to be sent, otherwise we should complain to the Sirdar. Two sheep were accordingly sent, but nearly as old and thin as the goats.

Upon the 13th we started at 8 A.M., and halted at the Udruck pass, after a march of fourteen or fifteen miles. I walked the whole of this march, carrying, much to the amusement of the Affghans, my little goddaughter, Georgie Anderson, in my arms, having given up my pony to another of our party, who required it more than myself. Mahomed Akbar, who accompanied us, seeing me on foot, sent one or two horses for me to ride, but I gave them over to those of the soldiers who were footsore and unable to walk without much pain. At the close of the march Mahomed Akbar sent for me, and asked me why I had not made use of the horses he sent me, instead of passing them on to others; adding, 'A man of your rank and consequence ought not to walk on foot.' I replied, 'Sirdar, a prisoner has no rank, and when you killed my chief you deprived me of all consequence.' 'I'll fine you,' he said, smiling, 'if you give away this horse I now make over to you,' and which I of course accepted. The Sirdar always took in good part whatever I said to him, and treated me invariably with marked distinction, rising on every occasion of my entering his durbar, and placing me on his right hand, above all his chiefs.

Upon March 14 we started early, and ascended, by a very steep and rocky road, the Badposh pass, 1,600 feet high. The ladies were forced to quit their kajahwahs and ride ponies, as being much safer than camels. The descent was short and less abrupt, and on reaching the valley we lay down for an hour to rest in the long grass. We then proceeded six miles along the left bank of the Cabul river, which is here very rapid, running between two precipitous hills. We crossed the river safely on a raft laid on inflated bullock hides, our animals having to cross at a ford four miles higher up. We found Sirdar Mahomed Akbar on the right bank, seated in his palanquin, watching the ferry with evident interest and amusement. Most of us, as we landed, went up and paid our respects to the Sirdar, and he chatted with me some time very affably, and then gave me some pieces of bread and sugar for the children, which the Affghans always carry about with them to allay hunger on a long march.

April 15.—We were delayed till noon waiting for our cattle, and when they did arrive there were no camels with kajahwahs. This was a serious matter for the ladies and the weaker men among us, especially poor General Elphinstone, who was much exhausted by the marching, and could not last much longer. Indeed he told me repeatedly he wished, and even prayed for death, as, he said, sleeping and waking the horrors of that dreadful retreat were before his eyes. We all felt deeply for him, and tried to soothe and comfort the old man, but it was of no avail, as he was worn out in body and mind, and evidently heart-broken by what had occurred. His wound still remained unhealed, but he heeded it not; his anguish of mind was too intense to be distracted even by bodily sufferings. Bygrave's feet were much better, and also Griffiths' arm, which at last was healing. We halted after a march of several miles at the fort of Surrobee, where we had passed the night of the 12th January, and where now Sirdar Mahomed Akbar had preceded us. Here was encamped a body of horse and foot soldiers, and some of our wretched Hindustanees who had survived the winter were among them. Our camp was pitched on a lovely greensward, surrounded with cultivated fields, and here we halted until the 19th, when we marched at 8 A.M. Mahomed Akbar gave up his palanquin to Ladies Sale and Macnaghten, as there were only two camels with kajahwahs available. Our road led up a narrow valley, and the air as we moved along was pestilential from the decomposed bodies of our troops scattered about, and lying in some places we passed in high piles, having probably perished by famine and exposure to the cold. The Affghans told us that many poor creatures had supported life by feeding on the dead bodies of their comrades. During the whole march we were drenched by rain, and were glad to arrive at Mahomed Khan's fort at Tezeen, where we halted for the night. The fort had been so much injured by earthquakes that the ladies had to be placed in a room which was already crowded with Affghan ladies, the wives and daughters of the Ghilzye chiefs, whom they were sending off to the hills, to avoid the advance of our expected army. They were kindly disposed to our ladies, making room for them by the huge fire, and showing great curiosity respecting their dresses and toilets. I was sent for by Mahomed Akbar, whom I found seated with the General and Pottinger in a comfortable room with a fire. A long and desultory conversation then took place about the treatment to which the female prisoners were subjected, in which Mahomed Shah Khan, who joined us, took part. Akbar, in reply to my complaints, retaliated by saying he had heard from India that one of his children had been starved to death, and the rest ill-treated. I instantly replied, ' I was confident he himself did not believe such a report.' ' It is written, however,' he replied. 'Whether written or not,' I answered, 'I don't believe a word of it, and I am sure you don't yourself.' 'Those about me believe it, at any rate,' he said. It was finally determined to depute an officer to General Pollock to negotiate for our release, and Mackenzie was selected for the duty. Towards evening Mahomed Akbar and his father-in-law left us. The ladies were then conveyed on the backs of Affghans to the apartment he had vacated, and which we were all forced to occupy that night, making as good an arrangement in the choice of places to lie down and sleep upon, as circumstances would permit. For myself I lay down, with nothing under or over me, at Lady Sale's feet, and many of the poor ladies had to pass the night in their wet garments. About 8 P.M. some rice and ghee were brought for our dinners, of which few of us were able to partake.

At dawn on the morning of the 20th we gentlemen left the apartment to the ladies, who, however, soon rushed out of it, alarmed by a smart shock of an earthquake which made the old walls shake and rattle. We remained here this day, and about mid-day Mrs. Waller gave birth to a daughter. Fortunately a room had with much difficulty been secured for her and Mrs. Eyre who took care of her. This was the fourth birth since leaving Cabul, three children having been born at the fort of Budeeabad. On hearing of the event Mahomed Akbar laughed, saying 'the more of us the better for him.'

On the 21st we still remained in the fort. I passed a wretched night. Pottinger had offered to share his rug and cloak with me, but was so overcome with sleep that I found it impossible to wake him, so I lay down on the bare floor near the poor General, who never appeared to close his eyes all night, so great was the pain he suffered. I spoke several times to him, but he only thanked me, saying I could do nothing for him, and that all must soon be over. This was the last I saw of him, as he, Pottinger, Mackenzie, Magrath, the Wallers, and Eyres were ordered to remain here, while the rest of us were to be sent to a place in the hills named Aman Koh.

About 4 in the morning of April 22 I was awakened and told to prepare our party to march. We were on our way by sunrise, the Affghans being evidently very anxious. We afterwards heard their anxiety was caused by a report that Futteh Singh, a son of Shah Soojah, intended to make a sudden attack from Cabul on the fort, while some of Macgregor's men were to advance simultaneously from Jellalabad to cooperate with him, with the view of releasing us. Our road lay up the bed of a stream, and shortly after starting we passed a cave, round the mouth of which many bodies of our camp followers lay strewn. Some of our party declared that they saw spectral figures moving about inside the cave, and heard them calling for help as we passed. We encamped at Goudah, in the Zubber Khail country, twelve miles from Tezeen. The families of Mahomed Shah Khan and other Ghilzye chiefs were encamped here also, but about 100 feet above our position.

Khojah Mahomed Khan, a brother of Mahomed Shah Khan, and Mahomed Afeek, a confidential follower of Akbar, with about a dozen Juzzailchees, were now associated with the Sikh Rajah and his men in charge of us. On Sunday, the 24th April, we heard that in consequence of the reported intention to attempt our rescue, the party who had been left at Tezeen were, after our departure, moved to Khuda Buxsh Khan's fort, some way off. Mrs. Waller and her baby, only a few hours old, were conveyed in an old kajahwah slung on a pole, and carried by two Affghans. The old General, unable to move by himself, was held on horseback, and did not survive his removal many hours, dying the same night. His suffering of mind and body had been intense, but he bore all with fortitude and resignation. He repeatedly expressed to me deep regret that he had not fallen in the retreat. His kind, mild disposition and courteous demeanour had made him esteemed by us all, and we could not but regret his removal from amongst us, although his death was to him a most happy release. Sirdar Mahomed Akbar, in spite of all we had told him of Elphinstone's precarious state, would never believe he was in danger, but after his death he expressed his great sorrow that he had not sent the General into Jellalabad, and now expressed his intention of forwarding the body there for interment.

Upon the 27th Mahomed Akbar joined us from Tezeen, and held a private interview with me for two hours. He showed himself most anxious to come to terms with the British authorities, but was evidently perplexed how to bring it about, expressing but little hope of any good results from the deputation of Mackenzie, whom he had already sent into Jellalabad. He then expressed his desire to know my sentiments, saying he had great faith in my truthfulness. I recommended, as his first step, and as calculated greatly to facilitate an immediate arrangement of affairs, to forward at once all the ladies and children to Jellalabad, retaining the men as hostages. The Sirdar shook his head at my proposal, saying he dared not, as the other chiefs would never consent to such a proposal. He then informed me that the chiefs had demanded that we should all be made over to them to be put to death, proposing to collect us all in one spot, and then each chief to kill a captive with his own hands, so that all should be equally criminal, and all placed beyond the pale of British clemency. He had, however, peremptorily refused to deliver up any one of us. He admitted to me that he ' now sorely repents the part he has taken in late events,' declaring that notwithstanding all he had done for his countrymen they were now deserting him.

April 28.—Mahomed Akbar intercepted this day a messenger conveying a letter from John Conolly in Cabul, to Macgregor in Jellalabad, which so exasperated him that he declared he would have Macgregor's life if he could catch him. Intelligence reached us this day that the poor General's body, which had been despatched to Jellalabad in charge of his servant, private Miller, of the 44th Regiment, disguised as an Affghan, had been seized on the road by the Ghilzyes, stripped, and pelted with stones, and Miller wounded. Mahomed Akbar was much incensed at the outrage, and sent a party out to the rescue, who returned with Miller and the body, which was then repacked and forwarded by a raft down the Cabul river to Jellalabad.

Upon April 29 a messenger came to Akbar from Naib Ameenoollah Khan to propose that Pottinger and I should either be required to sign fresh bills on India for the 14½ lakhs of rupees which had been, he asserted, granted on January 5, as the government had repudiated those signed on that date, or that we should be made over to him. Mahomed Akbar sent for Pottinger, who had rejoined us, and myself, and after a stormy discussion the messenger was sent back to Ameenoollah with the final determination of the Sirdar not to give us up, as we were under his protection.

Upon May 3 the Eyres and Wallers joined us, and also, much to our delight, Mackenzie, who had returned from Jellalabad, bringing us letters and papers, but no very satisfactory intelligence respecting ourselves.

On May 10 the hearts of the Andersons were made glad by the restoration of their long-lost child, whom Mahomed Akbar, who had gone to Cabul with Pottinger and Troup, despatched from thence, under an escort of two juzzailchees and an old servant of Troup's. The child had been seized by an Affghan horseman on the second day of the retreat, and carried by him to Cabul. Conolly, hearing of the child being in the city, induced Nuwab Zuman Khan to purchase her for 400 rupees, and place her in his own seraglio, where she remained well cared for until Akbar sent her back to her parents. She looks fat and well, but has acquired quite Affghan manners, and speaks nothing but Persian, although still understanding English.

Upon May 10 Mackenzie returned from a second visit to Jellalabad, bringing us money, letters, and papers, but still no definite intelligence respecting our prospects of release. He informed us that at last the poor General's body had arrived safe at Jellalabad, and had been interred there with military honours.

CHAPTER XV.

ARRIVE AT THE FORT OF SHEWAKHEE—COMFORTABLE QUARTERS ASSIGNED
TO US—VISIT FROM THE MURDERER OF SHAH SOOJAH—MAHOMED AKBAR
OBTAINS POSSESSION OF BALA HISSAR—GHILZYES ATTEMPT TO MASSACRE
THE HOSTAGES—ATTACKED BY SEVERE ILLNESS—ON RECOVERY DEPUTED
TO JELLALABAD—MEET MY BROTHER—MISSION UNSUCCESSFUL—RETURN TO
CABUL.

UPON May 22 we received orders to march, but sent a
message to Dost Mahomed Khan saying we would not
move until camels with kajahwahs were furnished for the
ladies. The Sirdar opened his eyes at this request, but
postponed our departure, saying, goodhumouredly enough,
' Well, you are strange prisoners ! '

We started at 10 A.M. on May 23, the ladies in kajahwahs slung on mules, as no camels could be furnished.
Our road led us past the Upper Tezeen fort, where poor
General Elphinstone had died, and we soon again came
upon the corpses of our ill-fated army, which thickly
strewed the road. Many of the bodies, from being
imbedded in the snow, were little altered, but the most
were reduced to skeletons. About dusk we reached that
part of the Khoord Cabul pass where the ladies had first
joined Mahomed Akbar during the retreat, and some
miles further we reached the fort where we were to pass
the night, having completed a march of twenty-one miles.
A crowd of Affghans were assembled to see us arrive.
One asked me if we had been made Mahomedans yet;
to which I replied, ' No, and by the blessing of God,
never shall.' Another, more friendly, touched me on the

shoulder, asking me in a low voice if I would have some wine, and on my answering eagerly 'Yes,' he pointed to a corner, saying, ' Then meet me in half-an-hour there.' This I did, and received from him an excellent bottle of sherry.

We resumed our marcn after a hurried breakfast on May 24, and crossing a stony pass, came into a plain with a fine pool of water, shaded by some large trees, where we rested for half-an-hour. We then ascended by the winding bed of a mountain stream for two miles to the ancient pillar called Minar-i-Seckundar, the Pillar of Alexander the Great, of which nothing is known except that it is said to have been built by his orders. The pillar stands on a pedestal, and is built of small stones, sixty feet high by twelve in diameter, and although somewhat out of repair may last for centuries yet. We had here a magnificent view of the town of Cabul, and the valley studded with forts and gardens, with the mountains of the Kohistan and the snowy peaks of the Hindu Koosh forming a superb background. All appeared peaceful below us, save when the silence was broken by the roar of a gun from the Bala Hissar, where Futteh Jung, son of poor Shah Soojah, still held out against Mahomed Akbar. Leaving the Minar we ascended for two miles of so steep and rocky a road that the ladies were obliged to dismount and proceed on foot. We rested on the top of the pass, by a deliciously cold spring, and thence on for three miles to the Fort of Shewakbee, about two miles from Cabul, belonging to Sirdar Ali Mahomed Khan, where we were to remain for some time. On our arrival we were shown some cattle-sheds, and informed they were the only accommodation we could have, which greatly incensed Lady Sale. I despatched a note to Sirdar Mahomed Akbar, expostulating with him on this harsh treatment, and a reply was promptly received, conveying his orders to Ali Mahomed's family to vacate their apartments and make them over to us. This was done, and we were put in possession of roomy, clean, and comfortable quarters. A fine large garden, with a stream of water running through it, was also placed at our disposal, to which we had constant and free access. The owner of the fort, Ali Mahomed, a Kuzzulbash, a polite, gentlemanly man, was apparently well disposed to us. He reminded me of the poor Envoy having in one of his morning rides during the last summer visited the garden, quoting some appropriate verses of Saadi, illustrating the ups and downs of human life and its great uncertainty.

Upon May 26 Troup, who was with Mahomed Akbar, and occupied with Pottinger and Mackenzie a room in his house, paid us a visit, and gratified us by the information that the hostages and all the sick and wounded who were left at Cabul before the retreat were safe and well. Scores of our poor Hindustanee sepoys and camp-followers, he told us, still crowded the streets in a half-starved condition. During the winter they were kept alive by a little bread doled out to them from time to time by Sirdar Mahomed Zuman Khan and Nuwab Zubber Khan. Troup in the evening returned to Cabul, taking with him a list of all our wants for submission to Sirdar Mahomed Akbar.

On May 29 we were visited by Soojah-oo-Dowlah, eldest son of Mahomed Zuman Khan, a good-looking. stout young man, by whom the poor old king, Shah Soojah, had been murdered. At his request he and I adjourned to the garden, and there, in the course of a long conversation, while walking up and down, he asked me what our

views were respecting the king's death. I frankly told
him that we all regarded it as a serious crime. So, he said,
his own father considered it, who had not forgiven him
yet. If our army came to Cabul, it was his intention, he
informed me, to fly to the hills. He was strangely enough
called after the old king, who was present on the occasion
of his receiving the name. Troup came out to see us on
June 9, bringing us letters and papers from Jellalabad, as
also the articles we had requested Mahomed Akbar to
send us. We also received some bottles of sherry and
brandy forwarded from Jellalabad by my brother Henry,
but we had been so long without these stimulants that few
of us cared for them. Mackenzie also visited us, bringing
the intelligence that Mahomed Akbar had obtained possession of the Bala Hissar, and that Prince Futteh Jung
was completely in his power. On the night of the 10th
we had a shock of an earthquake, which happily did no
damage. On the 13th I received a letter from Sir
Richmond Shakespeare at Jellalabad, who held out hopes
of our speedy release; but in the meantime our guard
was increased by thirty men. We enjoyed the garden and
the bathing in the stream very much, and I kept myself
in health by running races with the Affghans, the most of
whom I found I could beat. Troup and Mackenzie paid
us a visit on the 25th, and informed us that Mahomed
Akbar had installed Futteh Jung as king, in room of his
father Shah Soojah, Akbar himself taking the post of
Wuzeer. He is all-powerful now in Cabul, and many of
the chief men, still friendly to the British, have in consequence deemed it prudent to fly from the city and take
refuge in the hills, among them our trusty friend Jan
Fishan Khan, known among us as the Laird of Pughman.
His forts have all been destroyed, his property confiscated,

and two of his sons killed. Nuwab Zuman Khan considered the hostages no longer safe in his keeping, as the Ghilzyes had made several attempts to break into his house and massacre them; so, as a measure of precaution, he made them all over to the charge of Meer Weiz, the head moollah of Cabul, whose sacred character could more efficiently insure their safety. Nothing could exceed the Nuwab's kindness and attention so long as the hostages remained under his roof, and he accompanied them himself to Meer Weiz's, lining the streets with his own followers to insure them from being attacked on the way to the moollah's house.

Upon the 26th, Sunday, just as prayers were concluded, we were joined, much to our surprise, by the English soldiers who had been left in the Budeeabad fort. They looked thin and hungry, having, as they declared, been very scantily fed since our departure and in every way badly treated. They were accompanied by Mrs. Byrne, wife of a soldier of the 13th, and her child, who looked like a skeleton. Sergeant Wade's wife, a half-caste from India, had deserted him after our departure, and behaved very cruelly to her husband and her other late companions by telling the Affghans where they had concealed any little money about their persons, even pointing out her husband's shoes, in which he had hidden a few gold pieces. Sergeant Wade declared he would petition to have her hung as soon as General Pollock's force arrived at Cabul.

Upon June 27 Sergeant Cleland and Gunner Dalton, of the Horse Artillery, who had hitherto been detained by Mahomed Akbar, joined us. The sergeant spoke highly of the treatment he had received, and had evidently ingratiated himself with the Sirdar, who sent me a note, desiring me to furnish Cleland with tea and sugar, and anything he might require, as he was a good man and in bad health. Dalton was an Irishman, full of fun and frolic even in the most desperate circumstances. He had been a terror to the Affghans, feigning madness, of which they have a superstitious dread, thinking the insane inspired. Whenever the Affghans desired Dalton to do anything he ran at them, butting with his head like a ram, and bellowing and stamping with his feet. 'Truly,' said they, ' he is an inspired man !' Probably to this impression respecting him he owed his life. Upon July 5 an Affghan named Fyze Mahomed Khan called on me by permission of Mahomed Akbar, and produced a note from his brother Osman Khan, stating we might fully confide in the former, and proposed that Pottinger, Conolly, and I should discuss matters with him and come to some arrangement. Dreading a trap, I replied we had no plans and knew nothing of General Pollock's intentions, so he took his departure. Conolly came in this day with Troup, and as we had not met since the retreat we had much of course mutually to hear and to communicate. On the departure of our army he was left in charge of the hostages and the sick and wounded. He found great difficulty in raising the necessary funds for their support, and had by stealth been the means of supporting many of our sick and wounded Hindustanees by drawing bills on India. On hearing of Anderson's child being exposed in the bazaar for sale, he tried to purchase her through his moonshee. So extravagant a sum was demanded that he abandoned the attempt, fearing it might form a precedent if similar cases occurred of others of our countrymen or children being exposed for sale, and thus render their recovery hopeless. However, by other expedients he succeeded in recovering the child and making her over to her parents, as has been previously mentioned, through Nuwab Zuman Khan and Sirdar Mahomed Akbar.

Upon July 16 I, as well as some others, was attacked with severe fever, and Dr. Campbell was sent for from the Bala Hissar, where the hostages and sick and wounded were then located, to attend upon us, by Mahomed Khan's express desire. Under his skilful treatment I recovered, and was able to walk about by July 27, on which day Troup returned from Jellalabad, to which he had been sent by Akbar Khan, and informed me he had seen my brother Henry, who was in charge of the Sikh troops, looking well and hearty. Troup then went on to Cabul to communicate his intelligence to Mahomed Akbar, and returned next day, the 28th, with a message to me from the Sirdar that he was desirous, if I were sufficiently recovered, I should accompany Troup in a second journey he was about to make to Jellalabad. Although strongly advised by Dr. Campbell, Lady Sale and others, not to make the attempt, as I was in their opinion far too weak to travel, I gladly intimated my willingness to accompany Troup, feeling assured that once on horseback and in the open country, I should speedily recover my strength. Accordingly I rode into Cabul with Troup to arrange matters with Mahomed Akbar, and receive his instructions before we started. The Sirdar received us very graciously, shaking hands with me and making me take a seat beside himself. He expressed his fear, from my pale face and weak state, that I was not strong enough for the journey, begging me, in that case, to give it up, adding that he could not afford to let me risk my life, as I was the only person who could manage the ladies and children. Upon my declaring myself quite fit for the journey, which I felt would do me good, body and mind, the Sirdar gave us our instructions, which were merely to get General Pollock to ratify in writing and by his signature the terms he had already verbally agreed upon with Troup—an exchange of prisoners and the evacuation of Affghanistan by the British. We then took our leave, and after visiting Conolly and the hostages in the Bala Hissar, we returned to the Shewakhee fort in the evening.

At 3 A.M. on July 31, Troup and I started for Jellalabad, with Hadjee Bukhtiar and two noted Ghilzye freebooters as an escort. We struck across the mountain range which bounds Cabul on the south-east, leaving the Minar-i-Seckundar some miles to the right. The road was a mere sheep-track, in some places almost perpendicular, so that our horses could hardly maintain their footing. The descent was happily more gradual, and brought us about 11 A.M. to a small village, where we halted, and alighting at a shepherd's black felt tent, received a very friendly welcome, and some fresh milk and coarse bread, which were most acceptable. An old patriarch lay in the tent groaning from fever; he asked me for medicine, so I administered to him two pills at once, and left two more to be taken the following day.

At 3 P.M. we mounted, and reached the lower Tezeen fort about 5. Here we found some 300 Ghilzye Juzzailchees *en route* to Cabul, to oppose our army. They crowded round us in so excited and suspicious a manner that Hadjee Bukhtiar and the Ghilzye guides became alarmed for our safety, and advised us to move on to the higher fort, which we did, and reached by sunset. Sirdar Khuda Buxsh Khan, its owner, received us kindly, and gave us a portion of his own dinner—rice swimming in ghee, with coarse bread—apologising for its homeliness, saying it was all a poor man like him usually had, and that as our arrival was quite unexpected, he had made no preparation for us. Here we met Corporal Lewis of the 44th, who to save his life had consented to turn Mahomedan, and at sunset went through his devotions like a good Mussulman. We spread our carpets at 9 P.M. and slept soundly until the call for prayer on the morning of the 31st, when we prepared to resume our journey. Lewis seized the opportunity to beg us to intercede with the Sirdar to allow him to accompany us to Jellalabad. I had the previous evening twitted the Sirdar with Lewis not being a real convert, when he assured me the man would not leave the place even if he could. Of this I expressed my doubts, and asked the Sirdar if he would allow the corporal to accompany us if he himself desired it, when he replied in the affirmative. Accordingly, just as we were starting, about 7 A.M., seeing Lewis standing a little apart, I said to Mahomed Buxsh, 'Now, Sirdar, will you allow Lewis to come with us if he desires it?' On his replying 'Yes,' I turned to Lewis, and asked him, 'Do you desire to remain with your kind protector, or go with us?' The poor man answered in his best Persian, in order that the chief might understand him, 'For God's sake take me with you!' 'Go,' said Khuda Buxsh; 'I did not expect this, but as I have promised you shall go.' On hearing this, Lewis jumped several feet from the ground in an ecstasy of joy, and then bounded forward like a roe, keeping a good hundred yards in advance of us, as if afraid that the chief might recall him.

After proceeding some miles we crossed a very high mountain by a most precipitous sheep track, so shelving that had our ponies slipped we must have been dashed to pieces. At 9 A.M. we halted to admit of the guides saying their prayers. They looked at Lewis, expecting him of course to join them. 'Shall I join them?' he asked me. 'Not unless you please,' I said. 'Then they may whistle for me,' he replied, and remained standing by us all the time. 'I wish I had known this,' said one of the Ghilzyes, turning to Lewis as he rose from his knees, 'and we should soon have settled you.' About 4 P.M. we reached the village of Tootoo, where we halted, and spread our carpets under some large shady trees. The guides in the meantime killed a sheep, and roasting portions of it on their ramrods at a large fire, brought them to us, and we made a hearty meal. About 7 P.M. we resumed our march, and reached Gundamuck about 12, when we were so tired and sleepy that we dismounted and took some rest, holding our horses' bridles in our hands. Remounting, we rode until 11 A.M. of August 1, when reaching Charbagh we heard that Broadfoot with his regiment of sappers was within two miles of us, foraging, so pushing on we had the great pleasure of meeting him, our old friend Dr. Forsyth, and Lieutenant Orr. We spent a delightful day, and at night I slept in a bed with sheets for the first time for eight months. Broadfoot entertained most hospitably Hadjee Bukhtiar and our Ghilzye guides, who expressed themselves much gratified by their reception. At sunrise of August 2 we left Broadfoot's camp for Jellalabad, distant fourteen miles. When about four miles from the place we met Sir Robert Sale taking his usual morning ride, and he accompanied us to General Pollock's camp, where I alighted at my brother Henry's tent. It is impossible to describe my feelings of intense thankfulness and delight at meeting my brother, and finding myself once more among British soldiers. Hadjee Bukhtiar, who knew I was to meet my brother after a long separation and after many dangers, expressed his amazement at seeing us only shake hands. ' Why, I thought you would at least rush into each other's arms, instead of merely shaking hands,' he remarked. ' We do not feel the less,' I explained, ' although we make but little show.' ' Well,' he answered, ' you are an extraordinary people, and I cannot make you out.' Shortly after my arrival in camp General Pollock sent for me, and the moment I saw him I augured ill for the success of our mission ; for since his verbal agreement with Mahomed Akbar Khan, the General had received fresh instructions from the Government in Calcutta, ordering him to advance on Cabul. In the letter which we brought from Akbar it was written, ' The General must fix the day on which he would depart.' This rather haughty expression was made by General Pollock a pretext for cancelling the previous verbal agreement ; and we were desired to return to the Sirdar, with the very unsatisfactory reply from the General, that ' he would not be dictated to.' A pretty kind of communication for us prisoners to have to make to the fiery Mahomed Akbar,—but there was no help for it. My good and generous brother Henry tried hard to induce me to allow him to take my place, while I remained with the army, arguing that if anything fatal happened to him, as he had only one child, it would be of small consequence compared with my death, who had four children. Of course I could not agree to this generous and high-minded proposal, but with a sad foreboding set out on August 6 to return to Cabul.

We spent the day in Broadfoot's camp, and with a full heart I rode away in the evening, bidding my friends what I really believed was a final adieu. As I rode past Gundamuck I heard Hadjee Bukhtiar calling to me, angrily, ' not to loiter behind. Do not you see,' said he, ' these lights? They are the matchlocks of robbers, who would think very little of taking off your own and Troup's heads. Let us hurry on to the guides.' This we did, and found them parleying with some thirty or forty most ferocious looking fellows, with matches alight, ready for action. On our explaining that we were Elchees—ambassadors proceeding from the English camp with a treaty for the chiefs at Cabul—they bid us pass on, as we were not the game they were looking out for, which was a party of travellers they knew were on the road, and to pass that way that night. A more villainous set of cut-throats I never met with, but they seemed on terms of intimacy with our guides, and I was much relieved when we passed on at a trot and left them behind us. We continued our journey all night, and dismounted at 7 A.M. of August 7, having been twelve hours in the saddle continuously. On the morning of the 8th we reached Tezeen fort, and were again hospitably received by Khuda Buxsh Khan, where we passed the night, and proceeded on the morning of the 9th, reaching the entrance of the Khoord Cabul pass at nightfall. We wished to push on to Cabul, but the guides thought it dangerous to do so, and led us to some shepherds' tents, where we got something to eat, and then spreading our carpets slept until morning.

On August 10 we started early, and pursuing the road over the mountains, reached the Bala Hissar at 10 A.M. We were there informed that as Mahomed Akbar was asleep we might go to the house occupied by the hostages until summoned to attend the Sirdar.

Hadjee Bukhtiar and our two Ghilzye guides here left us. The Hadjee had been very morose and reserved since our leaving Jellalabad, hinting darkly that the result of our ambassage would arouse the displeasure of Mahomed

Akbar. As to the two freebooters, they were perfectly indifferent on the subject, and on our giving them a few rupees, left us, singing our praises.

On arriving at the house of the hostages, I heard to my inexpressible grief of the death of my dear and valued friend John Conolly. He had gone to visit his friends at the fort of Shewakhee, where being attacked with fever, he expired after five days' illness. In him his country and government lost a most valuable officer, and all of us a friend not to be replaced. Though young in years he was remarkable for his cool judgment, moral courage, and fine temper, and his intimate knowledge of the Affghans, whose esteem and affection he had won by his chivalrous bearing.

After some hours' rest, Troup and I were sent for and ushered into the presence of Mahomed Akbar, who received us kindly, though it was evident from his flushed face and bright eyes that he was placing considerable restraint upon himself, having already heard from Hadjee Bukhtiar of the unsuccessful result of our mission. Mahomed Shah Khan, Sùltan Jan, Dost Mahomed Khan, and other chiefs, were present, looking also disturbed and angry. 'Look!' said Mahomed Akbar to them, 'these English have returned. I never asked if they would come back.' 'But you knew we would return, Sirdar,' I said. 'Yes, I did,' said Akbar; 'though my chiefs assured me you would not.' 'Would you have returned?' he said, turning to them. 'Certainly not,' they replied; 'we are not such fools.'

When we were seated, Mahomed Akbar held out General Pollock's letter, and in a loud voice asked, 'Why, what is this you have brought me? It is no reply to my letter! I see the General is playing with me! He in no way confirms the verbal message he sent me by Troup Sahib respecting a mutual exchange of prisoners and evacuation of the country by the British. I had thought you English were men of truth; that your word once given was as good as law. I now see I was in error, and so end all my hopes of an amicable arrangement, and now it must be war.'

Mahomed Shah Khan, half drawing his knife and grinding his teeth, here broke in with, 'I knew this would be the result; the Feringhees were only deceiving us. War they want; let them have it; war to the knife. What is the use of talking? Let us destroy them all.' Then turning to me, 'Lawrence Sahib,' he added, 'you have not done us any good.' 'Thank you, Sirdar,' I instantly replied; 'you always put in a good word for me.' Some desultory conversation then took place, by which time Mahomed Akbar had recovered his usual composure, and expressed to me his deep regret at Conolly's death, lauding him highly, and offering to send his remains into Jellalabad for interment. I thanked the Sirdar, but said I thought he had better be interred where he died. The Sirdar then asked me after my brother Henry, and why I had not brought him with me, as he would have been quite welcome, and allowed to return to Jellalabad when he pleased. I smiled, and asked him 'whether he did not think it sufficient to have one of the same family;' adding, 'my brother proposed to take my place, but I would not consent; would you, Sirdar, have accepted him instead of me?'

'No, no,' replied the Sirdar, 'I prize yourself too much.' Then telling us to prepare for a march, he dismissed us to return to our old quarters at Shewakhee, which we reached the same evening.

CHAPTER XVI.

THE HOSTAGES JOIN US AT SHEWAKHEE—INTERVIEW WITH MAHOMED AKBAR —ARRIVAL OF OFFICERS FROM GHUZNEE—LEAVE SHEWAKHEE—SALEH MAHOMED—DR. BERWICK AND CONVALESCENT SOLDIERS JOIN US—PRO-POSALS TO SALEH MAHOMED REJECTED BY HIM—KINDNESS OF MUSTAPHA KHAN—REACH BAMEAN—SALEH MAHOMED'S COMMUNICATION—MEASURES FOR OUR RELEASE—ARRIVAL OF SIR RICHMOND SHAKESPEARE—RELEASE OF PRISONERS—ARRIVAL IN CABUL.

WE were cordially welcomed on our arrival at Shewakhee by our fellow prisoners, who had just buried poor Conolly in the garden of the fort. I was disappointed in being too late to pay the last tribute of affection to my departed friend, and to read the service over him, as I had done the preceding year over his brother Edward. Several of the prisoners were ill of the fever, and some of them in a very critical condition. We distributed the letters and papers we had brought with us, and also some gold Mohurs we had contrived to convey safely by carrying them tied round our waists. We had of course much to communicate to them of interest, and underwent, as was natural, a very severe cross-questioning as to all our proceedings at Jellalabad, so that it was very late before we could betake ourselves to our beds, which consisted of a horse-rug to lie upon and a sheepskin cloak over us.

Upon August 12 our party was increased by the arrival of the hostages from the Bala Hissar, Captains

Drummond, Walsh, Webb, Warburton, and Airey, who told us that we were all to be sent in a few days to Bamean, and detailed the great perils and hardships they had undergone in Cabul.

Upon August 16, I, accompanied by Lieutenant Melville, visited Mahomed Akbar in the Bala Hissar, and finding the Sirdar in a friendly mood, I ventured to propose that if the prisoners were sent off to Bamean, Captain and Mrs. Anderson might be left behind, both being ill from fever—and Dr. Campbell also, to attend them. To this the Sirdar readily agreed; but when I expressed my hope that I myself might also be allowed to remain behind, he peremptorily refused permission. I then requested that at least two days' previous notice might be given to the ladies for preparation before they had to leave Shewakhee, but he shook his head, saying it was impossible to give them more than two hours' notice, adding, it was also contrary to the Feringhee customs to do so, as they never even told their prisoners where they were to be conveyed, far less gave them time for previous preparation. He then informed me that General Nott had evacuated Candahar, first destroying all the guns, stores, ammunition, and grain supplies not required for his army on the road. He then inquired 'if it was our custom to give out one thing and do another;' 'for,' said he, 'the General has declared it to be his intention to march for India by the Goolaree pass. Do you think he is coming to Cabul with his army?' We replied that in war it was not unusual to give out one course of action and to follow another, but that we were entirely ignorant of the General's plans or what he intended doing. 'If he is coming here,' added Akbar, 'as I suspect, why destroy the fortifications of Khelat-i-Ghilzye, as he has done, which were completed with so much labour and cost ; and why destroy and blow up so much valuable Government property? Can it be proposed to leave Candahar for good? But you are an incomprehensible people ; there is no understanding you or your intentions.' We then took our leave, and rode under an escort of some of Akbar's men through a portion of the bazaar. We were stared at and abused by the Ghilzyes, who called out that our army dared not advance from Jellalabad to Cabul.

On August 17 one of the soldiers died of the fever, and Mrs. Smith also, the widow of a sergeant who had been killed on December 6. Both were buried close to Conolly in the garden, and I read the funeral service over them.

August 23.—This morning we were agreeably surprised by the arrival among us of Colonel Palmer, Captains Barrett and Alston, Lieutenants Harris, Nicholson, Poett, Williams, Crawford, and Dr. Thompson, who had been taken prisoners on the surrender of Ghuznee to Shumshoodeen Khan on the previous 6th of March. Their joy at getting among us was great, for they had suffered severe hardships and been treated with much indignity, being deprived of all their servants. Although lean and hungry-looking, they were all in good health. Their treatment had been very different from ours, which was soon exemplified by their amazement on seeing me suddenly rush downstairs and summarily eject from the square sundry of their guards who had followed them inside the building. 'Why,' said they, ' if we had even asked them to go out, instead of pushing them as you have done, we should have been killed on the spot.' The guards themselves were not a little surprised at their own speedy ejectment, but walked -quietly out without any remonstrance. Before their arrival we thought we could not find room for even one more among us, but we soon contrived to locate the new comers much to their comfort and content.

Shumshoodeen Khan had since their capture steadily refused to give them up to Akbar, but as he had started with all his followers to oppose Nott's advance from Candahar, his brother, Gool Mahomed, taking advantage of his absence, sent the prisoners on to Cabul, where Akbar Khan had received them graciously, directing them to proceed to Shewakhee to join us.

August 24.—Captain Troup and Dr. Campbell visited Mahomed Akbar in the Bala Hissar, and returned, bringing medicines and the Sirdar's sanction to the doctor's remaining with the Andersons when the rest marched for Bamean. They informed us that we might receive any moment the order to proceed, as they had seen Sùltan Jan setting off with some horsemen to oppose Nott, who must therefore not be far off. I was to-day, much to my gratification, relieved of my arduous and most thankless duty—for it was impossible to please everybody—of presiding over the commissariat. A committee, consisting of Pottinger, Webb, and Johnson, was nominated for that purpose, and I was asked to join them, but declined to do so, even although the ladies expressed their hope I would become a member. August 25.—While at dinner, about 3 P.M., orders were received to march, and a supply of yaboos and camels arrived immediately after for our use, under the charge of our old custodian, Mirzah Baha-oo-deen Khan. At Troup's request Mrs. Trevor, who was very dangerously ill, was, with her eight children, allowed by the Mirzah to remain behind with the Andersons, subject to Akbar's approval. A body of about eighty horsemen were sent to escort us, under an officer in whom I recognised Saleh Mahomed, formerly subahdar of Hopkins's regiment of the Shah's infantry, and who had deserted with his whole company to Dost Mahomed. Saleh Mahomed had also accompanied me with an escort once from Cabul to Bamean, so we were well known to each other, and on my addressing him as ' Subahdar,' he said, ' Lawrence Sahib, I am a general now, so you must now style me General!' ' Oh, certainly,' I replied, ' and why not Padshah ?'—king. ' Well,' he said, ' I am as good a'Padshah as many of those who now are calling themselves so in the city. Any man who can collect a few followers aspires to be Padshah in Cabul.'

Great was the bustle and confusion in preparing to march, and great the difficulty in providing the necessary amount of yaboos for the party. The new committee had no easy time of it, and thankful was I the distribution no longer fell to my lot. As only two out of my own four yaboos were sent, I got one from Captain Anderson and another from the Mirzah to make up my number. After taking a mournful leave of Anderson and his poor wife, who was unconscious from fever, and of Troup and Bygrave, who had suddenly been ordered to remain with Mahomed Akbar, I mounted and rode out of the fort with the rest about 11 P.M., after the moon had risen, hardly knowing where we were going, and quite uncertain as to what would be our fate.

This certainly was the most mournful of all our moves, and many of our number were quite despondent and abandoned all hope for the future. The moon did not last long, and as I wended my way in the darkness, thoughts of home and all my treasures there crowded upon my mind, filling me with sadness. But then came the consoling reflection that they were safe in their native country, and among loving relations who would well supply my place if it were God's will to remove me from them, and that my brothers would be ever kind and tender to them. Above all, the thought that I and they were in the hands of Him who is 'mighty to save' strengthened and supported me, as it had done in many previous dangers, difficulties, and trials.

We marched all night, and avoided the city of Cabul, passing through gardens and orchards, the escort plundering them as we went on. About 7 A.M. of August 27 we halted near the fort of Killah Kazee, under some trees, as we were not allowed to enter the fort, which was occupied by some of Sùltan Jan's horsemen *en route* for Ghuznee to oppose Nott's advance. We had no better shelter from the sun than we could make by spreading blankets over the branches above our heads; even then we found the sun very hot and oppressive. Towards evening we were joined by Dr. Berwick and fifty-seven sick soldiers, who had been left at Cabul when our army retreated, and who were now able to march. At 1 P.M. of the 27th we resumed our march, Lady Macnaghten leading the way in a kajahwah, and the other ladies and children following, two on each camel, the officers and soldiers riding or walking. The horsemen and infantry formed advance and rear-guards under Saleh Mahomed and Ahmed, Akbar's Master of the Horse, who had probably been sent to act as a spy on the former. The infantry portion of our escort was composed of some 300 men of Hopkins's old regiment, armed with British muskets. They made a great display of their discipline, mounting guard, planting sentries, beating the reveille and the retreat in the English fashion. They were a good-humoured set of fellows, and laughed and chatted with us as we marched along. Their commander, Saleh Mahomed, dressed in a blue frock-coat, and mounted on a large white horse with flowing mane and tail, was disposed to give himself great airs and aped the commander-in-chief. After a march of nine hours we halted at Khote Ashroo, where three small tents were provided for the ladies. There are three forts at this place, the proprietors of which are at continued feud with each other, and plunder travellers. We met to-day many camels and asses laden with assafœtida from Turkestan, their drivers regarding us with much amazement. Our march led us near Urgundhab on the road to Ghuznee, and Pottinger, Johnson, and I tried to induce Saleh Mahomed to make short marches, so as to allow Nott's forces to come up and rescue us, by promising him a considerable sum, of which each prisoner was to contribute his quota, to be adjusted by a committee. He affected to be very angry at such a proposal and refused to listen to us.

August 28.—We marched at 2 P.M. and reached Tock-hana at half-past 8 A.M. The road ran through a well-cultivated valley, and we passed many forts. We camped under a double row of poplars, on fine green turf, and apples, pears, and grapes were brought to us by the people, also a few small fish from the clear stream flowing near.

August 29.—We marched at daybreak and passed Sir-i-Chusmah, where there is a fort and walled town. I sighed as I thought of the previous occasion of my passing this same place when in pursuit of Dost Mahomed Khan, when I was a pursuer, instead of, as now, a miserable captive. Nevertheless I did not despair that all would yet turn out well. After advancing some miles we passed under a large fort belonging to Mustapha Khan, a Kuzzul-bash, who had the courage and humanity, in spite of

Saleh Mahomed's threats to report him to Mahomed Akbar, to come out and salute us, bringing us bread and fruit, at the same time sympathising much with us and comforting us, saying, ' Keep up your spirits ; all will yet go well with you.'   After a march of eight or nine miles we halted at the fort of Nazirkhan.

We marched at 2 P.M. August 30.   A kossid, as he passed, informed us that our troops had retaken Ghuznee, and that some of them were following after us.   We then passed a fort whose walls were crowded with well-armed men.   Our leader, Saleh Mahomed, fearing they might sally out upon us, halted, closed his ranks, fixed bayonets, and then moved on with drums beating and colours flying.   No attempt, however, was made to interrupt our march, and after a very fatiguing journey of ascents and descents, crossing the Hadjee Yuk pass of the Koh-i-Babu, 12,500 feet above the level of the sea, we reached the fort of Kaloo.   Our commissariat committee not being found to work satisfactorily resigned their functions here, and I assented, at the earnest request of the party, and being anxious to make myself of use as long as I could, to resume the sole management as before.

At daybreak of September 1 we marched, and crossing the Kaloo pass, an ascent of four miles, came in sight of Bamean, and halted after a fatiguing march of seven miles at the fort of the Topchee Bashee (head of the ordnance), situated in a narrow, well cultivated valley.

At daybreak of September 2 we marched to Bamean, seven miles distant, and pitched our tents close to the ruins of a fort and town, not far from the caves and colossal figures for which the place is famous, at which our guards fired as they passed, cursing them as idols. We were not allowed to remain long here, as our guards got into a row with the villagers, and Saleh Mahomed thought it best to move on another mile.   He then wished us to occupy a miserable fort containing only cow-sheds, and after a long altercation, in which he lost his temper, by no means good at any time, and abused me, he at last consented to our camping outside.   From September 2 to 9 nothing occurred of any interest, but on that day Saleh Mahomed, from some pretended alarm, forced us to move into a fort previously occupied by Dr. Lord, when political agent at this place.   The only accommodation it afforded was some miserable sheds, which were divided among the ladies, we gentlemen settling ourselves as best we could in the open square.   I made another attempt to induce Saleh Mahomed to permit our remaining outside the fort, which swarmed with bugs and fleas, but he again lost his temper, declaring that I was at the head of all mischief, and that he would shoot me if any of us escaped ; to which I merely replied, ' Shoot me, if you dare.'

Among our guard we found several Hindustanee, and some Heratee servants of Pottinger's, with whom we opened communications.   Rumours of all sorts were continually reaching us, one day elevating, another depressing our hopes.   I endeavoured for the poor ladies' sakes to put a good face upon matters, and to appear cheerful. To their continual query of ' Oh, when shall we be released ? ' I always replied gaily, ' Very soon, very soon, I am confident.'   My chief annoyance here was from the continual braying all night of an enormous jackass, which the guards had picketed close to where I lay down to sleep.   I let him loose several times, but they as often tied him up again, and declared they would brain me if I did it again.

On the morning of September 11 Pottinger told me that Saleh Mahomed had informed him that he had received from Mahomed Akbar orders to take us off to Khooloom in the event of the Affghans being defeated by our army then advancing on Cabul. Saleh Mahomed further stated that some of Moonshee Mohun Lal's agents in Cabul had sounded his friends there and offered a large sum of money for our release, and that Shah Mahomed Reza, Kuzzulbash, had now sent his agent, Syud Moortuzzah Shah, to confer with him on the subject. He added that 'he had no faith in Mohun Lal, the Kuzzulbash, or any one besides ourselves; that his mind was now changed respecting the prisoners since we had previously spoken to him, and therefore he now wished to know what we would do for our liberation.' On hearing this I immediately ran to Lady Sale, and awakening her daughter, Mrs. Sturt, and herself, told them the good news, and asked them to let us have the use of their room to hold a private conference with Saleh Mahomed, to which they gladly consented. Pottinger, Mackenzie, Johnson, Webb, and myself then met Saleh Mahomed and Syud Moortuzzah Shah, and, after some discussion, we agreed to guarantee to Saleh Mahomed a pension for life of 1,000 rupees per mensem, with 20,000 rupees to be paid on our arrival at Cabul. The following bond was then written in Persian by Syud Moortuzzah Shah: 'We, Pottinger, Johnson, Mackenzie, Webb, and Lawrence, in the presence of God and of Jesus Christ, do enter into the following agreement with Saleh Mahomed Khan. Whenever Saleh Mahomed Khan shall free us from the power of Mahomed Akbar Khan, we agree to make him, Saleh Mahomed Khan, a present of 20,000 rupees, and to pay him monthly the sum of 1,000 rupees, likewise to obtain him the command of a regiment in the Government service; and we attest this agreement to be true, or if otherwise that we shall acknowledge ourselves to be false men, even in the presence of kings.'

We all signed this bond, and afterwards took it to Brigadier Shelton and Colonel Palmer for their signatures, but both declined to sign it, the Brigadier alleging that it was premature, and might compromise him with Mahomed Akbar, and the Colonel urging it might do us harm, and could do us no good. A second paper was then written out by Captain Johnson, and eagerly signed by the rest of the captive ladies and gentlemen, agreeing to pay whatever amount might be fixed for each of us, to make up the amount payable to Saleh Mahomed, should the British Government object to fulfil the agreement we had entered into with him. When this was done, and the Persian bond made over to Saleh Mahomed, he produced the written order from Mahomed Akbar, directing him to convey us to Khooloom. Once there we knew that the Wullee, the ruler of the place, would seize us as his own spoil and sell us for slaves at Bokhara, and that we should never return thence. Saleh Mahomed then hoisted the flag of independence on the fort, and frightened away Mahomed Akbar's Master of the Horse and his horsemen, who indeed gladly availed themselves of the excuse to get off and look after their own families and affairs at Cabul, now that the English army was advancing, and all was in confusion in the city.

Upon the morning of September 16 we made our first retrograde march, and a very joyful one it was, from Bamean to the fort of the Topchee Bashee, *en route* for Cabul. On setting out, Saleh Mahomed offered us some of his spare muskets for our Horse Artillerymen and

the privates of the 44th, to use in case of our being
attacked by the way. The Horse Artillerymen gladly
seized the opportunity of arming themselves, but such
was the apathetic state of the men of the 44th, that although Lady Sale endeavoured to shame them into taking
the arms by offering to carry a musket herself, they would
not accept them, alleging they did not want arms, and
had quite enough to do to carry themselves along. Lady
Sale paid me the compliment of making me over poor
Sturt's sword, saying 'it was in safe hands, and would be
well used if needed.' We were aroused about midnight
by a horseman bringing a note from Sir Richmond Shakespeare, announcing that he had left Cabul with 600 Kuzzulbash Horse, to attempt our rescue. Our joy and thankfulness at the receipt of this intelligence are not to be
described, and little sleep did any of us have for the rest
of that night.

At day-break of September 17 we marched, arriving
at the fort of Kaloo at noon, and were all seated on
the shady side of the fort wall, when a cloud of dust
announced the advance of our friends to succour us.
Saleh Mahomed drew up his men immediately in line, in
single file, so as to make the most of them, and saluted
Shakespeare as he passed. Oh, what a joyful moment was
that when I saw my old friend Shakespeare, and felt that
we were really delivered! We made the hills around us
ring again with our cheers of delight and thankfulness.
Shakespeare then told me that my brother Henry had
intended accompanying him, but was prevented by some
pressing duty at the last. We then presented Saleh Mahomed to Shakespeare, recounting the good service he
had done us, and how much we were indebted to him for
our deliverance. We then resumed our march and crossed

the Hadjee Yuk pass, halting at Gurdun Dewal, the
Kuzzulbash horse keeping close by us; among them I
recognised many old friends of our prosperous days, and
had much interesting conversation with them on late
events.

We started at 3 A.M. of September 19, and as there
were rumours that Mahomed Akbar and Sùltan Jan intended to intercept us, we pushed on rapidly. As we
passed the fort of Mustapha Khan Kuzzulbash, the old
man again came out, and regaled us with cakes and delicious milk and curds, expressing much joy at our release,
and reminding us how he had encouraged and comforted
us on our sorrowful journey to Bamean by assuring us
that we should soon be at liberty again, his words having
proved true.

On the 20th we marched at daybreak, and after advancing some miles were met by the gallant General
Sale, my brother Henry, and other officers, with the 3rd
Dragoons and the 1st Light Cavalry. On reaching the
top of the Sufed-koh we met Backhouse with his mountain train, H.M. 13th Light Infantry, and Broadfoot's
Sappers. Oh, the joy of such a meeting, who can describe it? I took care to introduce Saleh Mahomed to
the especial notice of General Sale and others, for now
that we were safe among our own people he seemed to
apprehend that he and his men might be neglected and
his services forgotten. It was indeed well that I did look
after them, for on our ascending the top of the pass I
found that Broadfoot's sappers had seized many of his
men, on the ground that they were armed with British
muskets and pouches, which it was supposed they must
have plundered from our troops. It was with some difficulty, and only after fully stating their case, that I

induced Broadfoot to release them and return them their arms.

On the 21st we marched to Killah Kazee, and in the afternoon to Cabul, passing through the great bazaar, where all the shops were shut, and scarcely an Affghan to be seen. In the evening we arrived in General Pollock's camp, and thus ended my eight and a half months' captivity. May the God who so graciously preserved me through so many dangers sanctify His great mercies to me.

CHAPTER XVII.

OUR ARMY WITHDRAWN FROM AFFGHANISTAN—PLACED IN CHARGE OF THE
FAMILY OF SHAH SOOJAH—REJOIN MY REGIMENT—SERIOUS ILLNESS—
PROCEED TO ENGLAND ON FURLOUGH—RETURN TO INDIA—APPOINTED
POLITICAL AGENT AT PESHAWUR—STATE OF AFFAIRS IN THE PROVINCE—
OUR POLICY IN REGARD TO AFFGHANISTAN—VISIT TO EUSUFZYE COUNTRY
—TRANQUILLITY OF PESHAWUR—PROCEED TO LAHORE.

THE withdrawal of our army from Cabul, after having
first, as a retributory measure, destroyed the grand bazaar,
where the mutilated remains of the Envoy had been exposed to the insults of the inhabitants, and the subsequent evacuation of Affghanistan, are matters of history,
and require no comment from me; more especially as the
return march of our army through the Punjaub to Ferozepore was destitute of any striking incidents. Previous to
our departure from Cabul, General Pollock had appointed
me to the charge of the old blind king, Shah Zuman, and
the family of the murdered Shah Soojah, all of whom had
requested to be permitted to return under the protection
of our army to Hindustan, as their remaining in their
own country under its altered circumstances would, they
were well aware, have resulted in their extermination.

On reaching Ferozepore I was relieved of this charge,
and after having had to appear as a witness before several courts-martial held on the officers, not having been
hostages, who were prisoners in the hands of the Affghans,
and which resulted in their honourable acquittal, I

proceeded to join my regiment, now the 11th Light Cavalry, at Cawnpore.

Although I had passed through the disastrous events in Affghanistan, and through an eight and a half months' captivity, without apparently any diminution of bodily or mental health and vigour, as soon as the necessity for exertion had passed and a season of perfect rest ensued, I found that the anxieties and exposure of the preceding year had seriously weakened my constitution, and after a very dangerous illness I was forced to return on furlough to England for the recovery of my health. I remained absent from India a period of nearly three years, and returned in September 1846.

During my absence events of great importance had occurred. The kingdom of Scinde had been conquered and annexed to the British dominions; the power of the Mahrattas had been broken by the victories of Punniar and Maharajpore, and the kingdom of Scindia had been subsidized. The Punjaub also had been vanquished, the famous battalions of Runjeet Singh subdued, and the greater part of their splendid artillery captured in the successful actions of Moodkee, Ferozeshahur, and Sobraon. The Governor-General, Lord Hardinge, had, however, deemed it inexpedient to annex the kingdom of the Punjaub, and had generously restored it to the Maharajah Duleep Singh, on condition of the State paying an indemnity of a million and a half sterling for the expenses of the war they had themselves provoked; of ceding Cashmere, to be erected into a separate kingdom, and conferred on Maharajah Goolab Singh; and also of making over to us the Jhullundur Doab, which was then formed into a British province.

The Maharajah being quite a child, the administration

of the country was entrusted to the Maharanee Chunda, his mother, as regent, to be assisted by her Vizier Rajah Lall Singh, and a brother of her own, Pundit Jooalah Purshhad. The new administration having been duly installed, felt their position so insecure that they besought the Governor-General, when the army evacuated the Punjaub, to leave for their protection a body of British troops until such time as their own army was reorganised, and the administration of the country brought into working order.

To this proposal Lord Hardinge had with much reluctance assented, and on quitting Lahore with the army of occupation, left behind a division under command of General Sir John Littler, at the same time nominating Major Macgregor as agent on the part of the Governor-General and as a channel of communication with the newly constituted government.

This arrangement did not last very long, for it was soon discovered that the regency had by their intrigues prevented the peaceful cession of Cashmere to Goolab Singh. The opposition organised by them was so serious, that the Governor-General was obliged to send a British force into the country to carry out that portion of the treaty of Lahore. Lall Singh was in consequence of his proved complicity in this treachery removed from office and banished to Agra, and the Maharanee was deprived of power. A new treaty was then concluded at Bhyrowal between the Governor-General and the leading Sirdars of the Punjaub in the month of December 1846. Under its terms a council of administration, consisting of eight members, was appointed under the general superintendence and control of a British resident, whose authority was to be unlimited, extending to every department of the

State, as well as to all foreign relations, until the Maharajah should attain his majority. My brother Henry, who was at the time Governor-General's agent on the north-west frontier, was appointed to this new office of Resident. Under him was placed a staff of political assistants to be located in different parts of the country to control and superintend the administration carried on by the native officials.

Shortly after my arrival in Calcutta, in September 1846, I proceeded to join my regiment, which was stationed in the newly-acquired province of Jhullundur, of which my brother John had been appointed commissioner and superintendent. In December following the Governor-General, Lord Hardinge, considering from my intimate acquaintance with the Affghans that I was suited for the post, appointed me principal assistant to the Resident, and political agent on the western frontier, at Peshawur. This province is 12 miles from the Khyber pass, 210 miles from Cabul, and 45 miles from Attock. From its convenience as a connecting position between India, Affghanistan, and Persia, Peshawur had always been of great importance both in a commercial and political respect, and was the third capital of the Dourannee dynasty, being the occasional residence of its sovereigns. When Dost Mahomed finally prevailed over the Suddozye prince, Shah Mahomed, the Baruckzye brothers divided Affghanistan among themselves, and Peshawur fell to the lot of Sùltan Mahomed Khan. This prince was a noted intriguer, and invited Runjeet Singh to assist him with troops in some of his designs. The Maharajah gladly closing with the request, sent his general, Hurree Singh, with a force, ostensibly to assist Sùltan Mahomed Khan, but really to take possession of Peshawur, which remained

afterwards a portion of the Lahore dominions.
Singh exercised merely a nominal sovereignty
province until 1838, when he nominated General Avitabile
to the government, who ruled over Peshawur with an
iron hand until 1843, when he retired from the Sikh
service and returned to Europe. The province then fell
into a state of complete anarchy and confusion under
the administration of a succession of corrupt and unscrupulous officers deputed by the Lahore durbar to administer its affairs. The governor at this time was
Sirdar Uttur Singh, a young man totally inexperienced,
and indeed incapable. Subordinate to him General Golab
Singh, an old officer of Runjeet Singh, commanded the
troops located in the province, consisting of 10,000 men
of all arms.

The duty assigned to the political assistants of the
Resident, located in different parts of the Punjaub, was to
act as friendly advisers of the native officials, but not to
interfere directly, except when justice could not otherwise
be obtained, when they were to enforce it in the last resort. But the Governor-General regarded the province of
Peshawur as so important in a political and military point
of view, that it was necessary to vest the political agent
there with greater powers and more independent authority
than was exercised by the Assistants located elsewhere. In
particular it was deemed imperative that the political
agent should have under his immediate control a large
and effective garrison, not less than one third of the
army of the Durbar, whom it would be his duty to see
maintained in a high state of discipline and in perfect
contentment.

Such being the duties generally I was called upon to
perform, I proceeded early in February 1847 to join my

appointment. Upon arriving at Rawul Pindee on the 13th, it was not without a feeling of regret that I received the intelligence of the death, at Jellalabad, of Mahomed Akbar Khan, who was supposed to have died from a dose of poison administered to him by his doctor, a native of India, who immediately afterwards absconded. At Hussein Abdal a number of notorious freebooters came into my camp under a safe-conduct—' Burcheim' as it was termed. These men were no petty robbers, but heads of clans, who kept in their pay large bodies of followers, Sikhs, Affghans, and Hindustanees, and levied black mail from the whole country, from the Margullee pass to the Attock, acknowledging no authority unless supported by regular troops. It was in the wholesome dread that I would soon send some regular troops to settle matters with them, that they now came in to make their submission. I made an agreement with the outlaws that they should cease from all acts of violence and depredation, until I received a reply from Lahore on certain grievances they complained of, and their offers to take service, if their past offences were overlooked and forgiven.

On Sunday the 20th Feb. I entered the city of Peshawur, being received in state by the governor, Sirdar Uttur Singh, and other Sirdars. The whole city poured out to meet me, and loud were the complaints of the poor people and their demands for justice, many of them carrying fire on their heads as illustrative of their extreme misery and grief. I could not get rid of the crowds after arriving at my tent until night, although I repeatedly explained to them it was not my custom to transact any business, except of the most urgent character, on a Sunday. Their complaints were loud of the unchecked rapacity and violence of the soldiery, of the grinding extortion practised by the Kardars, and the heavy and incessant fines levied upon them on all pretexts and occasions. It was grievous to hear the lamentations and cries of the people, and I began to foresee that I had no easy task before me in endeavouring to introduce justice and order, after years of rapine, violence, and misrule. I had also to discipline a mutinous soldiery and police, and while strictly enforcing the just demands of the government, to put a stop to all exaction and oppression on the part of the durbar officials. To add to my difficulties I found shortly after my arrival that the treasury was empty, while the army, regular and irregular, were from three to eight months in arrears, and clamouring for their pay, threatening their officers with their vengeance unless their demands were speedily satisfied.

Hitherto it had been the custom to give the soldiers orders for their pay on the different revenue collectors throughout the province, which amounted of course to allowing the soldiery to live at free quarters on the country and enforce their own demands. As soon as a supply of cash was received I had the men paid in my own presence, which pleased them much and gave them confidence for the future. At the same time, by a few necessary acts of severity, a wholesome dread was established among the troops, who soon understood that while prompt obedience would be rigidly enforced, every consideration would be shown to their just complaints and grievances.

Several of the heads of clans and villages in the province showed little inclination to pay their revenue, refusing to obey the orders I sent to them ; it became therefore necessary to make an example of one of them for the intimidation of the rest. Accordingly, an expedition under my assistant, Lieutenant Lumsden,[1] consisting of

[1] Major-General Sir H. Lumsden, K.C.S.I., C.B.

200 cavalry and 200 infantry, was secretly organised, and sent off suddenly to surround the village of Mashoo Khail, the chief of which, Dawur Khan, openly defied the government, and had been guilty besides of many outrages. The troops reached the place at gunfire, and at once proceeded to surround the village. Dawur Khan, hearing the tramping of the cavalry, mounted, with some followers, and galloped out of the village, but coming on the cavalry in their front they threw themselves off their horses, cast away their arms, and fled into a field of standing wheat, from which Dawur Khan managed to escape in the dress of a woman. Lumsden arrested this chief's son, brother, and nephew, and brought them back to Peshawur. The expedition was conducted so rapidly and successfully that Dawur Khan, finding further opposition hopeless, came in and made his submission. Several other malcontents were overawed by this example and gave in their adherence also.

About this time intelligence reached me from Affghanistan, which was in a state of complete anarchy, that the chiefs— previously aware of the presence of a large force at Peshawur—having heard that I had arrived there, had made up their minds that our government was about again to enter their country in force. Many of the Sirdars sent me friendly messages, among others, Mahomed Shah Khan Ghilzye. This man had planned the Envoy's murder, and had repeatedly desired to put myself and the other prisoners to death, and yet had the audacity to send me a letter by a special messenger, requesting my aid to establish his authority in his own country. I summarily dismissed his servant, refusing to receive his letter or reply to it.

The Ameer Dost Mahomed Khan, who was at Jellalabad, endeavouring to reduce the Ghilzyes to obedience, sent me at the same time a vakeel, ostensibly for another purpose, but really to ascertain whether our government had any designs on Cabul. I thought it right to assure his messenger, that while we had no designs on Affghanistan, and were quite indifferent as to its politics, we were yet desirous to remain on terms of amity with the Ameer. I then dismissed his agent with due respect, conferring on him the usual dress of honour. As it was probable that formal overtures might be made to me by the Dost, I deemed it right to request the instructions of my government for my guidance in that event. I was accordingly informed that the Governor-General approved the reply I had made to the Dost through his messenger, and considered that it was more becoming our government to allow the Ameer to satisfy his own fears, if he had any—which Lord Hardinge doubted—than to be making professions of our intentions. Still the Governor-General had no objection to giving verbal assurances to any vakeel —who might come and go as he pleased—that we were quite indifferent on the subject of Affghanistan, for courtesy is to be reconciled with complete indifference. If, however, the Dost sought the friendship of our government by any specific overtures, the Governor-General was prepared to hear, but not to encourage them, or court any interference in the affairs of Cabul.

To these wise and statesmanlike instructions, which were in entire accordance with my own previous views, I strictly adhered in all my future communications while at Peshawur with the Ameer and the chiefs in Affghanistan.

On June 25 I was obliged to take very decided measures with another refractory chief, who refused to give up a woman who had been carried off forcibly by some of his villagers, replying to my demands by saying

he had never paid any attention to any orders of even
Avitabilè himself, and he did not see why he now should
regard any of mine.

The very night I received this message I started with
a force of 300 cavalry and 600 infantry, and by daybreak
we had surrounded his village of Mashoo Gugur, seized
the recusant Baron and brought him into Peshawur, very
much crestfallen and deeply penitent for his previous
contumacy.

A singular communication was about this time made
to me by some members of an Armenian family residing in Cabul, which illustrated the lawless condition of
society in that unhappy country. One of the young
daughters of the house was of singular beauty, and a
son of Dost Mahomed having heard of her, sent to her
father to demand her to be given up to him for his wife.
The father in vain urged the obstacle of their faith being
different from that of the Affghans, but he was only told
in reply that the prince would take the girl by force
unless made over to him peaceably. Upon this some
friends of the family begged my interference, and asked
whether in event of their flight from Cabul I would give
the girl and her family shelter and protection. I wrote in
consequence, as a private individual and personal friend, to
Dost Mahomed Khan, begging him to extend his protection to the family and to prevent his son's carrying out
his designs against the young woman, and my interference
was happily successful.

My hands were at this time greatly strengthened by
the removal of the young Sirdar Uttur Singh—who was of
very little use and mixed up with all the corruptions
formerly prevailing in all departments—and by the nomi-
nation of General Goolab Singh in his room as governor
of the province—a man much respected by the troops and

the inhabitants generally. I read out the orders of the
Durbar for the General's appointment at a grand parade,
pointing out to the officers that their Commander's eleva-
tion to so high a post was the result of good and tried
service to his government, expressing my confidence that
all would emulate his example, and my hope that some of
themselves might, in due time, obtain similar valuable
marks of the approbation of the Durbar.

Early in the year several chiefs from the Eusufzye
country had paid me a visit, and after exhorting them to
abandon their mutual feuds and devote themselves to the
cultivation of their lands, I promised, much to their
apparent satisfaction, to visit their country in the autumn,
when I would reward those of their number who had
been most successful in extending cultivation in their districts. Accordingly, a considerable force under the Sikh
General John Holmes, and accompanied by Lieutenant
Lumsden, started in September for Eusufzye, I myself
following with a small escort on the 24th. Just as I
was leaving Peshawur a kaffilah of merchants arrived from
Cabul, one of whom came offering me an English sword
for sale. On examining the blade I found to my great
satisfaction and surprise that it was my own sword, which
had been snatched from me on the fatal December 23,
1841, when the Envoy was murdered and I was myself
made a prisoner.

I joined the force in Eusufzye on September 27 at the
village of Kaloo Khan. Hitherto it had been very difficult
to obtain any revenue from this wild and half-cultivated
tract of country. It was the duty of the Mullicks, or
heads of villages, to collect the tribute due to the State
from each village; but although they were ready enough to
collect, they showed a great antipathy to paying up their
quotas, invariably replying to the demands of government

officials, that ' if they wanted the money they must come and fetch it.' When the government officers appeared, the Mullicks either openly resisted them, if they felt themselves able, or if not, they took to the hills, where it was difficult to follow them, leaving the officials to collect their dues from the unfortunate cultivators who had been already mulcted to the uttermost farthing.

With a view of endeavouring to amend this state of things I issued a proclamation desiring all absentee Mullicks who had taken to the hills on my arrival, to return to their villages within a month, on pain of forfeiting their lands and rights, and announcing that equitable rates would be fixed on all lands with due reference to their situation, quality, proximity to water for irrigation, &c., beyond which no demand would be made, while the Mullick's own dues would be fixed at one sum permanently. I marched for some days through different parts of the country, which, from the small amount of cultivation, was admirably adapted for the movement of troops and field exercise. I succeeded in making satisfactory arrangements, far beyond my expectations, for the payment of the revenue, with several chiefs. All supplies were paid for, a most unusual thing, and no trespass of any sort committed by the troops on the crops or villagers. The cultivators were surprised and delighted at the change. On all former occasions they had been so plundered and tyrannized over, that, driven to desperation, they made reprisals whenever they dared, by murdering all individual soldiers they fell in with.

The result on the present occasion was satisfactory for both parties, as shown by the following conversation I overheard between some Sikh soldiers reclining by a well, under the shade of some trees.

' How comes it, brother,' said one, ' that not a Sikh has been murdered this time ? Formerly when we visited Eusufzye not a day passed without several of us being killed.'

' It must be,' replied a comrade, ' because these people are afraid of the two white faces ; ' meaning Lumsden and myself.

Although I had succeeded in coming to terms with the majority of the Sirdars of this wild district, there was one chief of a village called Baboozye, who prided himself on never having paid any revenue to the Sikhs, and who had signally defeated, the previous year, a body of durbar troops sent to coerce him. He now refused either to visit me or pay the government revenue, so there was no course left but to coerce him. Accordingly I took measures for assaulting his village, and if possible capturing himself. With this view I reconnoitered Baboozye on the evening of October 9, and found it a very formidable place, built in the cleft of a hill, and so fortified by the spurs of the hill running down on each side, that to attack it in front would have been highly hazardous and occasioned much loss. The villagers were perfectly prepared to oppose us, and fired several shots at my party by way of warning. Hearing that there was a footpath through the Shadoon district, whose chief was friendly to us, by which the hills in the rear of the village and commanding it could be reached, I sent some men to reconnoitre, who reported it practicable. I detached in consequence a party of the Guide corps to proceed by that route, with orders, on gaining the heights, to attack the village in rear while we attacked it in front.

On the night of the 11th we marched, and arrived at 2 A.M. within a mile of Baboozye, where we halted till daybreak, when we advanced to the attack. A company from each regiment, under Lieutenant Lumsden, acting as skirmishers, cleared the jungle of all concealed enemies, while the guns opened a well-directed fire on the village in front. The Guides who had reached the heights above Baboozye opened fire at the same time, and the villagers finding themselves unexpectedly attacked in front and rear, fled at once to the hills, and this strong position, deemed impregnable by the Sikhs, was taken with very trifling loss. Our success had the most salutary effect, for the recusant Mullicks speedily came in and made their submission, binding themselves to pay the government demands in future without fail.[1]

Upon October 29 I returned to Peshawur, and received

[1] While engaged at Baboozye my Munshee, Hadjee Mahomed, a Candaharee, who always attended me in the field of his own accord, suddenly called me to notice some of the enemy deliberately firing at me from one of the adjoining heights, and urged me 'to alter my position and move out of range, otherwise I would certainly be shot.' As my attention was fully occupied at the time I took no notice of the circumstance, but shortly afterwards I found the Hadjee had quietly moved his horse and taken up a position immediately between me and the line of fire, so as effectually to shelter me, as no shot could reach me without previously passing through himself or his horse. When I rebuked him for his rashness, he observed 'his life was of no value, but mine was of much importance.' This is but one of many instances of devotion and courage on the part of this excellent officer. He had been in the service of Captain John Conolly, whom he faithfully served until that officer's lamented death at Cabul in 1842, when a hostage ; he then joined me, and during all my subsequent difficulties and dangers at Cabul, Peshawur, and Rajpootana followed me as my shadow ; and was, I believe, under Providence, by his fidelity, sagacity, and untiring vigilance on more than one occasion, the means of saving my life. Hadjee Mahomed was murdered at Jhodepore, of which state he was Prime Minister, out of revenge for his too faithful adherence to his master's interests. I pay this tribute to the memory of a true and faithful servant, whose career is a comparative refutation of the allegation too often made that our Oriental fellow-subjects know not what fidelity and gratitude mean. I have had many good and true Hindustanee and Afghan followers, but none like the Hadjee.—*Gen. S. P. Lawrence.*

a very hearty welcome from the people, who seemed really glad at my return among them, and to appreciate the security and peace they now enjoyed, to a degree unknown to them for many previous years of terror and misrule.

I was gratified by hearing that the head moollah, the high-priest of Peshawur, had, after concluding the public prayers, addressed more than 2,000 people collected on the occasion, saying, ' I have for years prayed that oppression should cease and justice be administered in this unhappy country. My prayers have now been granted, and do you yourselves all offer up prayers that this state of things may continue.' In the province affairs were now apparently so tranquil that I was able to quit my post for a season to proceed to Lahore, in order to take leave of my brother Henry, who was about to proceed to England for the recovery of his health, with Lord Hardinge, on that nobleman's resigning the office of Governor-General.[1]

---

[1] Lord Hardinge, before leaving India, addressed to Major Lawrence the subjoined letter, conveying his Lordship's approval of his administration of the Peshawur Province :—

' My dear Lawrence,— I cannot leave India without assuring you of the interest I take in your success, and the satisfaction it has given me to approve of all your acts in every instance since you have occupied the foremost post in the Trans-Indus frontier, in which prominent position the promptitude of your action and the soundness of your judgment have been most creditable to you and gratifying to me. Rely upon it the occupation of the Punjaub in peace is so intimately connected with the vigorous retention of the Peshawur district up to the Khyber Pass, that you cannot, in these times of peace, be in a better condition than in the command of 8,000 Sikh troops. It keeps you in the eyes of the authorities both in India and in England ; and as you are entrusted with the key of the only vulnerable entrance into India, I advise you, notwithstanding the banishment, to exercise your patience, for your conduct and the importance of your post are both justly appreciated in the proper quarter.

' Ever yours very sincerely,

(Signed)   ' HARDINGE.'

CHAPTER XVIII.

I RETURNED to Peshawur from leave in the end of January 1848, and so profound was the tranquillity prevailing there and through the entire Punjaub, and so complete the absence of all causes of alarm, that I was accompanied by my wife and children. Sir Frederick Currie had joined his appointment as Resident during my brother Henry's absence in England, and my brother John, who had acted as Resident in the interval between Sir Henry's departure and Sir Frederick's arrival, had resumed his own duties as Commissioner of the Jhullundur Doab. This favourable and gratifying state of affairs continued until the beginning of April, when a storm suddenly broke upon us, as violent and overwhelming as it was unlooked for and unexpected. It originated at Mooltan, the capital of a district lying between the left bank of the Indus and the right bank of the Sutlej rivers. The position of Mooltan as an entrepôt between central Asia and Hindustan, gave it much importance in a political and mercantile point of view. It had formed a portion of the Affghan empire originally, but the town was taken and the district subdued by Runjeet Singh in 1818, who incorporated it with his

Punjaub territories. Runjeet Singh entrusted the government of this valuable acquisition to a person named Sawun Mull, a native of the neighbouring state of Bahawulpore, who continued to administer it until Runjeet's death. During his long and successful incumbency Sawun Mull had acquired great power and influence in the province, amassed great wealth, and was almost independent of the Sikh durbar during Khurruck Singh's disturbed reign. In 1843 Sawun Mull was either accidentally or intentionally wounded by a pistol fired by one of his own guard, and dying of the wound, his son Dewan Moolraj was nominated by Khurruck Singh to succeed his father in the government, an appointment which was afterwards confirmed by the Regency at Lahore on the conclusion of the Sikh war in 1847. The Vizier Lall Singh soon after issued a summons to Moolraj to appear before the durbar. The Dewan obeyed the command on the guarantee of the British officers at Lahore for his safety, and a very favourable settlement being made with him, he returned to his province fully satisfied. On the downfall of the Regency and the appointment of a British resident, Dewan Moolraj was confirmed in his government. Suddenly, in November 1847, the Dewan revisited Lahore and communicated to my brother John, the acting Resident, his desire to resign the government of his province. My brother endeavoured to dissuade him from the step, but Moolraj persisted in his determination, requesting my brother to keep his resignation a profound secret from the durbar, to which my brother consented. Sir Frederick Currie becoming Resident on ascertaining these facts, was of opinion that the durbar should receive intimation of Moolraj's determination, and be consulted on the measures to be taken in consequence, as the Dewan's resignation, so far from being a secret, was talked of in the bazaars, and he had heard of it at Agra on his way to Lahore.

Sir F. Currie then addressed a letter to Moolraj, hoping he would alter his intentions and retain his charge, but in reply Moolraj expressed his fixed determination to resign. Sirdar Khan Singh was then nominated as his successor in the government, and two British officers, Mr. Vans Agnew and Lieutenant Anderson, were sent to accept Moolraj's resignation, settle with him the accounts of the province, and instal his successor in the government. The British officers arrived at Mooltan on April 5, and were both shortly after murdered. The postal communication between Mooltan and Lahore was immediately interrupted, showing that the movement was not local, but general. To meet this emergency a force of 6,000 men, with eighteen guns, was ordered to march at once on Mooltan from Lahore. Had this force moved when ordered, as Moolraj had then only 8,000 men with him, the insurrection might have been put down at once. Unfortunately the departure of the army was from one cause or another postponed, and on the 27th it was directed to halt for the present at Lahore : thus, as in the case at Cabul, what was originally little more than an émeute assumed speedily the proportions of a formidable rebellion. Although the advance of the army was postponed, orders were issued to Lieutenant Edwardes, then in the Deràjàt, with a Sikh force, collecting revenue, to cross the Indus and march on Mooltàn. Our ally the Khan of Bahawulpore was ordered at the same time to co-operate with his forces and assist Edwardes. In obedience to these orders the Sikh troops under Edwardes crossed the Indus on April 24, into the province of Mooltan. At the

same time the Resident, Sir Frederick Currie, communicated to Lord Gough, the Commander-in-Chief, then at
Simla, his opinion that, in a political point of view, it was
of the highest importance that a force should move immediately upon Mooltan capable of reducing the fort and
occupying the city, irrespective of the aid of these native
troops, and even in the face of any opposition which the
Sikh troops in the neighbourhood, if they mutinied, might
offer. The Commander-in-Chief, however, was of opinion
—and the Governor-General concurred with his Excellency
—that the season precluded any active operations in the
field with European troops, who were alone to be trusted;
that everything must, therefore, be deferred until the cold
season in October, when his lordship would take the field
in person, at the head of a force powerful enough completely to crush all opposition in Mooltan or elsewhere in
the Punjaub.

Upon April 27 the news reached me at Peshawur of
the outbreak at Mooltan, and the deplorable murders of
Agnew and Anderson. The intelligence did not appear
at first to have any evil effects on the people or troops at
Peshawur, then numbering 10,000 men of all arms, with
thirty-six guns. My assistant Lumsden had been recalled
to Lahore to organise a corps of guides, and two other
officers, Lieutenants Bowie and Herbert, were sent to
Peshawur, the first to aid in organising the artillery, and
the latter to act as drill instructor of the infantry.
Although everything remained tranquil, I received from
several friends recommendations to send away my family
to a place of safety; but I considered that any such measure might only precipitate matters, as evincing doubts in
my mind of the fidelity of the troops. I was at the same
time aware that some emissaries from Mooltan had been

endeavouring to corrupt the regiments, and that some Sikh fanatics had been heard abusing the Feringhees, and urging the soldiery to wipe out the disgrace they were under from their late defeats on the Sutlej by our troops, which I well knew they were burning to do. I was glad therefore to receive the Resident's instructions to raise a corps of Mahomedan Puthàns as a counterpoise to the Sikh element, and I accordingly enlisted at once 600 of these men. I took the opportunity of distributing ammunition to the new levies to lay up a store of powder and ball in the Residency in case of emergency.

About May the district began to be disturbed, and several murders were committed in different parts. Hearing of six men and a woman having been murdered by the villagers of Adeyzye, and feeling the necessity of taking immediate steps to quell the first signs of revolt, I despatched Lieutenant Nicholson[1]—who had lately joined me as assistant—with a body of Sikhs, to seize the murderers and punish the head men. Nicholson by a rapid march surrounded the village before the Mullicks were able to organise any resistance, and succeeded in apprehending the murderers, seizing at the same time a quantity of arms and ammunition stored up in the place.

On June 25 intelligence of Edwardes' success at Kewajec, and on July 9th of his victory at Suddoram over the Mooltan troops, reached Peshawur. I fired royal salutes on both occasions, and for a time I entertained hopes that these brilliant successes might prevent the spread of disaffection which had already, I was aware, commenced among the Sikh troops. I considered it at the same time my duty to warn, in the strongest terms, the Resident at Lahore, that the only way of maintaining

---

[1] Brigadier-General Nicholson, killed at Dehli in 1857.

tranquillity in the Peshawur province, and the fidelity of its large garrison, was to adopt immediate and stringent measures, notwithstanding the season of the year, for the suppression of the revolt at Mooltan and the seizure and punishment of the ringleaders of the insurrection. Further delay would produce, I assured him, very disastrous consequences, and a general rebellion which would require all the resources of the British Government to subdue.

Upon July 27 one of the chiefs of the Eusufzye country brought in a fakir whom he had arrested in the act of endeavouring to excite the chiefs of that country to revolt and join the Sikhs in getting rid of the English, promising them in that event jaghires, and remission of revenue for several years. On being interrogated by me, this man admitted that he was in the employ of Moolraj, and had been sent by him with letters to Dost Mahomed Khan at Cabul, soliciting aid, and promising to restore the province of Peshawur to the Ameer as a reward of his alliance. The Dost had, however, dismissed the messenger, declaring himself to be an ally of the British, and declining to have any further communications with Moolraj. The emissary stated that on his dismissal from Cabul he had come to Peshawur, and thence proceeded, as ordered, into the Eusufzye country, in order to raise that district and induce the people to join in the insurrection. I reported this man's arrest to the Resident at Lahore, recommending that he should be executed for his treason, as an example was greatly needed. Sir F. Currie concurred in my proposal, and the fakir was executed on the 8th August, in presence of a large concourse of people, who evinced no sympathy whatever in his fate.

As I had anticipated, the unfortunate delay in putting down the revolt at Mooltan caused the disaffection—notwithstanding all my efforts—at length to spread over the province under my charge. It first showed itself unmistakeably in the turbulent and wild district of Hazàrà, of which Chutter Singh, an old influential Sikh chief, was governor, and of which Major Abbott was in political charge. Chutter Singh was much dissatisfied at the loss of power and influence he and other old leading Sirdars had suffered by the assumption of the supreme administration of the Punjaub by the British Government, and he was willing to join in any attempt to restore a pure Sikh sovereignty to the country. Among his officers was a Colonel Canara, formerly a trumpeter in our cavalry, who commanded a body of artillery. This officer about the end of July reported to Major Abbott that a bad feeling was showing itself among the troops, and recommended that timely measures might be taken to meet any emergency that might occur. Shortly afterwards Canara, refusing to obey an order from Chutter Singh to remove his guns from their usual position in order to place them where they would have been completely under the control of Chutter Singh's troops, was cut down and murdered by some of that Sirdar's followers, and doubtless by his own orders. Upon the 9th of August I received intelligence of poor Canara's murder, and that Chutter Singh was concentrating all the Sikh troops in the Hazara and Bunnoo districts, with the view of marching on Lahore and joining the rest of the Sikh army there in a general rebellion, which he himself was to head. I immediately communicated the news to my assistant, Lieutenant Nicholson, then unfortunately confined to his bed from illness, and mentioned my deep anxiety to anticipate Chutter Singh's movements, by occupying, with some reliable troops, the important fort of Attock, and thus prevent its falling into the Sirdar's hands. Nicholson fully coinciding in my views, and seeing the importance of the measure, although suffering from fever at the time, insisted on my authorising him to proceed at once on this duty.   He accordingly started with a party of Puthàn Horse and arrived at Attock with only thirty men—the rest being unable to keep up with him—just in time to prevent the gates of the fort being shut against him. Chutter Singh had already been tampering with the garrison, and would have got possession of the place, had not, very fortunately for us, the governor, lately appointed by me, remained staunch, and prevented their carrying out their design of seizing the fort on Nicholson's approach. I next day sent some reliable troops, placed at my disposal by the Eusufzye chiefs, to reinforce Nicholson, who then turned out the mutinous Sikh garrison and thus made his position comparatively secure.

On the 10th August I requested the Sikh governor, General Goolab Singh, and all the Colonels of the regiments composing the force at Lahore, to meet me at my quarters, when I addressed them, appealing to their feelings of loyalty, pointing out to them that the preservation of the Punjaub—as a separate and distinct kingdom under their own Maharajah—was now in their hands and that of the other officers of the Sikh army. If *they* remained true to their salt, all danger would pass away ; if, on the other hand, they and their troops were faithless, nothing could save the independence of the Punjaub.   They all assured me of their own loyalty, and that they hoped to keep their troops to their allegiance, saying they had every reason themselves to be satisfied with the present administration, and wished for no change. I then dismissed them, well satisfied with the result of the meeting, although in my own mind I reposed no confidence in the assertions of any of them except the governor, General Goolab Singh, and his son, Colonel Alla Singh. My servants who had been with me at Cabul, and well remembered Sir A. Burnes's fate from his house being situated in the city, entreated me at this time to remove to the fort; but this I declined doing, as I felt it necessary to avoid everything which was calculated to give the impression to the troops that I began to distrust them. I therefore continued to occupy my usual residence. The Governor, however, as a matter of precaution, removed to a house close to mine, so that we might be in constant communication.

By his advice I addressed a letter to Sirdar Chutter Singh on the 13th August, mentioning that he was reported to have instigated the mutiny of the troops in Hazara under his command, and requesting him as a friend to communicate to me the full facts of the case. Scarcely had I despatched this letter when a confidential messenger from Chutter Singh himself arrived, bearing letters to myself and General Goolab Singh, requesting that three regiments of infantry and some cavalry might be sent immediately to aid him in putting down an insurrection of the country people which had broken out. Discerning that these letters were a mere blind, and surmising that the messenger had probably some verbal confidential communication to make to the Governor, I retired from the room, telling the General to take the opportunity to elicit the truth from him. This he did, discovering that the messenger's real object was to communicate with the regiments at Peshawur, and induce as many of them as he could to throw off their allegiance and return with him to Chutter Singh. On ascertaining this, I gave the messenger a receipt for his letter, telling him a formal reply would be forwarded afterwards, and sent him back across the Indus with a small escort, so that he had no opportunity of communicating with the troops.

I reported the state of affairs in the Hazara, and the treasonous proceedings of the governor, Chutter Singh, to the Resident, urging him at the same time to detach without delay a strong brigade of British soldiers to coerce the Sikh troops in that district, as all attempts to do so through the levies of the country people must be futile, and to send also a second brigade with a light field battery as a reserve, so as to obviate all risk of failure. The Resident intimated to me that he was fully alive to the expediency of sending a force to coerce the mutinous troops, but would not consent to send a single brigade without a reserve in support, and this latter he could not do without the sanction of the Commander-in-Chief and the Governor-General. On communicating with these authorities, the Resident was informed that both concurred in considering that no small force could be safely detached into the Hazara, while to send one sufficiently large to crush all opposition was at the time impossible, with reference to the disturbed condition of the Punjaub generally.

I could not but perceive a growing spirit of disaffection among the troops, shown by their insolent bearing towards myself and my assistants. While passing on one occasion with Lieutenant Bowie through the lines of one of the regiments, a subahdar and half a dozen men sitting together neither rose up nor saluted us. I immediately ordered their arrest, and the next day they were brought up for punishment. I thought it wise to proceed no further, but ordered their release on account of the general excellent conduct of their regiment up to that period. A little incident occurred at this time which

showed how sensitive the troops were of the least thing
which could be construed into a doubt of their fidelity.
Lieutenant Bowie had directed that some of the guns
should be brought up to the Residency for trifling repairs
to their carriages. The troops hearing of the order began
to murmur, saying the Sahib evidently wanted to keep
the guns at his own house, and so great was the excitement that it was thought advisable to send them back
again at once.

Nicholson's fortunate occupation of Attock had for
a time checked Chutter Singh's movements; but seeing
that no measures were being attempted to coerce the
Hazara brigades, he now openly raised the standard of
rebellion, 'devoting his head to God and his arms to
the Khalsa.' Nicholson was able, with some of the Mahomedan troops I had sent him, amounting to 800 men,
to take the field and co-operate with Major Abbott in opposing Chutter Singh, but it was scarcely possible for these
raw levies to resist effectually the regular battalions under
the Sirdar. Upon August 30 I received, at 11 P.M., an
express from Nicholson, urging me to send either Lieutenant Bowie or Herbert, with some additional levies, to
take charge of the fortress of Attock, as he was himself
required to operate in the field against Chutter Singh,
who was expected to reach Attock the following day, to
invest the fort. I immediately roused up Herbert, who
started in an hour, with 200 men, and reached Attock in
the morning, when Nicholson made him over charge of
the fort. The garrison then consisted of between 800
and 1,000 Mahomedans, recently raised, and whom I considered staunch, with eight guns and three months' provisions, which Nicholson had succeeded in collecting and
storing.

The troops at Peshawur, although not yet openly mutinous, were now in a most unsatisfactory and dangerous condition, clamouring for their pay, which had fallen three months in arrear. I was fortunate in being able to disburse the amount on receipt of bills on the bankers at Peshawur, forwarded to me by Sir F. Currie. But notwithstanding the removal of this grievance, the troops were evidently ripe for mischief, and at 8 p.m. of the 4th September intimation was brought to me that two of the Sikh regiments intended seizing the guns that night, and then attacking the Residency. I instantly communicated with the Governor, who summoned the colonels of the two Sikh corps, and also those of the Mahomedan and Hindustanee regiments. The Sikh colonels expressed their belief that their corps had no such intention, and that their men would be found to be asleep, which on enquiry was the case. I ordered the colonel of the Mahomedan regiment to take immediate possession of the guns, with four companies from each corps, which was at once done. I likewise called upon Sùltan Mahomed Khan Baruckyze, the former governor, to attend with all his d'sposable men, and he brought up in a short time 160 horse and 700 foot. It was an anxious night for us all, but passed off quietly, the measures so promptly taken having overawed the conspirators, who for the time deemed it advisable to abandon their enterprise.

On September 7 I received a warning that there was an intention to assassinate the governor, Goolab Singh, and myself; but of course it was useless to take any notice of this, for no precautions could prevent our assassination if the soldiery desired to kill us. On the same day a letter addressed by Chutter Singh to Sùltan Mahomed

Khan Baruckzye was intercepted and brought to me. Its contents seemed to prove that the Sirdar, notwithstanding that he owed so much to our government, was really in league and communication with the rebels. Sùltan Mahomed Khan had been the last governor of Peshawur under the Affghans, and had been arrested by the Sikhs and kept prisoner at Lahore. My brother Henry, at my suggestion, directed his release, and permitted him to return to Peshawur, restoring his jaghires to him on condition of his maintaining certain levies of horse and foot for service when required. In this letter Chutter Singh stated that it behoved Sùltan Mahomed Khan to leave his most competent son at Peshawur, while he himself with all his troops and officers should join Chutter Singh in Hazara. He was encouraged ' to put away all misgiving, and putting his trust in Providence to come quickly.' After reading the letter, I caused it to be conveyed to Sùltan Mahomed Khan, who, I learnt, exhibited great delight on its receipt, and promised to send a reply in a few days. That the Sikhs and the Affghans might form an alliance seemed so probable and so alarming that I again applied to the Resident to send a strong detachment to Peshawur to overawe the troops before they committed themselves by any overt act of insubordination against the Government. Sir F. Currie, fully concurring in the expediency of such a measure, ordered a force of 5,000 men, under Brigadier Wheeler, to hold themselves in readiness, and on September 22 they were ordered to march without any delay. The Commander-in-Chief, however, considering that the force was insufficient for the duty, countermanded its advance while already on the way to our aid.

In the meantime Sirdar Chutter Singh, with a force of 5,000 infantry, 600 cavalry, and 16 guns, had arrived at

Nowashur.   Abbott and Nicholson had to the best of their power endeavoured to oppose his advance, but their troops, with the exception of a few Mahomedan levies, deserting them and going over to the enemy, they were obliged to return.   My great fear was that Chutter Singh would cross the Indus to Peshawur, in which case the troops would certainly join him.   With the view of preventing the Sirdar making the attempt, I desired Herbert to send away all the boats but three from Attock, and directed Sùltan Mahomed Khan to proceed with his men to oppose the passage of the Sikhs, should they attempt it.

On the evening of September 21 the news of Shere Singh and his army having joined the insurgents, and the consequent raising of the siege of Mooltan by our troops, reached Peshawur and increased tenfold the danger of our already perilous position.   Fortunately, the troops remained in ignorance of this disastrous news for two days after it was known to myself and the Governor.   I took advantage of the lull to send off my wife and two children, one of them only a month old, to endeavour to reach Lahore, under charge of an escort of 500 Affghan horsemen furnished by Sùltan Mahomed Khan, and under command of his son.   The party were to proceed by Kohat, to which place Sùltan Mahomed had some weeks before despatched the females and children of his own family.   Although I entertained grave suspicions myself of the Sirdar's fidelity, I could not but trust him on this occasion, especially as he took the most solemn oaths on the Koran to protect my family, and see them himself safe across the Indus.

They proceeded on their journey as far as Churuckwal, where reports reaching the officers in command that Chutter Singh had sent out a body of cavalry to intercept them, it was thought expedient to return to Kohat, where Sùltan Mahomed Khan received them hospitably, and assured them of safety. The intelligence that my family had been sent away caused great commotion among the troops, as it was reported that I myself and Bowie had also left the station. To counteract the evil consequences of such a report, I deemed it necessary for Bowie and myself to ride through the town, which we did with perfect safety, and apparently with good effect in allaying the prevailing excitement among the troops and people. Upon September 27 I made known the Governor-General's proclamation confiscating the estates of the rebel Sikh Sirdars, which created a great sensation. On that day I directed a troop of Horse Artillery to proceed to Attock to oppose Chutter Singh, should he attempt to cross; and to my surprise the order was obeyed with alacrity, and without creating any opposition among the main body of the troops, who I feared might prevent their departure.

I received on the same day the sad and ominous intelligence of the murder during his sleep, by some of their own troops, of Colonel John Holmes at Bunnoo, and a few days later of that of Futteh Khan Towannah, who had incurred their resentment by unflinching loyalty. My own position, and that of the officers with me, by these events became of course exceedingly critical. I knew that a plot existed for seizing and conveying me as a prisoner to Chutter Singh, but owing to the disagreements among the conspirators nothing was actually attempted. I had only to put as bold a face as I could on matters, and carry on my duty as if the troops were all loyal and to be depended upon. With this view I inspected on September 28 two regiments of Sikh cavalry and one of infantry, putting them through their usual manœuvres as on ordinary occasions, and all implicitly obeyed me. I promoted some men and rewarded others on the spot, and placed two native officers in confinement for having paid their respects to a rebel Sirdar. By this means I managed to maintain my hold over the troops for some time longer, and restrain them from open mutiny. On October 13 I informed the Resident that 'I had still very reasonable hopes, even at this the eleventh hour, if only a British force advanced in the direction of Peshawur, to hold the troops to their duty. As yet I had not, in any way whatever, relaxed the reins of discipline, was fully supported by the officers, and had fortunately been able to retain possession of the artillery by placing them in charge of the two Mahomedan regiments. I intend,' I stated, 'to keep my people to the last moment at the Residency: when I can hold out no longer, I will take to the fort of Shameerghur, which I have provisioned for a thousand men for one month, and if driven from that position will do my best to secure my own safety and that of the persons attached to this agency.' The Resident was, however, powerless to detach a force to my aid, much as he desired to do so, as such a measure was strictly prohibited by the Commander-in-Chief, in whose views the Governor-General coincided.

The march of Shere Singh with his army from Mooltan towards the Salt range in order to form a junction with Chutter Singh's force, rendered abortive all my endeavours, and frustrated all my sanguine hopes of preventing the Peshawur force from breaking into open mutiny and joining the confederacy, and the crisis had now arrived. On the morning of October 23 Lieutenant Bowie rode into the city. I was about to mount my horse and follow him, when the Governor recommended me to remain at the Residency, as he had good reason for believing that the troops were about to break into open mutiny. I accordingly remained, and sent off a messenger to Bowie ordering him to return immediately to the Residency. Fortunately for him he promptly obeyed my summons, for some dragoons of the Shere Singh regiment charged him as he galloped out of the city, and he only escaped their sabres by the fleetness and activity of his horse, leaping two ditches which lay between him and the gate of the Residency. I then ascended the roof of the Residency, and could see the Sikh portion of the force, consisting of two regiments of cavalry and three of infantry, assembled on the parade and evidently in a state of open mutiny. The only thing to do was to endeavour to prevent their getting possession of the guns under the charge of the two Mahomedan regiments of the force, and with this view I immediately sent to their assistance some of the Hindustanee regiment and the Mahomedan Ramgole corps. The mutineers tried to induce the two Mahomedan colonels, and General Elahee Buxsh, commanding the Artillery Brigade, to join them with the guns, but they refused unless they received orders from myself, and warned the Sikhs they would fire on them if they approached the guns. Khan Singh Mujeetiah, commanding the Goorchurrahs, returned a similar reply, refusing also to join them. I then summoned Sùltan Mahomed Khan to join me with his troops, but he failed to appear, and towards evening sent a message by his son, excusing himself on the ground that he must at such a crisis look after the safety of his own family. The mutineer officers then sent a message to the Governor that they would march away from Peshawur without hurting anyone, provided he supplied them with carriage and the pay of Uttur Singh's regiment.   By my advice the Governor sent a reply promising to accede to their demands if they would only first prove their sincerity by marching immediately to Chumkunnye, seven miles from Peshawur.   The mutineer regiments not being able to make up their minds to attack the guns, at length moved away from the parade to the east side of the city, and were joined by the Sikh Ramgoles [1] on duty there, seizing as they proceeded some treasure and two guns which had been kept in Avitabilè's fortified residence.

This long and anxious day at last wore away, and in the evening Sirdar Khan Singh Mujeetiah, and two other Sirdars, came to the Residency to consult what was best to be done.   I knew that I could not depend on the Mahomedan regiments to act against the mutineers, but it was necessary for me to show that I still did not doubt their loyalty, so I visited both as well as the artillery that night, to encourage the men and keep them if possible to their duty.   The night passed without any further movement among the mutineers, and on the morning of October 24 I issued pay to the Mahomedan regiment commanded by Shere Singh, but no sooner had I done so than the men began to desert in large numbers.   Nothing, however, occurred until evening, when the Governor reported to me that the Mahomedan corps were no longer to be depended on to defend the guns, and he could not answer for their safety if they remained under their charge during the night.   On receiving this intelligence I sent off two or three hundred Puthàns, under their commander, and accompanied by my Meer Moonshee, to aid in protecting the guns and preventing their surrender to the

____
[1] Irregulars.

mutineers. But on this detachment approaching the spot the commandant swore that no Puthàns should ever approach his guns, and immediately wheeled them round so as to bear upon the Residency. It was now 8 P.M., and two shots were fired by the infantry, upon which signal the guns opened fire with shot, grape, and shrapnel on the Residency, to which I replied with musketry from the walls from my Puthàn guard. Several lives were lost on both sides, and at this moment the Governor and his son rushing into the Residency implored me to fly, as no dependence was to be put for a moment longer on any of the troops. The old man offered himself to accompany me, which I thought it best to decline, on account of his age and infirmities, and he then left me. As I heard an attack in force was about to be made on the Residency, and knowing that the rebel troops on the other side of the city would soon reach the spot, I felt that it would be absurd to think of opposing such a body with only the Residency guard. I therefore deemed the time was come for consulting my own safety and that of the two officers with me—Mr. Bowie and Mr. Thompson, in medical charge of the Residency, who was accompanied by his wife. We accordingly mounted our horses, which stood ready for us, and with an escort of fifty men rode out of the Residency. We were not a moment too soon, as the troops on duty only allowed us to leave the place under the idea that we were merely about to go out to reconnoitre and then return. The road to Attock was, we knew, closed by the enemy, so that our only course was to proceed to Kohat and place ourselves under the protection of Sùltan Mahomed Khan, who had repeatedly offered me an asylum in event of my having to quit Peshawur. We were not molested on the road, and safely reached Kohat at 10 A.M. of October 25.

CHAPTER XIX.

REPORT TO RESIDENT MUTINY OF THE PESHAWUR TROOPS—SÙLTAN MA
HOMED KHAN BINDS HIMSELF BY OATH TO SEND US TO BAHAWULPORE
—SÙLTAN MAHOMED KHAN IS MADE GOVERNOR OF PESHAWUR—DELIVERS
MYSELF AND PARTY TO CHUTTER SINGH AS PRISONERS—MY FAMILY SENT
TO THE FORT OF SUKKOO—I AM SENT TO SHERE SINGH'S HEADQUARTERS
—BATTLE OF CHILLIANWALLAH—SENT TO LAHORE ON PAROLE—BATTLE
OF GUJERAT—REJOIN THE SIKH CAMP—LIBERATION OF PRISONERS—
FINAL SURRENDER OF THE SIKH ARMY—RETURN TO PESHAWUR.

ON arriving at Kohat, where my wife and children already
were residing, I was hospitably received by Khojah Mahomed, son of Sùltan Mahomed Khan, the Sirdar himself having remained at Peshawur in order to receive
charge of that province from Chutter Singh, according
to an arrangement made between them. I reported to
the Resident that the Peshawur troops had, notwithstanding all my endeavours to keep them to their allegiance,
fraternized with the rebels, and that it was only at the
last moment that Lieutenant Bowie, Mr. Thompson, and
myself had abandoned our post, and when the delay of
but five minutes would in all probability have sealed our
fate. Previous to our departure Sùltan Mahomed Khan
had sworn in the most solemn manner on the Koran,
and offered to give me a writing to that effect, that he
would provide for the safety of my family and myself,
and of the several officers attached to the Residency,
and forward us to Bahawulpore, from whence we could

join the British camp before Mooltan.   Upon October 26
I addressed a letter to the Sirdar, to forward to me the
written agreement he had promised.   Upon the 27th I
received a reply, stating that the Sirdar had detached
one of his sons with an escort of horse to convey myself
and party to Esakhail, on the Indus, where a detachment
of British troops would be prepared to receive us.   The
promised agreement was however not forwarded, and the
Sirdar, through his sons, strongly dissuaded me from
attempting to proceed to Mooltan, as it would show I had
no confidence in him and would bring trouble and
disgrace upon him.   The following day Khojah Mahomed
brought me another message from his father, reiterating
his objections to my proceeding to Mooltan, and stating
that if I persisted in my resolve he could not be responsible
for my safety, as the road was now become too dangerous.
At the same time the guard which had accompanied me
from Peshawur was recalled, and a guard of his own men
substituted in their place.   It was clear that though
nominally guests, we were actually prisoners, for on my
walking out some distance to inspect a rather remarkable
well in the neighbourhood, near the Teera Hills, it was
reported that I was endeavouring to make my escape, and
a party of horse was sent out after me, who escorted me
back again, my walking out being thenceforward strictly
prohibited.

Upon October 31 Sirdar Chutter Singh entered Peshawur in state, having been received at some distance
from the city by Sùltan Mahomed Khan.   Chutter
Singh promised to make over the province and government of Peshawur to the Sirdar, provided he agreed to
deliver up myself and family, and the British officers at
Kohat.   Sùltan Mahomed, notwithstanding his solemn

promises to me, acquiesced at once, with the usual treachery of his race, in this arrangement, and directed that I should be sent back to Peshawur. I accordingly started with an escort, accompanied by Lieut. Bowie, leaving Mrs. Lawrence behind at Kohat, and was met some miles from Peshawur by Chutter Singh and other Sikh Sirdars escorted by a regiment of cavalry and a troop of Horse Artillery. Each presented his Nuzzur, and a salute of nineteen guns was fired. I expostulated with the Sirdar on this display in my honour, as absurd and quite out of place, considering that I was a helpless prisoner. ' Why is it absurd ? ' replied the Sirdar ; ' we have no quarrel with *you* ; on the contrary we feel highly indebted to you, as we never received anything but kindness and consideration from your two brothers and yourself. Although it is for our interest that you should be with us, and we must therefore detain you, we desire to treat you in all respects as if you were still governor of Peshawur.' We then proceeded to tents prepared for me, where a guard of honour received me with a salute as I dismounted. The Sirdars then left me, but the officer in command of the guard, Colonel Khan Singh Rosa, followed me into my tent. He and I were previously on friendly terms, and he assured me that although sentries would be placed all round the tents, I must consider them as only honorary guards for my protection, adding, ' I have served you as governor for the last two years as a duty, now I serve you as a pleasure, and you shall judge how I can acquit myself.' In a few days afterwards I was joined by Mrs. Lawrence and Mr. and Mrs. Thompson. We were very well and kindly treated, but though told we were honoured guests, were in reality captives, no less than thirty sentries surrounding our tents day and night, and two officers remaining always in attendance in the tent which Bowie and I occupied.　Chutter Singh, in the end of November, moved to Attock, and was very urgent with me to direct Herbert to evacuate the fort and make it over to him, which of course I declined doing.　While encamped here Chutter Singh returned for a few days to Peshawur, to meet the Ameer Dost Mahomed Khan, who, notwithstanding his previous protestations to Moolraj's vakeel of being an ally of the British, had joined the Sikhs on condition of receiving back the province of Peshawur, which was now to be delivered over to himself, Sùltan Mahomed Khan being continued as governor under him.

Upon December 3 we marched towards the Jhelum, and on the 5th Mrs. Lawrence with the children, and the Thompsons, were sent to the fort of Sukkoo.　Bowie was detained in the Sikh camp at Attock, and I was directed to join Sirdar Shere Singh's force, as the Sikh Sirdars wished me to become the medium of communication between them and the Commander-in-Chief, they being desirous to come to terms with the British.　I accordingly communicated their wishes to Lord Gough, and in reply to these overtures I was on December 13 informed by Major Mackeson, the Governor-General's agent with the Commander-in-Chief, that his lordship would grant no terms whatever to rebels with arms in their hands, but required unconditional surrender.　This answer of course put a stop to all hope of any satisfactory arrangement, and Shere Singh determining to fight it out, I was sent to the small mud fort of Dummoo, about twenty miles from that of Sukkoo.

Intimation here reached me, to my great regret, that Herbert, owing to the treachery of his garrison, had been obliged to fly from Attock, which fell into the hands of Chutter Singh's force, and was by them made over to

the troops of the Ameer Dost Mahomed Khan, who had
sent a force of 3,000 infantry and 1,500 cavalry to aid
the Sikhs against the British. Intelligence also reached
me that my brother Henry had returned from England,
assumed charge of the Residency from Sir F. Currie on
January 9, and was in the Commander-in-Chief's camp.
From the damp of the mud fort and the confinement I
suffered at Dummoo I became seriously ill, but though
otherwise well treated by the Sikhs was not permitted to
rejoin my family at Sukkoo. Upon January 13 I heard
heavy firing from 1 P.M. until night, but did not ascertain the cause until the 18th January, when it was reported that there had been a very severe battle on the
13th, in which the Sikh troops were defeated with great
loss at Chillianwallah, and Shere Singh himself seriously
wounded. Sirdar Chutter Singh, hearing that my health
continued very bad at Dummoo, allowed me on the 19th
to rejoin, as a great favour, my family at Sukkoo. On
arrival there I heard that the fortress of Mooltan had
been taken and the defences blown up, which accounted
for the chief's kindness to me, feeling as he did that his
cause was a failing one. I found also that in my absence
my own and my wife's riding horses had been taken by
Chutter Singh and generously presented by him as a
gift to Dost Mahomed Khan.

As soon as Sirdar Chutter Singh received the intelligence that my brother Henry had resumed the office of
Resident, he addressed him the following letter, enclosing
one from me to my brother :—' The Sikhs both high and
low, who were grateful to you in former days for the kindness and consideration you then showed them, are greatly
pleased at the intelligence of your safe arrival at Lahore
from Europe. As the seasons revolve and change, and do

not always continue the same, Major George Lawrence is
now residing in the Sikh camp. Everyone treats him
with attention and respect, and neither he nor his wife
suffer any hardship. I enclose a letter from him to you,
which I hope will reach you. I shall be happy to forward
to him anything which you may write in reply.'

In reply, the Resident forwarded to the Sirdar a copy
of the proclamation just issued by Lord Dalhousie to the
Sikh nation, which demanded as the only terms of peace
the immediate unconditional surrender of the army, the
soldiers on laying down their arms to be allowed to
return to their homes, and the Sirdars possessing estates
and jaghires to have them confiscated, but yet to be
allowed the means of subsistence. The only person to be
excepted was Sùltan Mahomed Khan, whose treachery in
giving up myself and my party to the Sikhs was considered by the Governor-General to debar that individual
from all terms of mercy.

'Your reasons,' observed my brother in his private
reply to the Sirdar, 'for detaining in imprisonment my
brother and other officers, as well as even ladies and children, are best known to yourself. You say that you are
rejoiced at my return, and that you and many other Sikhs
are grateful for the kindness which I have shown you.
You are quite right in saying that I have treated you
with kindness, for in truth you have never received from
myself, my brothers, or Sir Frederick Currie, anything
but the utmost kindness. Your messenger says you are
ready to follow my advice. My advice, then, is that
which has already been given you on the part of the British Government, *immediately* on receipt of this letter to
deliver over to Major Mackeson the British officers, ladies,
and children at present in confinement ; and secondly, to

come yourself into the British camp, trusting to the mercy of the Governor-General.'

My brother forwarded to me at the same time a copy of the proclamation, adding, ' You will observe that the proclamation promises that no man's life shall be touched for the part he has taken in the war (Sùltan Mahomed — Khan excepted), and that the soldiers, &c. will not be molested in their homes. These may appear small boons, but life, security, and food ought to be considered something by men who, if they meet our army once more in battle, will certainly be fugitives and wanderers, attacked on all sides, even by the Mahomedan population, and probably by many of the men now in their own ranks. Indeed, I understand that if the rain and other circumstances had not prevented our following up the victory of January 13th, the whole Sikh army would have been destroyed or dispersed. God knows that I earnestly wish to see the misguided soldiers return in peace to their homes and live there in comfort and security. They will probably ask you if they can hope to be employed again. Your answer must be that the terms of the proclamation offer no hopes for themselves of service either under the Maharajah or the British government, but this will not prevent their fathers, brothers, and sons from finding employment with us. Indeed it will be my earnest endeavour, as it will be my duty, to endeavour to find means of subsistence for all who are really anxious to live peaceably and in submission to the laws. You will of course make no promises for yourself or for me, but you may with perfect truth declare that I feel very great commiseration for the deluded soldiers and their families, and for the misery that has been brought on the country, and that I would not remain at Lahore if I had not hopes of doing something to amend matters. I trust that the Sikhs will be wise and release you at once. Tell them that if they do so willingly and honourably, it must be remembered in their favour; whereas if any injury is done to you, our vengeance will be great on them and theirs. You will say this as your own opinion, and as what they must feel is true; but I am not authorised to send any messages, so you can say nothing as coming as a message or promise from me. Yes, you may give one message if you like, it is to Milkah Singh, " that if a hair of Charley's[1] head is touched, he and his, with kith and kin, shall be rooted out of the land," and on the other hand that kindness to her and any of you now will be warmly remembered by me hereafter. So far I have full right to say as an individual, and apart from my official position. The Governor-General is well pleased with your conduct at Peshawur, and would do anything consistent with duty and propriety for your release; but he is averse to anything like treating with men with arms in their hands, and who have detained you and others, their best friends, given over to them by the basest treachery. Sùltan Mahomed Khan will get no terms whatever, because he betrayed you; he might have earned a rich reward by being your friend.'

Upon receiving the Resident's letter and the Governor-General's proclamation, I was sent for by Sirdars Chutter Singh and Shere Singh to join their camp near Gujerat, as they wished to send me to the British head-quarters to endeavour to procure for them some better terms than it contained. I arrived at the Sikh head-quarters on February 12th, and shortly after my arrival in their camp Shere Singh took me up to the roof of a house in Gujerat, and pointing out, with evident pride, his army

---

[1] Mrs. George Lawrence.

of 60,000 men and 60 guns, drawn up in the plain before us, exultingly asked me what I thought of them, and how I supposed the British army would meet the attack of such a superb force. I told him very plainly that 'if he had 200,000 instead of 60,000, they would avail him nothing in the day of battle against our troops.' Observing at the same moment a considerable body of cavalry manœuvring in the plain, I asked what they were. Upon which the Sirdar replied, 'Oh, these are the horsemen of Dost Mahomed who thrashed you so soundly in Cabul.' 'No Affghans, either horse or foot, ever thrashed us in Cabul,' I at once rejoined; 'we were beaten by cold and starvation. But as for these fellows I know them well, and depend upon it, fine looking body as they are, they will be your destruction; they will be the first to fly, and then your men, who otherwise would fight well, will follow their example.' For some days after my arrival the Sirdars were very undecided as to sending me on their behalf to the British camp, and they seemed resolved on trying once more another battle, the result of which could not be doubtful, as the British force from Mooltan had already joined the Commander-in-Chief. Bowie had by this time joined me in the Sikh camp, and we used to have a visit each night from Shere Singh, who conversed very freely, and expressed his great surprise that we did not make much more use of our splendid artillery than hitherto, instead of depending so entirely as we seemed to do on our infantry, which, he let us know, his soldiers had much less dread of than our guns.

Upon February 16 we marched with the Sikh army to Chakkore, some six miles from Gujerat, as the Sikhs said they anticipated an attack on their previous ground from our troops. It was a great pity that our army did not attack the Sikhs during this movement, as they would have gained a very easy victory. Chutter Singh at last determined that I should proceed to Lahore to confer with my brother and ascertain if any better terms would be given. I was for this purpose allowed eight days' leave of absence, but the Sirdar told me that if in the mean time there was a battle and their army beaten, I need not return, and that he would send Mrs. Lawrence and the rest to join me. I however assured him I *would* return under any circumstances, and begged that Bowie might be allowed to proceed to Sukkoo, to remain with my family, to which the Sirdar consented. During my absence at Lahore the battle of Gujerat was fought on February 20, and resulted in the complete defeat of Shere Singh's army, with immense loss and the capture of fifty-three of their sixty guns, their whole camp and stores falling into our hands. The survivors fled towards Peshawur, and General Gilbert, with 15,000 men and twenty guns, was sent in pursuit. I left Lahore on February 22, and I reached the Commander-in-Chief's camp on February 24, and thence I wrote to Sirdar Chutter Singh, reporting that I was about to return to his camp in terms of my parole.

On the morning of the 25th I proceeded on my journey to Gilbert's camp, which I reached on the afternoon of the 26th, pitched on the left bank of the Jhelum. The Sikhs were on the right bank, and both armies were firing into each other. As I went down alone to the bank of the river to join Shere Singh, I waved a white handkerchief as a signal for a boat to ferry me across. One immediately was sent, the firing ceasing on both sides until I landed. I then joined the Sirdar, and surrendered myself in terms of my parole, much to Shere Singh's surprise, and that of the Sikhs, who cheered me long and loudly, applauding me for returning to them, now that they had been defeated.

At this time the following notification, issued by the Resident at Lahore, by direction of the Governor-General, reached the Sirdars.

' If within eight days Major Lawrence, Lieutenants Bowie and Herbert, and Dr. Thompson, and the ladies and children now in captivity, are not made over in safety to one of the British camps, I will send Sirdars Gholab Singh, Bishen Singh, and the other Sikh prisoners now in confinement at Lahore, also their families and the families of such other rebels as may fall into my hands, into Hindustan. Such will be the first step taken ; the next will depend upon circumstances. You should understand that this proclamation is made by the orders of the Governor-General, and will be thoroughly carried out.'

The intelligence of the overwhelming defeat sustained by the Sikhs at Gujerat on the 20th February duly reached the fort of Sukkoo, and caused, as Mrs. Lawrence afterwards informed me, a great commotion among the garrison, some of them, ' old whitebearded men, going about weeping and sobbing like children.' The sentries were doubled in anticipation of a party of British troops coming to rescue the captives, and nearly all the servants in attendance on Mrs. Lawrence and the others were turned out of the fort. On the morning of the 2nd March orders were received for the immediate removal of the captives from Sukkoo to Attock, and notwithstanding Bowie's earnest expostulations, they had to march quite unprepared, leaving most of their baggage behind them, and were sent to Rawul Pindee, where the Sikh army was then encamped. I was not allowed to see them, although in the same camp. In the meantime I had been sent twice to Gilbert's headquarters to communicate with Mackeson as to the exact meaning of ' the unconditional surrender' required by the Governor-General's proclamation, the Sirdars entertaining serious doubts as to what that involved, and whether they would be guaranteed from imprisonment and banishment. Gilbert assured the chiefs they would be subjected to neither the one nor the other punishment, nor even required to leave the Punjaub if they gave sufficient security for their good behaviour, but on condition of themselves and their army surrendering, with their guns and arms, and giving up the prisoners. Each night the Sirdars used to come to my tent and discuss matters with me, asking my advice whether they should thus submit, or cross the Indus and proceed with their immediate retainers to Cabul. I told them that once in the power of the Affghans, I was certain, from my knowledge of the people, they would be considered and treated as prisoners, and probably forcibly converted to Mahomedanism. These arguments I could plainly perceive produced a deep effect on the minds of the Sirdars, who were perfectly aware I had not by any means exaggerated the risk they would incur by placing themselves in the power of the Affghans. Still they could not make up their minds to surrender, and vacillated from day to day. At length Shere Sing made up his mind to give up all the prisoners but myself, whom he desired to retain to assist him in any future negotiations with our Government. Upon the 6th March I had the intense gratification of seeing my wife and children, accompanied by the other captives, forwarded to General Gilbert's camp, whence my wife and family proceeded to Lahore, which they reached in safety on the 21st

March.   Shortly after her arrival she received the following kind and characteristic letter from Lord Dalhousie :

'Madam,—Since I cannot have the pleasure of seeing you here, I am sure you will permit me to take the liberty of addressing to you myself my hearty and cordial congratulations on your being once again in the midst of your family, and of those who have been long watching your fate with painful interest.

'The kindness of your friends has permitted me during that time to see many of your notes which you never meant for any mere official eye, and I trust you will not think I take too great a liberty in saying—for, even at the risk of your displeasure, *I must say it*—that the perusal of them during the long course of your captivity, showing to me the gallant heart you kept up under it, the cheery face you put upon it, and the uncomplaining and confiding patience with which you bore it all, has filled me with a respect for your character and admiration of your conduct, which if I were fully to express them you would perhaps suspect me of flattery.

'In the hope of one day paying my respects to you in quieter times than the past, and some pleasanter place than Peshawur,

'I am, &c.,

(Signed)   'DALHOUSIE.'

When the prisoners proceeded to Gilbert's camp they were directed to intimate to the General that the Sirdars themselves intended immediately to surrender, and accordingly some hours after their departure Shere Singh followed and surrendered himself with 450 soldiers.   The next day he was allowed to return to his camp at Rawul Pindee in order to arrange for the rest of the army laying down their arms. Again, however, the Sirdars began to vacillate, and Gilbert, hearing that they had changed their minds and were hesitating, immediately pushed on to Rawul Pindee, which he reached on the 14th March, receiving on the way the submission of several Sirdars, who with their retainers proceeded to his camp.

At last, on the 16th March, Sirdars Chutter Singh and Shere Singh, seeing that all hopes of escape or obtaining better terms were useless, determined to surrender also unconditionally. I accompanied these two leaders when for the last time they went down the ranks of their army. The soldiers were infuriated, and heartily abused them for having sold them to the Feringhees. It was perhaps fortunate for the Sirdars that they took the precaution of making me walk between them and their troops, as otherwise some of the soldiers might probably have used violence to them. When this was over, I accompanied the Sirdars to our camp, where they surrendered themselves formally, and gave up their swords to General Gilbert; and thus ended my second captivity of five and a half months.

I stood by Gilbert as the Sikh army, consisting of 16,000 men, passed him, each man, on throwing down his arms, receiving a rupee to enable him to support himself until he reached his home. From Gilbert's camp I proceeded to Lahore, where, after the annexation of the Punjaub, which was then erected into a Lieutenant-Governorship presided over by my brother Henry, I was employed in paying off and pensioning some of the old Sikh cavalry, and making other arrangements for the disposal of the disbanded soldiery. I then proceeded in April to Peshawur, of which province I was appointed Deputy-Commissioner under the government of the

Punjaub.   I found the province perfectly tranquil, and with apparently every prospect of remaining so.   My old friends the chiefs of the Eusufzye country came in to tender their allegiance, expressing their great joy at the annexation of the Punjaub to the British territory. There occurred nothing of sufficient interest for me to notice here in the administration of the affairs of the province from the time I joined my appointment in April until December, when I was obliged to depute a force into the Eusufzye district, which I myself accompanied, for the purpose of punishing some refractory landholders.   The operations were entirely successful, and the troops were back in the cantonments by the end of the same month.   My health began now so seriously to suffer from the climate of Peshawur, that I expressed to the Governor-General my earnest desire, on this account, to be transferred to some other post, and Lord Dalhousie kindly promised to meet my wishes on any appointment suitable for me becoming vacant and at his disposal.   One of the earliest measures taken by me on entering on my duties at Peshawur was to commence the construction of a road suitable for cavalry and guns from thence to the Kohat pass, in order to keep in check the hill tribes of that turbulent region, and prevent their making forays into the plains.   The road had been carried on without interruption until the beginning of February, 1850, and the greater portion had been completed, when the Afreedies, alarmed at the progress of a work which by rendering their hitherto diffi-cult country easily accessible, would put a stop to their predatory habits, made a sudden attack on the sappers employed on the line, killing twelve and wounding eight, and plundering their camp.   As soon as intelligence of

T

this untoward affair reached me, I requested General Colin Campbell,[1] commanding the Peshawur Division, to despatch immediately a body of troops to pursue the hill-men, and prevent the pass of Kohat falling into their hands.

The General lost no time in complying with my request, and proceeded himself in command of a considerable body of infantry, cavalry, and horse artillery. I accompanied the force, taking under my own immediate command the 1st Cavalry under Colonel Daly, and the 1st Infantry under Colonel Coke, of the newly-raised Punjaub force, and 1,500 Irregular Militia, the whole force being under the general control of the Commander-in-Chief, General Sir C. Napier, who had arrived at Peshawur on the 30th January. We succeeded in reaching Kohat on the 12th without meeting with much serious opposition, and the post having been reinforced by some of Coke's and Daly's men, the troops commenced their return to Peshawur. The Afreedies, by no means intimidated by the amount of punishment they had received, and which I had never regarded as sufficient, hung on the rear of our troops as they returned, and attacked our flanking parties, inflicting some losses upon us. No sooner had the army returned to Peshawur than the Afreedies again closed the pass, effectually stopping all communication with Kohat. Very soon after this, having again been attacked by illness, I proceeded to Simla for the restoration of my health, and as it was now clear that the Peshawur climate was unsuitable for my constitution I begged the Governor-General to remove me to some other suitable appointment, and his lordship, in July 1850, was

---

[1] Afterwards Lord Clyde.

pleased to nominate me political agent in Meywar, in Rajpootana.[1]

[1] In conferring this appointment upon Major Lawrence, Lord Dalhousie wrote to him the following gratifying letter:

'I have considered the claims of the several officers who have applied for the appointment of the Meywar political agency, and I regard your claims as superior to any others which have been proposed. I feel sure that the office is one which will be satisfactory to yourself, and that you will fill it to the satisfaction of the Government. I shall be heartily sorry to lose you from the Punjaub, where you have played your part so much to my satisfaction, as well in peace as in war. But as that was to be from the first, I am glad to have it in my power to offer you this public mark of my satisfaction with the past.

(Signed) 'DALHOUSIE.'

CHAPTER XX.

STATE OF MEYWAR IN RAJPOOTANA—FAMILY FEUD OF THE MAHARANAS—
WAR BETWEEN JEYPORE AND JOUDPORE—PRINCESS KISHNA KOONWUR—
SIR HENRY LAWRENCE APPOINTED GOVERNOR-GENERAL'S AGENT FOR RAJ-
POOTANA—TRANSFERRED TO OUDE—APPOINTED TO SUCCEED AS GOVERNOR-
GENERAL'S AGENT—COMMENCEMENT OF REBELLION—DEFENCELESS STATE
OF RAJPOOTANA—AJMEER FORT OCCUPIED BY MHAIRWARRAH BATTALION—
SEND FOR A FORCE FROM DEESA—MUTINY AT NUSSEERABAD—APPOINTED
BRIGADIER-GENERAL.

THE state of Meywar, the capital of which is Oodeypore, is
ruled over by a race of princes bearing the high title of
Maharanas, and esteemed as the most illustrious and
ancient of the Rajpoot royal families. The Emperor
Baber in 1526 had, with the view of strengthening his
government, introduced the practice of marrying members
of the imperial family to daughters of the chief Rajpoot
princes, the most of whom considered these alliances as
conferring very great dignity on their families, notwithstanding the difference of faith. Not so, however, the
Ranas of Meywar, who regarded such matrimonial alliances as contaminating their pure Hindù blood, and
therefore steadily refused through many generations to
form any matrimonial alliances with the royal house of
Delhi. They even ceased to intermarry with the Rajpoot
families who had given daughters in marriage to the
imperial family. This exclusion was keenly felt by the
Rajpoot princes, and their readmission to the honours of
matrimonial alliances with the Oodeypore family was

always stipulated in the coalitions formed by the Rajpoot chiefs against the emperors; and it was further agreed among them that the sons of the Oodeypore princesses should succeed the father in preference to elder sons by other mothers.

In 1806 the Rajah of Jeypore requested in marriage the Princess Kishna Koonwur, noted for her extraordinary beauty, daughter of Rana Bheem Singh of Meywar, who favourably received his suit. Man Singh, Rajah of Joudpore, at the same time advanced pretensions to the lady on the plea that she had been betrothed to his predecessor, and that the engagement was with the throne, and not the individual occupant. The dispute led to a bloody war between Jeypore and Joudpore, which was ruinous to both states. As there was no hope of reconciliation between them, the Rana of Oodeypore was persuaded to sacrifice his beautiful daughter for the peace of Rajpootana, and poison was administered to the ill-fated princess. From this time until 1817 Meywar continued to be ravaged by the Mahrattas and the Pindarrees under the noted leader Ameer Khan. On the suppression in 1817 of the predatory system which prevailed in Central India, it was resolved, chiefly with the view to prevent its revival, to extend British influence and protection over the states of Rajpootana. The chiefs were accordingly invited to ally themselves with the British Government, on the basis of acknowledging its supremacy and paying a certain tribute in return for external protection and internal independence. The Rana of Meywar eagerly embraced the invitation, and a treaty was concluded with him in January 1818, under the terms of which a political agent on the part of the supreme government was stationed at his court. To this office I had now succeeded.

Shortly after assuming charge of the Meywar agency, my brother Henry, having left Lahore, was appointed Governor-General's agent for the whole of Rajpootana, comprising eighteen principalities. The whole country at this time was in a state of profound and, to all appearance, permanent tranquillity, the only events occurring to vary the usual routine of official life being some differences between the nobles of Meywar and the Maharana. These were satisfactorily settled as soon as it became apparent that the supreme government would suffer no disturbance of the general peace of the country, and was determined, if necessary, to send a force to coerce the recusant nobles if they persisted in their opposition to the just demands of their liege lord.

In March 1857 my brother was removed from Rajpootana to occupy the more important position, at that time, of Chief Commissioner in Oude; and on his proceeding to Lucknow, the Governor-General, Lord Canning, was pleased, at Henry's suggestion, to nominate me as his successor, as agent for the whole of Rajpootana. It had been heretofore usual for the Governor-General's agent to proceed to the Hill Station of Aboo for the hot season. In April I had proceeded there with my family, anticipating no evil or any disruption of the general tranquillity. On May 19 we were suddenly aroused from our state of fancied security by the appalling intelligence of the mutiny of the troops at Meerut and Delhi, and the massacre of numbers of the English community at both places. Feeling convinced from that moment that the mutiny was general, and that no portion of the native Bengal army could be relied upon, it was not without dismay that I contemplated our position in Rajpootana. The Province was garrisoned by about 5,000 native troops of all arms, belonging to the Bengal Presidency exclusively, and without a single European soldier, except the few invalids at Aboo, nearer than Deesa, in the Bombay Presidency, distant 150 miles. Rajpootana, therefore, comprising an area of 100,000 square miles and a population of ten millions, was but ill prepared to meet the coming storm, for the native troops, instead of adding to our security, only enhanced our danger, unawed as they were by the presence of any European force to keep them to their allegiance.

Under the circumstances I felt that the maintenance of British supremacy in Rajpootana, and the general tranquillity of the country, mainly depended on the loyalty and fidelity to their treaty engagements of the native princes, and their maintaining their control over their own subjects and troops. With the view, therefore, of securing their co-operation, I issued on May 23 a proclamation to all the chiefs, requiring them to concentrate their troops on the frontiers of their respective states, so as to be available if called upon to aid the paramount power, desiring them, at the same time, to be alert in destroying or capturing any body of rebels and mutineers passing through their territories. I also offered rewards for the apprehension of any persons known to be concerned in the atrocities at Delhi and Meerut.

One of the chief objects of immediate and pressing concern was to provide, as far as practicable, for the safety of Ajmeer, with its large magazine and treasury. The importance of this place could scarcely be over-estimated, for what Delhi was to North-western India, Ajmeer was to Rajpootana, and an insurrection breaking out there would soon turn it into a focus for all the disaffected of the country. Ajmeer is not only a place of pilgrimage for Mahomedans, who resort there from all parts of India, but a very holy locality in Hindù estimation, being distant only six miles from their sacred city and tank of Pokur. In Ajmeer also is concentrated the most of the wealth of Rajpootana, the richest merchants and bankers having for years resided in the town. The fort, which was in a very dilapidated condition, was at this time garrisoned by a company of the 15th Bengal Native Infantry, a regiment which I knew was not to be depended on, and a company of the Mhairwarrah Battalion, which being composed of a different race and class of men from the regular sepoys, and not therefore likely to sympathise with them, might, I hoped, be expected to remain true to their duty. It was of course a matter of the most immediate necessity to remove this company of the 15th regiment, and replace it by an additional company of Mhairs, and this delicate and perilous operation was entrusted to Captain W. Carnell, second in command of the battalion. This officer, making a forced night march from Beawur, his head-quarters, reached Ajmeer, a distance of thirty-seven miles, in the early morning, and relieved the company of the 15th before they had time to concert any measures of resistance or to communicate with the rest of their regiment at Nusseerabad. To the success of this well-timed operation I attribute mainly the safety of Ajmeer during the rebellion. The measure was not adopted one moment too soon, for this very company of the 15th took a leading part in the mutiny which occurred at Nusseerabad a few days later, and was the first to take possession of the artillery at that station. It had been my intention to garrison Ajmeer by the Kotah contingent, regarding it as a loyal and trustworthy corps, but my measures were happily, as it turned out, frustrated by the Lieutenant-Governor of the North-west Provinces, Mr. John Colvin, who required the corps to advance towards Agra, where it subsequently mutinied and did much mischief. Finding the Kotah contingent not at my disposal, I made an urgent requisition on the officer commanding at Deesa, the nearest cantonment of British troops, to detach a light field force as soon as practicable to Nusseerabad, in order to overawe the native troops there, and if possible to keep them to their allegiance; and this officer promptly despatched as many troops as he could spare. At the sáme time I urged the government of Bombay to direct all the available European troops, then returning from Persia, to be landed at Pooree Bunder, and to proceed with all possible expedition to Agra *viâ* Gujerat and Rajpootana.

The garrison of Nusseerabad, consisting of the 15th and 30th Regiments Bengal Native Infantry, and a Native Horse Field Battery, had been some weeks on the verge of mutiny. As soon as they heard of the approach of the force from Deesa, they determined to anticipate their arrival, and about 4 P.M. on May 28 broke into open mutiny and seized the guns. The 1st Bombay Lancers, which formed part of the garrison, and up to that time had behaved with exemplary loyalty, was ordered to charge and retake the guns, as it was expected they would not refuse to act, having shown no sympathy with the mutineers. The regiment obeyed their orders and charged, but turned threes about when within a few yards of the guns, shamefully abandoning their brave and devoted officers to continue the charge alone, which they did nobly but ineffectually, losing two of their number killed and having two wounded.[1] The Brigadier having thus no troops whatever

---

[1] It was said the Lancers had an understanding with the Bengal mutineers not to charge home on condition that the latter would not harm their families who were in the cantonment.—*G. S. P. L.*

to support him on whom he could rely, very properly retired from the station with all the European officers, ladies, and children, and proceeded to that of Beawur, thirty-two miles distant, situated on the road leading to Deesa.   The mutineers burnt and plundered the cantonment and all public and private buildings at Nusseerabad, and next day marched for Delhi.   A force of Meywar and Marwar troops, under my assistants, Captains Hardcastle and Walter, started in pursuit of the mutineers, but these officers were unable to induce their men to attack the sepoys, thus proving, what I always anticipated, that the troops of native states could never be got to encounter our regular regiments, more especially when these were backed, as in this case, by artillery.·

The intelligence of the mutiny at Nusseerabad reached Aboo on the 1st June.   On the same day I started, with two assistants, Hardcastle and Impey, by carriage post, for Beawur as a more central position, and arrived there on the 5th, finding the country as I passed through less disturbed than I expected.   I found on my arrival a warrant from the Lieutenant-Governor of Agra, nominating me Brigadier-General to command all the troops in Rajpootana, and thus the chief military as well as political authority was vested solely in myself.

The garrison of Neemuch, consisting of one Native troop of Bengal Horse Artillery, one wing of the 1st Bengal Cavalry, the 72nd Bengal Native Infantry, and the 7th regiment of the Gwalior contingent, had been for some weeks in a very disaffected state, causing the greatest anxiety and alarm.

Upon the night of the 3rd June these troops, notwithstanding the most devoted efforts on the part of their officers to restrain them, broke into open mutiny, burning the cantonment, breaking open the jail, and plundering the public treasury of a large sum of money. Most fortunately the officers, ladies, and children were allowed to escape, and the only lives lost on the occasion were those of the wife and children of a sergeant of artillery, murdered by the sepoys in their own house. The mutineer brigade next day marched for Delhi *viâ* Agra in the most orderly manner, taking all their plunder with them. The intelligence of the mutiny reached me immediately on my arrival in Beawur. It was quite expected by me, and I could only be thankful that so few European lives had been sacrificed. The superintendent of Neemuch, Captain Lloyd, and his assistant, returned to the station the day after the brigade marched, and re-established the civil government, which had then only been in abeyance a few hours, and by this prompt and resolute conduct they prevented the spread of disorder any further at that time.

Colonel Dixon, the Commissioner of Ajmeer, died at Beawur a few days after my arrival, and by desire of the Lieutenant-Governor of Agra I assumed charge of the office and carried on the daily duties in open court just as in times of profound peace, and thus I maintained confidence in the district and the authority of the government.

On June 12 I had the gratification of hearing of the arrival on that date at Nusseerabad, of the light field force from Deesa, consisting of 400 of the 83rd Queen's regiment, the 12th Bombay Native Infantry, and one troop of Horse Artillery. I immediately ordered 100 men of the 83rd, as many as could be spared, to reinforce the native garrison at Ajmeer, which was by this means placed in a position of comparative safety, its defences having been repaired, and the fort provisioned for six months. To place the arsenal, however, in a complete state of security, it would have been necessary to garrison the small fort on the Taraghur hill, which commands the magazine and the city. Not having sufficient men for this purpose, I entrusted the defence of the post to the Mahomedans, who having a shrine on its summit were interested in its safety. Their chief priests happily volunteered their services to guard it, which duty they regularly performed for many weeks, until all danger was over.

Early in June I received a letter from the Lieutenant-Governor, Mr. Colvin, requesting me to march with all the European troops, officers, and treasure I could collect, on Agra, for the defence of that place. I deemed it, however, my duty to decline compliance unless positively ordered, as such a move would undoubtedly entail the loss of Ajmeer, with its important arsenal and stores, and also lead to a general rise in Rajpootana. The Lieutenant-Governor, acquiescing in my representations, did not press the matter any further. During June and July I resided alternately between Ajmeer, Beawur, and Nusseerabad, as I deemed my presence necessary at each place with reference to my military as well as civil and political duties. My head-quarters were, however, at Ajmeer, where I resided in the Dowlut Bagh, close to the city, with a native officer's party of the Mhairwarrah battalion as my only guard. When at Ajmeer I never once allowed the routine of civil duties to be interrupted, but held open court, almost daily visiting the city, where, although fierce and sullen faces were often to be seen, I was always treated with the greatest respect. Occasional panics occurred, and the bankers sent away their families more than once during these months, but as often recalled them, as the stringent measures I enforced allayed their fears and restored their confidence. Notwithstanding all my precautions, an outbreak occurred on the 9th of August in the jail, and fifty prisoners escaped, who were promptly pursued and cut down by a party of mounted police. On my riding out on the track of the runaways, several of the leading Mahomedans of the city joined me and rendered assistance, thus showing their good feeling.

At Nusseerabad on the 10th August symptoms of disaffection appeared among the Hindustanee portion of the 12th Bombay Native Infantry, one of the corps sent to my aid from Deesa. A trooper of the 1st Bombay Light Cavalry, under the influence of opium, saddled and mounted his charger, and riding up and down the lines, endeavoured by cries and threats to excite his comrades to join him in mutinying; none joining him, he discharged his carbine at a native officer of his regiment, while trying to arrest him, and then fled to the lines of the 12th Bombay Native Infantry, where he was received and sheltered. The Brigadier ordered an assembly of all arms at the guns, but only forty of the 12th Bombay Native Infantry obeyed it and followed their officers, the rest of the regiment refusing, saying they were only being led to the guns to be slaughtered. The Brigadier then proceeded with a company of the 83rd to the lines of the 12th, and drove them out of their position. The trooper, who was still there, fired at the Brigadier, but fortunately missed him, and the man was then cut down and killed by some artillerymen. The Brigadier then paraded the 12th, and disarmed all who had failed to obey their commanding officer, when it was found their muskets had been loaded. The ringleaders were tried by court-martial, five of their number hanged, and two native officers and one sepoy sentenced to imprisonment for life. Twenty-five Hindustanees deserted;

the remainder, twenty-two in number, who were concerned in the mutiny, were summarily dismissed the service. Their arms were then restored to the remainder of the regiment, whose subsequent conduct in the field and in quarters was unexceptionable.

After the troops at Neemuch had mutinied I was obliged to garrison that station by some of the Meywar, Kotah, and Boondee troops. I soon found that these men were not to be relied on, as among them were many disaffected Hindustanees, ready for any mischief. As soon as possible, therefore, I ordered a force, consisting of one squadron of the 2nd Bombay Light Cavalry, 100 men of her Majesty's 83rd Regiment, and 200 of the 12th Bombay Native Infantry, to proceed to Neemuch and relieve these native troops, in order that they might return to their respective states. Soon after the arrival of this force, upon the 12th of August a few disaffected men of the 2nd Light Cavalry and the 12th Native Infantry endeavoured to get up a disturbance which might have been very serious had not timely notice of their intention been conveyed to Colonel Jackson, the commanding officer, by some men of the cavalry. He promptly proceeded to seize the ring-leaders with the men of the 83rd. A few of the mutineers were arrested, while eight escaped, and in the operation one man of the 83rd was killed and an officer and two privates wounded.

About this time I received from Agra the sad and distressing intelligence of the death on the 4th July, of a wound received two days previously, of my brother Henry, at Lucknow, and of my eldest son George,[1] one of the Assistant Commissioners, having been severely wounded. The following extract from the letter of my son George,

---

[1] Now Judge of Allyghur, N. W. Provinces, India.

received subsequently, gave me full and deeply interesting particulars of the death of his beloved uncle.

' . . . You would like to hear the true account of uncle's death, so I will try and tell you. On July 2nd about eight o'clock, just before breakfast (which had been laid in the next room at my suggestion), when uncle and I were lying in our beds, side by side, having just come in from our usual morning walk and inspection, and while Wilson, the Deputy Adjutant-General, was standing between our beds reading some orders to uncle, an eight-inch shell, thrown from a howitzer, came in at the wall exactly in front of my bed, and at the same instant burst. There was for an instant darkness, then a kind of red glare, and for a second or two no one spoke. Finding myself uninjured, though covered with bricks from top to toe, I jumped up. At the same time uncle cried out that he was killed. Assistance came, and we found that Sir Henry's left leg had been almost taken off, high up by the thigh—a desperate wound. We carried him from the Residency to Dr. Fayrer's house amid a shower of bullets, and put him in one of the verandahs there; he seemed to feel that he had received his death wound, and calling for the head people he gave over the Chief Commissionership into the hands of Major Banks, and the charge of the garrison to Colonel Inglis, at the same time giving them his last instructions what to do, among which was "never to give in." He sent for others, such as G. Hardinge,[1] of whom he was very fond, told them what he expected from them, and spoke of the future; he also sent for all those whom he thought he had ever, though unintentionally, injured or

---

[1] Son of the late Major-General Hardinge, K.H., and nephew of the late Field-Marshal Viscount Hardinge. Died subsequently of wounds and exposure.

even spoken harshly to, and asked their forgiveness. His bed was surrounded by old and new friends, and there were few dry eyes there. His old servants he spoke to. He mentioned the contents of his will, and who he wished to look after his children, and he spoke also of yourself and mother with great affection. He was pleased to say that I had been like a son to him, and that though he used to think me selfish, he had not found me so, and lastly gave me his blessing. We all received the Communion with him, and at one time the doctor thought of taking off his leg, but it would have been of no use. To drown the pain they gave him chloroform constantly, and then he cried out rather incoherently about home and his mother. He seemed to me at times to be in great pain, but he said he was not. He spoke, of course, of dear Aunt Letty, and a good deal, at intervals, of his wife, repeating texts she had been fond of. He took part in the prayers read by Mr. Harris the clergyman, when he thought he was going, but more than once he rallied, though getting weaker and weaker. After the evening of the 2nd he scarcely spoke at all, and the next day was, I think, nearly unconscious. Dr. Ogilvie was very kind in watching with me, and giving him drink when thirsty, and two ladies also waited upon him—poor Mrs. Dash-wood, who has since lost her husband and brother, and Mrs. Harris, the clergyman's wife, and I must not forget Mrs. Clarke. About eight o'clock on the 4th he died, quite quietly ; I scarcely knew when the breath left him, for I was sitting at his feet, having just been wounded. Dr. Ogilvie first told me all was over. A better man never stepped, but we must not grieve for him, but try and follow his example. · He was buried in the church-yard where all the rest were, but no one save the Padre could attend, as the place was under fire and everyone had to be at his post.'

It is not for me to pass any encomiums on my beloved brother, but I may be allowed to say that the government never possessed a more single minded, zealous, or fearless servant, and sure am I that his countrymen will not fail to appreciate his character, and for many a year continue to honour his name and revere his memory.

Scarcely had I·recovered from the severe shock this intelligence caused me, when events occurred which threw me into a state of the deepest anxiety for the safety of my own family.   I had left at Aboo my wife, two daughters, and my son Alexander, recently arrived from England to join the Bengal Civil Service. Captain Hall, commandant of the Joudpore Legion, and his family, as well as those of several officers absent in the field, were residing there also. A guard of sixty or seventy men of the Legion was on duty at the station, and there were also thirty convalescent soldiers of the 83rd Regiment, who had been sent from Deesa to Aboo for the hot season.   The distance from Ajmeer to Aboo was 150 miles. I was in almost daily communication with my family, and entertained no anxiety whatever on their account, as the loyalty of the Joudpore Legion had never been doubted. From the 21st to the 26th no posts arrived from Aboo, but this gave me no concern, as I considered they must have been delayed by recent very heavy and continuous rains. Early, however, on the morning of the 26th I was greatly alarmed by receiving an express from the political agent at Joudpore, enclosing a hurried note from the adjutant of the Legion, Lieutenant Conolly, from their head-quarters at Erinpoorah, dated 4 A.M. of the 22nd, stating that an intercepted letter addressed by some men of the Legion to their comrades had just been brought to him, in which they called on their comrades to mutiny and join them at once with the guns, as 'they had been to Aboo, fought with the Europeans, and had taken all precautions.' The adjutant, in forwarding the note, expressed his belief that the company stationed at Anadea, near Aboo, must have mutinied and attacked the place in conjunction with the detachment on duty there, and as he fully expected the rest of the Legion to follow the example of their comrades, he begged that some aid might be sent to him immediately to protect the station of Erinpoorah. On receiving this very alarming intelligence I issued orders to disarm immediately the company of the Legion stationed at Nusseerabad, and this was effected, without any resistance, by the men of the 83rd Regiment. I also sent off a squadron of the 1st Bombay Lancers to Erinpoorah to rescue Lieutenant Conolly.

No further intelligence of what had occurred at Aboo was received until the afternoon of the 27th, when a messenger brought me a letter from the postmaster of Erinpoorah, a Parsee, stating that all the men of the Legion there had mutinied, making prisoners of the adjutant, Lieutenant Conolly, and two European sergeants with their families, and that he had reason to believe that Captain Hall and the English families at Aboo had been all murdered by the mutineers there. Scarcely had I read this disastrous intelligence when my anxiety and alarm were in a measure removed by the arrival of another messenger bringing me a Persian letter from the superintendent of Serohi, stating that the mutineers who had attacked Aboo had been defeated and driven down the hill, that no European lives had been lost, but that my son Alexander[1] had been severely wounded.   A few hours later this intelligence was confirmed by the receipt of a letter from the political agent at Joudpore, Captain Monck Mason, dated August 26, forwarding me one from Captain Hall himself, giving details of the attack on the station. Upon the afternoon of the 26th Hall had visited the detachment at Anadea, seeing then no signs of mutiny or insubordination among the men, and after the inspection had ridden back to Aboo, distant two miles. At that time these villains had arranged to join the detachment at Aboo next morning, murder the Europeans, plunder and destroy the station.   Accordingly, under cover of a heavy mist, they ascended the hill early in the morning of August 21, and joining their comrades attacked simultaneously the barracks where the thirty convalescent men of the 83rd were asleep, and the house of their own commandant, Captain Hall.   Fortunately, none of their shots fired into the barracks took effect, and the soldiers, awakened out of their sleep, seized their arms, and rushing out on their assailants, drove them off. Captain Hall and his family were also unhurt by the fire, and managed to escape to the schoolhouse, which had been fortified for a rendezvous in case of an attack, and where a guard of one corporal and three privates of the 83rd was stationed. The rest of the families, alarmed by the firing, had already congregated there.   My son Alexander on the first shots being fired ran to Captain Hall's to ascertain what was going on, and was almost immediately shot down with a severe wound in the thigh, from which he would have bled to death, but for the skill and prompt attention of Dr. Ebden, the Residency surgeon.   The thirty convalescent soldiers had by this time reached the schoolhouse, and

---

[1] Now Magistrate and Collector of Etawah, N. W. Provinces, India.

headed by Captain Hall, attacked the mutineers, who fled down the hill, and did not, fortunately, renew their attack. Thus by the great mercy of God were the murderous designs of these bloodthirsty villains baffled, and my own and the other families saved from a sudden and terrible death.

The mutineers then joined their comrades at Erinpoorah, and all united in plundering and burning the station. They then marched towards Ajmeer, intending to attack it, taking their adjutant, Lieutenant Conolly, with them, but releasing the sergeants and their wives without doing them any injury. After proceeding three marches they released Lieutenant Conolly, who came into Ajmeer attended by five sowars who remained faithful. The Maharajah of Joudpore sent a force to meet the mutineers at Palee, and the latter in consequence diverged from the Ajmeer road, and entered the service of the Thakoor of Awah, the second noble in Marwar, who being disaffected to his own government took this opportunity, with their help, of openly rebelling.

The Joudpore troops were on September 8 attacked by the Legion and the Awah men, and put to flight, without any resistance on their parts, and with the loss of their commander killed, and their guns, camp, and ammunition taken.

Considering that it could not fail to have a very injurious effect on the country generally if the rebels were allowed to remain unmolested in such a position as Awah, situated on the high road between Deesa and Nusseerabad, thus cutting off the communication between those places, I assembled as soon as possible a force at Beawur for the purpose of co-operating with the Joudpore troops in dislodging the rebels. I felt pretty confident that if we could only allure the mutineers into the open country and away from the stronghold of Awah, we were sure of beating and dispersing them; although it was vain to expect, with the means at my disposal, to attack with any prospect of success Awah itself, which from the nature of its defences would require heavy guns and a large force to besiege and reduce it.

Upon September 18 the force under my command reached Awah. The town, surrounded with a high wall, was only to be approached through a thick jungle, and was quite invisible until within about 600 yards of the walls. As soon as our force emerged from the jungle a heavy fire was opened on us from the guns in the fort and a battery posted on the high bank of a tank outside.

Our guns replied quickly and effectively, obliging the enemy to withdraw their battery within the walls, although a howitzer and one gun of ours had been temporarily disabled. As my object, which was only a reconnaissance, had been gained, and the enemy showed no intention to attack us in open ground, I withdrew the troops as night came on to the village of Chulawass, about three and a half miles from Awah. The political agent of Joudpore, Captain Monck Mason, had started from that place on a camel to join me before Awah, and arrived as the action was going on. He was seen to dismount from his camel about 300 yards from where I was standing, and to proceed to join me on foot. Unfortunately he mistook the bugles of the mutineer Joudpore Legion for our own, the calls being the same, and went up to a party of the enemy, by whom he was immediately killed: thus miserably perished a most valuable and able public officer. I encamped for three days at Chulawass, hoping to induce the enemy to move out and attack us, but hearing from spies that they had no intention of doing so, and were busy strengthening their own defences, I returned by slow marches to Ajmeer and Nusseerabad. The advance on Awah, although not so successful as I had hoped, was not without its favourable results, as for the three following months, with the exception of an outbreak at Kotah, all Rajpootana remained quiet and tranquil.

CHAPTER XXI.

MAJOR BURTON AND HIS TWO SONS PROCEED TO KOTAH—INTERVIEW WITH THE MAHARAJAH—TROOPS ATTACK RESIDENCY—MAJOR BURTON AND HIS SONS MURDERED—REBELS ATTACK NEEMUCH—AWAH TAKEN AND DEFENCES DESTROYED—SIEGE AND CAPTURE OF KOTAH—TANTEA TOPEE LAYS SIEGE TO TONK—PLUNDERS JALRA PATTUN—IS AT LAST CAPTURED AND EXECUTED — POLICY PURSUED IN RAJPOOTANA — ITS SUCCESSFUL RESULTS—RETIRE FROM THE SERVICE.

MAJOR BURTON, the political agent at Kotah, had accompanied the troops of that state when they were sent by me to garrison Neemuch. On their return to Kotah Major Burton remained behind at Neemuch, as the Maharajah requested him to postpone his return for twenty days or so, as 'in these unsettled times he could not have entire confidence in his troops.'

On October 5 Major Burton, accompanied by two of his sons, one aged 21, the other 16, started for Kotah, leaving his wife, daughter, and three other sons at Neemuch, and on the 12th he reached the Residency. The following day the Maharajah visited the Agent in state, and on the next day Major Burton, accompanied by his sons, returned the visit. On this occasion, after the public reception, the Agent had a private interview with the Maharajah at which no one was present but a vakeel who was subsequently blown away from a gun by the rebels. The Maharajah states that Major Burton urged him to punish and dismiss several of his officers who were known to be disaffected, and it is probable the vakeel after the meeting made the advice known to the troops and their officers, who all at once determined to avenge themselves on Major Burton. Accordingly, the following day, October 15, bodies of the troops, accompanied by a rabble from the town, suddenly surrounded the Residency, killing the doctor, Mr. Salder, and a native Christian doctor, who resided in houses in the Residency grounds. The guards and servants fled from the premises and hid themselves in the ravines close by. Major Burton and his two sons were left alone with a single servant, a camel-driver, and all took refuge in a room on the roof of the house. The mob then fired round shot into the Residency, and for four hours these four brave men defended themselves, till at length the Residency was set on fire, and Major Burton, feeling the case to be desperate, proposed to surrender on condition of the mob sparing his sons' lives. The young men at once rejected the offer, saying they would all die together. They knelt down and prayed for the last time, and then calmly and heroically met their fate. The mob had by this time procured scaling-ladders, and thus gaining the roof rushed in and despatched their victims, the servant alone escaping. Major Burton's head was cut off and paraded through the town, and then fired from a gun, but the three bodies were by the Maharajah's orders interred the same evening. The Maharajah at once communicated to me what had occurred, deeply lamenting the fate of the Agent and his sons, and deploring his own inability, from the mutinous condition of his troops, to do anything to save them. The rebels took possession of the city, and kept the Maharajah a prisoner in his palace. They then forced his Highness to sign a paper consisting of nine articles, one of which was to the effect that the Agent and his sons had been killed by his own orders. The Maharajah was compelled to temporize with the rebels until assistance was sent to him from the neighbouring state of Kerowlie, with the chief of which he was connected. These troops proved themselves bold and trustworthy soldiers, and drove the rebels from the part of the town where the palace was situated, and of which they were able to retain possession.

In October a party of rebels from Mundesore, under the leadership of a pretended member of the Delhi royal family, seized the town of Jeerun, within ten miles of Neemuch. To have allowed such an insult to pass unnoticed would have been productive of the worst consequences to the peace and loyalty of Rajpootana, so, despite the weakness of the force at my disposal, it was determined to attack the insurgents. Upon October 23 our troops moved from Neemuch and attacked the enemy's position at Jeerun, which was found to be very strong and was well defended. In the attack two officers were killed and five wounded, and our troops, disheartened by the fall of their leaders, gave way and retreated. The rebels, not waiting for a renewed attack, evacuated the place, and the authority of our government was at once restored. The rebels, however, were not disheartened, and a body of 4,000 of them advanced on Neemuch on November 8, taking possession of the station, and causing the Europeans, with two companies of Bombay Native Infantry, to retire into the fortified square, where, under Captains B. Lloyd and Macdonald, they successfully defended themselves for fifteen days during which the siege lasted. At length the rebels despairing of taking the place, and hearing of the advance of a force from Mhow, raised the siege and retreated, after a vain attempt at escalade.

In January 1858 reinforcements from Bombay reached Rajpootana, and it was in the first place necessary to make an example of the Thakoor of Awah, who had taken into his service the mutineers of the Joudpore Legion, and had opposed British troops in the field, causing the death of Captain Monck Mason, the political agent at Joudpore. The Thakoor besides was known to have made overtures to the Emperor of Delhi. Accordingly, on January 19 a force under Colonel Holmes, of the 12th Bombay Native Infantry, invested the place. After five days' siege operations a breach was pronounced practicable, and the assault ordered for the ensuing morning. During the night a fearful storm raged, and the noise and darkness were so great that sentries only a few paces apart could neither hear nor see one another. Under cover of this storm the garrison evacuated Awah with such secresy that almost all escaped. The fort was found to be of great strength, consisting of a double line of defences, the inner of strong masonry and the outer of earthwork, both being loopholed. Thirteen guns, three tons of powder, and 3,000 rounds of small arms ammunition were found in the place. The keep, the bastions, and all the masonry works were blown up and destroyed, so as effectually to prevent the stronghold becoming a nucleus of rebellion in future.

It was not until March 1858 that a sufficient force, with guns, could be collected to punish the Kotah rebels, who still held the greater portion of the city, and appropriated the revenues of the district. A force of 5,500 fighting men of all arms under command of General Roberts, who, as my senior, had since his arrival assumed the command of the forces in Rajpootana, accompanied by his staff, proceeded on March 23rd to Kotah, which was invested on the 25th. A portion of the force was sent into that part of the town held for the Rajah by the Kerowlie troops. Some heavy guns and mortars were placed on the parapets and in the streets of the same part of the city, and on the 29th a heavy fire of shot and shell opened on the quarter in occupation of the rebels. On the 30th three assaulting columns proceeded from the fort simultaneously and cleared the different quarters of the town, meeting with little opposition, the greater part of the garrison having evacuated the place, and the whole city was in our hands by the afternoon. The cavalry brigade attached to the force failed from various causes to intercept the rebels, who almost all escaped.

Kotah had been famed for many years as a secure emporium for treasure and all sorts of merchandise, but the mutineers and rebels had during the months of their occupation so completely pillaged it that the place presented a most desolate appearance, much damage having been also done to the houses by our shot and shell. The British force evacuated Kotah on April 20, the Maharajah finding himself by that time well able to protect his city and preserve the peace of his own dominions.

During the next two months Rajpootana remained in comparative tranquillity, nothing occurring beyond petty local disturbances caused by small bands of plunderers who were easily put down. This pleasant state of things was not, however, long to continue, for suddenly news reached me from the Governor-General's agent at Indore, reporting the flight of the celebrated rebel leader Tantea Topee from Gwalior into Rajpootana, with an army of some 12,000 men. The next intelligence I heard was that they had made for Tonk, to which they laid siege, but retreated precipitately on hearing of the advance of an English force to the relief of that place.

Several British columns were directed to co-operate from different quarters in pursuing Tantea and his army, who apparently had no distinct line of action beyond that of immediate escape from their pursuers, taking from time to time any route which appeared most expedient for that purpose. After doubling backwards and forwards the rebel army was overtaken and defeated on August 13, 1858, by General Roberts's column, at Bunnass, from whence they fled to Jalra Pattun, the capital of the Maharajah of Jhullawar, whose troops fraternised with them, the chief himself with difficulty making his escape in disguise to the nearest British camp. At this place Tantea obtained a large amount of jewels and treasure, stores and material of all kinds, and also a train of artillery of twenty-seven guns, with elephants and horses sufficient to replace his exhausted cattle, and thus was enabled again to take the field, notwithstanding his severe losses at Bunnass. After a halt of eight days at Jalra Pattun the rebels abandoned Rajpootana, and fled beyond my jurisdiction into Central India, closely followed by the pursuing columns. During the months of September, October, and November, Tantea and his army traversed nearly the whole of that part of the country. By the fertility of his resources and the marvellous rapidity of his marching, he succeeded in eluding his pursuers, and suddenly reappeared at the close of November in the Bagur, a district of Meywar. I had proceeded to Joudpore in that month, and there heard of Tantea having again returned to Rajpootana. This Bagur comprises portions of the states of Purtabghur, Banswarrah, and Dongurpore, is covered with dense jungle, and, abounding with impenetrable natural fastnesses, presented most serious obstacles to the operations of regular troops. I lost no time in directing the chiefs to whom this tract belonged to adopt immediate measures for closing the passes leading from the Bagur into their respective territories. This was immediately done, and as our columns were converging upon this tract, there seemed a fair chance of surrounding and overwhelming the rebels. Tantea's resources were, however, not yet exhausted; for hearing that the British force had been temporarily withdrawn from Purtabghur, probably by a ruse of his own, he availed himself of the only opening left, and dashing through, passed the flank of the British column sent to intercept him and made good his retreat to the eastward.

In January 1859 Tantea and his army, estimated at 8,000 men, chiefly cavalry, crossed the Chumbul, and for the third time entering Rajpootana, threatened Tonk and Jyepore. A force under General Showers, sent from Agra, overtook the rebels, notwithstanding their rapid marching, on January 14th, at Dowsa, just as they were preparing to move, and taking them completely by surprise, inflicted on them very severe loss. A few days later a column of British infantry under Colonel Holmes, to which Captain Beynon, Assistant Agent Governor-General, was attached, after a most extraordinary march of more than fifty miles in twenty-eight hours, came upon the rebel camp at Seekur before daylight and entirely dispersed them. From this place they broke up into separate bodies, of which one of 345 and the other of 215, under their respective leaders, shortly afterwards surrendered under the amnesty. The remainder fled into Central India, never, however, again to concentrate or disturb the peace of Rajpootana, for their celebrated leader Taotea was soon after betrayed, and falling into our hands was executed for rebellion.

During the momentous period between May 1857 and

February 1859, when our power in India was shaken to its foundation, not one of the nineteen states or princes of Rajpootana wavered in loyalty or withheld a cheerful and hearty support to the paramount power. Neither they nor their people sympathised with the revolt, and while our own provinces were ravaged with fire and sword, the vast tract of Rajpootana, extending over 100,000 square miles, with 10,000,000 of inhabitants, notwithstanding the occurrence of mutinies of our troops within its limits, continued comparatively tranquil. Life and property remained secure, trade and agriculture were carried on as usual, and scarcely any call for armed interference occurred for the support of order and legitimate authority.

The just and generous policy so long pursued by our government towards these ancient and influential principalities now bore its legitimate fruit. The princes felt that their interests were identical with ours, and that their own positions of power and dignity were best secured by the maintenance throughout Hindustan of British supremacy.

My own policy, following that of my brother Henry, during this anxious and critical period, was one of non-interference, letting well alone, and allowing the princes to work out their own plans for the preservation of peace and security within their respective territories. I made every effort compatible with the dignity of my own government, which was always the chief consideration, to maintain peace at any price, carefully to avoid all causes of discontent and collision between our government and any of the states, and to prevent all quarrels and encroachments among the principalities themselves.

This policy proved successful, and in carrying it out I was ably seconded by the different political officers under my authority. By their uniform firm, resolute, and at the same time conciliatory bearing, often in very isolated positions, far from European support and in circumstances of unparalleled difficulty and danger, they one and all maintained the confidence of the chiefs and their people in British prestige and the ultimate successful issue of the struggle which has now happily terminated.

In consequence of the fatigue, anxiety, and labour of the preceding two years my health was completely broken, and I was forced to proceed in April 1859 to England for eighteen months to recruit.   In November 1861 I returned to India and resumed my duties in Rajpootana, but the experience of a few months too clearly convinced me that my work was done, and that my strength was no longer equal to carrying on satisfactorily the arduous duties of my high and very important office.   I accordingly, in April 1864, resigned my appointment, after a service of forty-three years.

And now, in closing these reminiscences of a chequered career, it well becomes me to record my deep thankfulness to God, by whose gracious and protecting care I was preserved through so long a period of service, and through so many scenes of anxiety and peril, and permitted at last to return in safety and in peace to my country.[1]

---

[1] The following are the surviving officers to whom I feel deeply indebted for their gallant and zealous services under me in 1857-8 in Rajpootana:—Col. J. Brooke, Off. Agt. Gov.-Gen.; Major Beynon; Major E. Impey; Capt. Walter; Capt. Newall; Lieut.-Col. E. Hardy; Major W. Carnell; Doctors Lownds, Moore, and Small.—*G. S. P. L.*

APPENDIX.

Copy of William Brydon's Account from memory, and Memoranda made on Arrival at Jellalabad, of the Retreat from Cabool in 1842.

IT was given out to the troops in Cabool on January 5th that arrangements had been completed for a retreat to Hindoostan. Such of the sick and wounded as were unable to march were left under medical charge of Drs. Berwick and Campbell and Lieutenant Evans, her Majesty's 44th, in command. Captains Drummond and Walsh, and Lieutenants J. Conolly, Webb, Warburton, and Airey were placed as hostages in the hands of Mahomed Zeman Khan. The sick were lodged in Timour Shah's fort, the hostages with the new king, Shah Shoojah.

January 6.—The retreat commenced this day about 9 A.M., a temporary bridge having been thrown across the Cabool river for the passage of the infantry; the guns, cavalry, baggage, &c. fording the river, which was about two feet deep. The 5th Native Infantry formed the advance guard, with a hundred sappers, and the guns of the mountain train under Brigadier Anquetil; next came the main body under Brigadier Shelton, followed by the baggage, in rear of which came the 6th regiment Shah Shoojah's force, to which I belonged. We did not leave cantonments till nearly dusk, immediately followed by the rearguard, composed of the 5th Light Company 54th Native Infantry,

x

two Horse Artillery guns, and part of her Majesty's 44th. All the guns, excepting those of the Horse Artillery and Mountain Train, were left in the cantonments, together with a large quantity of magazine stores. I saw Lieutenant Hardyman, 5th Light Company, killed by a shot from the enemy, who had entered the cantonments and fired upon us from the walls immediately the troops left the gates, and in a short time set fire to all the buildings. Each officer carried away what little baggage he could on his own animals. I having six ponies, reserved a favourite chesnut for myself, and mounted all my servants; but before I left cantonments I saw my best horse, which was carrying my boxes of clothing in charge of my groom, seized by the enemy, who dashed in among the baggage and carried off a great quantity of public and private property without resistance between cantonments and the Seeah Sung hill, at which place the two guns with the rearguard were abandoned. We moved so slowly that it was near midnight before we reached our encamping ground across the Loghur river, a distance of only about five miles; but even this short march, with the darkness and deep snow, was too much for the poor native women and children; many lay down and perished, and the cries of others who had lost their way were truly heartrending. On arriving at our ground the scene was sad indeed: the snow several inches deep; only one small tent. saved from the general pillage, was pitched and occupied by the General, and as many more as could find room in it, and the troops lying in the snow, or sitting round .fires mostly fed by portions of their own clothing. I rolled myself in my sheepskin cloak, and taking my pony's bridle in my hand, lay down among the men of my regiment and slept.

January 7.—When I awoke in the morning I found the troops preparing to march, so I called to the natives who had been lying near me to get up, which only a very few were able to do; some of them actually laughed at me for urging them, and pointed to their feet, which looked like charred logs of wood. Poor fellows, they were frost-bitten, and had to be left behind. This day, advanced guard ·54th Native Infantry, rearguard her Majesty's 44th, and mountain train, our march was to Bootkhak, a distance again of about five miles, and the whole road from Cabool was at this time a dense mass of people. In this march, as in the former, the loss of property was immense, and towards the end of it there was some sharp fighting, in which Lieutenant Shaw, 54th Native Infantry, had his thigh fractured by a shot. The guns of the mountain train were carried off by the enemy, and either two or three of the Horse Artillery were spiked and abandoned. I saw a gallant but fruitless charge made by Lieutenant Macartney to try and recover a horse of his own that was being carried off; he with difficulty rejoined the troops. Few had anything to eat except those who like myself followed the Affghan custom of carrying a bag of parched grain and raisins at their saddle-bow. There was rather less snow than on our former encamping ground, and the night was passed like the former, the pony only getting a few bites of grass from the ground and having the saddle-girths slackened. Up to this time I had seen nothing more of my servants or their ponies. We were tricked into encamping here instead of at once pushing on through the pass by Akhbar Khan, who sent to say he must make arrangements with the chiefs to let us through, but in truth that he might have time to get the hills well manned before we entered the pass, and some of his horsemen who accompanied us are said to have called to the enemy in Persian ' to spare,' and in Pushtoo, which the hillmen speak and few Europeans understood, they exhorted them ' to slay the Kaffirs.'

January 8.—This morning we moved through the Khoord Cabool Pass with great loss of life and property; the heights were in possession of the enemy, who poured down an incessant fire on our column. Great numbers were killed, among them Captain Paton, and Lieutenant Sturt of the Engineers, by a shot in the groin; many more were wounded—of them were Lady Sale and Captain Troup, and when we arrived at our ground at Khoord Cabool Captain Anderson's eldest child was missing. All the stragglers in the rear were cut up by the enemy, who descended as soon as the main body had passed. The pass is about three-and-a-half miles long, with a small stream running through it, which had to. be crossed about thirteen times in transit; it was covered with ice, but not strong enough to bear a man, and I had an awkward accident about the middle. I suppose I had forgotten to tighten the girths, and my saddle turned, tumbling me into the water at a place where the enemy's fire was particularly sharp. I managed to get close under a rock to right the saddle, and both I and my horse escaped untouched.

January 9.—We halted at Khoord Cabool this day, scarcely annoyed by the enemy at all; and I was glad to find three of my servants out of the five that had been with me in Cabool, the bheestie (water carrier), khidmutgar (table attendant), and sweeper; those missing being the syce (groom), carried off with the horse the first march, and a tailor. To the bheestie I had given a bag of barley to carry on his pony, and he had filled his mussuck or water-skin with pistachio nuts, so the animals got a feed of corn, and myself and the servants made a hearty meal on the nuts. At this place by treacherous promises Akhbar Khan induced the General to make over to his care all the married officers and their families and some wounded officers.

January 10.—Resumed our march about 10 A.M. and were immediately attacked, and numbers fell in a small rocky gorge, Tareekee Tungee, just outside the camp, before we ascended the Huft-Kotul (Seven Hills). At the moment of starting the Sergeant-major of our regiment brought some eggs and a bottle of wine, which he got from a box left by some of the ladies, and gave them to Captain Hawkins, who divided them with Captain Marshall, Lieutenant Bird, and myself: the eggs were not boiled, but frozen quite hard, and the wine also to the consistency of honey, a little only in the centre being fluid. This was a terrible march, the fire of the enemy incessant, and numbers of officers and men, not knowing where they were going from snow-blindness, were cut up.   I led Mr. Baness, a Greek merchant, a great part of the way over the high ground, and often felt so blind myself that from time to time I applied a handful of snow to my eyes, and recommended others to do so, as it gave great relief. Descending towards Tazeen the whiteness was not so intense, and as the sun got low the blindness went off; but the fire of the enemy increased; and as they were able to get very close to us in the passes, which we now again entered, it was very destructive, many of the enemy indeed running across our line and cutting down any they could.   So terrible had been the effects of the cold and exposure upon the native troops that they were unable to resist the attacks of the enemy, who all the way pressed hard on our flanks and rear, and on arriving at the valley of Tazeen towards evening a mere handful remained of the native regiments which had left Cabool.   Amongst those wounded I saw Drs. Duff and Cardew placed on a gun-carriage, but they did not long survive.   Dr. Bryce, just on entering the pass, was shot through the chest, and when dying handed over his will to Captain Marshall.   At Tazeen when we halted we found there were killed or missing, besides those named, five officers of the 5th Native Infantry—Swayne, Miles, Dees, Alexander, and Warne; one of the 37th, Ewart of the 54th, and Dr. Magrath.   After a short rest, when it was quite dark, our diminished party moved on, setting fire to the carriage and leaving the last of the Horse Artillery guns on the ground, and a great number of the remaining camp followers who would not, or many could not, move further. We passed pretty quietly through the Tazeen valley, but were again fired upon when we entered the hills, especially near a small river where the enemy had a large sungah on a hill, and where Brigadier Shelton unfortunately halted his men to return their fire, thereby losing severely.

January 11.—We marched all night, the cavalry advanced

guard, and arrived at Kutta Sung this morning, having sustained more loss from the enemy firing on us from the heights all the way ; we halted a very short time, being only a valley surrounded by hills. Here Captain Dudgin, of her Majesty's 44th, gave me a biscuit and a sardine : very acceptable indeed they were, as I had eaten nothing since the frozen eggs the morning before. As we pushed on to Jugdulluck we found wild liquorice, chewing the roots of which refreshed me much. We reached it about noon, still hard pressed by the enemy from the hills, and close to the camp ground Lieutenant Fortye, of her Majesty's 44th, was killed. Shortly after our arrival the General, Brigadier Shelton, and Captain Johnson went to Akhbar Khan, and were detained as hostages for the march of the troops from Jellalabad and safe-conduct for us. We were encamped in an old enclosure, which however gave us very little shelter from the enemy, who had possession of the surrounding hills, from which they never ceased firing. Captain Skinner of the commissariat was killed, and many men and officers wounded : among the latter, whose wounds I dressed, were Captains W. Grant and Marshall ; the former had his jaw shattered, and Marshall a shot through the chest. Poor Marshall, Bird, and I had dined on a portion of a fat Arab charger that had been shot, slices of which we grilled over a fire of brushwood, during which operation Marshall lost the only bit of rock salt we had, and looked on it as a very bad omen. I suppose it fell in the snow and melted. Shortly afterwards he volunteered to lead a party to try and drive the enemy from a hill from which they specially annoyed us, and he was wounded before he had gone many yards. We did not move from Jugdulluck till about an hour after dark on January 12th, when an order was given to march, owing I believe to a note being received from General Elphinstone, telling us to push on at all hazards, as treachery was suspected. Owing to this unexpected move on our part the abattis and other impediments which had been thrown across the Jugdulluck pass were undefended by the enemy, who nevertheless pressed on our rear and cut up great numbers. The confusion now was terrible; all discipline was at an end. I started, leading poor Marshall's horse, who was too weak to guide it; and Blair, Bott, and another wounded officer, all of the 5th Light Cavalry, were on a camel close to me. We had not gone far in the dark before I found myself surrounded, and at this moment my khidmutgar rushed up to me saying he was wounded, had lost his pony, and begged me to take him up. I had not time to do so before I was pulled off my horse and knocked down by a blow on the head from an Affghan knife, which must have killed me had I not had a Blackwood's Magazine in my forage cap. As it was, a piece of bone about the size of a wafer was cut from my skull and I was nearly stunned, but managed to rise on my knee; and seeing that a second blow was coming, I met it with the edge of my sword, and I suppose cut off some of my assailant's fingers, as his knife fell to the ground. He bolted one way and I the other, minus my horse, cap, and one of my shoes; the khidmutgar was dead; those who had been with me I never saw again. I regained our troops, scrambled over a barricade of trees made across the pass, where the confusion was awful, and I got a severe blow on the shoulder from a fellow who rushed down from the hill and across the road. Here I picked up a 44th cap. Soon after I came up with Captain Hopkins, and alongside his horse I walked for some distance, holding on to his stirrup. In this way I overtook a Hindoostanee mochee (saddler) of the Shah's cavalry, who told me he was dying, and begged me to take his pony, or some one else would. I tried to encourage him, but he fell off, carrying away one of the stirrups, and I found the poor fellow was shot through the chest and dead. I then mounted his pony, and riding towards the front I met Brigadier Anquetil, who asked me how they were getting on in the rear. When I told him he rode back, and was never seen again. The men were running up the hills on the sides of the road and on in front, throwing away their arms, &c. to lighten themselves, and could not be kept together or controlled, so Captain Bellew, the Quarter-master-General of the force, assembled all he could find mounted, and formed us into an advanced guard, about forty; only one trooper of the 5th Cavalry could be found. We moved steadily on, fired at from the hills, which were blazing with watchfires, but we in the dark, so few hit as we passed along, only once losing our way in the darkness, but regaining it again after a short détour. During this night we all suffered intense thirst, and my shoeless foot, which was unfortunately in my only stirrup, felt as if it were being burnt, so I was glad to find in a bag with other things at my saddle-bow a piece of list which I wound round the iron. At daybreak we found ourselves at Gundumuck, and had lost all trace of those in our rear. Here a dispute arose as to the road, there being two, one over the hills and the other through the Neemlah valley, in which was a large village. I having been encamped for about three months in quiet times in this neighbourhood, and knowing both roads, recommended the former, while a Mr. Bailis, a clerk in one of the public offices, said the other was safest and best. So our small party split, half going each way; those by the valley were attacked and killed by the villagers, except Mr. Bailis, who was taken prisoner (and afterwards I heard taken to Peshawur, where he died of fever). We proceeded over the hills without seeing a single individual. Shortly before entering on the plain we rested a little while in a small grassy glen, and let our horses have a bite of such grass as it was. My saddle was a wooden one, of a kind then common in the Punjaub, with a high peak in front, and from it I now re-moved the bags, which were very heavy, containing saddler's tools, bullets, a pistol (which none of the bullets would fit), a chain and spike for picketing a horse, &c. All these I threw away except the pistol, which I put in my pocket. On starting after half-an-hour's rest, our party consisted of Captains Bellew, Hopkins, and Collyer, Lieutenants Bird, Steer, and Grey, Dr. Harper, Sergeant Freil, and five or six other European soldiers. We shortly came in sight of the village of Futtehabad, on the plain, and about fifteen miles from Jellalabad; all here seemed quiet, and Captain Bellew said he would go and enquire into the state of the country. In a short time he came back and told us that all was quiet, and that if we would wait he would bring us some bread promised by the headman of the village. In about a quarter of an hour he returned again, and said he was afraid he had ruined us, as from the village, which was on a mound, he could see cavalry coming up on all sides, and he had no doubt that some signal had been given to gather them while we were kept waiting; probably a red flag we saw ourselves. He begged us to keep together and move slowly on, the armed villagers following, and calling to him to come back, as they were friends. Captain Bellew did so, and was immediately killed. At the same time the villagers fired on us and the cavalry charged among us. One fellow cut at me, which I guarded, and he then cut down poor Bird, and it became a case of utter rout, out of which all that got clear were Captains Hopkins and Collyer, Dr. Harper, Lieutenant Steer, and myself. The three former being well mounted left Lieutenant Steer and myself behind, telling us they would soon send us help. After riding on a short distance Lieutenant Steer said he could go no further, as both he and his horse were done (the latter was bleeding from the mouth and nostrils); he would hide till night in one of the many caves we knew were in the hills about half a mile to the right of the road. I tried hard to persuade him to push on, as the plain was sprinkled with people tending sheep and cattle, who must see him, but he would not. So I proceeded alone for a short distance unmolested; then I saw a party of about twenty men drawn up in my road, who when I came near began picking up large stones, with which the plain abounded, so I with difficulty put my pony into a gallop, and taking the bridle in my teeth, cut right and left with my sword as I went through them. They could not reach me with their knives, and I was only hit by one or two stones. A little

further on I was met by another similar party, who I tried to
pass as I did the former, but was obliged to prick the poor pony
with the point of my sword before I could get him into a gallop.
Of this party one man on a mound over the road had a gun,
which he fired close down upon me, and a large stone broke my
sword, leaving about six inches in the handle; but I got clear of
them, and then found that the shot had hit the poor pony, wounding him in the loins, and he could now hardly carry me, but I
moved on very slowly and saw some fine horsemen, dressed in
red. Supposing they were some of our Irregular Cavalry I made
towards them, but found they were Affghans, and that they were
leading off Captain Collyer's horse. So I tried to get away, but
my pony could hardly move, and they sent one of their party
after me, who made a cut at me which I guarding with the bit of
my sword, it fell from the hilt. He passed me, but turned and
rode at me again; this time, just as he was striking, I threw the
handle of the sword at his head, in swerving to avoid which he
only cut me over the back of the left hand. Feeling it disabled
I stretched down the right to pick up the bridle. I suppose my
foe thought it was for a pistol, for he turned at once and made off
as quick as he could. I then felt for the pistol I had put in
my pocket, but it was gone, and I was unarmed, wounded, and
on a poor animal I feared could not carry me to Jellalabad,
though it was now in sight. Suddenly all energy seemed to
forsake me; I became nervous and frightened at shadows, and I
really think I should have fallen from my saddle but for the peak
of it, and some of our people from the fort coming to my assistance, among the first of whom was Captain Sinclair, of her
Majesty's 13th, whose servant gave me one of his own shoes to
cover my foot. I was taken to the sappers' mess, my wounds
dressed by Dr. Forsyth, and after a good dinner, with great thankfulness enjoyed the luxury of a sound sleep, most hospitably
lodged by Captain Francis Cunningham, whose quarters I shared
during the whole siege. On examination I found that besides my

head and left hand I had a slight sword wound on the left knee, and a ball had gone through my trousers a little higher up, slightly grazing the skin, but how and when these happened I know not. The poor pony directly it was put into a stable lay down and never rose again. Immediately on my telling how things were, General Sale despatched a party to scour the plain in the hopes of picking up any stragglers, but they only found the bodies of Captains Hopkins and Collyer and Dr. Harper. The second night after my arrival poor Mr. Baness was brought in by a fakeer from near Futtrabad, to whom he had done a kindness on a former occasion; in marching up to Cabool he saved the fakeer's mulberry grove from being destroyed by some Sikh soldiers. Mr. Baness only lived one day, being perfectly exhausted by his sufferings from cold and hunger.

LONDON: PRINTED BY
SPOTTISWOODE AND CO., NEW-STREET SQUARE
AND PARLIAMENT STREET

www.ingramcontent.com/pod-product-compliance
Lightning Source LLC
Chambersburg PA
CBHW031153120726
47905CB00006B/1932